THE SECOND BLOOMING

By W. L. George

THE SECOND BLOOMING

A BED OF ROSES

THE CITY OF LIGHT

UNTIL THE DAY BREAK

THE MAKING OF AN ENGLISHMAN

WOMAN AND TO-MORROW

DRAMATIC ACTUALITIES

THE SECOND BLOOMING

BY

W. L. GEORGE

Author of "The Making of An Englishman," etc.

BOSTON

LITTLE, BROWN, AND COMPANY

1915

Published, January, 1915
Reprinted, January, 1915 (twice)
February, 1915 (three times)
April, 1915

Printers
S. J. Parkhill & Co., Boston, U.S.A.

TO THE WRITER WHO TURNED THE STRONGEST LIGHT UPON THE COMPLEXITIES OF HIS DAY; SHOWED ME MY FELLOW-MAN STRUGGLING THROUGH ENDLESS MISUNDERSTANDINGS AND PAINS TOWARDS A HIDDEN GOAL; RESTORED TO ME A TRUST I THOUGHT DEAD IN THE GOODWILL THAT WILL NOT DIE; SHOOK SCALES FROM MY EYES AND FILLED THOSE EYES WITH DREAMS; BADE ME HARBOUR NO ILLUSION AND YET NURSE HOPE; SHOWED ME I MIGHT LOVE THAT WHICH I DESPISED, BECAUSE MAN MUST NOT BEAR THE BURDEN OF MY ARROGANCE;

TO

H. G. WELLS

I DEDICATE THIS BOOK

CONTENTS

BOOK THE FIRST

Clara, Grace, and Mary

BOOK THE SECOND

Grace and Clara

BOOK THE THIRD

Grace

BOOK THE FOURTH

Grace, Clara, and Mary

BOOK THE FIFTH

Mary

BOOK THE FIRST

CLARA, GRACE, AND MARY

Here lies the body of
Lady O'Looney,
Great niece of Burke, commonly
Called the Sublime.
She was
Bland, passionate and deeply religious;
Also she painted in water-colours,
And sent several pictures to the Exhibition.
She was first cousin to Lady Jones,
And of such is the Kingdom of Heaven.

(Epitaph in Pewsey Church.)

THE SECOND BLOOMING

CHAPTER THE FIRST

"IT'S A LARGE FAMILY," SAID MRS. WESTFIELD

I

MRS. WESTFIELD was smiling as her grey, rather inquisitive little eyes took in, one by one, these seven people who were making, she thought, a gratifying amount of noise. Seven were not a very great many, but then they knew one another well, were parted by no reticences; indeed they were linked by interest and the desire to astonish one another a little; this dinner had caused competitions to meet. There were sisters hoping that a dress might be envied; brothers-in-law flaunting a reputation or a car. Mrs. Westfield was amused; she did not understand everything, but what she understood she understood clearly; her shrewdness had a finite scope and was no scalpel to dissect the seven souls about her, but she knew the nature of her daughters' domestic rivalries, the ambitions of her sons-in-law and the modest passions of her old friend Sturry. She drew inferences from the inflections of voices, could speak the private slang her daughters had evolved when they were schoolgirls. "It's a large family," said Mrs. Westfield, "still the boys will be all right, and the girls . . . will marry — "

Something within her seemed startled. The smile faded from her large lips, and a general air of seriousness overspread the vast, creamy rosiness of her face; the sharp little eyes became intent behind the glasses, looked searchingly but unseeing into the stolid blue of Mary's pupils. Her daughter shifted a little in her seat under this scrutiny, wondered whether her mother was displeased with her because she was not talking; she reflected that this was not her fault: her mother should not have seated her next to her own husband; and, besides, when eight people dined, one person must be left out if another ceased to speak. Mary felt injured, threw sidelong glances to her husband, Tom Stanley, on her left, to Edward Kinnersley on her right; her husband, she saw, was speaking to Grace as uneasily as usual, laughing very loudly to fill in the pauses. And Edward, with a fixed, complacent smile upon his small, well-cut features, seemed to talk endlessly to Clara. Mary surprised herself in a little giggle, for she knew that Lady Govan also liked talking . . . but Edward could be trusted to cope with her.

Mary need not have speculated. She had in her mother's thoughts only the place due to her as one of the family. Mrs. Westfield was wondering why, so unexpectedly, the queer thought had occurred to her, and at this moment. It was a very old thought, and she wrinkled her sparse eyebrows together in an effort to remember its origin. She had a vision of the nurseries, the big rooms at the top of the house, now empty, but in those days like a ward in a children's hospital. In the first stood little twin beds where slept Hubert and Johnny — an ache came out of the past as she thought of Johnny, for she poignantly remembered the tiny snore of her dead son. Then, in the second room, she glimpsed the netted cots of Grace and Clara; she was conscious of Mary in her cradle.

"She looked very fat that night," thought Mrs. Westfield.

She smiled as she remembered the thumb she had gently drawn out of Mary's mouth. She saw herself from an outer plane, a young matron in blue silk trimmed with jet, her hand against the door lintel as she looked into the nurseries at the beds outlined by the glow of the night lights. How long ago! Over twenty-five years! She remembered her blue silk evening frock, her ridiculous "bustle," and that night — she had been with Horace to see *Barbe Bleue* at the Avenue — she seemed to hear Horace on the lower floor — his loud whisper on the stairs: "Laura! I can't find my slippers."

For some seconds she thought of her dead husband. No ache here, but a regret that was decorum's due. Then she wondered why the old phrase had leapt out of the past as a Drury Lane demon from his well. Why had she suddenly switched back time? Heard herself, on her fifty-ninth birthday, whisper to herself a sentence she had whispered before her five little children a quarter of a century before? It had been a true forecast, for her son Hubert had just been gazetted to his company, and Johnny, the sailor, was dead. Death, among the well-to-do, is almost as good as a career; it is so final. And all the girls had married; they too were settled. Mrs. Westfield's brief fit of introspection passed away; she reverted to her more normal condition of interest in the affairs of other people. The heaviness of her gaze lifted from Mary, and she met with a smile Sturry's quizzical eyes.

"What is the great thought?" asked her neighbour. "The plump perfection of Mary? a dream of grouse still six weeks off? or the washing?"

"I was," said Mrs. Westfield, "thinking of Westminster Cathedral."

The old man burst into delighted chuckles. For thirty years Mrs. Westfield had twitted him with his morbid interest in churches, found saintly smells in his clothes and ecclesiastic degeneration in his collars. And the jokes were perennially fresh; ancient quips, that had made Mr. Westfield laugh, still charmed him. He was of those for whom old jests are old times.

"You flatter my mania, my dear," he said, rather fondly. "That is wrong of you; you are being considerate to me, as if I were over thirty. You make of me a candidate for the bath-chair."

"You will never sit in a bath-chair," replied Mrs. Westfield; "you're more likely to push me about in one."

The two laughed together. They could not be modern,

for they carried their past; with the young they could spar about art or politics; with each other they had to be sprightly, Victorian, for they mutually evoked a bygone age: Mrs. Westfield made Sturry feel he wanted to bow, and he faintly influenced her to ogle.

"Mary," said the old man, inconsequently, "is getting stout."

The talk suddenly became confidential and murmuring, coy. It glided, arch and dated as *Vanity Fair*, under the sonorous periods of Sir Henry.

"It is a shame, as you say, Grace. I quite forgot to ask you to tea, and yet the Terrace is short of flowers."

He was a handsome man of about forty-five, so tall that, as he spoke to his sister-in-law, he leant over her, his heavy, fair moustache close to the dark, warm gold of her hair. She looked up at him amusedly, wondering what there was so comforting in his bigness, the brick-like sunburn of his cheeks that threw a paleness of contrast over his moustache and his thick grey hair.

"Do you know, Harry," she said suddenly, "you're really a very handsome man."

"My dear Grace!" protested the man, rather loud in his surprise.

"Is she being naughty?" fluted across the table Edward's high voice. The proprietorial smile became more complacent on the husband's features. "Daddy will spank her and put her to bed," he added, and the smile grew arch. He shook his head; had he been a woman he would have shaken brown curls which would well have accorded with his warning finger. He appealed to Clara for support.

"I expect Grace has said what she really meant," said Lady Govan. "That always startles Harry."

There was a general laugh, in which the victim joined.

"Well," he said, still stolid and good-humoured, "what do you expect after two years in Parliament? You know, it really wouldn't do. One can't say what one thinks about a bill. Now there's these old-age pensions, for instance; I think they're a capital idea, but —"

The little speech developed; as Grace watched him, she was conscious of his quiet, solid importance. It was not only his fine body, the shapeliness of his long muscles in repose, and the regularity of his large features; nor was it the perfection of his tailoring, the incredible gloss of his high collar and shirt-front: it was some quality of balance, a sense of adequate but limited intelligence, good intentions subject to reserves, energies tempered by the rules of good form. Sir Henry, in Parliament, was rather like the elephant tied up to the little peg; he might have broken away if he liked, and thought for himself, but it never occurred to him to do so.

As she smiled up at him, Grace was surprised, for she realised her brother-in-law for the first time; she liked him and thought it curious that she should still like him as she understood him better. She wondered why she was analysing him, and as she did this, she let a slow gaze wander round the table, meet for a second the bright blue of Clara's eyes as she determinedly tried to thrust into one of Edward's bar anecdotes her own impression of a judge who had taken her in to dinner. How alive Clara was! She looked at Edward: her own husband seemed separate from her, and when he twinkled at her, she looked away as if caught prying. Her eyes passed over Mary, who was talking to Tom with the air of indifferent content that comes to the passably wed. And then, conscious of a certain rigid good humour joining her mother with her old friend, she returned to Sir Henry. The analytical fit passed away. It had been no more than a flash, and now she was no longer in the light, yet not in darkness. Her mind stumbled.

"You see, Grace," Sir Henry was saying, "when it comes to old age pensions, we have to take into consideration that Chamberlain said in 1892 . . . Now was it '92?"

He paused, as he struggled with memories of Hansard; his mind flew back to Grace's blunt compliment. He decided that she was a very pretty woman and dismissed the topic. Soon he was developing, point by point, a contributory amendment to the bill. Something of his fleeting admiration had appeared in his eyes, and Grace was amused when, so soon, his subject recaptured him. She was, she thought, worthy of more sustained interest. As she looked at her hands, idle upon the table, for she had refused the ice which the parlour-maid had offered her, all the conversations about her became separate; she heard her mother wrangling with Sturry as to the colour of an absurd overcoat Mr. Westfield had worn at Brighton before she was born; Tom, laughing rather loudly with Mary; and Edward, being jocular with Clara over the audacity of her low-necked dress. But it was of her own hands, rather short, flat-nailed and capable, of her face and breast, reflected in the polished silver flower-stand before her, that she was most conscious.

The savoury, shrill caviare, was handed round. As she put to her lips the glass of champagne, she maintained over-long the pose of her arm, just to see mirrored in the silver the length and secret strength of it. That night, she knew, she was beautiful. Her hair, dressed low over the forehead, glittered in those places where touched it the light of the electric bulbs. And she observed gladly the sheen of her firm arms, the ivory and amber warmth of her skin, the gentle curves of her breasts under the chiffon. Ungratefully, she regretted the height of her cheekbones, the irregularity of her nose, the slight sideways tilt of her mouth, all the charming incongruity of her features.

But dessert had come, and as the port began to pass, sacerdotal, in the wake of the sun, the growing noise drew her from her self-analysis. Tom told her two anecdotes, straight from the City, where the humorous character had had a drop too much. Clara became more metallically bright as Sturry reminded her of the great day when she climbed the poplar with John's irons, vowed she would do it again for fun, rallied him for a moongazer and an amateur verger. The old man, amused by her nervous merriment and energy, laughed shrilly. And Edward had ostentatiously taken Mary's hand, was stroking it, vowing that he had married the wrong woman. Then, in calm, formal tones, Sir Henry announced that it was Edward's turn to make the annual birthday speech.

Mrs. Westfield leant back in her chair, her hands folded where she ought to have worn a stomacher, smiled as Edward Kinnersley stood up, the Edwardian smile upon his face. As Edward smoothed his short, curly hair and cleared his throat, there was a slight increase in the noise, for Sir Henry boomed a few "hear-hears," while Clara energetically clapped her hands. And through the rather too boisterous knife-rapping that Tom contributed came an ironic whisper from Sturry that Edward would now orate.

"Ladies and gentlemen of the jury," Edward began. He stopped, and to obtain silence raised a deprecatory little hand. "It is my duty this year to lay before you the recurrent crime of our mother by deed or by adoption, — that of having compassed another year without giving us an opportunity to quarrel with her, of having proved that lovely woman improves with time as does good wine." His smile expanded: "And I realise how delicate is the position of one who so addresses his mother-in-law — "

Edward spoke through titters as he cast a veil of badinage over the broader humours of the music-hall. A little too generous of gesture, legally nimble and lucid in phrasing, he strung together in compliments that always seemed near a tangle and yet always somehow resolved themselves, expressions of their general love for Mrs. Westfield, of their hopes for her happiness, wealth and health. As he spoke, Grace watched him intently, then sought in the other faces for impressions that did not appear. Kinnersley forgot the metaphor of a family jury, adopted an inn-dinner style tinged with gaiety.

"And so," he concluded, with a little air of triumph, "ladies and gentlemen of England — "

A thin streak of positive liking for her husband filtered through Grace's mind.

" — ladies and gentlemen of England, I pray you charge your glasses, which you may not break when you have drunk, for our Home Ruler is not the Queen, and I pray you drink the health of our mother."

While all laughed, and cried out approval and drank, a curious thought came winging towards Grace: she positively liked her husband — it was curious that conjugal love should vary, that —. But further she could not follow it, into some dim recess of her brain where she might long have wandered, trying to understand why a woman might suddenly feel a liking where there had been nothing, where she thought that there must be something, trying to draw some truth out of the half-confidence her soul held out to her. Instead, she smiled at her mother, drank.

The old lady stood up. "Thank you, thank you very much," she murmured, a little shyly. Then, while Sir Henry, by right of courtliness, held open the door, she led her daughters towards the drawing-room.

II

The men did not very long stay together. Sir Henry and Tom Stanley were not unwilling to dally, the former to discuss with Edward the status and bar earnings of the legal members of the House, the latter to pass round the port with solemn gusto and to persist in the vain effort to make Sturry take up golf. But their victims did not respond very well. For some minutes there was listless conversation of the "I suppose so" and "I wonder" kind; Tom swallowed his coffee and then his chartreuse in two gulps, so as to be free to return to port. As he drank, he began to talk more stodgily: he had not had too much, in his own phrase, though what he had had might have been too much for most men, but enough to make him ponderous rather than jovial. He was addressing himself to Sturry.

"You know," he said, confidentially, "you really ought to go in for it. It'd make a new man of you. Now I — "

While he explained to Sturry the intricate workings of his liver, the old man looked at him and listened to the other couple. As those others talked, Sturry smiled, more and more mischievous; his keen little grey eyes, set very deep, twinkled like those of a mandrill, and his pointed white beard twitched with his mouth. Narrow skull, sparsely hairy, thin, long nose and high-set ears, he was as a very old faun that kept its own counsel. Tom had abandoned his liver, skimmed morning throats and smoker's heart, was now safely at work on last Sunday's fifth hole. "Thirteen more to go," thought Sturry, cheerfully, and listened to Edward, who instructed Sir Henry Govan.

"My dear Harry," said the barrister, fluently, "you political people are amazing; you think that when a man's in politics, he's got to heaven and will renounce the world. Harton will take a judgeship any day."

"He wants to be Solicitor-General," said Sir Henry, obstinately, "he told Melton — "

"I know. Melton told me too, but, my dear fellow, it's bluff." Edward laid an affectionate hand upon Sir Henry's knee, and there left it, though the knee twitched to be free. "Harton took silk twenty years ago; he knows that it's no use being Solicitor-General unless one's going to be Lord Chancellor by and by, and, quite apart from the other man, Southrop, as Lord Middlesmore will last for ever. . . ."

They laughed. The eccentricities of Middlesmore and the luck of his relatives were discussed. A forensic repartee was entered; a promising junior was placed on probation for five years.

As Sturry listened, mechanically helping Tom from hole to hole, he sorted impressions in his mind. Sixty years of the world had not habituated him to men's after-dinner talk: politics, their work, golf, motor-cars, foreign travel, dogs, horses and, a very, very little, women. The old man yawned, concentrated on the Morland which hung opposite the chair. Yet he was oppressed by realities, saw that these three men did not talk nonsense, that they were solid, earnest, doing each one of them something rather well; free from women, they became themselves: Sir Henry was simpler, Tom ceased to strain, and Edward Kinnersley forgot to be arch. It was, he thought, woman tainting man, making him strut, just as he, in return, made her look through her eyelashes. He yawned: this seemed endless; man by himself was sound, but he was very dull. Then he listened more intently, for the object of his neighbours' attention had shifted.

"Of course," said Sir Henry, "she'd be charmed to go to Court . . . and in front of all the poor baronets' wives. It's the women push the men on."

"Ah," said Edward, with secret relish, "marriage is one of the dangerous trades." He threw out his chest, well-pleased.

"Port?" said Tom. "No? Send it round, then." He abandoned golf, threw himself into the rival conversation, intending to make it humorous. He failed; soon he was following.

"A woman will never rest," said Edward, "until her husband gratifies her ambition. If he's not ambitious, she's no use for him. Now Grace has quite made up her mind that I must be Lord Chief Justice, at least."

"And Clara must be a Cabinet Ministress before she dies," said Sir Henry, "no matter what I suffer. What does Mary plan for you, Tom?"

"I don't know." Tom was profoundly serious; his large, coppery-red face was set in fat folds, and the good-humoured, clean-shaven mouth seemed compressed. "I don't know that she plans anything that I can think of, unless it's an extra day-nursery."

"Mary," said Edward Kinnersley, rather sententiously, "is a good mother. Not that I complain of Grace. Far from it: dotes on the two brats, and she's as keen as mustard to know what's going on in the Courts. And when a woman's keen, she's keen. Isn't she, Harry?"

"Oh, yes," said the big baronet. "Clara'd frame my questions for me if I'd let her. The other day, for instance, when they promised to introduce that Butter Bill — "

Clara's efficiency appeared. Tom interrupted to show that Mary remembered the dates of insurance policies;

Edward quoted a touching case where Grace, on her own initiative, had had new silk facings put on his dress-coat. They grew mildly excited; too well-trained to interrupt one another, they watched for pauses as eagerly as runners for the fall of the flag. The talk became a chorus:

"Grace won't let anybody else dust my desk — "

"If I 'phone Clara that I left my Erskine May at the club — "

" — and as she knows that I oughtn't to touch game — "

" — sat up all night with Horace. . . . Now you know what whooping-cough — "

They exhausted themselves, together became silent. There was a pause; then old Sturry's thin, high pipe came, rather startling.

"That's all very well; there they are, all the three of them, ordering your dinners and looking after your professions, and your politics, and your old boots and your children. But what d'you think they're up to? Themselves?"

"What do you mean, Sturry?" asked Sir Henry, rather coldly.

"Well . . . where do they come in? Will it last?"

"My wife," said Kinnersley, solemnly, "is absorbed in my affairs."

There was another pause. Tom announced:

"Anyhow, Mary never seems short of something to do."

The three men looked at Sturry blankly. For, hunched-up in his chair, the old gentleman was weakly giggling, as if possessed by some inscrutable, revealed joke, more and more like an absurd, elderly faun that kept its own counsel.

III

The women sat in the big drawing-room, ostensibly interested in one another, actually waiting for the men. It was a very comfortable place, for Mrs. Westfield had been born just late enough to dodge the antimacassar; and Mr. Westfield, espousing the prevalent view that the wife owns the drawing-room while the husband controls the dining-room and hall, had not interfered with her plans. Thus the drawing-room was very white and gold, chintzy and knickknacky; there were good rugs on the parquet floor, and fat cretonne cushions and hard footstools. The Chesterfield and its attendant armchairs were large: when sat upon, their sturdy springs resisted. There was a touch of taste in the many English colour-prints, in the rather etiolated water-colours of Kentish seascapes; a touch of fancy in the collection of Chinese ivories in the tall Chippendale cabinet; a touch of Victorianism in the plum damask curtains and the drawing-room table. Mrs. Westfield had not lived in the wax-fruit period, but she was old enough to respect the big chandelier that hung twoscore crystal bangles over her head. And she kept, on the drawing-room table, a large book of family photographs, a very old book upholstered in red velvet, with a silver back and clasp, and lettered " ALBUM " in bold sloping characters. By its side were *The Spectator, The Queen,* Rackham's *Peter Pan,* a little book illustrated by his young rival, Dulac, and two volumes bearing the Mudie label, one of them a novel, the other " serious."

Mrs. Westfield's drawing-room table was the meeting-ground of the nineteenth and the twentieth centuries. The two epochs did not collide as a river and a sea roaring at the bar: they gently merged into each other as two converging streams.

Clara stood at the table, turning over the pages of the serious book, somebody's travels in Mexico. Hers was a slim, rather meagre but elegant figure, on which the rigid blue and black *moiré* gown hung in straight folds. Indeed the whole impression of her was one of straight lines: strong, rectilinear brows, absolutely symmetrical eyes, long, exactly-centred mouth, rather thin but well-moulded limbs. Alone, the slight outthrust of her jaw to the right and left marked her out as her mother's daughter. And she had exaggerated in her bright blue eyes the shrewdness of her mother's grey ones — unless this was not shrewdness but a nervous activity, an activity that made her turn the pages very fast, as if she were a magpie, inquisitive rather than in search of treasure.

"This seems rather trash, mother," she said. Mrs. Westfield was talking to Mary, did not hear. Clara, book in hand, came to Grace, who seemed unconscious of what she did as she teased the petals of the peonies in the big jar. "Have you read it?" she asked her sister, showing her the book.

"Read what? *Me and Mexico?* No. What a funny title!"

"It's by a globe-trotting lady, and more Me than Mexico," said Clara, laughing and putting the book down, as if her quip had given an obvious clue to the writer's name. "She drank *maté* with the President, unless she ate *banderillas* or something; one gets so mixed up in the local colour. Still, one has to read these things. Keeps one up to date."

"I suppose one has to," said Grace. "And yet I don't. I suppose I'm too busy."

"Oh, rot!" cried Clara, suddenly schoolgirlish. "You don't know what it's like to be busy."

"I've got two children; you seem to forget—"

"Well, it's only a question of organising your time. Now I—"

Clara developed a strenuous plan of life. An M. P.'s wife had to respond to so many calls, bazaars, visits, garden parties, opening things, and christening future constituents. And there were other people's children, care committees—

"What's that about care committees?" asked Mrs. Westfield, drawn out of a conversation with Mary that was doubtless intimate, for it was a little whispering. "Don't move, Mary, I'll get you a cushion."

Clara explained that she had "gone on" the local committee; it would help Henry, and it was rather fun getting those children washed and amused and doctored. She became quite enthusiastic about dental inspection and laid down views on vermin with perfect scientific aloofness.

"What we want," she declared, "is more inspection.

Not only teeth and heads; there's sight and the Fraga test for uric acid, and — "

Clearly her care committee cared.

" It's a pity you haven't any children of your own since you're so fond of them," said Mrs. Westfield, at last.

" She wouldn't be so fond of them if she'd got four," said Mary, faintly malicious.

Clara flung a spiteful glance at her pretty, but heavy sister propped up against the cushion. " Well, I wouldn't have four," she snapped.

Mrs. Westfield and Grace laughed together at the sisterly spar. For some minutes Mary's coming baby was discussed; the debate became so frank that Clara, with a little sniff, rather ostentatiously took up *Me and Mexico* and began to read, while Mrs. Westfield pursued the catechism of her sisters.

" How does Horace like the kindergarten? " she asked.

" He loves it," said Grace. " Since they took to teaching him to count, he's got a new monomania; yesterday, at tea, he said to me: ' Mummie, one red ball is five blue! ' and since then it's never stopped. He sings it in the bath."

" Horace was always one for monomanias," said Mrs. Westfield. " Do you remember ' puffers '? "

All three laughed together, for it was true that between the ages of two and four Horace had said " puffer " or " puffers go on lines " several score times a day.

" You should take his mind off it," said Clara, suddenly dogmatic; " it's an obsession."

" Take his mind off it! " cried Grace. " You don't know Horace. He already knows what he wants."

" I suppose you mean he doesn't bother about you? Personality at age five? "

" Not exactly — " said Grace, and hesitated. " But still he seems to be getting ideas of his own — not coming to me so much . . . you know."

" My dear," said Mrs. Westfield, " of course he's not needing you so much. He's turning into a man. He'll be wanting a wife soon, not a mother."

While the others laughed, Grace once more had one of

those peculiar, novel sensations. She could not fix it, and yet it was sister to the feeling she had had about her husband; Horace had been so close to her, for a long time she had felt all his little diseases . . . and now, somehow, their business was not quite the same. This idea she expelled as she thought of Susan. Yes, her little girl was helpless enough; she was four. And yet, even Susan . . . now that she came to think of it, Susan was beginning to play all alone at being postmistress, the result of a recent holiday in a village. Grace struggled in vain to find out what was this feeling. It was a sort of — outsideness. She heard Mary discussing her progeny.

It seemed that Rose could now read one-letter words; Maud threatened adenoids. Of Ella there was nothing at all to say, but Gladys was getting uglier every day.

"Tom says she's ugly enough to be a boy, and yet — " Mary sighed. For these four girls born in six years were the tragedy of the Stanleys.

Mrs. Westfield became optimistic on the score of what would happen in February, vowed that "Jack" would be born. Clara said something about Schenck, then turned away, nervous and disturbed by this maternal atmosphere, redeemed it by invoking science.

"I ought to read up some Schenck," she remarked to herself.

Then the men came in.

IV

Mrs. Westfield was sleepy. As she beamed, she nodded and winked. Grace could hear her husband talking to Mary:

"So you're going to Folkestone? Capital place for the children. We? Oh, we're going abroad, to Trouville. Grace has been given a blank cheque for frocks; you see, we're going away on a second honeymoon."

He looked at his wife. Grace answered with a slow, small smile the archness of his lips. He was gay and generous. Of course she loved him. She smiled broadly. He twinkled.

CHAPTER THE SECOND

"— AND THE GIRLS WILL MARRY"

I

MRS. WESTFIELD's house was in Campden Hill Road. It was a deceptive building, for its small, white-painted stucco front, its narrow portico and front garden suggested it as a high house strangled between two neighbours. It did not look like the rearing-ground of five children, but exploration showed that it was very like those little colonies on the West Coast of Africa that press a tiny mouth against the sea and extend towards the interior in a vast hinterland. For, the long, solemn hall and its great hatstand passed, the house suddenly expanded; behind the dining-room, which faced the street, was the drawing-room, a place thirty-five feet by twenty, abutting by glass doors on a garden that seemed to roll away endlessly towards the ivy-grown back wall. Above were five bedrooms and the bathroom which had caused so great a sensation in 1868. Yet higher, the two big day-nurseries and the servants' quarters. The spacious days of Queen Victoria.

The house would never have been built if the owners of the neighbouring buildings had not, in the days of George IV, begun an acid dispute over their party-wall. The king died. The struggle did not abate. King William IV intervened through his Chancery Courts: the struggle became venomous. There were injunctions, also interlocutions; the owners became elderly and very violent; the servants were encouraged to throw dead cats over the wall. Queen Victoria succeeded to the throne; the documents of the combatants filled many despatch-boxes; then one old gentleman died, and the other, finding the executors anxious to compromise and his occupation gone, also died, presumably of a broken heart. And then the executors, breathing sighs of relief, swore that no walls should ever more trouble them; old friends of both families, they had grown rather tired of the subject in the course of a generation: they sold the site and its hinterland to John Westfield, for him to build his house.

John Elba Westfield was born in Mincing Lane, where he lived above his father's oil warehouse. He owed his curious name to having stared into the world on the fatal day when Bonaparte suddenly soared with eagle wings across the sea. Banished to Harrow, and then to Oxford, where he grew moustaches and hoped he looked like a military man, he returned to find himself travelling every day from Highgate upon a gaily-trotting public coach that took him to Aldgate Pump. He was the first of his commercial line to go to Oxford, and he repined a little when confronted with the oil, for he had hoped, legally-gowned, to take the air at Temple Bar and fees at the Old Bailey. But not long: philosophic, he expressed already that which he learned, in a more concrete form, many years later, from that clever young man, Mr. Alfred Tennyson: His not to make reply, His not to reason why —

At thirty, John Westfield, now a junior partner, met Martha Broughton and created a great scandal because he figured with her, the same night, in four square dances. A very little later, careless of exceedingly tight cream-coloured trousers, he knelt upon the path of Mrs. Broughton's little garden at Camberwell. Martha blushed red as the roses on the bush that hid them from Mrs. Broughton (who was dozing in the parlour over Mr. Dickens's new work, *Martin Chuzzlewit*), and let drop on her crinoline a small, white hand upon which John Elba Westfield printed ardent but modest kisses. Then John Westfield built his house. His father objected very much, for his daughter, Lucia, having married into the East India Company, had as good as disappeared, while John's younger brother, Thomas, had come to a bad end. What this end was nobody knew, for nobody dared ask Mr. Horace Westfield, but there was a hideous rumour that the young curate who had so suddenly vanished from Rochester two days after Frances Kemble and her touring company had honoured the town was Thomas and no other.

"Damme, Sir," shouted old Horace. "What's this I hear about Campden Hill Road? Highgate's not good enough for you, I take it. It's Miss Martha, I take it. Gadding and gallivanting! I'll have you know, Sir —"

But John Westfield, stricken with love madness or inflamed by the democratic spirit of the age, came very near replying in the "Damme, Sir" style. He built the house in Campden Hill Road, married Martha Broughton, who gave him one child. Until he died, old Horace chuckled savagely over the small size of this family; it was, he declared, God's judgment on his unruly son. But John only laughed, said that families were growing smaller and that the Reverend Tobias Fullet boldly printed in the *Morning Post* that impious man and not an angry Deity was to blame. Resigned to the oil and to Mincing Lane, he sent the boy, whom he forgivingly called Horace, to Harrow and then to Oxford. Then, when Horace had finished his grand tour, which included a view of the Emperor of the French and a loss of two hundred napoleons at Homburg, he called the boy into his study and asked him what he wanted to be.

"I want to be a painter, Sir," said Horace, who knew that his chances of emulating Sir Edwin Landseer were small and used "Sir" instead of "Father" as a forlorn emollient.

The father looked at his son for a long time. A faint memory of his own desire to read for the bar flashed through his mind. Then he remarked: "Tush, you hussy," to memory and said:

"You're going into the business. It's a good, respectable business with no fallals about it. Do you understand? Damme, Sir —"

Horace went into the business. Later he inherited the house. He worked most diligently, extended the activities of what he made with many misgivings, Westfields Limited, into Greece and Spain, and the importation of animal fats. He married a lady called Laura Bedwyn, and it was this Laura Bedwyn who, nearly forty years later, beamed upon her birthday party, her three well-wedded daughters and the thought of their growing children.

For Mrs. Westfield had no cause to complain of Horace. He was rich, and when he died, during the stormy winter of the Boer War, there was no reason to think that he had been anything but a completely happy man. He had not been unhappy, in the strict sense.

He had been genuinely in love with Laura Bedwyn and, for a very long time, seemed quite content with Mincing Lane and the house in Campden Hill Road. Though, under his sway, the business progressed and he showed himself shrewd enough to operate (a little late) in that new-fangled commodity, petroleum, he left upon the City no mark at all. He was just one of the Westfields, one of those Westfields whose firm, since the days of Queen Anne, had always had an oleaginous reputation. He was a small, quiet, dry little man, a Whig because Mr. Disraeli's waistcoats struck him as in rather bad taste; he liked every Wednesday night to shut himself up with *Punch*, firmly believing that none of the women of his household could be interested in it. Though he had accepted the house and furniture that his father had left him, and took gentle pleasure in the numerous George Morlands which had somehow accumulated about him, Horace Westfield's life, extending to sixty years, consisted in a series of mild little protests.

Mr. Westfield's attitude towards the world was very much the same as his attitude towards his wife. "My dear," he would say to the world whenever it suggested anything new, and then, a few minutes later: "Well . . . if you really think so."

For Mr. Westfield did not need to assert himself; he was always working at life from over the way and, in a quiet, mouse-like style, doing very much what he liked. He had his tiny rebellions against the front garden. It was, he thought, a little formal behind its well-clipped box hedge; he disliked the stone flags separated by moss, the steps, the little bushes of box cut in the shapes of ducks and peacocks and toy-trees. All these things jarred a little upon the mild bohemianism of his soul. They were not quite in accord with the revolutionary attitude of the man who voted for Mr. Gladstone in '84. In a soothing, insidious way, Horace Westfield preserved peace by respecting the rigid front garden, while enjoying himself to the full at the back. It was due to him that, behind the herbaceous borders, little by little and year by year, there appeared by the side of the regulation roses and hollyhocks the less formal rosy chains of the foxglove, the obtrusiveness of carnations, the vulgar flaunting of self-advertising geraniums, and of peonies that looked like music-hall stars. He loved the untidy, the columbines, like tumblers upside down, the straggling lupins and larkspurs, and the clematis which, shocking to say, did absolutely what it liked on the wall. And, when Horace Westfield took his little girls into the garden to open and shut the yellow or purple mouths of the snapdragon, it is quite certain that he wearied of the game less soon than they.

"You never know when you have got Horace," said Mrs. Westfield, sadly, to one of her friends, and she was right. For Horace, having been foiled in his desire to be a professional painter, managed to be an amateur. Not only did he quietly escape with a paint-box on Saturday afternoons to the fields beyond Hammersmith, whence he returned with water-colours that showed that he would have starved if he had painted for a living, but in a sly, peace-making way he bought. He bought a Burne-Jones which his wife called elegant. Much later he induced her to accept a Furse, and, just before his death, there was a wrangle because he had brought home a sketch by an unknown young man, Robert Brough. There were a few worse things against him: incredible to think, at the age of fifty, this respectable City merchant kept in a private drawer in his study a certain number of Aubrey Beardsleys: they were burnt behind locked doors by Mrs. Westfield when she cleared his desk after his death. For she was not one such as the Westfields. The Bedwyns were not the heirs of a long commercial line which had somehow repeated itself, generation after generation, for two hundred years, always very much the same. Some of the Bedwyns had been in the Church, others in trade; one had had a commission bought for him.

Among the Bedwyns were fellows at Cambridge, and solicitors' clerks. They had no tradition; only one of them had gone to the devil, not one of them had made very much money: they had just been intelligent, had lived, married and died.

II

If the house at Campden Hill belonged to anybody at all, it belonged to the three girls, for John very early went to the Royal Naval College and Hubert to Harrow; then John joined his ship and, except for brief intervals, was not seen again, for he died of fever in an Eastern port. Hubert was disgorged by Harrow and Sandhurst into the Indian army; his appearances were purely meteoric.

And so it was the three girls who made holes in the little lawn, tore their skirts in the rose-bushes and broke the swing; they grew up faster than their father, who seemed a queerly appropriate figure when, linked by the hands with his three little girls in Kate Greenaway frocks, he ran round and round the little lawn. The girls grew up very different. There was Clara, with the beautiful brown pig-tail, the brilliant blue eyes, and the sharpness of tongue twenty years in advance of her times; Clara, well-beloved of Horace Westfield because she was to him very much like a large and mischievous kitten that, at any moment, might claw him; Clara, Clara burning bright, "Crystal Clara," as he called her. There was her younger sister Grace, already quiet and thoughtful, inclined to speculate in embarrassing ways as to the origin of babies and the existence of God. But Grace always accepted her father's humorous and nebulous answers. She took up Burne-Jones when the Burne-Jones arrived, and she had to submit to a great deal of chaff when, for the first time on record, she substituted for the word " pretty " the word " beautiful." Already then, there was in her hair the streakiness of dark worn gold and of autumn bracken, and there was indefinite wonder in the greenness of her eyes and the pretty, uncertain curves of her red lips. Lastly there was Mary, a calm, steady child with enormous pig-tails of fair flaxen hair, a skin of pink and white velvet, a great appetite for bread and butter and a capacity for doing nothing with commendable concentration.

Their father loved them, played with them. Their governess educated them. They learnt to play Beethoven, Chopin and, to show how modern they were, a little Wagner. They spoke French. Grace drew acanthus leaves. They went to tea-parties, all three in white; Mary with a blue sash, Clara with a pink sash, and Grace with a green sash. In the late afternoons the victoria drove them round and round the Park. On great days they were taken to the Zoo, also to Madame Tussaud's, but not to the Chamber of Horrors. Times became more liberal: they assisted at the performance of an oratorio at the Albert Hall. . . .

Then something happened. One May evening, in 1896, Mrs. Westfield remarked: " Horace, don't you think that Clara ought to have her hair up? "

" My dear! " said Mr. Westfield, as a little pang shot through him. He thought that he would never more see the pig-tail, and that the flying, brown-stockinged ankles would vanish under long skirts, and then again, looking into the future, that Grace's warm gold tresses would be hidden, also Mary's sturdy flax. But he sighed and said: " Well, my dear . . . if you really think so . . ."

III

A change came over the entertaining at Campden Hill Road. The conversation in 1896 had happened just before dinner at seven o'clock. Mrs. Westfield was in grey satin with large pouffs upon her shoulders, her hair dressed upon the back of her neck in an abundant bun; a handsome matron of forty-seven, she was preparing to conduct one of Mr. Westfield's queer, mixed, protesting little dinner-parties. There was to be an alderman and his wife, the rector of St. Aldate's and a daughter who kept his house, a stockbroker whose trousers were military and too tight, Mrs. Westfield's spinster sister, Miss Bedwyn, and . . . four of Horace's friends, very unsatisfactory people: a crumpled artist who seldom had his hair cut, with a wife who had no waist so far as one could judge from her clothes; also a poetess who ate more than the alderman, and a very young, dark man who made epigrams and liked *Lady Windermere's Fan.*

That was the sort of party through which Horace Westfield gave a hint of the parties he would like to have had if he had been allowed, twenty-five years before, to go to Paris and try to win the Prix de Rome. Horace Westfield's self would out: that evening it "outed" in the shape of a black tie that was too large for him.

Now that was all over. The parties changed. Clara came out at her ball, danced all night and slapped the face of a young man who tried to kiss her in the back garden. She had never seen him before and never saw him again. Then she forgot all about him. The dinner-parties became more purposeful in their planning. Some secret force seemed to act upon the people who came to the house; the aged were discouraged and a new kind of young man appeared, a kind of young man between twenty-five and thirty-five. The type came in twos and threes, fair or dark, mainly from the City or the Temple; it had fathers in Good Positions, uncles in the Civil Service, in an indefinable way, it had Prospects. One year later Grace came out: she was kissed at her coming-out ball by one of the eligible young men, and thenceforth harboured for him an attachment which was ended only when he married somebody else. The eligible young men grew more numerous. Clara and Grace were escorted to many dances in Kensington and to one in Mayfair. Mary came out after having been informed by her sisters that nobody would want to kiss her: she was kissed by three of the young men and submitted with an equanimity which, though pleasing to them, should have taught them wisdom.

The girls began to pay calls with their mother, to sit at home and sometimes pour out tea. They learnt to talk of Mr. Pinero and to enquire privately about *The Second Mrs. Tanqueray,* they went to Folkestone in the summer and to Bournemouth in the winter. Then, one day, Clara's boot-heels began to grow, and a very tall, big man, with a moustache that looked as if it would drag him to the ground, began to tramp heavily in the wake of those growing heels.

IV

Mr. Westfield died quite quietly of a cold upon the lungs, which ended in pneumonia. Clara wept herself sick for three days. Grace went about the house with a set face and dry eyes. Mary found that grief increased her appetite and began to carry, hidden in her breast, a locket containing a wisp of her father's hair. And then the big man began to matter. The big man was Sir Henry Govan, fourth baronet and late of the Lancers. He had appeared, together with the other young men, in response to those secret forces which had pushed out the untidy people who liked the *Yellow Book.* He had come with a small group whose members had the distinction of being a little more significant than the other young men. It was a group of five to which the adjective "serious" was applied by Mrs. Westfield when she considered it in the quietude of her bedroom. In addition to Sir Henry there was Edward Kinnersley, a barrister of about thirty, with close-cropped brown curls, small, good features, a rosy, smug little mouth; he radiated a cheerful archness which would have been boisterous if he had not been well-bred. There was Mr. Moresby, who hunted and wore volcanic tweeds with such an air of detachment and modesty that on him they did not look at all Roseberyish. Mr. Moresby had nothing to do; also, judging from his club, he had plenty of money. He passed his time between country houses, race courses and first nights; in fact, he had so little to do that Mrs. Westfield hoped he might take up matrimony as an occupation. There was also Tom Stanley, already a little rotund, though he had not touched thirty. His black hair, high nose, coppery-red face, and extraordinary thickness between chin and neck, made of him a figure of burly brutality which hid his childlike gentleness of soul and his extraordinary unawareness of the strength of his attractions. There was Mr. Dallas too, a newspaper man, the last vestige, perhaps, of the Horace Westfield influence; but he was a respectable vestige, who did not write essays upon the use of the peacock in wall-paper, but excellent and sober articles to show how right we were to make war, or on the improvement of the people through Sousa's music, or on bimetallism. Mr. Dallas was very busy and flashed through the house at Campden Hill Road only in the intervals of going to press. And he was so busy that he was always in a hurry to say what he had to say, always concentrated: it was not wonderful that Mrs. Westfield found his appearances profoundly significant.

But little by little the field began to scatter. Greater purposefulness appeared in Sir Henry's movements. There was a tendency on his part, and also on Clara's, to go into the garden in December to see whether there were any roses left. When, one night, Mrs. Westfield observed them simultaneously paying attentions to the Persian cat, attentions which ended in their accidentally, but frequently, stroking the cat in the same place together, she made ready for the event which she desired.

Sir Henry was the fourth baronet. The first had been created by the Regent, owing to Algernon Govan's anatomical merits. Sir Henry's ancestor happened to have feet exactly the same size as those of His Royal Highness and, for the sake of friendship, made a practice on Brighton Front of easing the Prince's new boots. So well did he perform this Samaritan service that the Regent made him a baronet. He did not live very long to enjoy his honours, for, a week later, he died, shot in a duel caused by the casual remark of a friend who asked him whether the new motto of the Govans would be *per pedes.* But his line succeeded him, and Sir Henry, not very rich and not at all acred, but thirty-seven, intelligent, agreeable and quietly political, was quite a good match. Clara was flattered by his attentions, liked his weight and his rather pompous good-humour. He did not bore her, and when for the first time he took her in his arms, she felt a content and an exhilaration that was in the nature of love. At least she had never felt more for anybody and, as she raised her lips to his, she was conscious of a quality in his kiss that had not been in the caresses of relations.

So Clara got married.

V

Mr. Dallas spoilt his chances when, the profound significance of his hasty conversations with Clara not having been properly understood, he transferred his attentions to Grace. She was then twenty-one and on the sweet eve of her womanhood. She was all contrast, for the soft droop of her shoulders, the question in her greenish eyes, clashed with a sudden brightness of enquiry which led her to " take up " in turn, art, society, and religion. And sometimes she was mischievous. It was not Lady Govan, suspected as she was by her mother, who put the new kittens in Mr. Moresby's overcoat pockets, but Grace. Next day Grace looked as much like a Madonna as her irregular features would let her, decided that she was leading an evil life, and that she had better go in for doing good to the poor.

Mr. Dallas proposed to Grace, was rejected and rebounded with extraordinary swiftness towards Mary. Edward Kinnersley became more urgent, brought to the house at Campden Hill piano pieces for four hands which Mary could not play. And in 1902, when Grace was safely engaged to Edward, a disturbing young Frenchman, called Lucien Cadoresse, who had only been three months in

England and was so determined to be English that he had already learnt to out-swear Tom Stanley, threatened for a time to turn her head by raving to her about the Impressionists, and telling her stories which she thought every minute were going to be improper but somehow saved themselves in the nick of time. As Cadoresse, who had been acquired through that prim girl, Gladys Raleigh, was a merchant's clerk earning ten pounds a month and, from the English point of view, detrimental, he was one evening practically ejected by Mrs. Westfield. She then went to Edward Kinnersley, pointed out that girls were flighty, and that the wedding had better take place soon.

"Well, little girl," said Edward, "your mother says we can get spliced when we like. All I can say is 'Barkis is willing,'" he tittered. "What do you say to that, Gracie-Bracie?"

Grace looked at him with a smiling mouth and rather sad eyes. He was, she thought, rather good-looking and rather nice. His morning coats fitted him admirably and he was gay, and he loved her, and she? she was always glad to see him, gladder than to see anybody else.

"As you like, Edward," she said.

"You mustn't call me Edward," he replied. "Call me Ned; Edward's so stiff. You wouldn't like it if I called you Grace." Then his attitude became more whispering, modestly suggestive, gay, arch, naughty. He threw his arm about her waist, drew her towards him and said: "We'll be happy, won't we? like two pussies in one basket."

Edward Kinnersley's attitude towards woman was an attitude to a toy. He conceived woman as the twin almond . . . only it was man, the major almond, who dictated the lines. She was to be sweet, he kind; she to listen, he to enlighten; and Grace was gay when he was gay, serious when he so felt; he loved her. He loved her because she corresponded: it was right that the wife of Edward Kinnersley should be young, accomplished, beautiful. It was more than right: it was only right.

There was no fever in his wooing, and Grace, of nights,

slept unracked; but he pleased her because he was man, and man in love. She did not question the quality of his love and gave him a love as unquestioning. He occupied many of her waking moments with the trousseau, the house to be found, and the choice of nuptial music. Romantic, she wove romance about him, found in herself a frightened urgency to wed, to accomplish herself. It was an experience to which she went blushing with shame and delight, reluctant, hurried, as a nymph eluding a faun and yet, strangely, running not straight, but in circles.

And so Grace got married.

VI

The pace grew. Mr. Dallas founded a newspaper and in due course became a bankrupt, while Mr. Moresby, who had apparently found things to do which he did not advertise, appeared as co-respondent in a divorce case so attractive to society's moral sense that Mrs. Westfield took Mary away with her for a fortnight to stay with Miss Bedwyn, in the hope that she would not see the newspapers.

When she returned, the new type of young man was still there, but the most evident eligibles had gone, and Tom Stanley, who had just been made a partner in his father's commission agency, suddenly realised a curious and novel importance in himself. He found that at dinner he generally sat next to his hostess and always next to Mary, and when, one evening, Mrs. Westfield, on leaving the dining-room, selected him to give to the men the message that they should not be too long over their port, a dilation took place in Tom Stanley's large, soft heart. That evening, having in his elation drunk more than usual, he looked with more assurance at the little figures that surrounded him, analysed the men and summed them up unfavourably; analysed the women and reflected that there was one of them, blue-eyed, white-skinned, white-shouldered and, so far as he could judge from the modestly-cut low dress, agreeably buxom.

Tom Stanley had always had thoughts such as these about the Westfield girls. He had looked a little hungrily at Clara's agile, boy-like figure, had laughed at some neatness of her speech, at the sharpness with which she criticised her friends. Then he had said to himself a little sadly: "Well, I'm not much." He had looked at Grace, had thought in a muddled way that languid upon its stalk a lily was not more graceful. Sudden desires to take her in his arms and to assure her that the lily should not droop while he held it had come to him now and then; but he had thought, and again sadly: "Well, I'm not much."

But here was Mary, so settled, so simple, and so frank. Mary, with her blue gaze meeting his, was gentle, was unready to snub him as Clara had been, much less mysterious than Grace, that almost exotic flower. Mary became important. Then she became obsessing. She did not move, but she waited. She liked him, and often she looked up with real admiration at this man in whom she dimly felt the strength of the bull and the gentleness of the dove. They laid no traps for each other, those two, as they glided into love. And it was quite artlessly that Mary waited when, at a dance at the Empress Rooms, which they had interrupted to "sit out" because Tom's feet were rather large and very heavy, he leant forward very anxious.

"Mary," he said, his eyes averted, less because they feasted upon the sumptuous whiteness of her shoulders and breast than because they could not meet her own mild eyes . . . "Mary, I've thought for a long time . . . always been so fond of you, you know . . . of course I know I'm not much . . . still, if you don't mind and you would . . . marry me . . ."

She had not replied, but had let him take her hand, then draw her towards him. After Stanley had kissed her and gained from her a "yes" which came readily enough, he felt very proud, much more masterful. And she, lying in the shelter of arms which with every second of security grew heavier and more insistent, she too, quietly, was glad.

And so Mary got married.

VII

They were hard, strong stock, these three young women. Two hundred years of clean living, of such education as their country could give them, had blended with the influences of their times, of art, romance and poetry, to make them what they were; all their energies and desires, their hopes and their anticipations were compounded of the subtle effluvia of the raging life that was breathing into commerce, society, politics, and letters. They were the first product of the fusion of the sedateness of the nineteenth century with the new and sudden spirit of enquiry which followed upon the disasters of the War. They were setting out, all of them, strong-bodied, armed with puritanical rectitudes, with stereotyped and uncertain faiths, like caravels, laden with illusion, sailing towards a coast still below the horizon.

CHAPTER THE THIRD

ROUND AND ROUND . . .

I

GRACE stood for some moments on the steps of her house. There still lingered in her ears the rattle of the fanciful little knocker, the Norwich imp, which had moved as she closed the door. As she slowly rolled up her umbrella, she looked across Kensington Square at the trees which had already shed most of their foliage, at a leaf upon the ground. A puff of wind snatched, now and then, another leaf and, after gently rocking the dead golden memory of what had once been green and vivid, softly laid it to rest upon the pavement to be gilded anew by the pale sun. Already something of the melancholy of winter was in the October day, some weakness in the sun, as if it were sleepy, having shone too much, and languid for the rest of the second solstice.

Grace's thoughts flew away from the beautiful leaf that lay, gilt and crimson, at her feet, and decided that she had done well to put on her blue coat and skirt. Also that it probably would rain. As she walked up Young Street towards the busier places where London joins with Kensington village, she was conscious of a quality of elusiveness in her thoughts akin a little to the uncertainty of the autumn day, of conflicting interests: Clara, with whom she was to shop, the golden leaves, the decay of the Shakespeare flowers in her little front garden, and the set of her coat, with which, she reflected as she stopped in front of the tall looking-glass outside the draper's at the corner, she was not quite pleased. For some seconds she stood in front of the glass, torturing her neck in an effort to see her back. She pulled nervously at the lapels, so intent that she did not notice a middle-aged man of the well-brushed kind who, sauntering past, lingered a little, using the mirror to look into her face.

"I don't know what's wrong with it," she remarked to herself at last; then deciding that next morning she would have to find time for a call at the Sloane Street tailor's, she stepped out nervously, conscious that life was really very wearisome. She glanced into the shop-windows where already furs were appearing, lingered in front of the florist's and, carried away by impulse, went in and ordered three large bundles of chrysanthemums, yellow stained with brown, and purplish white, and faint rose. She idled in front of the book-shop, wondered who bought those funny books on Christian Science and Higher Thought; then, having laughed at herself as she passed the confectioner's because a desire had come to her to go in and have a maid-of-honour, assuming that the Kensington shopkeeper sold anything so schoolgirlish, she went on. The shops vanished into the broad solitude of the Gardens, of Kensington Gore, of Queen's Gate, running away endlessly towards the south.

She seemed small in the morning emptiness of Kensington, small because the roads were broad, the Albert Hall and Memorial so towering. But yet she was a tall, slim figure, and the close cut of the blue serge brought out fine moulded lengths in her limbs, a roundness in her breast and hips. Walking quickly, almost soldierly, upon feet that were not too small, with a little of the hockey girl's swing in her shoulders and arms, her mouth set under the close veil, Grace was not that day the adventurous caravel setting out upon the sea for the unknown; rather she was a trim frigate scudding under little sail on some errand of business, for she was to fetch Clara to help her to shop. Also, because she had not seen her sister for a week, it had become quite necessary that they should discuss Mary, the husbands, children, friends and concerns of the family. And so it was with a pleasant anticipation that was almost excitement that she rang the bell at Albert Hall Mansions and waited in the drawing-room until Clara was ready.

She had hardly sat down when Clara came in; she too dressed in blue serge, but, somehow, there was in the very plain pleats of Clara's blouse, the simplicity of her shoes, which were not patent leather, but glacé kid, an air of business and of rather purposeful plainness which was not belied by her words: "Oh! Grace, I'm so sorry. Wait a minute, will you? I'm just writing a letter." Clara rushed to the settee, snatched up a book which was lying there. "That's what I was looking for. Yes, wait a minute, will you? Oh! bother, there's the telephone."

Clara ran out of the room towards the hall, where the instrument was ringing as if growing angry while it waited. As Grace half listened to Clara's questions and answers, she was faintly annoyed. In those ten seconds Clara had, as usual, managed to start three or four ideas and to leave them all unretrieved. Hands folded in her lap, she waited, looking at the bumps which her rings made under the white kid gloves.

"No, you haven't got it at all. You know what I told you about the envelopes. . . . Well, I can't help it if you have printed five thousand." A long pause. Grace vaguely envied Clara for being so busy with some scheme. "Well, anyhow, you can choose," said Lady Govan's voice. "Either you supply them to fit the envelopes or you supply five thousand envelopes free." The receiver came down with a sharp click, Clara's head appeared for a second at the door. "Perfectly ridiculous," she snapped. "Printers are fools. . . . Did you see Lord Cromer's appeal in the *Times* this morning . . . ? Well, I'll tell you about it . . . but, oh, I forgot my letter."

The door closed. Grace heard beyond it the muffled sound of a passing argument with the parlour-maid. "Telephone the garage!" screamed the voice.

Clara sat down hurriedly at the secretaire in her bedroom, dropping the book by her side and accidentally pushing it with her elbow into the waste-paper basket, where it lay undisturbed, apparently not being wanted after all. She had been up and dressed at nine, had breakfasted in twelve minutes, read the *Times, Daily News,* a number of cuttings affecting the recent International Congress of Sanitary Engineering. She had ordered dinner in these rapid words to the cook: "We're alone to-night; same as this day last week. No port? Tell Sir Henry." And then plunged into her correspondence: begging letters, requests for her attendance at two sewing-classes, one mothers' meeting, one bazaar. She had manicured herself at great speed. She had invited three people to dinner by telephone; they were only politicals and did not need any notice. She had herself answered the telephone five times and in three cases told the callers that her number contained double fives, not double nines, and that she was not the power-station. Lady Govan found it very difficult to let a maid answer the telephone: servants were so slow about it.

And now she finished her letter-writing quickly, in good, straight, angular characters. She signed her name and flung down the pen so that it made a blot on the mahogany, and, as she closed the envelope, leapt up to put on her hat. As she stood before the swing mirror she did not take the slightest notice of the very pretty, tight-featured, rosy face. She tied on her veil quickly, pouting rosily as all women pout when they put on their veils. She seemed to have more than two hands for, almost simultaneously, she found her umbrella, her gloves, her little bag and her gold purse. And yet, when she whirled into the drawing-room, the hurry had not made her untidy; her brown hair accorded perfectly with the numerous additional curls which were demanded of her by the fashion of the Edwardian day. Somehow, incredibly swiftly, her gloves were on, fully buttoned, her veil perfectly edged the brim of her large black hat. As she swept in, Grace was looking at a pastel landscape on the white wall. She had tired of sitting on the chintz sofa and of the serious book, *Woman In Politics,* which she had found on one of the chairs. Then, after casually opening *Peter Pan* and the book of memoirs which showed that Clara was very much her mother's daughter, she had examined the collection of Lowestoft china which satisfied some need of Sir Henry's soul. And she had reflected that, considering the size of the flat, its few and small bedrooms, its moderate dining-room, this enormous place of entertainment was really a little disproportionate.

" Come along," said Clara. " We mustn't keep the car waiting. We've lots to do before lunch, hurry up."

She plunged into a corner, snatched up a newspaper: " How did this get here? I'll show it to you in the car."

Grace found herself mildly hustled out, listening abstractedly while Clara talked and for nearly ten seconds pressed the lift-bell to encourage the man below to hurry up.

II

Slowly in sensation and swiftly in effect the big electric glided out towards the east, solemn and assured as an ocean liner. Steadfastly Clara talked. Not enough, Grace thought, of those topics which Grace had intended to discuss.

" Yes," she said, " Mary's pretty well. She's looking a bit awkward, of course, but then she's so used to it — "

They laughed together. And again, when Grace suggested that poor Mary had her evening frocks cut on maternity-gown lines, well knowing that she couldn't pass a season.

" Well," said Grace, " she seems pretty happy. If it's a boy — "

But Clara had already eluded her, was choosing a more serious subject. As they turned into Sloane Street, the more serious subject became predominant; Clara had an unusual kind of concentration: fitful concentration, intense for very short intervals; her mind worked like an alternating current, continually switching from one preoccupation into another and throwing into varying channels a constant supply of energy. Thus she was as intent on the afternoon dress to be chosen as on the Cromer appeal, and it was only because Sloane Street was about her, possessive and suggesting clothes, that the afternoon dress at last triumphed. Her mind tried to leap away to her husband's affairs, to Mrs. Westfield's difficulty with her cook, to a small scandal . . . but the electric glided onwards and the shop fronts, the signs, the discreet doorplates so often shouted through the windows: "Hats! Frocks! Underclothes!" that clothing imposed itself on the blurred pattern of her brain and its fugitive impressions.

"Here we are!" she cried gleefully, as the car pulled up.

She leapt out and Grace followed more carefully; she strode, boyish and resolute, past the saluting page, into the big show-room. It was not a busy day. Not more than half a dozen women seemed to require service of the equally numerous assistants. There were no mannikins, but, hung on lay-figures, a number of Paris models, a few rather daring, high-waisted, close to the moulded busts, but most of them tame enough, perhaps a little backward, varied with fichu effects, with transparent yokes; and some, rather overloaded with bows or brandenburgs or broken in the shoulder line, were clearly destined for ladies who had followed their husbands' fortunes from Wandsworth to Belgravia.

Clara and Grace settled with the agreeable assistant at the central table, where lay the Paris fashion plates.

"This is about it," said Lady Govan, pointing to a confection.

"My dear," said Grace, "I don't see you in it."

"Why not?"

"I can't tell you, I just don't."

The assistant contributed that the confection was delightful. It was discarded. Another confection was discussed. It was too mild.

"No good for platform work," said Clara. "What's this?"

She turned over a coloured engraving, pronouncedly Directoire.

"Heavens!" she murmured.

"It's lovely," said Grace.

It was lovely; light blue silk apparently, hanging in straight lines from the breast. And slit — almost to the knee, shamelessly exhibiting a silk-clad leg.

" I'd be mobbed if I wore that in St. Panwich," said Clara, laughing. " Show me something quiet, something a lord-mayoress who'd been to Brussels with the Polytechnic would like."

The assistant smiled dutifully, produced other patterns and plates. But Grace was still looking at the daring picture. It made an appeal to her, as if it held out hands. Its beauty mattered less than its audacity. She sighed, wishing she could wear it, wondered why she could not, decided that to know she could not was enough.

" What are you poring over?" asked Clara, briskly. " That? You're not thinking of it for yourself, are you?"

" Well — " Grace faltered.

" My dear G.! It really wouldn't do," cried Clara in consternation.

" No." Grace's voice was regretful. " I suppose it wouldn't."

She would have liked to discuss why it wouldn't do, but Clara had forgotten, and already the assistant was leading them towards one of the lay-figures. At once two women detached themselves from their contemplation of another dress, came a step closer, interested in the dress because rivals were interested. They glanced at it and at Grace and Clara, still nodding towards the first object of their attention, but irresistibly drawn to the one other women favoured. Eyes crossed, polite but watchful. And insensibly Grace and Clara found that it was the other dress drew them. Still more insensibly they came closer to it. Positions were reversed and a vast content seemed to fill the four women. They had cut one another out; like cats at meat, they robbed one another's plates.

" I think I'll have something like that," said Clara.

The assistant returned, became enthusiastic.

" Yes, I think I would," said Grace. " But we'd better raise the band a little."

" We must raise the band," Clara agreed. " But should I have it caught up here? "

Three fingers made for the same spot. Colours were talked. Patterns flickered; silk and crêpe de chine rolls flowed over the long table, purple, plum-coloured, mauve, garnet, amethyst, all contributing to the scheme. There was an argument as to whether the foundation should be white or cream silk.

" We can fit on Tuesday, your Ladyship," said the assistant.

Doors seemed spontaneously to open, the carpet to caress their feet. It had not been a long business, twenty minutes; Grace was interested, Clara a little excited.

III

The car stopped; veils were selected.

IV

Clara gave a Bond Street address.

" I want a wedding present for the Hellidons," said Clara. " Now if we could only make up our minds before we see the things — "

But one does not make up one's mind like that when one is about to shop in Bond Street, and to choose a wedding present for one who shall have all that is sweet and fair, and have a house in St. James's Square. As the electric slowly threaded its way among the motor-buses which never put anybody down or took anybody up in the costly region, and as the glass of the car reflected for the moment the ten thousand things which they sell in that street, all of which Epictetus could have done without, their perturbation seemed to increase.

" Silver, of course," said Clara, following the line of least resistance.

" Or leather," said Grace, a little more inspired.

For some moments they did not speak, occupied with thoughts of dressing-bags and sugar sifters, shrinking back from the thought of mustard pots with a delicious sense of originality.

" Oh, well," said Clara at last, with a sigh, " I suppose we shall see something." And her swift thought winged away to Lord Cromer. The electric pulled up outside Torrey's. " I suppose we shall see something."

They did. For here was Torrey's with everything that had ever been thought of and a great deal that had never been thought of before. Here shrank away into the insignificance of the obvious the sugar sifter and the fruit spoon. The dressing-case was abashed, the cruet invisible. The assistant, who bought his clothes in Savile Row and his ties in Jermyn Street, leant forward across the glass cases in which everything shone, glittered, twinkled. The assistant said: " Madam," and so admirably that his speech was almost a silence. All round were little groups, women in couples and mixed couples, all earnestly engaged in confabulation with assistants clad as the lilies of the Piccadilly valley. Hushed words. A carpet so discreet that it absorbed but never returned the sound of footsteps; sometimes a laugh, clear as the occasional tinkle of silver on crystal. In the air, a little scent, a very little, one of those scents which are detected in Bond Street and not in the Quadrant.

The urbane presence bent across the glass case and, as Grace looked into his imperturbable eyes, all her ideas seemed to desert her. She wondered whether, if he chose, this young man could sell her a coffin or an elephant. As she looked about her uneasily, she was oppressed, for Torrey's did not flaunt its goods as a bootmaker who crowds, hangs, festoons, garlands his show-case with boots. No! Torrey's goods, many and every, were in their show-cases, glass-shrouded, unobtrusive but established, and all of them lurking as if some magician had turned spiders into liqueur-bottles or sets of brushes. Even Clara felt it, for it was without her usual certainty that she said: " I want a wedding present."

" Yes, Madam," said the urbane, but did not ask what she would like, for that was not his business, nor what she would pay, for that was nobody's business. In one single and harmonious movement he seemed to produce six objects, and more objects, and more objects. There were cut-glass bowls with wire frames for flowers, and draw-bridge sets, and mechanical card-dealers, and perpetual cigar-lighters, and calendars endless as time. A dressing-case opened to show gold tops; a manicure set to boast of solid amber handles.

"I want—" said Clara, hurriedly.

"Yes, Madam," said the urbane.

There came hair-brushes of tortoise-shell and cigar boxes of tortoise-shell and silver; there came Bradshaw and a telephone directory bound in white calf; there came a pocket edition of a typewriter in a purple morocco case.

"Oh, I don't know what I want," said Clara.

Grace found herself listening to another urbane whom she could just hear telling a military-looking man that they did not stock that sort of garter, and that he must go to the Arcade. Clara stood by nervously. "I don't know, I don't know," she murmured.

Grace was fingering cigarette cases, vest buttons, sleeve-links of red Russian enamel. Somehow, this familiar atmosphere was no longer familiar to her. She was conscious of unaccountable disconnections between herself and all these useless, luxurious wares. As if she were standing on the pavement outside, she looked at herself through Torrey's windows, a simple and quite incomprehensible figure, lost in the midst of possessions. "It was," she reflected, "too much; she could not see the things for the things." And, her objective mood increasing, she seemed to see Torrey's and Clara, the urbane and his fellows, and all those others shadows buying things they did not want, or things for people who didn't want them, as if her soul had suddenly been snatched up out of her body, and was now whirling through space, looking down upon the world from its seat upon a molecule.

The cosmic dream passed away. Could this be she? she thought. She, actually saying to the urbane: "Do you happen to have any—mustard pots?"

Clara's heels went tap-tap so hard that the carpet reluctantly confessed to the noise.

"I must hurry, I must hurry," she murmured, "I can't wait."

V

Clara leant out of the window as the car swooped round the corner into Dover Street. Upon the cold wind her words flowed back towards Grace: "Hurry up, Tyler."

An old soldier saluted as they went into the bookshop. *The Spirit Of Parliament* was bought. Then three copies of an illustrated *Pickwick Papers,* to be despatched in time for Christmas to different colonies. Grace bought *The Little Flowers of St. Francis of Assisi* because it was prettily bound, calmly telling herself that she knew she wouldn't read it.

A winking doll was bought for Rose, as Mary's little girl was to have a birthday. The car stopped. Somebody was telephoned. Grace was set down at Naseners to buy some Grieg, and came out with some Liza Lehmann. Big Ben, very far away, boomed one o'clock.

"We shall never get through," said Clara anxiously.

The car stopped at the Hyde Park Hotel, for the *Academy* had to be snatched up from the book-stall.

"Hurry up," said Clara.

VI

The two sisters were lunching alone at Kensington Square. Grace's house had a tall, narrow front of small Georgian brick. Beyond the door and its Norwich Imp and its little fanlight stretched the long hall, oak-panelled half-way to the ceiling; upon the cream distempered walls were sporting English prints of gentlemen, all red-coated, some falling over five-barred gates, and of hounds in full cry behind fleeing foxes. No hatstand here, but an oak cupboard, dim in the distant lobby. All alone the incongruous red and orange of a Jugend picture in a rough green frame. The dining-room, where they now sat, repeated the vague, artistic impression of the hall. Here was a Turkey carpet, but not red and blue: more subtly, it was red and green. They sat, uncomfortably, at a gate-leg table on ladder-back chairs whose rushes caught at their gowns. A Welsh dresser, suitably defaced by age, bore many blue plates and a set of jugs, graduated in size, decorated with pictures of ships. Plain green canvas curtains broke the whiteness of the walls upon which, aloof and lonely, hung an engraving of "The Trial Of Charles I," and one oil representing obviously English girls picking grapes in the South of France; a copper warming-pan hung upon a nail. Upon the mantelpiece, under the mirror in the rim of which were stuck half a dozen invitation cards, were a model of a lawyer, arguing, in Staffordshire pottery, and two Dutch copper coffee-pots. The room had a quality of art and error. It had the air that comes to rooms when an artistic impulse becomes predominant in society and is adopted by those who like it without quite understanding it.

It was anachronistic, and yet not of its period; it was reconstructed and transplanted from another age. This Jacobean room was Jacobean because James had come to town, as in other days it might have flaunted pampas grass and wax fruit under a glass case or, as in days yet to come, it might be decorated after Picasso or Wyndham Lewis.

This room in which now, lunch being done, the sisters sat over their coffee, silent as one is a while after a meal, was Edward and Grace and their matrimonial bond and the time that made it. It was the resultant of several forces: some desire in Grace to live in the midst of white and of green, of restful, pleasant colours; of the effect upon the Kinnersleys of rooms which were Jacobean before theirs was Jacobean; of some veneration for the ancient; and of an uncertainty expressed by these very English girls petrified in the act of picking grapes in the south of France.

Grace found herself looking at it more critically.

" I wonder," she said to Clara suddenly, " why we've gone in for oak."

" Well," said Clara, " lots of people have."

" I know," said Grace. " I suppose that's why we did. I like it," she added after a pause, " but I wonder if I shall always like it."

" I don't suppose you will," said Clara, cynically. " But then what does that matter if you like it now? Now, Henry, you know, he likes all that Chippendale stuff — "

While Clara related how Sir Henry had found the Chippendale sideboard which was in her own dining-room, Grace, who did not listen very intently, wandered on in her mood of doubt. She remembered how she had loved that Burne-Jones of her father's and then, a little later, discovered Rossetti for herself; how, two months before her marriage, she had chosen good solid modern suites, and how, a little more recently, the Jacobean impulse had come to her, sweeping away the snows of yester year. For a second she had a vision of life, swiftly unrolling like a cinematograph film that had suddenly gone mad . . .

But again, as was now usual with her, the vision passed. No other vision imposed itself upon her mental retina. There was just a blankness or a doubt, a grey screen upon which Clara obtrusively flashed her own concerns. For now Clara was talking of her husband and her occupations.

" Anyhow," said Clara, " you can keep that furniture of yours if you choose, or change it if you choose. Not like me."

" Surely," said Grace, " there's nothing to make you do anything you don't want to."

Clara laughed a little shrilly. " My dear girl, anybody can see you aren't in Parliament. I don't mean to say I am in Parliament, but it's the next worse thing. An M. P. can do anything his supporters like, but an M. P.'s wife can only do what the M. P. thinks his supporters will like, and that's a good deal more complicated."

" I suppose," said Grace, " you mean that . . . if

Henry wanted to powder his nose, badly I mean, well he'd chance it, but if you wanted to, he might be a bit more severe."

"That's about it," said Clara. She laughed shrilly. "I shall never powder my nose, even if I feel I want to. Never, never," she added, in accents of woe. "There isn't a parson's wife in the whole constituency powders her nose, and if I were to do it, my dear, it simply wouldn't Do. . . . When Henry is in the Cabinet, I shall not only have to leave it unpowdered, as I do now: I'll have to polish it with a selvyt!"

"That's what they call democracy," said Grace, laughing. "I'll be the same when Edward's Lord Chief."

"Pooh," said Clara, "when Edward's Lord Chief, he won't look at your nose."

There was a little pause, and just for a second Grace was conscious of some disillusion. And yet, a moment later, of a curious feeling: would she look at the Lord Chief's nose. . . . What was Edward's nose like, anyway? It was horrible to think that this once wonderful, well-moulded nose had become so habitual that she could hardly remember it at all. Does one cease to see things when they are too close?

But Clara was whirling on. "We'll have to move soon, I think. A flat, you know, it's . . . it's not Solid. When the secretary of a ward-committee comes up from St. Panwich, he looks round . . . well, how shall I say . . . ? as if he were frightened. . . . A London flat, you know, it's . . . rakish, immoral."

"But why did you go into a flat?" asked Grace, smiling.

"We had it, for one thing," said Clara, "and then in the beginning, you know, it's sort of modest, unassuming. A young member mustn't overdo it. The whips don't like it. By and by, in a year or so, when Henry has made his maiden speech, it'll be different. We'll be Established."

Grace was granted a vision of extraordinary complexities, of a mysterious process where lack of assumption combined with adequate assertions, with judicious subserviencies, with strategic compromises between the fashionable entertainments that amuse aged Cabinet ministers and a virtuous demeanour that placates constituencies. All sorts of things came in: the right dwelling, not too smart, for that's frivolous; not too dowdy, for that's not powerful enough; not too small, for that's poor; not too large, for that's threatening. And the attitude of the member's wife: a knowledge of bills for the serious young man; a joke, just faintly naughty (but oh! so faintly) for the buffers on the committees; a gown, just smarter than the St. Panwich gowns, and yet not so smart that St. Panwich could not copy it; support of the Church; interest in Nonconformity; respect for the Jews; broad-minded tolerance of the agnostics, and a ready ear for adventitious religions; charity without patronage and, if possible, patronage without charity, for that's cheaper; a knowledge of cricket, football, the plays of Shakespeare, the contents of the *Daily Mail,* of Tennyson (but not Swinburne), of political finance (excluding the sale of honours), of everybody's name and of everybody's face, and of everybody's street, and of everybody's aunt by marriage, of babies, of rheumatism, of cures for chilblains, and of the historic sayings of Mr. Disraeli. . . . Behold! the perfect member's wife.

But Clara did not mind. "There are lots of things one can do, you see; it's a complicated business. . . . All those things one mustn't do — "

"Yes," said Grace, "it's the things one mustn't do that matter, not the things one must. It's hard on Henry too."

"It is," said Clara, fervently. "Do you know, he said 'hear, hear' the other day when Balfour was up. He heard the Speaker didn't like it; didn't like it at all. It's being a young member. Still, he won't always be a young member." She flushed prettily; her blue eyes shone: "And I am going to Help."

For some minutes Clara expounded the satisfactions of helping. Helping socially, entertaining in the constituency, dinners to useful people, with a few nice ones thrown in to make the evening possible; and being, in a general, busybody sort of way, very much there among the mothers and the babies and such of the men as weren't too rough.

"Well," said Grace, at last, "I suppose it's all right; it's interesting in a way. I suppose getting-on's always interesting, wherever it is you get to. And I suppose you like the children?"

"I don't know that I'm so fond of them," said Clara, "between ourselves, the play-centre's rather smelly. It can't be helped, of course; they're so poor. Still . . . when we've got tariff reform — "

Her last words made her fervent, but then again the fervour lapsed; her brows knotted; a little listlessly, she said: "And it keeps one busy; gives one something to do."

"I wonder," said Grace, after a long pause, "whether women of our sort do want something to do. We haven't much, you know. When we've ordered the meals, and bought our clothes, and drunk tea with somebody, and been to a theatre or something . . . well, the day's over somehow, and yet . . . well, I suppose it's all right."

"It isn't all right," said Clara, suddenly aggressive. "What you want, G., is something real to do. Something to get you out of all this 'I wonder, I wonder' sort of way. Of course you get bored and morbid with nobody to look after."

"I've got my two children," said Grace, a note of protest in her voice.

"Oh! go on," said Clara, almost rudely, "you know what that means too. Playing with Susan and Horace from five to six, if you happen to be at home, assuming they did want to play with you, but you know they don't."

"Yes," murmured Grace, "they're beginning to look after their own business."

"And that's not the end of it," said Clara, more trenchantly. "The nurse is going to hand them over to the governess, and the governess to the preparatory, and the preparatory to the public school and the high-school, and Brussels and the 'Varsity. Why, you talk, you talk as if you were Mary with a rabbit warren on the third floor. My dear, you don't come in at all."

Grace's eyes fixed rather sadly upon the curtains; the reflected light illumined her pupils with a deep green that was almost that of the sea. As if puzzled she tugged at her hair with her short white fingers.

"Yes," she said, hesitatingly, "perhaps you're right. Of course, when they were babies — "

"It's different now," said Clara, rather brutally.

VII

Soon Clara had gone. She had gone hurriedly, after confessing that her haste of the morning had been so well rewarded that she had nothing particular to do that afternoon. This seemed to disturb her, and Grace put it to herself that she could see in Clara's eye that she was going out to find an outlet for her energy. Before going she had roped in her sister as a member of a care committee, and made her pledge herself to attend the play-centre. Now it was half-past three. She too had nothing to do. Soon it would be teatime. That would be something; of course she might go and see somebody, but she felt too languid to telephone. The children were out, she supposed. Well, perhaps somebody would come. She took up *The Little Flowers of St. Francis of Assisi,* tried to read the book. She found it amazingly dull.

VIII

At five o'clock Horace and Susan came in. They were pushed into the room by their nurse and there left, close to the door, two little figures stranded in what seemed to them an enormous space. Both were clad in rather vivid blue; flannel for Horace and some woolly substance for Susan. In his short knickers, exposing his sturdy little calves, and his tunic belted in with white patent leather, Horace looked curiously like his father. He had the close brown curls, the small features and the fine brown eyes of the Kinnersley breed, and that day his little mouth was smiling. As he looked at the model steamboat which he held the smile was complacent, proprietorial; satisfaction radiated from Horace. He took a few steps forward and slowly pushed the steamboat along upon its keel, accompanying its progress by "puffer" noises. From time to time he looked up. "Mummie, look at my steamboat. Haven't I got a fine steamboat? Do you think they'll like my steamboat when I sail it on the pond?"

"I'm sure they will, darling," said Grace. "Susie, come here and tell mummie what you've been doing."

Susan came slowly, careless rather than reluctant. She was big for her age; though but four years old, she was taller than Horace, and Grace was sometimes a little anxious, for *The Mother's Book* told her they ought to have been the same height. She was a pretty child, and resembled exactly neither her father nor her mother, for she combined with Grace's beautiful greenish eyes and her autumn hair, the small nose and satisfied mouth of the Kinnersleys.

"Well, what have you been doing to-day?" said Grace.

"Been a dood girl," said Susan carelessly. "Have you got any sweeties, mummie?" Her small hand fluttered towards the tea-tray, where were chocolate and biscuits.

"Did Nannie say you were to have sweeties?" said Grace. But Horace interrupted. "Mummie," he asked, "have other little boys got steamboats? Do you think they have steamboats like me?"

"Not all of them," said Grace.

"I am very glad," Horace enunciated with great care.

"Horace!" cried Grace, horrified, "what a dreadful thing to say!"

"Mummie, I want sweeties," said Susan, plaintively. "Horace mustn't, he's been sick."

Horace dropped his steamboat, leapt to his feet. "It isn't true! it isn't true!" he cried, passionately, and stamped.

" Horace," said Grace, " you mustn't say ' it isn't true '; that's rude."

" Well," grumbled Horace, " it isn't 'nackeret."

At this Grace had to laugh. Clearly the blood of the Kinnersley ran here, but Horace took no notice. Forgetting the insult in his greater preoccupation, he was now pushing his steamboat along the carpet, making " puffer " noises, and repeating at intervals: " My steamboat, my carpet; " or from time to time, as his thoughts wandered to other concerns of his own: " Five blue balls make one red one, five blue balls make one red one."

Susan was tugging at her mother's sleeve. " Mummie," she said, breathlessly, " I want sweeties and biscuits and . . . and sugar and ' matses,' and . . . and— "

" Whatever do you want all that for? "

" To play ' sop.' "

" To play shop? "

" Yes, ' sop.' "

Indulgently the stock was provided for the shop. Susan gathered it into her small hands and settled near one of the windows.

" Now," said Grace, " Mummie will play ' sop ' with you. What will Mummie buy? "

Susan turned upon her a green eye that was hostile. " Susie play ' sop,' " she declared, " Susie play ' sop ' all alone," and turned her back upon her mother.

For a minute or two Grace, from the sofa, watched her two children: Horace pushing his steamboat up and down on his carpet, and Susan purchasing her own stock from her own shop. Then, with a little sigh, realising their intentness upon their own affairs, she once more took up the *Little Flowers of St. Francis* that so exceedingly bored her.

IX

Very slowly the door opened and, with a hushing finger upon his lips, Edward appeared in the doorway. The children, still busy with their private games, had not noticed him; Edward, smiling a smile mysterious, boyish, mischievously arch, raised his arms in the air. Suddenly he let out a piercing hiss and, as his children turned, a little surprised, three times in succession he leapt into the air. Another piercing hiss and he flung himself upon the floor on the top of Horace, vowing he was a large serpent about to eat him. With another movement he gathered Susan into his arms, upsetting by a kick the whole of her shop. Susan gave a loud scream, and Horace cried out, for his father had sat upon his steamboat. But already Edward was on his feet again, carrying one child under each arm and solemnly prancing round and round the room, singing at the top of his voice a hideous pot-pourri: "The boy stood on the burning deck whence all but he had fled, and always kept his napper down save when he was in bed—"

"Mummie! Mummie! Mummie!" screamed Susan.

"Down the valley of death rode the three hundred . . . hey diddle-diddle, the cat and the fiddle . . . (Tune interposed, one from *The Merry Widow*) . . . the cow jumped over the moon, the little dog laughed to see such sport, the dish ran away with the spoon."

Round and round the room he pranced, his face all radiant, joggling the recalcitrant children, beaming, assured of the good effect of his fatherliness. He was not wrong: already the children had forgotten their games and were gasping in delighted gurgles, but as Horace had dropped forward and was now being held almost head down, Grace at last interposed: "Let them go, Edward," she said, "I think they've had enough."

"Enough!" cried Edward, boisterously. "Enough is as good as a feast, but who says 'enough'? Horace, you're a true Englishman, aren't you? You'll never say 'enough,' will you? Ha, Ha," he laughed, uproariously. "Horace is the champion of England, he'll never say 'enough' while he can stand up."

But at last Grace rescued her crumpled and laughing children. No sooner had Edward released them than he seized her by both hands.

"Gracie-Bracie, now I'll treat thee likewise."

"Don't be ridiculous, Edward."

But Edward was dragging her round and round the drawing-room in a pretended and inadequate waltz to an obbligato contributed by himself, based on *Waltz me round again, Willie.*

For Edward was always funny and always fond. That night he was impersonating a working-man comin' 'ome, as he put it to his "old Dutch." This he kept up for some time. Said he was 'avin' a night orf. Wished to know if there was anything to eat in the 'ouse. He was full of vapid gaiety, at its best when partnered with some reluctant auditor but yet possible without assistance. Gaiety was his society manner, or rather his society manner was a burlesque of gaiety.

While the children were removed from the room, he was loudly imitating a bell-ringer.

"Good night, Daddy," said Horace, with polite cordiality.

"Good night, Daddy," said breathless Susan.

"Ding-dong, ding-dong," Edward shouted. And as the children were taken up-stairs by dark, solemn Nannie, Edward stood on the threshold, looking up the stairs, his arms extended in imitation of a parson, and loudly exhorting his dearly beloved to be good in the bath.

He returned to the drawing-room, and as Grace upon the sofa, *The Little Flowers* in her hand, watched him with a fond smile in which was a little embarrassment, as if she were exhausted by this outburst of vitality, some seriousness seemed to come to him.

"Well, Gracie-Bracie," he said more quietly, but still benevolent, "and what have we been doing with our little self to-day?"

"Oh, nothing in particular," said Grace. "I went shopping this morning, and Clara said — "

"We've been rather full up," said Edward. "No end of excitement with the new K. C.'s. So you saw Clara."

"Yes," said Grace. "I — "

"Some of them are rather sore about it," Edward interrupted. "There are only twenty-four this year, and it's been rather a shock to a few of them to be left out."

Evidently he did not want to hear about Clara. For again: "Of course I only put in as a matter of form. I haven't a ghost of a chance for another four years. No." And his manner for a second resumed its archness. "*Non, mon amie, pas un phantom.*"

He laughed loudly to himself. He had a fondness for French translations, for distortions of words, distortions of phrases and of all accents. But one week before he had suggested to Grace when leaving for the week-end that they should take the train — the *chemin de fer.* But now his conversation was of the Temple and of the Courts which had just reopened. News was abundant, for a friend had taken the Commission of Assizes on the Western circuit as a speculation for a judgeship. And a promising junior, whom Edward described as "swollen-headed," had been taken from the Parliamentary Bar as his marshal. Walking up and down, his hands buried deep in the pockets of his perfect trousers, for minute after minute Edward held forth on the gossip of the Griffin, the cases he had in hand, the heaviness of the lists, the temperaments of judges, the reputations made and in the making. At times he asked Grace a question, but took no notice of her answer. His occasional attention to his audience was nothing but a nervous habit. He wanted no replies to his questions; he wanted to talk. But suddenly he seemed to become aware of his wife's existence; the gravity went out of him; he strode up to the sofa on which she sat and, with a great air of demonstrative affection, threw one arm round her shoulders, while his other hand seized her by her arm and began to fondle it. For Edward always fondled. He was one of those men who have a continual need of physical contact, as if something sensual in them had been left unsatisfied or, perhaps, as if the potency of his interest in himself preventing him from letting others speak, he had to establish by the link of an arm or the contact of a shoulder the fact of the existence of the sedulous hearer. So he stroked Grace's arm as he had seized and pawed his children, as he had maintained his hand after dinner upon Sir Henry's reluctant knee. As he stroked, from facetious he grew flirtatious. "And what have we been doing with our little self?" he asked again, evidently forgetting that he had asked the question before and quite unaware that it had been partly answered. But it was not yet to be answered, for Edward went on: "Has my lady-fair been flirting? That would be very naughty, with hubby dear rescuing criminals from the gallows all day long to buy diamond tiaras. Gracie-Bracie, I see it in your green eye, you've been out with a fascinating man!"

"Don't be silly, Edward," said Grace, making a slight movement to free her arm. "As if one husband weren't enough to try a woman."

But Edward did not hear. And now, judiciously and morally, he discussed a fashionable divorce case which was the pride of the cause-list. He outlined the details. A little lecture was delivered on the nature of evidence. Then he shifted from law to the higher ground of morality.

"It's a clear case," he said. "I think it a very wrong thing for any married man to behave like that."

"I suppose so," said Grace. "Still, if he loved the girl."

Strangely enough Edward's answer coincided with her implied question: "It's all very well talking of love and all that sort of thing. I don't say that some impulses aren't too much for any of us, but still, when it comes to an unmarried girl! When you think that all the risk and shame fall upon her. . . . I think a man ought to restrain himself. He ought to think beforehand. You see, Gracie, we can't do what we like in this world, we've got to respect things: the law, and the conventions and all that. Why, one might think one was living in a state of nature judging from the cases that come along—"

Other cases were put forward, cases nearly all within Edward's own experience, illustrated by his own attitudes, his own performances in court, his own addresses to the jury, and the scintillating things he had respectfully hurled at the judge. For all roads in Edward's mind led back to Edward. Mainly his thoughts were of his profession, his reputation and his advancement. Not that he lacked heart, for he loved the children he played with, the wife who had given them to him, but they, with politics, morals, general ideas and the rest of the world, hung in a state of suspense in an atmosphere into which he had to plunge. He was his own life. They were addenda, addenda that, when observed, became significant, for which he could feel deeply, but yet addenda, things not essential, that could be taken up or discarded at will. And when he took up child, wife, or idea the effort at once grew perceptible, threw about his deed a veil of archness or farcical humour. He had to transplant himself from the soil of his self into the soil where those others grew.

While Grace brushed her hair before the looking-glass, she could hear Edward in the dressing-room, making noises that the practised ear of the wife connected at once with acts: the dropping of boot-trees, the opening of the tight top drawer where he kept his shirts, and even the sound of the brushes when he put them down on the marble top of the washstand. As she slowly drew the comb through the thick dark gold of her hair, her arms raised above her head, she was unconscious of the supreme beauty that is given almost every woman by that action. The light from the bulb upon her head brought out upon her arms a gleaming milkiness, and all about the cheekbones, the exquisite narrow bridge of her high nose, a faint spatter of freckles made more dazzling the whiteness of her brow, melted imperceptibly from brown into the lightest ochre, into the hesitating rosiness of her cheeks, into the warm white of chin and neck. And there were deep, dark shadows about the hollows of her elbows and breast, tender shadows tinged with bistre that flitted in the light.

With serious face, as her strong short hands manœuvred the brush and comb, two silver facets glittering in the light, she tried alternately to analyse and to expel from her mind the confused impression left upon it by Edward, his antics, his pursuits, his absurd, lovable boisterousness. Lovable or absurd? Or neither? or both? She wondered how she was affected, was surprised to be affected, yet more surprised not to know how she was affected. She knew that, somehow, for three months, she had been analysing him, herself, their relation, without arriving at anything more definite than that her individuality was disentangling itself from the duality which is marriage. "And they shall be of one flesh," she thought. And smiled. Yes, that was all very well, but could they be of one spirit?

Shocked a little by her own boldness, her hair being coiffed, heavy-piled on the back of her head, she slowly powdered the whole of her face, lightly, and yet so negligently that she smiled at herself when, a little later, having taken up the stick of lip-salve, she found that she had powdered her mouth. She seemed to think of Edward with a coldness in which was something that did not relent, something almost cruel. She thought of August at Trouville, of the "second honeymoon" as Edward called it, of Edward morally frowning at the French smart set, anxious lest she should be looked at, inimical to her mild desire to risk a gambling franc at the *petits chevaux*, vetoing her entry into the baccarat room . . . and yet incomprehensibly trying to convey that he had the joy of life, that he was a bad, bold rake and conducting his wife on the *planches* with a winking, naughty air, jocularly hinting that doubtless Trouville thought they were an irregular couple —

"An irregular couple . . . Edward!" Grace smiled, rather contemptuously. But at once her mood passed to a bewilderment in which was some sadness. What could this mean? this new mood? Why could she see Edward detached from herself? Six years before he had come to her, gay, smiling, with the joy of life in his hands, causing her throat to swell. And now, here he was, gay, smiling, with the joy of life in his hands, but her throat no longer swelled. She had explored him, and he her. . . . A mutual life had come without discoveries, without possible discoveries. . . . Children too, wonderful once, but now actual, separate human beings, unrelated to her. . . . She stood up, hands upon her breast, full of intolerable, vague sympathy for herself.

"I don't understand," she murmured. "He's got his own affairs, of course, and I too."

But had she? She reviewed her day, the round of it, and the previous day, and the chance of the morrow. Round and round, always round and round. Could it always be round and round?

The dressing-room door opened. Edward came in, singing a tune, flat as usual. He was in his shirt and trousers, carried his tie in his hand.

"You better tie it, Gracie," he said, "since you say I do it so badly."

Without a word she took the tie, passed it through the loop and round the collar. As she tied it, their faces close together, she was conscious of his eyes upon her, rather intent. He laughed, increased the intimacy of the attitude by banteringly caressing her bare arms.

She laughed, but she knew that his touch irritated her. Her hands trembled, as if her nerves had gained some independence. She tied the tie badly.

"I don't think much of that," said Edward, looking into the mirror and, with assumed carelessness, roughly pressing his shoulder against her. "I must punish my lady fair."

He seized her in his arms, kissed her. She was conscious of some very faint, insidious revulsion of feeling. For the kisses were only two, one upon her neck and one upon her lips: they had no lingering or possessive quality; he kissed her as he might have smacked her — playfully. Without intent she freed herself, pushed him away.

"Hullo, hul-*lo!* What's this, scratchy kitten?"

But his jocularity vanished before the angry, set mouth. There was a silence, soon broken by Grace's nervous laugh.

"I don't know. I'm sorry, Edward. I didn't mean it . . . Ned."

His smile returned, secure. Only in most sentimental moments was Edward called Ned.

"You've got the jumps," he said, sagely. "You want a change. Would you like to go away for a bit? to Brighton, say. I could get down for the week-ends. Or we might do a theatre to-morrow night."

She shook her head. And again, when he suggested a doctor, a rest-cure, nerve foods. She did not know what was the matter. Suddenly Edward, with a cry of: "Oh, I forgot," dashed into the dressing-room, returned with a little case.

"I noticed it in Piccadilly Arcade a day or two ago. I thought you'd like it."

It was a necklet of jade. Green jade to match her eyes.

"Oh, Edward," she faltered, horribly guilty. She kissed him quickly upon the cheek.

He took her in his arms, kissed her behind the ear. Then she heard him hum, as he rocked her: "Hush-a-bye, baby, on the tree-top." Gently she freed herself. She looked at him dumbly, grateful, ashamed, disturbed, unable to disentangle her emotions, the exasperation from the affection.

Edward said nothing. Hands in pockets he smiled broadly upon his lovely wife.

CHAPTER THE FOURTH

. . . AND ROUND AND ROUND . . .

I

As the Underground carried her from Gower Street towards the West with that quiet swiftness which has done away with the old sense of motion which it had when, dirty and smoky, it wheezed on protesting, Grace reflected that this had been a big afternoon. The play-centre, this odd development of Clara's activities, was a very large room, the extraordinary cleanliness of which singularly contrasted with the usual air of St. Panwich. She remembered it by reconstruction: a boarded floor, unpolished so that little feet might not slip; whitewashed walls, decorated with pictures of Louis Wain cats, with long Dutch landscapes in which danced little boys and girls; there was a frieze of large roses, also a picture of a bulbous little girl cradled in something that looked like a champagne glass, a little girl, serious and goggling, and intimating that hers were "happy days." But mainly, when she thought of pictures, Grace had in her mind a solemn group of four little boys and four little girls, all rather ragged and all very dirty, who stood in a row with linked hands, admiring a large reproduction of a little girl standing on a pile of books against an enormous St. Bernard. That picture was called: "I'se Biggest."

There had been a piano in a corner, and Grace had played little tunes from a book, little tinkling tunes such as the Elizabethans loved, so that the infants might form a circle and solemnly wander round and round the countess who had come in for ten minutes to look very uncomfortable in their staring midst. Grace laughed as she thought of the countess, of her sables, of her "how delightfuls," and of her sweet, soft, scented womanhood, of the contrast between the long white glove and the rough paws of the charwoman with whom she shook hands in the sacred cause of charity and votes. She laughed again as she changed at Edgware Road for the Hammersmith line, so much so that a clerk, returning early from the City, looked longingly at her charming figure and wondered what she would say if he ventured. He would not have been snubbed. He would merely have been stared at in a surprised way, for the whole of Grace's impression was too humorous and too pathetic to leave any room for indignation. Somehow it had all been very dirty. Not obviously, normally dirty, for on the whole the ragged pinafores were fairly clean, and the faces freshly polished, while the mothers had snatched a minute from the washtub and the holystone to put their hair right. But she had had a sensation of under-linen absent or unwashed, of bodies uncared for, of a general lack of food, of coal, of an unbridgeable gap between her boudoir and their back room. And Clara, she thought, bright, metallic, whizzing, seizing upon unoccupied children and compelling them to play kiss in the ring, or solemnly leading them round and round the mulberry bush, Clara had conveyed to her little more than a hectic, forced activity. It was artificial, the whole thing.

Four mothers only had been there, doubtless because they were unemployed. The thirty children seemed to have drifted to the room out of the street because it happened to be warmer than the street, or they had been dumped on the door-step like foundlings. That is what they were, socially, temporary foundlings, to be left till called for. And as the train rumbled on towards Hammersmith, Grace remembered something lamentable in the faces of those four women, their scanty hair, the cheeks fallen in over their ravaged gums; they had not gloated over their children at play, these four. They could only reply, hard and incoherent, "No, Mums," or "Yes, your ladyships," to Clara, her countess, and the three West-enders, guaranteed bright, who had been imported for the afternoon. One mother had said it was a fine day; the others had perspired with emotion when accepting tea. And not even the ruthless suppression of a tendency on the part of some of the larger boys to force the little girls to play leapfrog had given the proceedings reality.

Reality! Was this reality? "Work," "occupation," as Clara called it? Or was it just something done? something artificial forced into the artificiality of the day? To amuse those little children, to keep them for a while out of the way of passing cabs, to put them beyond the reach of a cold in the head, that was all right. One could see where they came in, these little ones from the slums of St. Panwich, but those who entertained them, what about them? "We don't come in," Grace reflected. "We play with them, but we don't know them, we're outside them. It's not real, somehow. . . . It's just something more done, from our point of view . . . as if it mattered whether we did anything or not."

II

The mood was still upon her when she reached Mary's house. As she pushed open the gate she determined to engage Mary Stanley in a discussion: do the rich get rewarded for looking after the poor? But she did not have her opportunity for Mary, who seemed to have been stowed away among the cushions with great care, was pouring out tea for their mother.

Tom Stanley, whose name was actually Thomas though nobody in his life had ever used it, had apparently chosen his house with a patriarchal purpose in his mind. It was a large three-storied, white-plastered house close to the King's Theatre, in the Hammersmith Road. Opposite stretched the dirty-dark wall of Nazareth House, but this ugliness was shut out from the windows by the front garden where two acacias and a big chestnut tree combined with the plane trees outside to give to the house that quiet air of aloofness which is so necessary to a patriarch who takes his house on a seven years' lease. There was a little portico round the quiet green door. Inside, the taste of the master at once became affirmative, for the hall was papered in red, set off by Axel Haig etchings of Venice. There was a vast hat-stand, decorated with so many hats that it seemed incredible that there was but one man in the house. And in the blue china jar stood sticks and umbrellas, some of the latter in a condition which made it safe to lend them to forgetful guests. Grace gave her umbrella to the parlourmaid whose cap had just that slight inaccuracy of angle upon rather rebellious hair which showed that Hammersmith was very near and Kensington not quite so near. She caught a glimpse of the dining-room, of the overmantel and its mirror, lit up by the fire which was burning below it, of the weighty sideboard with its tantalus, of the corner bookcase with its pile of bound volumes of *Punch,* its litter of papers on the top, of the rack of pipes above.

There was an indomitable air of solid comfort, of careless, jovial untidiness; an air of pipe, slipper and fox terrier; and indeed the fox terrier came to her, wagging his stumpy tail.

"Hallo, Spot," she said, bending to stroke him as she entered the drawing-room. Spot followed, breathing excitedly, violently wriggling his thin hind-quarters. Spot was one of those fulsome dogs that lay insistent and rather muddy paws upon the dresses of women as they sit down. She answered Mrs. Westfield's questions: Edward was well and busy. Horace gave no ground for report, but Susan had fallen down-stairs and cut her lip. For a while Mrs. Westfield pursued more minute enquiries: whether Horace should this year be admitted to the Christmas dinner as he was so grown-up for his age; whether Mary would be well enough to come; and did Grace think that maids preferred silver-backed brushes as Christmas presents or just money?

When everything had been answered, Mary in her turn gave her news: "Tom's pretty well; of course at this time of the year he's rather busy with all the Christmas trade. I never seem to see him now except on Sundays."

"Never mind, my dear," said Mrs. Westfield, with rather Victorian sprightliness. "One generally manages to see enough of one's husband."

Mary shook her head. "I don't think so, Mother," she said, laughing rather broadly. "You don't know Tom; he's always so jolly when he comes back from the City. Besides, after a whole day with that large family of mine, all girls too, and seeing nobody but the servants and the callers, it's quite a relief to have a man about."

"Yes," said Mrs. Westfield, gravely veering back to the realities of life. "One does need a man in the house."

Grace avoided considering whether one needed a man in the house; somehow she seemed to be avoiding a good many things in these days. Rather hurriedly she plied Mary with questions, while she sipped her tea and made a very healthy meal of sandwiches which did not quite please her, because her taste, accustomed to mustard and cress or salmon, rebelled a little against gentlemen's relish. She listened to Mary's recital of what the doctor had said. Mrs. Westfield became more deeply interested. The gynecological spirit pervaded the drawing-room, and very vaguely, Grace perceived a faint disgust in herself. Mary, in her loose blue gown, her face a big flower of pink and white, her beautiful fair hair piled high over her forehead, was certainly at her best. There was a clearness in her skin and a bright blueness in her eyes. She seemed satisfied, at rest, but it was just her quality of smugness, her rather stupefied satisfaction in restfulness which exasperated Grace. For Mary was so obviously contented with her large, dowdy house, with her comfortable drawing-room, the heavy Chesterfield upon which she lay. As Grace looked about her, she was conscious of a heaviness which to her mind was almost ugliness, though in reality it was rather comfort. There were many armchairs, all fit to sit upon; they stood on a rose-sown carpet; there were many bronzes, and palms in green or swathed pots; a great many photos in silver frames; a cerise window-curtain fell carelessly over the music piled on the top of the piano. It was all large, sprawling, horribly content.

Grace mentally decided that Tom's house did not bear witness to the three or four thousand a year he was making in his commission agency. "But then," she reflected, quickly, "with four children . . . and that isn't the end of it."

Mrs. Westfield was now talking of things in general. "Have you been to a picture palace yet, Grace?" she asked. "They've just opened one in Oxford Street, and they're talking about it in all the papers."

Grace showed herself a little haughtily superior.

"Well," said Mrs. Westfield, "I don't see any harm in it. Of course the servants are mad about it. I'm going to let them all out together next week and get the sensation over. It's better than the music-halls anyhow, and the chapels, judging from the trouble they get into there."

Grace turned away her head and stared at one of the bronzes. She thought that her mother mixed very curiously with the gentility of the 'seventies the grossness which she supposed was quite of the period, but yet seemed to clash with it. Mrs. Westfield then wondered whether the picture palaces would prove popular and whether more of them would be built by and by. Their influence on the lower classes again began to bulk. The conversation became more specialised, to be dominated by the servant question, for Mrs. Westfield, whose servants had seldom stayed with her less than ten years, was oppressed by the modern fear of suddenly being deserted by the whole household.

"Girls are so discontented nowadays," she sighed. "I don't know what we're coming to."

She did not find out, for neither Grace nor Mary had servant problems, except that Mary's nurses were considered a little uppish by the other servants and complained of having their meals so cunningly set outside the nursery door that they fell over them if they didn't look. The heaviness of it all seemed to grow upon Grace and overwhelm her. The weight of material preoccupations, unimportant, unduly valued. So she was not sorry when her mother got up, and she refused the lift in the brougham which was offered her, affecting to want to talk to Mary. She did want to talk to Mary though she hardly knew of what. And curiously it was of Mary's health, her health, that is, in a broader, different sense from the one which interested their mother.

"How are you?" she asked. "I don't mean how you're feeling about the baby and all that; generally, I mean."

"Oh," said Mary, and she was careless, "I'm all right."

There was a pause. Then suddenly Grace asked:

"Happy?"

Mary's blue eyes stared at her a little surprised, as if she had never before been asked so odd a question: "Of course I am," she said, a little pompously. "What do you expect?"

Of course, what else should she expect from a well-fed young mother? But still—. Those words, "but still," seemed to hang over all her impression and conclusions. "But still," was the ghostly footman who opened doors for her as she went, giving her extraordinary peeps into new rooms of that unexplored building which was called the world.

"Well," she said at length, "of course you would be with the children all right, and you feeling all right too, and Tom in a good temper. He always is in a good temper."

"I'm not so sure," said Mary, cheerfully, and quite unaware of some faint irony in Grace's words. "You've never heard Tom give me what he calls a 'mouthful.'" She laughed. "He's got a large mouth. But then that's marriage, isn't it?"

"Yes, that's marriage," echoed Grace.

"After all," said tolerant Mary, "he's got a lot to try him in the City with his nine to six when it isn't nine to nine. When he's had a hard day, of course he expects to find everything going well at home and everybody pleased to see him, even if he's a little grumpy. It's only natural. And we're pleased to see him, all of us."

"Mary," said Grace, suddenly, "are you ever sorry you married?"

"Sorry I married?" Mary repeated, incredulously. "What ever do you mean, G.? Of course I'm not sorry I'm married. Are you?"

"No . . . I don't know. Only one gets uncertain, sort of aimless after five or six years. . . . Edward's got his own things in life, and the children growing up on their own and all that."

"I don't see what you're driving at," said Mary, "I'm not aimless. This house and five servants, and four children, — there'll be five soon, — there's nothing aimless about that. Not that I mind."

"Mind?" said Grace, rather harshly, "but Mary, d'you mean to say you *like* it?"

"Of course I like it," said Mary, ponderously. "I'm very fond of Tom and the children; besides, what else is there to do? I'm sure I don't want anything else to do. I'm too busy to think of anything else."

Busy! Yes, that was it. Mary was too busy to bother with highfalutin nonsense about something that wasn't there and might be nothing. Her words created in Grace a curious impression, half of envy, half of disdain, for evidently Mary was happy in her fashion, suitably loving her husband, giving birth to his children, seeing that he and they were comfortably fed. And she was happy because she had no time to be unhappy. Perhaps she had no time to live, unless what she did was living. Yet it made her angry that Mary should be so — soddenly content. That she should have no intimations of any problems, that no evidence of unrest should upheave the smooth surface of her thoughts . . .

"Queen Bee," said Grace, laughing.

"I don't see what you're driving at," said Mary.

No more did Grace, quite clearly. She was herself too

uncertain as to what she liked, disliked or sought. The conversation became desultory, and soon Grace said that she must go, but consented, before so doing, to view the nurseries where the domestic pageant was in full swing.

In the immense night-nursery, made up of two rooms which had been deprived of their partition, the four little girls were being put to bed. Seated on the floor in the midst of a chaotic array of picture-books, bricks, dolls and india-rubber balls, the two eldest, Rose and Maud, were patiently waiting their turn while Ella and Gladys, the former loudly paddling in her bath, the latter kicking and screaming on her nurse's flannel apron, were being prepared for bed. As their mother appeared, there was a slight disturbance. Rose and Maud rose quietly though rather hurriedly, and came to their aunt to be kissed. They were, both of them, fair, ruddy children, very like Mary, calm and unobtrusive. Silently, each one of them took one of her mother's hands and stood looking at her with an air of repose that might be stupidity, and yet akin to her own sensible manner. They did not, Grace thought, resemble her own egotistic, self-centred children. But Ella, who was dark and spoilt as to looks by a big nose, evidently Tom's, developed a hysterical fit of splashing and a persistent demand that: "Mummie should sit in 'barsch;'" while Gladys, at the sight of Grace whom she looked upon as a terrifying auntie, began to squeal as a dying pig. The cries of the children mixed with the expostulations of the nurses, one of whom held Ella down in the warm water, while the other, in the intervals of vainly endeavouring to hush Gladys, explained to Mrs. Kinnersley what a grand nurse she was, and how she didn't care what she did for the children . . . didn't mind work . . . night and day . . . wear herself to the bone for them—

In the midst of her young, Mary, stolid and smiling, was as some benevolent Juno who had graciously consented to come to earth to become the mother of the race of man. As Grace stole away, she felt that Mary did not want to accompany her to the front-door.

"Don't trouble," she said.

And Mary, smiling, stayed in the nursery, while Grace, running down the stairs and closing the door behind her, felt that she had somehow intruded upon a rite in which she played no part. She too had her nurseries, knew that smell of violet powder, of clean young bodies, but hers were not on this magnificent scale; they were not an enterprise, a sort of sex-justification, a triumph. She knew that she was only a wife, that she had become a mother without consciousness or purpose. It was true that Mary could not either have decided to take up the rôle of mother, but she had accepted it when it came her way.

So Grace felt she was slinking away, almost guilty, as if she had done wrong. And more acutely, she was envious of all this ease. She thought vaguely of a French rhyme which she misquoted: *"Là tout n'est que beauté, joie, calme, et volupté."*

III

For a long time Mary remained in her nursery, taking no share in the work, allowing the now soothed Gladys to be laid in her cot near Ella who, powdered and glowing, had fallen asleep as soon as her head was laid on the pillow. Rose and Maud were taken from her; they were washed more formally, as befitted their ages of five and four. In her presence their hair was plaited. Under her patronage the Almighty was invoked. Then, for a while, she sat smiling back at the two rosy faces that watched her from the pillows. The nurses deftly cleared away the basins, the implements of toilet; curtains were drawn, the night-light glowed out. At a word the attendants abandoned the workshop, and Mary, her back against the space between the windows, looked at her little children. It was not pleasure she felt. It was not anything so definite, but the nothingness of sensation which is content. She turned out the electric light, went towards the cots and, in turn, very softly kissed each one of the four little flushed faces. Then, treading lightly, she went to the door and, as she very softly closed it behind her, heard far below the sound of her husband's latchkey in the lock.

IV

Mary met Tom at the drawing-room door. She had gone down so carefully and so slowly that he had had time quickly to wash his hands in the lobby.

With a cheerful "Hallo! old girl," he put his arms about her shoulders and kissed her. She too kissed him. There was no stir in these caresses. The hard, heavy grip of his arm about her shoulder, the sense of his propinquity, of his rough coat, his reddish face and the sturdy assertiveness of his mouth as it touched hers: these were no lover-like things. They were not formal or distant, nor seductive. But, as they went into the drawing-room, his arm still about her waist, Mary found no change in the placid content of her mood. The husband had come home.

"How are you?" asked Tom, and there was a delightful, humble anxiety in his eyes. "Feeling all right? Yes? You weren't up to the scratch this morning. Quite sure?"

He was smiling but solicitous. He really wanted to know. When at last he was assured that his wife was well, and she had lied to him several times, concealing little ailments as women will, he passed to other topics, also near to his heart. One by one the children were reviewed.

"So Maud has been scratched," he said. "Serve her right; I've told her to leave the cat alone. And Rose. How's Rose?"

There was no change in Rose. Reported for obstreperousness. "Oh, well, well, shows her spirit." Small details were given as to the babies' health.

Then, sitting on the sofa by his wife's side, he stretched out and announced that he had had a hard day. Christmas orders, he declared, were keeping him on the run.

"Has that bother been cleared up?" asked Mary. "That American business, I mean."

"Oh, yes, that's all right."

Tom Stanley was one of those men who give their wives as little information about their business as they can, but expect them to be interested in it. Mary had only a faint idea of what the American bother meant, but somehow she was interested in it, because the bother that bothered Tom bothered her. Tom declared that he had had a hurried lunch and was longing for his dinner, but he stayed, for he did not dress. Instead, he read out to his wife extracts from the Christmas Books supplement in the evening paper, suggesting that it would come in useful. And so, slowly, the clock travelled on towards the half-hour. Tom went up-stairs to put on his slippers. Just before he left the room he turned, his big red face smiling, looking like a very fat, middle-aged boy.

"By the way," he said, "Mary, I saw a stunning pineapple this afternoon in Old Broad Street; simply couldn't resist it. It's on the way."

They were content, these two, or far from their own problems; they seemed even forgetful of that son whom they so desired. There is no room for the business and for the dream. Soon, very quietly, so that the children might not be awakened, the gong was struck in the hall.

V

At that moment of time when Mary, standing at the door of her nursery, heard her husband's key in the lock, Clara, clad in a plain, white dressing-jacket, was lying back in a large chair while her maid, Germaine, did her hair. She was restless under the operation. If she had had her way, she would have had no French maid to worry her with attentions and to thrust upon her cares which she did not feel. But then every Lady Govan had had a French maid. Sir Henry ordered one for Clara together with the furniture, and the bride had not then the courage to rebel. The pretty, rosy face pouted into the mirror, for Clara, even when she had nothing to do, could hardly bear the waste of time entailed by all this hair-combing and brushing, and pulling, and crimping, and twisting; all this ridiculous rolling of curls, all this fussing with irons. But Germaine went on, stolidly working, parting the thick, brown strands and drawing them back across the crown, cunningly fixing in where she chose the few false curls her obstinacy had forced upon her mistress. Then, suddenly, she gave vent to a violent "*zut*" and, with one tug, drew the whole of her mistress's hair down again upon her shoulders.

"Germaine!" Clara screamed at the mirror, "this is too much! this is three times. I won't have it! I won't have it!"

"It is *nécessaire,*" said Germaine, unperturbed.

"I won't have it! I won't have it!" Clara protested feebly. "Here, let me do it."

With thin, rather febrile hands, she herself piled the hair upon the crown, roughly twisted the ends into short coils and attempted to hide them by thrusting them out of sight over her ears; she stabbed her hair with hairpins, stuck in the combs anywhere. In one minute the hair was up and, rather triumphantly smiling, she turned to Germaine and said: "Now, what do you think of that?"

"It is very like a—what you call it, miladi?—a suffragette."

"Well, I am a suffragette," said Clara, rigid.

Germaine's heavy, black eyebrows rose very high up her olive forehead; she shrugged her shoulders; she clearly meant that one needn't look like a suffragette if one was such a fool as to be one, and as she did this, the power of her hard French will made itself felt. Germaine considered that hair should be properly done, that is to say, as it was done in Paris. If one rebelled, one was not *chic;* if one were not *chic* one might as well be dead. Her small, brown hands closed upon her waistband, and she assumed the attitude of a martyr ready to be burned at the stake for the sake of her principles. And so Clara, feeling the pressure, suddenly flung herself back in the armchair:

"Oh, dear!" she murmured. "Do what you like, Germaine."

And, as the nimble hands worked in the hair now lowered for the fourth time, Germaine let forth a stream of approving chatter, little compliments on the texture of miladi's skin; on the moulding of her ears, which she considered ought to be pierced; she expatiated on the delights of serving a lady so *raisonnable*.

Clara did not listen very intently. The travail of beauty bored her. As, little by little, the rebellious coiffure took shape, the events of the day passed through her mind. That play-centre had been a good idea; evidently the children liked it, and if the children liked it, the mothers would see to it that the men voted right; and the countess had been very nice. There ought to be no difficulty in getting her to take the chair at the St. Panwich Women's Unionist Association when they had a big meeting. It never occurred to Clara that the countess had been rather embarrassed; she had not noticed the pretty gesture with which the scented handkerchief had been persistently held against fastidious nostrils, nor the bewildered air of the great lady as she wondered what the impertinent little girl was going to do with the powder-puff which she had abstracted from her bag: Clara had been too busy; there had been too many people to run, too many howls to stop, and hands to shake; hence perhaps her satisfaction. She had had nothing but an impression of movement and, though she would not have acknowledged it, she was happy only when in movement.

"Yes," she mused, "it's a good idea. We'll have to have some more — other things. Something original that the papers might take up. I must think about it."

Her thoughts took another turn, for here was Germaine again at one of her outrageous beauty-parlour tricks, attempting to powder her nose.

"I won't have it. I won't have it," she expostulated, dodging from side to side to avoid the powder-puff.

"Oh, miladi, a little, a very little. . . . After a day in St. Panwich — *Voyons,* miladi."

"No, no."

It was impossible to say what were Clara's objections. Some vague puritanical idea that powder was somehow sinful, fast, oppressed her; or some rough contempt for the care of the body. It was not a security in the charm of her body: Clara never thought of herself as youthful, almost girlish. She accepted herself and, perhaps rather smugly, objected to face-powder because she thought herself good enough like that. But Germaine was obstinate and cunning. She put down the powder-puff and gently reduced the slight glitter of the nose with unobtrusive *papier-poudré,* while Clara again resigned herself into her hands, thinking of her own affairs, a little of Grace of whom she had not a very good opinion. Grace had been rather absurd at the play-centre. Fancy expecting the children to admire her chrysanthemums, and dangling her gold purse in that silly way! What the children wanted was games; good, organised, regulation games, with somebody to tell them what to do. One didn't want self-government in the nursery. But that silly, artistic attitude of Grace, really . . .

She was on her feet now, and Germaine, having taken off her dressing-jacket, was encasing her in an evening dress of blue silk, with an overlay of pink chiffon. Clara chafed and stamped a little, so interminable seemed this doing up of hooks; then, at last, Germaine was satisfied and stood back to look at the picture. It was a charming picture: that of a tall, slim, woman with nothing of the matron in the delicate curves of her breast, nor in the shapeliness of arms that were still youthful and a little angular. In the blue satin shoes the feet were narrow and arched. Lady Govan, somehow, had breed, a touch of the greyhound, but she wasted no time over her looks. Without a glance at the mirror she turned and hurried into the drawing-room. There she walked aimlessly round and round, for it was only twenty-five to eight and here were ten unoccupied minutes.

Fortunately, at that moment, she heard Sir Henry close the door of his bedroom. He came in deliberately, very handsome and very large, his thick hair perfectly ordered, his yellow moustache looking almost white on the deep sunburn of his cheeks. He came towards her slowly upon legs that seemed unusually long in his black trousers; an imposing figure, with a sheen that was metallic upon his shirt-front.

"Good evening, darling," said Clara, casually.

This, of course, was a courtesy title and Clara had no sensation at all as she confronted the handsome figure.

Sir Henry took her hand and, bending low, kissed her wrist. He had a fancy for solemn, stately manners. His taste for Lowestoft china indicated it and, perhaps, there was still in him the blood of the courtier who had gained the baronetcy by wearing the Regent's boots. He was forty-five, but carried off his age with an air in his evening clothes: it was evident that he could use any implement of sport, ride a broncho if required, and be at his ease with a cowboy or a bishop.

"My dear," he said, "you look charming. We must get Clausen to paint you for the Academy."

Clara laughed.

"I've no time even for Sargent, Harry, and don't try and make me believe that a picture of me is worth a thousand pounds . . . but don't let's talk about me. What happened in committee? In the Butter Bill committee, I mean."

He explained in detail. She quarrelled with an amendment. His caressing approach did not mean that he was playing the lover, any more than her rebuff meant that she wanted him to persist. He was not pursuing his wife, and she was not inciting him, as other women might, to pursue her. They were busy with other things, those two, and husband and wife only by the way. And it was characteristic of Clara that, when it occurred to her, while Sir Henry was explaining Clause 9 which affected the strengthening of margarine tests, she should have but a very short vision of the past; of a time, eight years dead, when she and Sir Henry went out into the garden at Campden Hill Road, in December, to see if the roses still bloomed. That night, she remembered, Harry had said something halting and quite delightful about some roses blooming all the year round. But then Clara's mind, more or less, said "pooh."

"But," she said, "you must be careful not to annoy the milkmen."

"Oh, well, of course," said Sir Henry. "We don't want to annoy anybody, but we've got to do the thing decently. I know what you mean; of course in St. Panwich, where they buy ten pounds of margarine for one of butter, it might cause trouble; but we'd better have no trade than have a dishonest one."

Clara did not reply. It was difficult to reply to such a remark, and, as they went into dinner, she was still brooding over it. "Really Henry was too quixotic; this idea of tinting margarine violet or pea-green, or some disgusting colour! Well, of course, it was a fair thing to do, so that people weren't swindled. But how would the milkmen like it? and the people themselves?"

She had no grasp of the mechanical, obstinately equitable working of Sir Henry's mind; of the ignorance and disdain which pervade the aristocrat when he deals with trade; of his indifference to the feelings of the buyer and the seller of goods which he himself can never conceivably buy or sell. As he talked now of other subjects, of the bad two hours of bridge he had had at the Portland, of the possibilities of a by-election, she was still resentful.

"Henry," she pursued, after a pause, "you wouldn't like to come in to tea and be offered purple bread-and-butter. It isn't only the milkmen; the people themselves won't like it, and they'll know you've had a hand in it. The St. Panwich Gazette watches you like a cat. Why! You could lose your seat on it."

"I might," said Sir Henry, laughing, "I can see the posters: 'Every Vote For Govan Is A Vote For Blue Butterscotch!' Still, my dear girl, I think you're exaggerating."

He always thought she was exaggerating. There was nothing in common between their ideas. They thought of the same things on the same lines, worked for the same interests, held almost the same views. But all this happened separately; they never tried together, or hoped together. They were as soldiers fighting under the same officer, with the same object, but no understanding; they were not partners sharing profit as well as loss. And so conversation continued in the rather solemnly comfortable atmosphere of the dining-room.

Upon the sideboard stood the cups that Sir Henry had won at golf; upon one wall was a Clausen. Good were the red rugs on the parquet, the Chippendale chairs, the silver appointments; and if the red damask curtains were a little skimpy, it was because there intruded into Clara's carelessness some fine streak of avarice.

Sir Henry asked his wife to send to the library for a travel book, and a work by Captain Mahan. He asked a few questions as to her day; he assumed its existence and its separateness from his own, but he accepted the rapid statement of her doings in a spirit that was almost judicial.

"Henry," said Clara, suddenly. "I'm hatching a scheme."

"A scheme!" said Sir Henry, and a coldness came into his voice. "Oh, yes — a scheme to — to what? my dear."

"I don't know yet. But I feel we want something at St. Panwich."

"You're busy enough, aren't you?" Sir Henry had spoken amiably these words which from another would have sounded curt. "There's the care committee and the play-centre. I should have thought you were doing enough."

"But that's nothing, Henry," cried Clara. "I mean, it's just the ordinary sort of thing."

"Do we want the extraordinary sort of thing?"

Clara did not reply for a moment. Evidently she wanted the extraordinary sort of thing. And she knew very well that Sir Henry disliked that. But all her reserved energy, her unrest, fruit of her aimless hours, seemed large within her as some living being clamouring to be born.

"I think we want something—," she hesitated,—"startling."

"My dear girl!"

Every bit of Sir Henry's body seemed to protest. "Startling!" he murmured. To him the word had an indecent sound.

"Clara," he said, quite firmly. "I hope you will do nothing of the kind. We do not want anything startling. We both of us have our duty to do, and we may do a little more, in a reasonable sort of way, but please do not let us be fanciful. Startling things are generally ridiculous, and I want neither you nor me to be ridiculous; and besides it wouldn't do. It wouldn't do us any good at all."

"How do you know?" Rather sharp, this question.

"Leave it to me. We don't want advertisements in politics."

"Well, we banged the tom-tom hard enough to get you in, Henry," said Clara, and her good-humour returned as she scored.

But Sir Henry was not to be put off. He developed his view. It was quite right that his wife should take an interest in his affairs, quite right that she should grace his platform. She was young, pretty, dressed well: constituents liked that. And he liked the idea that she should often visit St. Panwich, it secured the seat; but that did not mean she must give up everything.

"Well, you don't want me to have tea at the Savoy every day."

"Of course not. But you needn't have tea at the workhouse on the Monday, at the hospital on the Tuesday, and so on. That's overdoing it."

The word "overdoing" was taken up firmly. Sir Henry grew almost excited with it, as a terrier worrying a favourite ball. A lifetime of habits, the Eastbourne preparatory, Harrow, Oxford, the army, the House, rose up, massed round him as a phalanx to repel the word. Clara must not go too far. She must do nothing unladylike. Clara, head a little down, listened rather mutinously. She felt snubbed but knew that she was in the right. (She always knew that.) A politician's wife ought to be active. She ended by snarling.

"Oh, well, if you object to my working for you—!"

Some tenderness, the calm, unebullient love he felt for his pretty wife, overwhelmed Sir Henry. Or perhaps she appealed to him more when childish, querulous, than when assertive and hustling. He crossed over to the sofa, sat down, took her hand.

"You mustn't talk like that, darling," he said, mixing severity and coaxing. "You know I'm only too glad. It's awfully decent of you."

He was still holding her hand loosely; he reached across her knees, seized her other hand. She did not resist. She was not offended; only irritated. She let him caress her, feeling that after all he was only doing what he ought to do. And anyhow she was in the right. Then she looked at him quickly through her eyelashes, was as usual agreeably impressed by his big handsomeness, his solidity and the kindly concern now in his eyes. She smiled. He released one of her hands, passed his arm round her shoulders and drew her towards him. As he bent to kiss her, rather solemnly, rather carefully and yet with a firm, confident possessiveness, he smiled. And the feel of his cold shirt-front against her bare breast made her shiver. "There," he said at last, when his cool lips had abandoned hers in which also was no fever, "you're not cross, are you? You mustn't, you know," he added, for the first time rather cumbrously rallying, "for I'm off to the House now."

He could be gay, make allowances for a petulant wife. Women were funny things; they had to be petted and humoured. Even the cleverest, and he took Clara to be one of them, wanted a little managing. Vaguely he wished Clara were easier to manage; she did not fight him, oh, no, nothing so fierce as that, but she eluded him. She broke out in unexpected ways. He could better have done with a woman of older tradition; this one's hurries and enthusiasms disturbed him. He was not sure that they were quite feminine. And though he believed in votes for women, he wished she were not a suffragette.

"You're not cross, are you?" he repeated.

"Of course I'm not cross," said Clara, brightly.

She kissed him on the cheek, listened to the clang of the outer door. She stood awhile, unoccupied, staring at the wall. She still felt injured: her husband did not grasp what a lot she did for him. She honestly thought that she espoused his interests; it never struck her that she was not working for him, that she was taking the easiest way to fill a life left empty because no household cares, no children, no responsibilities had been given her, that she was working for herself in the only way she knew. She was conscious only of dissatisfactions which she put down to his lack of insight. She did not correlate them with the aimlessness of her life, with the deprivations of activity inflicted upon her by childlessness and wealth.

VI

Upon the sofa she tried to read, but two books and a review successively bored her. She tried to think out a scheme, but the idea did not come. There was nowhere to go to; nobody was likely to come and see her. It was half-past nine. There was nothing to do.

CHAPTER THE FIFTH

. . . AND ROUND AND ROUND AGAIN . . .

I

A COLD wind filled the garden, spitefully clutching at the dust and gravel of the paths and freezing the grains of earth that now became separate and sharp like little black crystals. It was a swift, fitful wind, coming from the east and yet all dry, as if in passing over marsh and field it had wept itself free of the tears of the sea. It came hurried and definite, laden with some mysterious urgency and business, blood-whipping, challenging, full of a brightness that could not fall, shouting that queens might not die young and fair. Shouting indeed that they must abandon queenly demeanour and, as dairy-maids, truss their skirts above their knees and trot about their queenly occupations.

For this was the London east wind, blowing white faces into red, anxious, impatient, and yet merry. Mischievous in its searching of weak bodies and benevolent in its firing of strong, rebellious young blood. For the London east wind is not soft and languorous as the Atlantic air that comes, all velvety and sweet, from the American shore. It comes hard and almost frozen, keen as a spear.

As Grace walked down the steps of Mary's house, the wind seized her, seemed to leap at her, to press her against a bosom such as that of the ancient virgin's studded with iron spikes, embracing her together with the acacia, the plane trees, and their bare twisted branches. It seemed to tear at them angrily because baulked of the sport of their leaves. It battled with Grace cheerfully, gambolled with her as some merry, kitten-like but dangerous tiger cub. As she ploughed into its face, head down, skirts furled about her ankles, steadying her hat with one hand, she could hardly see, for moisture had filled her eyes and, between her parted lips, the cold air was painfully biting at her teeth. At first this battling air added some of its weight and unrest to the two hours of discomfort by Mary's side. For she had been to see Mary on this Saturday afternoon. Tom had gone to golf, so they had been alone and, for two hours, Grace had tried to force some energy out of her sister, to make her pretend that she cared what happened, that she was interested in something that was not herself or hers.

She was still angry as she thought of her sister, lying full-length upon the sofa, two large cushions under her head and shoulders, another under her feet, reposing upon this bed with an air of passivity so complete that it was almost aggressive. Everything in Mary, her quietude, her silence, her acquiescence, seemed to proclaim that within a few days she would be important, a mother triumphant, and that she knew it. Indeed knew nothing else. In her absorption in the child that was coming, Mary's egoism grew enormous. She was not altruistic because her thoughts were of her race: she was egotistic because everything about her said, not: "my child is coming," but: "*my* child is coming." Grace thought herself unfair because she had not sympathised enough with Mary's secret anxiety, her fear that once more it would be a girl. Then again she became resentful as she reflected that this one was yet another of the moments when Mary gained a majesty which was not hers on ordinary days.

As she lay upon the sofa, the great, untidy masses of her fair hair undulated upon the blue cushion, like ripples on a still pool gilded by the setting sun. A whiteness had come to the neck and breast which the loose gown exposed; a gleaming whiteness, translucent and delicate, and yet rich as ivory; the beautiful rose-petal colour, the peach-like softness of her cheeks enhanced the transient brilliance of her blue eyes.

As Grace went on, slim and moulded by the air, all

beaten and buffeted, she felt a rage in her in which the wind was her partner, a contempt for this woman, this contented mother upon her domestic throne. What did Mary care whether empires fell or genius rose? or picture palaces were built? what did Mary care for the fashion, the poem, the passion and the crime? She cared not at all. This day she was Olympian and on Olympus, the mother of the gods.

It was, thought Grace, base, earthy, and yet—

As she struggled on alone towards the west, she found herself envious . . .

But not envious of easy maternity, of this dull repetition of physical discomfort, of fear and of agony; nor did she love little cares and preoccupations, baby-linen, bottles, the quarrels of nurses. She too could have all that if she chose, but it was not that she wanted. If she grudged Mary her content, she did not grudge her the means to her content, but, humanly enough, she too wanted satisfaction, a satisfaction designed for her own temperament, the incomprehensible something which could stimulate and then satiate her, make life resound when it had been empty, make time precious instead of burdensome. What was it?

Here were the shops near the Earl's Court Road, rather mean and rather cheap; then others, slowly growing in wealth and charm as she went toward the East. She did not feel impelled to buy anything; she did not even stop to look at a show-case full of furs. And here was Holland Walk, with the gates and the big, mysterious houses, the tall trees; here was Phillimore Place, with Campden Hill towering over it: this was the ease of life, and these were the riches and the dignities. . . . Beyond were greater riches in Kensington and greater dignities in Belgravia and Westminster; but again it was not that. Now she had passed the church and entered the Gardens, reluctant to go home, as there was nothing to do that day. Not even Edward would be in, for he had gone to an intellectual play with an intellectual man, and would doubtless come back to talk about it intellectually at dinner. But in the

Gardens, where the brightness of the sun still lingered, though night already threw out threats, here indeed was the wine of life: nursemaids wheeling perambulators, chattering with little charges that were packed and muffled in blankets and furs, showing naught save small fresh faces and bright eyes as those of white animals; elderly gentlemen with close-cropped moustaches, tanned skins, that day stung to redness, and the sharpness of parade in their steps; and young couples, arm in arm, close-hugged for warmth and satisfaction, laughing into each other's eyes because, that day, all eyes were bright . . . the girls and boys of the people with hoops, and the little ladies and gentlemen in leggings, and a great many dogs, disreputable fox terriers chasing stones, a Pekinese condescending to pursue a three-and-sixpenny indiarubber ball.

A new vigour seemed suddenly to come into Grace: she had walked across the frosty, crisp grass near the Round Pond, and it was as if her feet, on touching earth, had drawn up strength into her body; across the water there was no mist, but the bare branches of the trees outlined, black as arabesques against the dead white brilliance of the sky. No hope here, but a present power, a present vigour that made hope unnecessary. Here were her two children, near the pond, playing with a ball with nice awkward movements like puppies. She went towards them smiling, glad of them, of their flushed faces, of the round, bulky effect of their little bodies in the brown fluffiness of their coats; of their laughing, parted lips; of their eyes, bright brown and luminous green; and of the hoydenish rushing of them as they deserted her after having forced her to throw the ball so that they might run for it. A dozen times she threw it for them along the grass, and they ran, shrilly crying out and wrangling, and together complaining of unfairness, sometimes together falling upon the ball and rolling in a heap, more than ever like puppies.

Quite suddenly, some private idea seemed to come to them; the ball was taken from her. Breathless they played with it alone, standing six feet from each other, both of them throwing it rather furiously at the opponent's feet so as to make him run. The ball rolled to Grace's feet; she stooped to pick it up. There was a double cry of "No!" Then Horace came to her, took the ball and, as he went towards Susan, said: "No, Mummie, it's my ball."

As Grace, turning, left the Gardens, she wondered whether it was the slow coming of the night that slackened the racing of her blood. Or something else, unsatisfied, unsatisfiable.

II

"What you want," said Clara, decisively, "is work."

And because of this, added to other and unexplainable unrests, Grace found herself, one afternoon, seated in the small room in St. Panwich which represented the heart of Lady Govan's activities. Somehow Clara had nullified her husband's desire that she should not overdo it. She had not explained to him that she needed an office from which to run the constituency: she had hired one and Sir Henry, faced with the fact, had assented. The soup-kitchen had quickly emerged from the political chaos: Sir Henry had subscribed ten guineas. This had entailed extra work; a typist had been introduced: Sir Henry was uncomfortable, but he did not know exactly what to do; he was like a man taking a very boisterous dog out for a walk upon the lead; he did have the dog upon the lead, but the animal was so irresistibly active that no one could say which of the two was being taken for a walk.

Clara's office occupied the first floor of a house in the St. Panwich High Street, over a small fruit shop run on the "three oranges a penny" basis. It sold also very small and dirty-looking apples, stringy rhubarb and such vegetables as were very definitely in season, while it festooned its front with bananas which, as they rotted, wafted a faint, sweet, rather sickly scent up the stairs and into the office. The office itself, floored with rough boards that the greengrocer's wife insufficiently washed at infrequent intervals, had walls painted the most repulsive shade of pea-green. There were no curtains, no easy-chairs; the furniture comprised one large table covered with papers, three chairs of the kitchen type, and a small table with a typewriter. That queer, mean streak in Lady Govan's nature which had cramped the fullness of her drawing-room curtains combined with her conscious desire that the whole thing should be very businesslike indeed. She never said: "no fallals," but she conveyed by her attitude that she knew there were no fallals about her.

Grace sat at the big table, slowly wading through the register and the local directory which embraced St. Panwich and the neighbouring district of Uppington. She had hung her hat and furs upon a nail, and now her short, shapely, white hands rumpled the warm strands of her hair, which every minute grew more untidy. A little frown had formed between her brows, and was delightfully surmounted by a single, large freckle; the small, open mouth was a little drawn in with worry, for her task was to sift out from among the St. Panwich list those whose houses, occupations, addresses or interests made it likely that they would subscribe towards the soup-kitchen.

"Bubwith, Bubwith," she murmured, "upholsterer, 44-51, St. Panwich High Street; Works, Hornsey. Seems pretty good." She reflected that everybody seemed "pretty good," until it came to asking them for subscriptions. And to ask everybody made the job so big.

The typist's back, in its slate-blue sweater, seemed hostile, turned towards her in aloofness as she tapped out for the thirtieth time that day the begging formula which Clara had dictated in the morning.

"Miss Lenzie," said Grace, "do you know Bubwith?"

The tap-tap ceased and, rather slowly, Miss Lenzie turned to look at her. She was a small, dark creature, with rather irregular features and an abstracted way, half-hesitant, half-dignified. Her rather humid, big brown eyes gave her a wistful air. A mass of very heavy, dark brown hair that went almost black in front seemed too heavy for her slender neck. Miss Lenzie looked at Grace as if bewildered and frightened by a question the answer to which she knew very well, as if once upon a time her family and her friends had frightened her a little too often.

"Bubwith?" she said. "Oh, they're quite big people." Her confidence returned. "They've got six shops in the High Street; they sell furniture mainly."

"D'you think they'd give anything?" said Grace.

"Oh, they might very well," said Miss Lenzie, with growing animation, as she discovered that Grace meant her no harm. For a while she dilated upon the Bubwiths and their goods; she had a tendency to dilate over much on things; she volunteered that they showed the Liberal window-cards.

"We'd better look for the canvass cards," said Grace.

A large box in the corner was opened and, for a while, the two women rummaged among the bundles of cards from which, at last, they drew one showing that Mr. Bubwith had been "doubtful" at the previous election.

"Oh, well, we can but try," said Miss Lenzie, cheerfully. The change from this monotonous typing into something more active seemed to feminise, to humanise her. When Grace turned to her desk, with an air of conclusiveness, Miss Lenzie seemed regretfully to go back to her machine, as if this interval of passing intercourse had made more heavy the monotony of her labour.

Grace put down the name of Mr. Bubwith with a query mark for reference to Clara. Here and there in the list she picked a clergyman, suitable for the improving of the occasion when soup was drunk. She discarded the Baptists, the Congregationalists and others, placing the Wesleyan ministers on a special list in the hope that one of them might be less Nonconformist than the others. Her pen was rusty and scratched the paper; mechanically the typewriter went tap-tap, and every five minutes there came a rolling rasp as a finished letter was withdrawn. Almost continuously the trams came by, roaring, sometimes four or five one after the other, the heads of the outside passengers making, in the dirty window, a curious frieze. This was the afternoon, and a dullness seemed to fall.

"I suppose," thought Grace, "that Clara's right. Work is good for one, one must do something." And resolutely she bent her head to the local directory in search of the dignity of labour. There was a knock at the door, but, before a reply could be given, a very large, abundant creature, radiant in yellow furs, entered the room like a genial, but majestic Atlantic billow. Grace and Miss Lenzie felt so small by the side of this apparition that for a second they remained staring at her. She did not mind. She had that smile which, her husband said, "never came off," set in a large, round, pink face, under twinkling little grey eyes. She wore an incredible number of yellow curls.

"Are you Lady Govan?" asked the being.

And, before Grace could reply, her hand was seized in a warm glove, padded everywhere with soft flesh.

"I'm delighted to meet you, dear Lady Govan, delighted, delighted." Her glance roved about the room. "Ah! I see how well you are attuned in spirit with all this ugliness, with all the misery of it. The poor," she sighed. "The *poor* poor!"

"May I ask to whom I am speaking?" said Grace, a little coldly. "I'm not Lady Govan; I'm her sister, Mrs. Kinnersley."

For a second the grey eyes suggested haughtiness.

"I'm Mrs. Willerby," she said.

There was a pause during which Grace wondered who Mrs. Willerby was, while the visitor gave her time to be properly overcome.

"I'm sure I'm delighted," said Grace, rather nervously. "Would you like — I mean — is it for the soup-kitchen?"

"It is," said Mrs. Willerby, beaming. "I feel, Mrs. Kinnersley, that we need something more than soup-kitchens. You know what I mean. The ethereal, the beautiful — something."

"Oh, yes! yes," said Grace, unsteadily. "You mean — "

"Exactly," said Mrs. Willerby, with great satisfaction.

And then it became manifest, little by little, that Mrs. Willerby wished to preach in St. Panwich the gospel of beauty, to address the outcast of the world, as they drank their soup, upon the beauty of paganism and the water-nymph which, she maintained, dwelt in the horse trough outside the King's Arms.

"There is no God," she murmured, fervently, "save beauty. Nothing is immoral if it is beautiful, and nothing is moral when it is ugly."

Grace and Miss Lenzie listened, more and more amazed, while this splendid creature enthusiastically lifted in the air, like wings, the yellow sides of her fox fur. As she spoke of Virgil's pastorals and how truly they embodied the Greek spirit, of the wild, barbaric mystery of that great Turkish book, *The Arabian Nights,* she swelled, her pink cheeks became pinker, and a suave, cloying mellowness seemed to fall from her tongue.

"Well," said Grace, at last, "I can't say exactly, Mrs. Willerby. I'll speak to my sister and let you know. I'm sure it's very kind of you."

She felt much inclined to laugh. This was so ridiculous, and she nearly gave way when Miss Lenzie flung her the queer side look which clearly said: "This is really absurd, but of course my opinion isn't worth much. Still if you do laugh, I'd like to join in."

Mrs. Willerby went towards the door, quite assured of her success. Her hand upon the door-knob, she stopped. "By the way," she said, "I suppose you need money for the soup-kitchen? The poor — the *poor* poor."

Grace wondered how she ought to beg when, suddenly, Mrs. Willerby came skipping back to the table, pulled a gold purse from her muff, shook out the contents. There were three sovereigns and a few shillings. She left the three gold coins upon the table and said:

"That's all I've got. You won't mind if I keep the silver to get home with, will you?"

There was hardly a pause. Then Mrs. Willerby said, a faint Irish accent in her voice: "It's good work you're doing, me dear."

And Grace was amazed to find that the large arm had been whipped round her shoulders, that she had been kissed on the cheek, and that Mrs. Willerby had gone, leaving behind her an impression of absurdity and egotism quite neutralised by a queer, generous sweetness.

But everybody was not like Mrs. Willerby. Notably the prosperous tradesmen's wives, when Grace went to call on them, seemed to view her with suspicion as if she were the sort of person who came round selling gold bracelets on the instalment plan; the clerks' wives in the villas were still worse. Grace laughed two days later when she discovered that she had acquired the canvasser's trick of unobtrusively sliding her foot between the door and the door-post. And Mrs. Bubwith was a great trial.

She had to go and see Mrs. Bubwith whose complexion suggested that she had been boiled in disinfectants, after which her grey hair had been twisted into a knot and left to dry. She clasped upon her belt two enormous knotty hands which had evidently scrubbed floors and never forgotten it.

"Are you Mrs. Bubwith?" said Grace, timidly.

"Bubwith's the name," said the woman, and her sharp grey eyes drilled into Grace as she explained her business.

"So what we want," said Grace, "is a little subscription."

"I don't 'old with it," said Mrs. Bubwith, decisively.

Grace persevered. She pointed out that Mr. Bubwith was on their political side.

"Don't 'old with politics," said Mrs. Bubwith. "Elbert wastes enough time as it is."

Grace shyly referred to the Wesleyan minister who had recommended.

"Don't 'old with parsons," said Mrs. Bubwith.

In the end Mrs. Bubwith lost her temper, told Grace that she didn't approve of young women gadding about like that. Suggested that she had better go home and mind the baby, and in general that hers was an attitude she didn't 'old with.

Grace never found out what Mrs. Bubwith did hold with, and she never got a subscription. She seemed to have a little quarrel with Clara, as the latter came whirling in and out of the office, reducing Miss Lenzie to a condition which would have approached tears if she had not proudly fought them down and comforted herself with the thought that she was a Lenzie of the Maclenzie clan and that nothing could do away with that. For Clara was censorious. Grace's doubts as to whether it was "quite nice" to beg from the moderately well-to-do, her shrinkings from the Bubwith type, irritated Clara. Clara settled Mrs. Bubwith in ten minutes by telling her that, if the soup-kitchen was not properly supported, the local association and its attached bazaars and socials would hire their furniture anywhere except in St. Panwich.

"Consider their feelings!" she cried. "Why should I consider Bubwith's feelings? He's only a doubtful."

Her business was going ahead in spite of Grace's hesitations. The soup-kitchen was beginning to have soup to distribute. There were hints of other plans in Clara's mind; she had many appointments with helpers; the telephone was fitted up in the office; the countess reappeared and said the smell of bananas was much nicer than that of the play-centre. All this activity seemed to satisfy a need in Clara and yet to irritate it. More and more conscious of her lack of occupation, with more and more time upon her hands as she snatched it from the sterile, social round which secretly sickened her, she seemed at the same time to be more urgent and more dissatisfied. It was not now only "something to do," but "quick something to do," as if, because in her life there was nothing, there must be something, anything.

Grace was not influenced. Just for one moment she had a vision of reality when an angry factory girl from Dwyran's, the jam people, violently entered the office during the lunch hour, and "told Grace off," because her small brother had been fed. She was a splendid girl with masses of rough red hair and big, wild breasts straining at her coarse blouse. She roared her complaint, stamped, shook her fist at Miss Lenzie, swore that for two pins she would wring her neck, which she probably could easily have done. She informed them that they were a dirty, psalm-smiting lot, that her brother was a blasted skunk and that it was their fault if he was, with their blasted charity. And then finally, hurling herself out of the room, she could be heard upon the stairs vowing that she would deal with her little brother in a way which would cause disturbance to his liver.

Somehow, this incident seemed to depress Grace, to fill her with a sense of inadequacy which she could not understand, unless it meant that she was not really in things but only on the edge of them. This she told Clara.

"Oh, my dear," said Clara, "for heaven's sake don't be fanciful just because a girl comes and blackguards you. What a fuss about nothing! What ever does it matter what people say or do? One's got to do something in life."

"Has one?" said Grace.

"Of course," said Clara, acidly. "One's much too unhappy if one doesn't."

A keen shoot of misery seemed to go through Clara as she said this, and Grace's hand unconsciously went out towards her sister's.

But already Clara had eluded her.

"I must telephone, I must telephone," she muttered.

And Grace, a little heavily, began to be quite sure of what she had suspected: that this thing she did was not the thing she was looking for, or that it was not enough.

III

In her need, as she walked through the slums all the way home from St. Panwich, as if to kill unrest through weariness, Grace had a ridiculous idea. People hurried past her: factory hands and shop girls on their way home, clerks, workmen with their tool-bags, and tramway-men, and policemen off duty. She nearly stopped a fair young person because his face was so rosy in the light of a gas-lamp. She would have asked him: " Have you any message for me, person? "

She laughed aloud as she went, thinking how he would have stared and yet she did not know what message she wanted. She knew only one thing for certain: that it would be written in some unknown hand, and be hopeful.

That night, as she sat alone with her mother in the drawing-room, she needed the message so much that she suggested to her mother that she needed it, as if forgetting that no mother ever has hope to give her daughter, because her daughter is only herself in another form, not a separate person. When she had stemmed Mrs. Westfield's enquiries as to health and doings, enquiries which threatened, little by little, to extend over the whole of the family, she tried to convey to her mother how ill at ease she was. Mrs. Westfield did not understand. Her little grey eyes became very sharp, and her thin mouth thinner with anxiety as she suggested that Grace did not look very well.

" I'm all right, Mother," said Grace. " It isn't that."

Mrs. Westfield's gaze concentrated behind her glasses. " I don't know about that," she said. " You're looking thin just there."

She touched the smooth cheek under the high cheekbone.

" And what's that little frown? " Suddenly her tone became excited. " Grace dear, are you quite sure that —? "

" Oh, Mother! " said Grace, acidly. And her mouth pouted in discontent. " Of course it isn't that."

She was irritated. This continual suggestion of maternity, this obsession, this mantle of small cares and small interests in which they were trying to swaddle her and to stifle her. . . . It was nauseous.

" Mother, I wish you wouldn't always be thinking of that. I'm not Mary."

" It would be a good thing if you were," said Mrs. Westfield, ponderously. " You wouldn't talk so much nonsense."

" I'm not talking nonsense," said Grace.

And the pity she felt for herself filled her eyes with a thin film of tears.

"Giving birth to a child every week, Mother, and ordering the dinner . . . and all that. Of course it's all right, but it isn't everything. It isn't Life."

"I don't understand," said Mrs. Westfield, severely. "When I was a young girl, we didn't talk like that, but in these modern days girls are different. Perhaps you'll tell me what women are for, if it isn't that."

"Oh," cried Grace, desperately. "How do I know what women are for?"

The conversation went on, the same things were said ten times over, Mrs. Westfield still maintaining the Victorian ideal and making of it not an ugly one. For her, marriage was an equable, permanent state; it was the justification of woman, the object of her existence, the shrine which sanctified her, the duty which was laid upon her, the satisfaction which should fill her. Men must work and women must marry. And still Grace stretched out hands that now were nervous and greedy towards the invisible.

"I don't know," she cried, at last, "I don't know what I mean, Mother. Clara says I need work, but work doesn't seem to make her very happy. There's something wrong."

"Isn't Edward kind to you?" asked Mrs. Westfield, her tone very definitely suggesting that if her husband failed her she would know the reason why.

"Oh, Edward!" said Grace, wearily. "He's as usual. He's very kind to me. Very, very kind. He's cheerful. Oh, I've nothing to say against Edward."

"Then," said Mrs. Westfield, "I don't understand. It isn't money, is it?"

Grace shook her head. No, there was money enough. Two thousand five hundred a year for themselves and two children. It was enough and Edward was not mean; she had only to ask to be given.

"There's something wrong," she repeated. "I don't know what it is."

Edward came in during the silence into which Mrs.

Westfield had been struck by these amazing remarks. He was smoking a cigar which he had begun alone in the dining-room. Though the cigar was stuck between his front teeth, he still managed to beam upon the couple. He took it from his mouth.

"Hope you don't mind my smoking here, Mater?" he said. "Though of course not; I forget that ladies are so modern in these days." He took his cigar case from his pocket. "Might I offer you one, or will you join me in a pipe by and by?"

Mrs. Westfield laughed. She liked him. To her he was still a boy. She liked the cheerfulness and even the obtrusiveness with which he entered rooms, she liked his little songs, his dances, his practical jokes, all the buffoonery with which he entertained the company.

"Well," said Edward, at length, settling in an armchair, so low that he nearly fell out of it, and sprawling so as to show he was extremely at his ease. "What have you been plotting, you two? Discussing the world in general, eh, what?" ("Eh, what?" had just come in in those days.)

"Yes," said Grace, "that's exactly what we've been doing."

"And how do you like it, Gracie-Bracie?" asked Edward.

Grace did not reply.

"I'm afraid Grace is a little discontented," said Mrs. Westfield, "and what about, I really don't know."

"Discontented? Dear me, that won't do. That won't do at all. The little girl must be bucked up. Hubby will take her to Earl's Court and she shall go down the chute —"

He took Grace's hand and fondled it. "She shall go down the chute with her hubby, the little girl shall . . . poor little baby-girl." He put his arm round Grace's shoulders, drew her to him and pretended to rock her, singing a little lullaby: "Poor little girlie-girlie."

"Oh, Edward," cried Grace, wrenching herself away, "don't."

He drew his hand over his close brown curls, manifestly surprised. "What's come over you?" he said, seriously. But his seriousness could not last. "Naughty temper? We shall have to have doctor in and girlie will have to drink nasty physic." Again he tried to take her hand. She snatched it away, and went to stand with her back against the wall.

"That's a good attitude," said Edward, "you're like the woman in the play this afternoon. It's a jolly good play —"

He forgot her. He began to talk about the play. He gave her an account of it, act by act. He told her the names of all the actors. He quoted choice passages. He emphasized curtains. He acted them. He told her what he had felt, what Brandon had said to him and what he had triumphantly replied to Brandon.

Grace was not listening. In her mind was but one thought: "This can't go on. This can't go on." And Edward went on, went on talking.

He remembered her. And, suddenly, as he remembered her, some sweetness came to him; he seemed genuinely anxious, and to perceive that a rigidity had come into the set of her mouth. He suggested that she should travel, go away with her mother for a while to Brighton, or even further, to the Riviera. This appealed to Grace, but Edward said: "That'll put the little girlie right." Then Grace shook her head. "Would she like some more money to play with? to go to the theatre? to buy clothes?"

Something vibrated in Grace, but still she shook her head.

"What are girls coming to?" said Mrs. Westfield, indignantly.

IV

But the sower who sows the seed sometimes sows at random. This idea of clothes seemed to settle in some intimate part of Grace's brain, for a few days later she found herself thinking of the clothes that, within two months, she must buy for the season. Clothes! Perhaps there was something in clothes; they could be so beautiful and one could be so proud, so fine, when one was well-dressed. A virgin enthusiasm seemed to seize her. She saw herself regal among her fellows, envied, admired, copied. She saw herself pioneering the art of clothes. Living and doing something worth while.

She had a dress to buy for the Cadoresse wedding. That should be her demonstration, her first step. The thought of the dress grew in her mind, became enormous as a djinn released from its bottle. It should be a wonderful dress, a dress of dreams. It should express her, enthrone her. Her brain was in a whirl as she lay awake thinking of the dress, as if something had unsettled her; she found she could hardly control her emotion. She wanted to laugh and to cry, for she was joyful in the face of this adventure.

V

And indeed it was a wonderful dress. She carried out in green the necessary correspondence with the warm tints of her hair. Of course it was an Empire dress, as was in those days compulsory. Long folds of pongee silk fell from the high waist, so that when she walked, her limbs free, she seemed to undulate; from waist to breast she hung in the broad girdle of pale blue and silver; she was like a great flower with petals of rose and amber resting in its grasp. The long, narrow sleeve of heavy green satin made an unexpected contrast with the thin, cloud-like material of the skirt. When it came home she thrilled as, for the first time, she put it on. Its clasp was warm and exciting as the embrace of a first lover.

And the dress kept its promise, as she walked down the aisle to see that young Frenchman who had once been one of her detrimentals married to slim Edith Lawton, so white and virginal. She knew that they were looking at her, these people, and not at the bride. And later at the reception, as she wandered round Mrs. Lawton's big drawing-room, all littered with silver, with leather-bound books and statements that so-and-so had sent a cheque, she knew that the men were looking at her. At the revealing outlines of her clothing, at her green eyes and their brilliance. As she stood in front of the bride, congratulating her, no spasm of envy shook her, for she knew that she was taller, more beautiful, more woman. She did not even envy the fleeting blushes which often stained the cheeks of little Mrs. Cadoresse, for it was not at the bride, even now when she stood in contrast, that the men were looking. And greater triumph still: it was not only the men, it was the women who were looking. . . .

BOOK THE SECOND

GRACE AND CLARA

They too, bound upon the wheel, go forth from life to life, from despair to despair. — (Kipling — *Kim.*)

CHAPTER THE FIRST

"WHITHER?"

I

CLOTHES! April, a deceptive freshness, heritage of the dead winter, sweet scents of earth and young grass, green bud, sharp-pointed, and skies smiling gaily through tears. As the hyacinth, still decked in clustering rosy bells, and the daffodil, bending under her golden crown, as the peacock growing new feathers, and the beasts sloughing the heavy coat of winter, the women, with the languorous touch of the wind upon the melting softness of their cheeks, thought of clothes for the summer Saturnalia.

Grace was a competent woman. She called at her bank for her pass-book and understood which side the balance was on. All alone in the dining-room, after breakfast, she sat down before the book, her hand rumpling over her white and freckled forehead some straying strands of hair. Twice a year she performed this rite: in April before the season, and in October before the cold. It was then she had to allocate her dress-allowance of a hundred and fifty a year to the best advantage and effect. Sixty pounds belonged to April and the whirling of London May; fifty pounds to the sober winter, the doing-up of furs, the coats and skirts and the out-door coats. And forty pounds were sagely spread over the rest of the year to pay for seaside linen dresses, for country clothes and the things that really mattered: the hats, the gloves, the veils, the boots, the translucent stockings, the relentless corsets, and all those other sweeter, softer, secret garments, all frill and film, clamorous for ribbon and for scent. She had not, so far, exceeded her allowance, though it was subject to a little jugglery: sometimes coal was cheap, and one ton meant two petticoat-bodices, unless the coal helped out the account which was still called "Baby;" and there were obscure economies, which sometimes led to as much as a hat, in that indiscriminate account: "House, Furniture and Garden Maintenance" which Grace pompously called "H. F. G. M."

But this morning Grace was not examining those other accounts with intent to despoil them, the year was yet too young. She was considering how to spend sixty pounds. She was excited, almost agitated. Rather feverishly she put down: one coat and skirt, eleven guineas. She sighed; coats and skirts were so dull. Then two afternoon dresses, say twelve guineas and nine guineas. Thirty-two guineas gone! She bit her pen. And she must have two evening dresses, say twenty-four guineas for the two; and she could have the black one done up of course. And the green afternoon dress too, the foundation was quite good. Her mind wandered off as she reflected: charmeuse draped badly . . . while crepe de chine . . . Of course if the cleaner . . .

Grace found that she had brought down her fist upon the table and said: "Damn the cleaner!" She was a little shocked. Never in her life had she said "damn" before. And, very dimly, she realised that she had passed some mental Rubicon, but she did not long dwell upon her own psychology. The glow, the delight, the almost joyful despair irritated her. The words "cleaner" and "doing-up" receded into the back of her mind, became imperceptible. Something seemed to boil within her head, an almost intolerable joy as she thought of the clothes that she would buy, the new clothes. In another half-hour she was in Sloane Street, in that shop where not many months before she had accompanied Clara. To enter it thrilled her. The spider-like detachment of the attendants, the surrounding crowd of dummies in their raiment of white and gold, of oyster-grey and opal slashed with blue . . . and the atmosphere, the hurry, a shrill voice, the little jostles about some triumph, for this was April, not the

Autumn now. But her delight lasted little. Unattended she considered the drama almost impersonally and, as she so did, a contempt came to her; with new eyes she saw these women, their pleated skirts just passing out of fashion, their uniform blue coats, their regulation hats and hair, faces, thoughts. And then she saw the models: they were too sober . . . too ladylike. Ladylike, yes, that was what it was, Kensington, South Kensington. The edge of Belgravia towards which Belgravia never looked. For some minutes she stood staring and, when an attendant came towards her, was wondering whether this were not St. Paul's Churchyard. "No, thanks," she said, "I've changed my mind."

In ten minutes a taxi had taken her to Bond Street . . .

Riot! With feverish steps she walked up the hill, then through Grafton Street, hesitated for a second before the word "Paquin," through Albemarle Street, then up Dover Street again to the corner of Hay Hill . . . she was hesitant and yet thrilled. All about her rose the powerful effluvium of all those silks, and laces, and jewels hidden behind obscure Victorian house-fronts: satisfaction, here it was. She ordered her coat and skirt: fifteen guineas. "Oh, well, I'll take it out of one of the evening frocks."

There was no evening-frock at nine guineas. She forgot the evening, for here was a postillion-coat with a fancy brown waistcoat, striped yellow . . . the Devil's gewgaw . . . fifteen guineas. And here another rather low-necked, shimmering blouse, mauve as the heron's wing, and faintly revealing underneath the rosy glow of the flamingo's —

She ordered both. In a maze she was measured. There were fumes, as of wine, in her head —

She lunched greedily, gulping as if something called her, some hunger of soul greater than that of her body.

She bought an evening-dress of cream and amber, of amber such as her hair, and of cream such as her neck. She did not ask the price. Then for a moment, in a day-dream of remorse and fear, she hesitated, remembered very vaguely the "little woman" in Earl's Court Road, who would give her an evening-dress so Belgian that some might think it Parisian, for eight guineas. She shrank, she thought of doing up old frocks, she almost ran out of the shop, but all that evening and all that night there was riot in her blood. She saw herself arrayed as the humming-bird, eclipsing the dahlia. She woke hot-mouthed . . .

And for three days the fever was upon her. Two more evening dresses were bought and, more insidious, there were silk stockings, shimmering as pearls, others pale as running water. She bought hats, no longer the hats of modesty, but hats for five guineas, one for six guineas, and one long, wild feather that could span her arm. She bought handkerchiefs framed with gossamer, jabots as the edge of a wave. She bought blouses, costly because so plain, gloves that moulded her to the shoulder . . . and little, high boots with white kid tops, and a tall black aigrette to stand in her warm hair, as a black pine-tree overtaken by the twilight against a glowing sky . . . and at home, in her drawing-room, sometimes with a little vein twitching in her temple, she waited: the bell, here again the bell . . . another parcel. Sharply she drew in her breath.

II

She was conscious of an obscure travail in her mind. Here indeed were intimations of unrest. It was complex. A desire to be beautiful, to be loved, envied, admired, to make men turn to look at her, and disdainfully to walk on flattered, to make women stop and enviously scoff. Here were the first shadows of some subtle decay; it was a wild search for a satisfaction, for something that would bridge a gap, for something to do, something to want and to have.

She had wandered into the labyrinth of purchase, there a while to be lost. She was going to buy without truly wanting, and merely because she wanted to buy, or wanted to want; to buy to whet her appetite for buying, and to buy to try to kill that appetite, to buy nervously, carelessly, and yet hungrily as if she were trying to force into her consciousness something that would occupy it; to buy because that meant movement, haste, thought, preoccupation, weariness and the excitement that comes when the body is too weary to sleep and can do naught, tossing in the night, but grapple with a mind still planning and still scheming, a mind trying to rest and yet thrusting away sleep lest the wasted hours of the night should steal from it its activity.

III

She was happy. The sense of impending triumph was upon her, that consciousness of worth creating success by creating the certainty thereof. There was, she knew, a change in the atmosphere that surrounded her in these drawing-rooms which she had frequented as the wife of a rising barrister. It was almost as if already the barrister had risen. As she went, in her fine clothes, her pleasure lay not only in the men who looked at her in the street and paid her the compliment of wondering whether she was quite respectable, nor even in the men who, warned that in spite of her elegance she was virtuous, asked to be introduced to her in the queer, mendacious way that men do these things. She knew those little tricks, could detect the side-look which the men gave to her hostess, could see their lips form the words: "I seem to know your friend —must have met her somewhere," which invited a reintroduction. And, at dinner, she knew very well that the man upon her right tended rather often to disregard his partner; from across the table, through the flowers, she caught little gleams in eyes.

No, it was not the men, it was the women who made the new atmosphere, this strange atmosphere of competing clothes, of quick, estimating glances. She could see women pricing her garments, tracing the address of the maker; she could hear the delicious hatred in the compliments they paid her, feel the envy of those who had not dared. Now she was in her stride, knew that she was going strong, knew that her rivals knew it. They were racing, these women of the town, racing for the first variation in style, a new wave for the hair, a new top to a boot, a new buckle, for the colour of a facing, or the texture of a vest slip.

Sometimes she wondered to what goal they were racing. To capture man? No, it was not that; it is not clothes that capture, so little do men in their uniform of cloth or tweed know that clothes vary, and so gladly do they wed the dowdy. Was it women? Hardly. For only those women who are not quite women can love beauty in their own sex. And Grace could not conceive that one should desire the hatred of women, incense of flattery though it be. Or was it for her, herself? Perhaps. Sometimes she was sure that it was for herself. For whom else should her petticoats be inserted with lace? and for whom else should she buy stays of green silk to set off the amber and gold of her hair?

Doubtless these things were not for her husband, though doubtless they might have been. One evening she was undressing, tired and a little languid, for she had come back from the theatre, bidden Edward good night, and it was late. He opened the door. She turned a little angrily; she hated this intrusion into her privacy, this opening of her bedroom door without a knock. Never had she forbidden Edward the room, but she had always felt that she ought to have had the right to forbid him and that a knock would recognise this.

He came towards her in a rough, blue dressing-gown, trimmed with red, which, he said, was good enough for a plain man. As he closed the door, there ran through Grace's exasperation a feeling that she could have forgiven him if he had slammed that door, come to her, seized her by wrist and body, purposeful and silent, conveying that her privacy was nothing to him, that he was her master, her owner, therefore her conqueror. But as he came, hands in pockets, the Edwardian smile upon his face, she was thrilled with anxiety as she told herself, remembering the topic of the day: "He is going to tell me about the compensation-case." As he opened his mouth, she clenched her fists. Edward threw her a look which included, with her, the mirror, the curtains and anything within the scope of his eyes. Then: "I say, I forgot to tell you the finest thing about that case —"

Grace stood before him, rigid, looking, in her green silk stays, with her bare arms and throat, like a boulevard statuette. Rage was upon her. In that minute she knew that he had not seen her, that she was not a woman to him, but an ear. And that was why he did not knock: he did not want to respect her privacy, nor to violate her privacy; he simply did not consider the question of her privacy. Slowly the recital of the case went on. Once more the evidence of Jones, the foreman, was sifted, while Edward walked up and down the room, his hands in the pockets of his dressing-gown, shouting the periods of the opposing counsel mimicking the judge's bass and the high treble of a female witness. He walked up and down, blind to the tender apparel of a woman's bedroom: soft garments, scents, delicate little tools of the cult of beauty, as if he did not know that it existed, because it was not his . . .

But stay, it was his in a sense. It was his wife's, therefore his. He became aware of his property; the story of the case stopped abruptly. The law of compensation against accident suddenly receded in his brain, gave place to a consciousness that he had here a beautiful possession.

"Hello, Gracie-Bracie," he remarked, "you're looking pretty fit." He came closer, put his arm round the stayed waist. "Aren't you going to give hubby a buss?"

Grace's eyes were hard, but she was not yet hard throughout. She smiled as Edward, drawing her closer, kissed her lips.

Much later the lights were out. Through the undrawn curtain the moonlight, streaming in, lit up Edward's sleeping face; his small, regular features were all silvered. As he slept, his breath came light. Grace sat up in bed, threw away from her face the heavy, untidy masses of her hair, and looked at the sleeper. Yes, in a way, he was beautiful. Like a mask in the rays of the moon he slept, her husband, already. He slept, and earlier than in those days long dead, when he was lover too. As she bent down to look at him, she wondered why she did not, before going to sleep, want to stoop lower and inspire his dreams with a single kiss, very soft, upon his brow. It was, she thought, unaccountable as she thus sat while he slept by her side and there still was, all through her, the consciousness of his brief caress. But again came the flush of anger. Yes, it was true, he was a lover still in a way. Still could he clasp her close in his arms, perhaps thrill her with fleeting delight. She was woman after all, and she could be his. But was he hers? Had he been conscious, all these years, that he was not alone in his joy? had he known that she was there at all? had he courted while he conquered?

A little bitterly she went through the events of the day. They had been to an at home, and she had worn the postillion-coat with the brown and yellow vest; everybody had looked at it, the men without understanding, but with vague interest, the women as judges; Edward had said nothing. He had made a reference to going on the razzle-dazzle with a lady of fashion, but had he seen her? Had she existed in his world at all? And in that minute she was quite sure that he had not seen her, that he had not known what she wore, thanked her for being beautiful any more than in that past minute, the warmth of which was now receding so fast that she began to forget it; he had not been conscious of her except as of something necessary for his pleasure and his self-glorification. He had patronised while he loved . . .

She bent over the sleeping face. She thought she could detect in the lips a smile that said:

"Behold me, Edward Kinnersley, husband of the most beautiful woman in the town, as is natural enough since I chose her. Behold me, Edward Kinnersley, the perfect lover who knows how to control a woman with the right degree of masculinity, to give her the consciousness of being loved. Behold me, father, lover, dispenser of all good things. I sleep, but still I am Eros; and, as I sleep, in my dream, I see my beautiful wife sleeping too by my side, dreaming in admiration, content and gratitude. My wife . . . but let me see, about that compensation case—Now I wonder what I should do, what I—? I—I—"

As if the rays of the moon were cold, a shiver went through Grace's bare shoulders. Suddenly she thrust herself low into the bed, drew the bed-clothes about her head, as if in the blackness to blot out the world.

IV

Mary looked up from the *Daily Mirror.* The cook stood at the door. "Please, mum," she said, "the butcher."

The meat was ordered. The cook was told to procure peas regardless of cost; the quality of the potatoes was animadverted upon. A dispute between the housemaid and the day-girl as to who was responsible for washing the lino on the servant's floor was settled. Grave reflections were cast upon the parlour-maid's capacity for cleaning the silver.

The morning list was made. A hat had to be bought for Ella, promoted that day from bonnets; a telephone call was decided so that one of the perambulators might be re-tyred, visits were planned to the plumber, the upholsterer and, very reluctantly, to the hairdresser.

"I suppose," thought Mary, "I shall have to have my hair waved."

She got up and went to the looking-glass set in the overmantel, for she carried none in her little bag. "I suppose I shall," she repeated, "I haven't been near him for two months."

She wondered whether the doctor had better come once more to look at Maud. It had only been nettle-rash after all and the spots had all gone in— Still—

She went through her letters, set aside the advertisements of patent foods and laundries, while throwing into the waste-paper basket a catalogue of the *Galeries Lafayette.* She accepted two invitations to dinner, laid the basis of an at home which she supposed she would have to give. She held upon the telephone a long conversation with Mrs. Westfield, the principal topic being Maud's vanished nettle-rash. She closed the door, then resumed her telephone conversation, so that her mother might miss nothing of the dispute between the housemaid and the day-girl. She dressed. Then, before she went out, she went up into the empty nursery. Her little children were now all in the Gardens; a sort of business-like content filled her as she surveyed the vast rooms, the glistening linoleum, the spotless curtains, the shining glass and crockery; the nurseries seemed as well organised as a bank. Or rather, they were as a quarter-deck. And Mary, as she stood and inspected them, felt much as may a captain when, all alone, in his gold lace, he stands upon the bridge.

It was in the afternoon she accidentally met Grace as she came out from the hairdresser's, her fair hair waved and making her look strange because these visits were so rare.

"Hallo, G.," she said, brightly; then, as if, for a moment, the fashionable proceeding of having had her hair dressed excited her, she added: "I suppose I look like a skinned rabbit, but I feel a rip."

Grace smiled. She thought that Mary dressed like a dowager. But she was languid that day, the memory of the past night hanging weary over her. She let Mary talk, of her children, her husband, her mother. She answered her questions as to her own belongings. And she was a little surprised when Mary intuitively said:

"What's wrong, G.? You don't look quite up to the mark, though you're pretty smart."

"Oh, well," said Grace, "I don't know. Perhaps I'm not. Silly worries, you know."

"Yes," said Mary. But she could not find out what these worries were. She alluded to Grace's clothes again. "I don't know how you've got the patience to bother about them," she said, "I'd never have time."

"Oh, you've got something else to do," said Grace, a little sarcastic.

But, as later, when she had left her sister, she thought of Mary's remark, she reflected that the sarcasm could have been turned on her, that Mary could have said: "You're not bothering much about your children, you're too busy, you've got something else to do." And she wondered whether her activities meant anything. It was that worried her, and something else too: the fact that she had spent not sixty pounds, but, so far as she knew, about a hundred and twenty-three. This was May, and in five months she had spent the dress-allowance for the year, all but twenty-seven pounds. There would be a crisis, it was certain, and she knew that she had no desire to avert the crisis, even if she had to go to Edward and ask him for some money. She wondered whether he would be angry, and just for one fleeting moment wished he would be; but she knew he would not, that she would be too crafty. She knew that for an hour before she asked for a cheque she would talk courts, law, judges, that she would ask Edward to tell her stories of the Inns and that at last, when he was smoothed and pleased, she would ask him for money, that he would give it her with a genial, kindly, patronising kiss. Or, much worse, she might tell him that the bills for the quarter amounted to so much and he would pay without enquiring, without wanting to know.

V

In the motley assembly which is modern society were other busy women too. There were many of those beautiful, well-gowned, detached women who seem a typical product of English civilisation. Carefully they preside over social functions; they assist at political meetings, those of their fathers' party when they are girls, those of their husbands' when they become wives; they read, without partisanship, the book of the day; they go to picture shows and buy pictures when the artist is an acquaintance; they love their daughters, send them to the right schools, marry them to the right men; they love their sons and direct their tastes towards the right regiments. Strictly they are the organisers of the governing class, they are the people who take orders from men and make them a little more human; they form against the threatening desire for reform which the working-class growls out now and then in the shape of an incoherent, impotent strike, a broad bulwark of refinement which is strong by the very fact of their luke-warmth, of their rather faded elegance. It is almost as if these ladies stood in front of the docker, clamouring for an extra penny, raised a deprecatory finger, and said: "Hush! what naughty words!" And so gracefully do they stand, so assured that their class will always stand, that, after a few growls, the docker goes, very much like the lion that noses its prey and, finding that it seems to be dead, leaves it alone. It is enough to make one wonder whether these ladies, and all those whom they represent, are not indeed corpses, shamming life with amazing skill.

Here and there, like trees jutting out of low-lying mist, is one not quite the same as the others. There is Mrs. Cheddon. She is twenty-five, flat-chested, regular-featured, and very like a handsome man. She drinks whiskey and soda; she carries her umbrella as if it were a hunting-crop, and she very nearly smacks it, as she walks, against an absent high boot. From her well-tanned complexion her eyes stare, blue and very beautiful; and her mouth, perfectly moulded, is made for kisses but kisses seldom. She has a husband somewhere. She never swears, for she has a man's restraint without a man's license, but in a high, soft voice she talks of dogs. She breeds dogs. She shows, she takes prizes. In her kennels there are no lady-dogs: Mrs. Cheddon's pets are bitches. And there is nothing equivocal in her absurdly girlish voice when she tells you that her Airedale, Crompton Rightaway, is at stud.

"Is it enough?" she replies, when Grace questions her. "What do you mean? huntin'? and dogs, and all that sort of thing? Oh, well, keeps one goin' somehow."

"But are you never bored?" says Grace. "Do you like dogs enough to do nothing else? I mean—is it nice?"

"Nice?" said Mrs. Cheddon, indignantly. "It's top-hole, that's what it is."

And Mrs. Leycett too has found something that is top-hole. Once upon a time she was an actress and got two lines to speak because, one day, though a vicar's daughter, she decided to slam the door and live her own life. She married and ten years have passed. Algernon is at the preparatory; Isabel has an efficient governess; and Tom has a nurse so fierce that the nursery is taboo. Ten years have passed! and Mrs. Leycett has returned to the stage.

Her hair was fair; it is now smothered in reddish ringlets; there is salve upon her mouth and always in the corners of her eyes a tiny black pussy-cat of make-up. Two frills are the fashion: she wears three. Parasols are tall to-day: hers reaches to her shoulder. She is gay; the footlights shine a little in her wake; the celebrated actor-manager is to her merely Georgie.

Grace does not ask her whether it is good enough; evidently it is. All she can do is to defend herself when attacked because she reads the wrong papers.

"What!" cries Mrs. Leycett, "don't read the *Era?* Nor the *Sporting and Dramatic?* Well, I never! What do you read then?"

And Grace must acknowledge that she reads nothing so significant as the *Era*.

There are others too, but more than any other there is Mrs. Shapwick. She is thirty years old, and really twenty. When she is forty she will be eighteen. She has a husband who dances, also a F. I. A. T. car, no house cares, but a suite in a hotel. She is gay and round, and rolls as a big white ball; she enjoys a week-end with nice people, and she enjoys a week-end with dull people; she likes the journey, she loves the packing. She likes post-impressionist teas at the Savoy, morris-dances in the East End, the novels of Mr. Henry James and those of Mrs. Barclay. She gets up as early as she can and goes to bed as late as she can. She belongs to every Sunday club; she plays tennis at Queen's and has a taste for new religions.

"Busy?" she cries to Grace. "Well, yes, I'm pretty

busy. Just dropped in here for a moment, but I must be off; I've got to dress."

"Are you doing anything to-night?" asks Grace.

"I don't know, but Charlie's sure to have thought of something when I get back."

And Mrs. Shapwick bounds out, extraordinarily busy with that something unknown which she must do that evening, a something which is very important, for it is a something to do. And, as Grace looks at the dining-room door closing behind her, some inner voice in her calls out:

"I say! Mrs. Shapwick! I say, do you like it?" And, as if some psychic link connects her with the visitor who has doubtless passed the front door and leapt into a taxi, Grace seems to hear Mrs. Shapwick's voice floating towards her: "Do I like it? My dear, it's top-hole."

VI

Clara put down the telephone, feeling that the day was getting on nicely. Three minutes past ten. Already she had read her letters, made notes on them, which Miss Lenzie would deal with by and by in her deprecatory but not inefficient way; she had read the *Times*, thought some hard things about Mr. Lloyd-George, and considered whether Lord Algernon Cust could be entangled; she had ordered dinner: same as that day last week. Now she had to go to Victoria Street, to the office in St. Panwich, to ring up the ball-furnisher, to drop in at her club in Albemarle Street and arrange for the afternoon she was hostessing. An easy morning. But no, there was a hat; she really must buy a hat. She made a little angry noise: these clothes! Why could not a member's wife wear tweeds and be done with it? She rushed to the telephone, rang up Grace. In a few moments she was stamping with rage; Mrs. Kinnersley was still in her bath.

"Bath, bath," said Clara, angrily. "Bath at ten o'clock in the morning, disgusting habit— Oh, is that you, Grace? So you've finished dressing, have you?" (Ironic).

"Oh, no," came Grace's voice, far away and rather languid, "shan't have done for an hour."

"You used to be quicker," said Clara, acidly. "I don't know what's come over you. You're such a spug now."

Grace laughed at the old familiar word of the nursery, "sleepy pug," contracted into "spug." "Perhaps I'm changing," she said. "I'm excited and tired at the same time, as if something in me were trying to get free and banging up against some bars."

"Oh, for heaven's sake don't talk like the young men from Chelsea; rather tell me what sort of hat I'd better buy."

"Hat?" cried Grace, more interestedly. "Oh, it's obvious just now; quite, quite small; right over the eyes; velvet with an aigrette. Or if you want it a little higher —"

The information seemed to go on indefinitely, and Clara found her mind wandering to more important cares. "Oh, never mind, never mind," she fumed at last. "I don't care."

"Well, what are you going to buy?" asked Grace. "Any damn hat?"

"Grace!" said Clara.

"I beg your pardon," said Grace, "it slipped out. You don't seem to care. But seriously —"

The hat question was settled. And, a little later, as Clara leapt into her car, she wondered how it was that Grace had said "damn." Dimly she realised that her sister was changing, and for a second asked herself whether she too were not changing, whether there was not something wrong with her. A terrible moment, but only a moment for, at once, her mind, swift and erratic in its flight as a gull, had forsaken such little concerns as her own soul and Grace's.

For here she was, in Victoria Street; those circulars would not draw twopence. And now in St. Panwich, straining Miss Lenzie's shorthand beyond the powers of

Pitman, enjoining upon her to telephone Mrs. Bubwith — to order the Liberal Year Book and the Navy League Annual — to beg one woman for cakes and to refuse another a ticket. Fierce altercation over rout seats — speech soft as honey for the club secretary. Conduit Street: the hat, a dozen hats inspected, bewilderment — any hat — "any damn hat," as Grace said. Hat chosen: time four minutes, twenty-five seconds.

Lunch: the *National Review* perused between courses.

Three o'clock. Drawing-room meeting. The chair. Speech on behalf of washerwomen who have seen better days. Smiles and recognition of total strangers. Moistly warm hand-shakes. Cold tea. Triumph.

Four-thirty. Home again: a valuable young man to be captured. Barrister, well-brushed, must be snatched before the Eighty Club gets him. Constituencies talked hard in spite of young man's efforts and desire to receive his teacup so clumsily that his fingers lightly touch those of Lady Govan . . . his attempts to make the conversation neurotic suitably baulked, but smiled at. Visit very long, as it is difficult to get business done when a promising young man insists on your needing cushions behind your back and puts them there in a lingering way. Very long hand-shake, granted with indifference, and a kiss upon the wrist. Kiss forgotten.

At six o'clock she was tired, but she told herself she was not, and that she loved her work, this fine, life-filling, exciting work, this running of the Empire, via St. Panwich. Besides, she had to dress.

She ordered more tea, having a conscientious objecttion to whiskey and soda. Fierce struggle with Germaine and her theories as to the garbing of a *femme du monde.* Sir Henry spoken to for the first time since the morning, and not for long; for here is a political dinner with a Cabinet Minister between débutantes, as his dislike of anything over nineteen is notorious. The hostess, rather anxious, wondering what will happen to the youth, recently down from Cambridge, who has determined to tell the Cabinet Minister how they thought he should save the country when he was at Cat's. Some M. P.'s, some candidates, some prospective candidates; the wives they married early and unwisely; the wives they married after consultation with the Central Office —

Clara found it hard work with the man on the right. He was a manufacturer called Holt whose name was a household word in cement circles; a queer, hard-bitten person with a house in the Finchley Road, a wife who, he declared, didn't care for society. His son, Jack, having, some time before, supplied a small scandal in St. John's Wood by making advances to a certain Mrs. Victoria Fulton, his mother's companion, the old man had taken to politics after sending his son up north. Clara expounded at length how much the party needed money; a cheque from Mr. Holt to the Central Office would yield the funds of St. Panwich a commission. She talked in her pretty, high voice, leant towards the old man, used her bright, blue eyes, quite unconscious that he had successfully resisted the far greater charms of Mrs. Fulton. Thomas Holt looked at her with sharp, humorous eyes. Every now and then he thought: "Do you think you're getting at me?" And said aloud: "May be."

"We need the support of the solid people," said Clara, strikingly.

"May be," said Thomas Holt.

"Support in influence and — money," said Clara, more daring.

"May be."

She plunged. "There's your own place, Mr. Holt. Rawsley, isn't it? You've never — had any Parliamentary ambitions?"

"May be," said Thomas Holt.

And the man upon her left was quite as bad. He was an enormously stout journalist whose rosy cheeks and neck drooped over his low collar. He twinkled at her amiably, swore he would not forget her in his society notes; indeed he swore it all too well, for Clara, accustomed to dominate conversations, found she could make no headway through the soft, sticky mass of his baronial, ducal, royal facts.

"But, of course, Lady Govan, of course I shall be charmed. I shall be *ravi,* as our gay neighbours across the Channel say. I shall be *enchanté.* It is so important that the Right People should be properly advertised in these degenerate American days. As I was saying the other day to the Princess Frederika — a charming woman, you know her, of course — the aristocracy ought to take a column in the *Pall Mall Gazette* every day to expound its policies, principles and opinions, and have it run by 'Demosthenes.' She was charmed, charmed, absolutely charmed. She repeated it everywhere, simply everywhere — "

The rosy flesh heaved amiably, and he went on repeating it: "Everywhere, everywhere — "

"I say," said Sir Henry, as the car swiftly sped up Sloane Street, "I wish you wouldn't throw yourself about so much, Clara."

"I'm not throwing myself about," she replied. "I don't know what you mean, Harry."

"Oh, well," said Henry, unusually acid, having that afternoon dropped thirty pounds at the Portland. "If you don't know what I mean, I suppose I must explain. All this rushing about. . . . When we're in the flat together, I never seem to hear anything except you rowing the exchange."

"Well," said Clara, brightly, "get the Government out and give us the old National Telephone back; then I shan't row the exchange any more. If you turn the Government — "

"Oh, damn the Government," said Sir Henry. "You talk of nothing but the Government." A furrow came between his eyebrows. "Damn the Government," he said again, furiously. "Damn politics!"

"Well, we'd be pretty slack without politics," said Clara.

"Slack!" said Sir Henry. "That's just what you want to be. You're a bundle of nerves. If you didn't do so much, you wouldn't always be looking for something to do."

A streak of self-pity passed through Clara's irritation.

"But, Harry," she said, more softly, "I must do something."

"Do less," said Sir Henry, obstinately.

"I can't," said Clara, weakly. "I must do something, Harry."

He turned away. He wanted to shrug his shoulders; as this was not one of his habits, without another word he lit a cigar . . .

As, little by little, she grew sleepy, Clara turned over in her mind the events of the day, the arrangements at Victoria Street, so unsatisfactory . . . the character of the club secretary. . . . Vaguely she planned new schemes for St. Panwich, local schemes, then broader, national schemes . . . imperial schemes. All through ran that streak of worry and self-pity. She thought of Mary who had become a suffragette, as soon as the movement ceased to be fashionable, and for a moment seemed about to be regenerated. Yes, when Mary became a suffragette, Clara thought there had been hope that she would turn into a human being, after all. But it has not lasted long. Already there was an idea that Mary might be going to have another child. As she fell asleep, Mary was still in her thoughts, fat, placid, stupid, maternal Mary. A contemptuous little laugh melted into the growing regularity of her breathing.

VII

When all the clothes had come home, Grace bought no more. She was as a sultan in possession of a new mistress, aware that the desire for a new love would come again but yet assured that the present love was sweet. Sometimes, in the late afternoon, before it was time to dress for dinner, she would lock herself in her bedroom and take out from the wardrobe and the drawers all those new and charming things which had come into her life. In those moments her bed was covered from rail to rail with afternoon dresses and evening dresses; the rails of the bed were festooned with silk stockings, with filmy, ribbon-threaded nightgowns, with foam-light ruffles; upon the mantelpiece she stood the shoes and the little boots, well-polished and all in a row; and upon her dressing-table were grouped the hats, except one, a very large black one, the one round which curled the immense feather: that one, quite alone, was on the floor, surrounded by linen, so that by contrast it might appear yet larger.

And then, in the midst of her fripperies, more than ever as a sultan among his favourites, she could feel a warmth rising into the atmosphere, something more living than mere beauty, more suggestive of power. These sterile, charming things were potential conquerors. Yet, now and then, a little coldness touched her heart, and she asked herself: "Conquest? Yes, but the conquest of what?" She quickly thrust that away. For Grace had her ghostly footmen that followed her on list slippers, insistent that she should partake of their meats. She was oppressed with debts. The thirty-seven pounds ten which had been paid into her dress account at the end of March quarter had melted before the cash purchases of April and May; as she was a new customer in Grafton Street she had been pressed for payment, and had aroused suspicion because she had not dared to give references to the tradesmen. It seemed almost as if she had felt her exultation to be guilty; she had wanted to hug her secret, to conceal the fact that such garments as these were not bought in Kensington. So she had juggled with her accounts. As Edward refused to deal with any bill himself, she had managed to pay the upholsterer out of the wine account, while making a new coal contract so as not to swell the previous bill. She had made the rates wait; the red notice had arrived; gas, electricity, rent were, in this month of June, coming down pitiless. Her mind was busy with apologies and offers of instalments; vaguely she thought of past lectures and, more distastefully every day, of the necessary explanation which she would have to give Edward. He would scold her gently, call her a naughty girl, declare that girls would be girls and, after gently inferring that the husband was the head of the wife, would pay . . . and kiss her. As she stood in the midst of the room that was beflowered with silks and lace, a shiver of irritation passed through Grace. The idea that her husband would kiss her awoke in her a strange repugnance. The kiss and the receipted bill — marriage or Leicester Square? And she was, perhaps, still more shocked by her own lucidity. She saw herself as useless save in one way, or in other ways not much more notable: housekeeper, companion, racial instrument and lover. Was it for all that she had to be young and pretty? And was it for all that silks and laces filled her room?

Sometimes she grappled with herself and listened to the other ghostly footman, the one who, upon a badly cleaned salver, offered her moral reactions. She told herself that she was a bad woman, frivolous, selfish, that she was a bad mother, a bad wife. In those moods she would run up to the nursery, and an obscure sense of decency, when she did this, made her throw off her high-heeled shoes with the enamel buckles, put on slippers, visit the nursery in a reverent spirit. But always she was the congregation, never the officiating priest. Horace and Susan had been seized by the vast mechanism of the rich child's education which begins with the monthly nurse at four guineas a week, passes through the Norland nurse or the Princess Christian nurse to the costly kindergarten, to the preparatory where a boy is not much if he is a commoner, to the public school and the immaculate establishments for girls on the South Coast, to the university, to the coming-out ball, the bar, the regiment, and marriage.

Sometimes Grace tried to interfere with a garment, a task; but always the expert knew better. If she put a finger into the machine, she upset its smooth working and hurt herself.

"There's no room for you, there's no room for you rich mothers," murmured the machine, as it smoothly worked on. "Just get your children born, and then run away and play; I'll do the rest. And, for heaven's sake, don't interfere, my dear girl; it isn't done."

Sometimes, very gently, she tried to assist Edward's

career. He never did anything for it himself, though he seldom thought of aught else; he was too continually prostrate before his own forensic performances to be aware of outer worlds. He too, in the legal profession, was like the actors, the literary men, who cannot conceive that the world exists outside the theatre or the publisher's office. So he did not complain when they dined alone, if only afterwards he were allowed to sleep in an armchair, or to rally his wife, or according to his mood to talk courts and cases for two hours. Now and then only, he would awake to the fact that they were not seeing anybody, that life was flat. He had become what all husbands become.

For a man who marries, like a woman, sets out as a caravel towards the unknown shore that lies below the horizon; he has to explore a new continent and to discover treasure; he will devote himself to that treasure and cherish it; he will be gay, tolerant, protective, generous. And all these things he is. But one day the treasure becomes a valuable possession. The valuable possession becomes a possession. The possession becomes part of the property. Then the treasure is only a wife. Once she was beautiful and thrilling; now she is beautiful. Once she was dressed: now she is clothed. Once her headaches were alarming: now she is begged not to cough so loud at breakfast. But, much worse, she has lost her power of intimacy; she has her own friends, her own club, her own pleasures, her own desires, opinions and revolts . . . and all these things she may keep to herself: they are not wanted. Meanwhile the power of intimacy falls away from the hands of the husband. Those bachelor friends, once forgotten, are taken up again. The club begins to call, politics excite, the career dominates. That creature so like man and yet so different, with her long hair, her softness, with the queer, quick, humid gleam in her eyes when she looked at him, that creature of unaccountable impulses, so prone to lie, and so ready to give her life for a man, so vain and so egotistic, and yet so thankful for a kind word — that creature has lost its mystery, and the man has turned away. He is not a man any more, but a husband; he has become what all husbands become. The "we" is dead, the "I" has risen again . . .

So Grace suited her dinners to her man. Solicitors were asked, for solicitors can give briefs; and K. C.'s, for K. C.'s can help promising juniors; and their wives, for wives must be asked. Grace did not ask her own friends, those desultory, preoccupied people, such as Mrs. Cheddon or Mrs. Leycett; her friends she entertained at club and restaurant, for she was sure their conversation would not amuse Edward. But Edward's friends she asked to her own table, not feeling entitled to wonder whether their conversation would interest her.

VIII

Mrs. Westfield was sitting in the dining-room, comparing the laundry list with that of the previous week, as she wished to check the extravagance of the maids. As Grace came, there was a slight frown between her thin eyebrows, and a general air of severity on her creamy-rose face. She warmly responded to her daughter's kiss.

"Well," she said, cheerfully, "and how's the family?"

This question always irritated Grace. Her mother had a way of asking: "How's the family?" as if she thought woman existed only for the family. Often she felt impelled to answer: "And how's the fancy-work?" as a scoff at Mrs. Westfield's only vice. But this morning she felt too listless to open up an argument.

"Oh, they're all right," she said.

"Horace?" asked Mrs. Westfield.

"Horace practically knows his letters."

"That's good," said Mrs. Westfield, and went on to a lengthy warning against the danger of pushing little boys too early, illustrated by a number of cases of meningitis and minor troubles which had come within her experience. Then she demanded an account of Susan.

"Susan is rather naughty," said Grace. "One hardly knows what to give her to eat; she refuses everything."

"She should be slapped," said Mrs. Westfield, severely.

" Spare the rod, my dear, and spoil the child. Now when you were a little girl — "

Several painful instances of Grace's early youth were recalled and, generally speaking, it was inferred that things were much better in the days of the dear queen.

" Well, Mother," said Grace, " I don't know that the whacking did me much good."

" My dear," protested her mother, as if Grace blasphemed, " I don't say you're perfect, but think how much worse you would have been if you hadn't been punished when you were naughty."

Grace felt there was a flaw in this logic, but did not pursue the subject, for she was so interested in herself as to want to consider rather the state in which she was then, than the causes which had brought about that state. She did not have an opportunity for a while, as Mrs. Westfield had more enquiries to make.

" Now," said Mrs. Westfield, " tell me all about it. I saw Edward's name in the paper the other day. He was defending somebody. Did he tell you? "

" I don't remember who you mean, Mother," said Grace, " but I expect he did tell me. Do you mean the burglar? "

" Yes," said Mrs. Westfield, delightedly, " that's the man. He picked him out, didn't he? "

" Yes," said Grace, " Edward was at Guildford Assizes, and as his case was settled out of court, he stayed for a little. Then they brought in the burglar and, as he was undefended, he just picked Edward out and put his fee down before him. So Edward had to take it. It's the rule, you know."

" Oh," said Mrs. Westfield, " I'm not surprised he took Edward; he's so winning, don't you think? "

" Yes, Mother," said Grace, dutifully. She did not want to discuss Edward. She feinted. " Tell me what you've been doing? "

Mrs. Westfield did not at once pick up this attractive glove. As if moved by some intuition, she dwelt on Edward, on his gaiety, his generosity, his good looks, and wound up on a peroration which showed that she had not only been a very successful mother in providing so good a husband, but that, in a vague way, Grace was ungrateful for not saying so herself.

"Well, I'm not saying anything against him," said Grace, rather acidly.

Her mother did not notice and, for a long time, having suddenly taken up another subject, gave her an account of the repairs necessitated by the leaky roof, a sketch of the temperament of an elderly doctor to whom she had been introduced. "And the servants," she said, "I'm having the old trouble with Louisa: break, break, break! I've got to hurry through the hall when I go up-stairs in case I may hear another smash. I'm sure it's bad for my heart."

"What's the matter with her?" asked Grace.

"Oh, she's got a young man. Girls are always silly when they've got a young man. But," Mrs. Westfield sighed a large sigh, "she's going to marry him soon. She'll get over her nonsense."

There was a pause during which Grace gloomily reflected that when one got married one did get over one's nonsense. So serious was her face that her mother noticed it.

"And you, Grace," she asked, suddenly. "You — you look rather pale."

"I suppose I forgot to put any complexion on."

"How can you talk like that? Complexion indeed! The way women paint their faces nowadays is simply disgusting."

"But, Mother, it isn't paint; a little powder perhaps. Everybody does it a little."

"I suppose they do," said Mrs. Westfield. "I don't know what we're coming to. In my time, when I went to the theatre with your father, we used to have to hurry out so that I needn't see too much of those creatures in their silks and satins, and their painted faces, but now . . . the way things are going, it's they will have to show natural skins or we shan't be able to tell them from the respectable women."

Grace laughed. "There's still a little difference, Mother," she said. "Any man will tell you."

Mrs. Westfield did not at once reply, but looked at her severely. "Any man will tell me!" she repeated. "Do you mean to say that you think I could discuss such a subject with a *man?* I suppose you do think so. I don't know what's come over you. Really, Grace, while I'm about it, I can tell you that there's something funny about you just now; there has been for a long time."

"What sort of thing?" asked Grace, in a tone which she strove to make firm.

"Well," said Mrs. Westfield, "I hardly know. . . . A sort of agitation. Are your nerves all right?"

"Quite, Mother," said Grace. "At least I never lose my temper, if that's what you mean."

"And there are your clothes; they look very expensive."

"Not very expensive," said Grace, uncomfortably.

"Well, they *look* expensive," said Mrs. Westfield, finally. "I'm afraid you're wasting a good deal of money."

"Oh, it's great fun."

"It may be fun," said Mrs. Westfield. "But I don't understand what you want fun for. You've got plenty to do with your house, and your husband, and your children."

"Oh, no, I haven't, Mother. The whole thing runs itself. Edward's got his own things to think of, and nurse and the governess look after the children."

"A mother's eye should be everywhere," said Mrs. Westfield.

"But it isn't wanted everywhere," cried Grace, desperately. "It can see that it can't see right."

"I don't understand," said Mrs. Westfield.

"Oh, Mother, can't you understand that when one's got money, one's got to bring up one's children in a certain way? and that the nurse and the governess do it much better than you do? A mother who brought up her own children would make . . . monsters of them. The boys would be prigs and the girls wouldn't know anything. In our class a mother's only in the way."

Mrs. Westfield rose to her feet. "In the way!" she murmured, solemnly. "I never thought anybody would say such a thing. And that a daughter of mine — "

She lectured Grace for a full half-hour. It appeared that there were two duties: the duties of the wife, and the duties of the mother. Rights were not mentioned. To be in the house was not enough; one had to know what the children ate, and if one cooked it so much the better. If, as a result, the children had indigestion through improper feeding, one dosed them oneself; if one dosed them wrong, so much the worse: one sent for the doctor, and not too often, for that was a modern, hysterical way. One administered justice, that is to say one saw to it that the children's birthdays were well-advertised so that other people might give them presents while one did the spanking oneself. One saw to it that the children gained general instruction and, if one had girls, one was careful to prevent them from frequenting the High Church or the chapel. A girl who talked of becoming a nun should always be taken to a pantomime. The flesh and the devil should always be kept in reserve, not too accessible but still handy if the other world became too appealing. (Short interval for the discussion of variety in breakfast dishes; lecture resumed.) A husband's tastes in food to be studied. Feed the brute, still true. And accounts! "Do your accounts balance?" asked Mrs. Westfield.

"So, so," said Grace. "They nearly balance, and if they don't quite I put the difference down as 'lost.'"

The lecture became financial. It appeared that the special account should not be called "lost," but "laziness and incompetency, spendthrift habits, extravagance in clothes." At last Mrs. Westfield came to her peroration:

"This is the beginning of the end. You girls have forgotten what you're in the world for. You're becoming self-indulgent, lazy, ostentatious. You show your stockings above the ankles, and I'm told that lots of women smoke, though it hasn't been done before Me. It is the beginning of the end. I'm not a prejudiced person; I know that times change, but they're changing a little too fast. Yes, women have forgotten what they're in the world for, that's what it is."

As Grace closed behind her the heavy front door, she asked herself without any success: "What are women in the world for?"

As she walked down Campden Hill Road, slowly, she was oppressed by a sense of rebellion which was slowly turning into fury. Was this what women were for? this function that her mother sketched out: to give pleasure to man, physically and intellectually, without much return, to give birth to children, to bring them up so that they might marry, give birth to more children, and bring those up, and so on for ever and ever towards no end. So intense was her emotion as she thought of this endless prospect of births, most of them the result of a smart manœuvre on the part of nature, that she stopped before a garden where stood two spreading hawthorn trees, laden with pink and white blossom which had shed upon the little grass-grown path between them a sumptuous shower of petals. "They too," she thought, "those trees . . . they live only so that the pollen from another tree, a lover, may be carried by the wind into the embrace of their blooms, that they may bring forth fruit, and seed, more trees, more life, and so on for ever and ever."

For a moment this sketchy botany cheered her. It was a law, after all. But at once she perceived a difference. She was not as a tree. Here she was, lonely and yet oppressed with cares, anxious, restless, desirous of something unknown, while the trees, more favoured of nature, flaunted in the sunshine in their white and rosy robes.

"Hawthorn," she murmured, aloud, "you know how to live."

Knowledge of life, she thought, is that the great mystery? To have life is easy; to live it, very complicated. There must be many ways. Had she the right one? and how should she live it? At the question her mood turned to activity: of course . . . she knew her clothes were not enough, she must have more clothes. Her pleasures were not enough. Then more pleasures, more change, more haste, more accumulation of excitements, more pride, more triumphs —

With her mother's sermon in her ears, she entered the High Street. Moved by an impulse, she walked into the theatre ticket office. She came out with four stalls for that night, admitting her to a play the name of which she had not asked.

IX

Grace laid the four tickets upon her dressing-room table. There they were, four little flags hoisted on a ship the name of which she did not know, bound on a voyage to an invisible harbour. It was not the first time she had taken theatre tickets, but in other cases there had been discussions, arrangements; lists of plays had been examined, hearts had been searched to find out whether the mood of the day was frivolous or earnest. This time she had decided to go to the theatre much in the spirit in which she might have decided to go to the devil. The only thing she had to do now was to fill three stalls, and it was characteristic of her attitude, of her quiescence, that she thought only of filling two. She assumed that Edward would go with her: a married woman accompanies her husband to the play. It was early yet, only half-past twelve. There was a good chance of finding many acquaintances at home, but she did not long have to search her mind, for the word "theatre" brought up at once that agreeable woman with the red ringlets that had once been yellow, Mrs. Leycett, and her husband, that Charlie who always found something to do. It was possible that at half-past twelve they would not yet have found something to do in the evening.

Before going to the telephone, some bourgeois remnant compelled Grace to examine the paper and to see what was the play to which she was committed. The title did not tell her much; it was " Miss Halifax, Lady." But it was evident, from the number of authors and composers who had contributed to it, that it was a musical play. She did not, as a rule, like musical comedy. She had been brought up in the vaguely superior tradition that a play or a book should blend instruction with amusement. Her generation was too recent to look upon the theatre as the home of evil, and yet not so recent as to consider that pleasure quite justified itself. She was half a Puritan. But, as she went to the telephone, she realised that she had changed, that she had no qualms, that she was not reproaching herself for having wasted two guineas, and that she wanted either to enjoy herself or to relieve herself. She did not quite know which. Nor did Mrs. Leycett complicate her arrangements. She informed Grace that she was jolly lucky to have got her and enthusiastically accepted, declaring that " she'd love to go, as Totsie Tibbets was the goods." (Mrs. Leycett had recently learnt American).

That left only Edward, and again it was characteristic of Grace that she did not think of telephoning until after lunch and, even then, that she deferred the operation a little. What should she tell Edward? She could hardly tell him that, moved by an impulse, she had bought four stalls. Edward didn't go in for impulses. For a moment she thought of telling him that Mrs. Cheddon had given her the tickets, but drew back: Grace had no dislike of lies as such, and all her life she had been told that lies were wrong, but though she quite realised that a lie would make things much easier, she hesitated. When you have been brought up as a lady, lies are not exactly wrong, but sometimes impossible. So she telephoned vaguely that she felt she wanted a change . . . that she had heard of the play. . . . She found the telephone very merciful. It was much easier to tell half-untruths when Edward was not looking at her. But crisis was upon her: Edward could not come. He had intended to dine at home as usual but, at nine o'clock, had to take part in a moot at his inn.

" Never mind," came the gay voice. " Never mind,

Gracie-Bracie, you'll have to take another man. Now no flirting . . . enjoy yourself, and don't be a naughty girl or hubby'll put you in the corner."

Before she could reply, Edward had put down the receiver. Evidently she had disturbed him in some work of his own far more important than her little affairs.

Another man! Here she was, actually forced by her own imprudence and by her own husband to treat a man to a stall at the theatre. But how would he take it? What would he think? Really it was too bad of Edward. Still she realised that the stall must be filled and that Mrs. Leycett would not thank her if they were two women to one man.

"I'm in for it," thought Grace.

Then she reviewed the men she knew: there was Mr. Sturry, quite safe of course, but would Mrs. Leycett like him? There was Mr. Shapwick; Mrs. Leycett would certainly like him but she was afraid he would like her a little too obviously. And what would Mrs. Shapwick say? She discarded a few promising barristers, as she knew how they gossipped in the common rooms; it would never do if Mrs. Leycett's ringlets — "But never mind Mrs. Leycett," she said aloud, "what about me?"

And for the first time in her life since her marriage, she looked for a man to suit herself. It was as if the Sleeping Beauty had been awakened not by the Fairy Prince, but by a complete regiment of Yeomen of the Guard and, casting upon all these men her astonished, opening eyes, had sought the man. For a second her mind flew back through the years like a bioscope film unrolling the wrong way. She thought of all those young men who used to come to the house at Campden Hill Road; of Mr. Moresby, and of the dreadful case in which he had been concerned, of Mr. Dallas, who was always in such a hurry; and even, with a little smile, of that wild young man with the blue-black hair, Lucien Cadoresse, whom her mother had thrown out of the house. She smiled, thinking of the recent wedding, and how annoyed her mother must be to think she had treated so ill one who was destined to become a partner in the important firm of Stanley, Cadoresse and Co.

"But no," she reflected, "Cadoresse was too recently married. In a couple of years perhaps — "

She laughed, and then was shocked. What was this she was laughing at? What was this suggestion in her mind? That Cadoresse, the bridegroom, was beyond her, while Cadoresse in another two years might not be. What was this cynicism? And then, suddenly serious again, she realised the importance of this business. The name of Saunton occurred to her. He was a young man whom she seemed to meet everywhere, as if he made it his business to know everybody. Well, it should be Saunton. To know a man who knows everybody is to rely upon the safety that lies in numbers. She sent him a telegram.

X

Mrs. Leycett sat at the end of their four stalls; next to her was Patrick Saunton; then came Grace and, at the end, Charlie Leycett. To Grace the play seemed incoherent and rather long. She was languid during the first act. Chorus of lady-gardeners appeared suddenly in a typewriting office . . . and the princess from Chicago sang in the Italian style of an English blacksmith under a chestnut tree. It did not seem to hang together, and this reassured Grace, for they had all dined in Jermyn Street, and she was sure that the extra crême de menthe had not been quite wise. She need not have troubled, for between the continual changes of grouping, between the breaks from dialogue into song, into parading, Saunton and Charlie kept up on both sides of her a continual flow of conversation. As Saunton was epigrammatic and daring, while Charlie was full of information, the result was a little complex.

"There's Archie," said Leycett. "See him? The one with no eyebrows. Topping, isn't he? Ever seen him in 'The Girl Without A Veil?' No? You ought to have, Mrs. Kinnersley. That's where Tootoo came out; you remember Tootoo — the little girl with the coffee-coloured eyes, Lady Roscrowther. That was last summer, a long time ago."

"Yes," said Grace, suddenly aware that somehow last summer was a long time ago. But she was not going to allow herself to meditate. Bravely she turned to Leycett. "She did pretty well for herself," she said, "especially as they say the House of Lords has given up the chorus."

"You mean," said Saunton, "that the chorus has given up the House of Lords. . . . Prefers a pig in a Chicago can to a coronet in pawn."

The gifted actor with the perfect trousers and the limbs of india-rubber began to dance, surrounded by many admiring girls.

> "Oh, he's a dandy, oh, he's a dandy,
> The dandiest, the nuttiest you ever knew.
> He's at the stage-door,
> Cursing the encore,
> Is Mr. Dandy, dandy, dandy-doo."

The two men were still contesting, Charlie with solid facts, Saunton with semi-epigrams. Mrs. Leycett bent forward to point out Lulu Malavine, the latest addition to the manager's harem. The gifted actor ended his dance, bowing, his trousers still miraculously creased.

"Cluster, girls!" he cried, "cluster!" and vanished within an enormous mass of pink, frilled, short skirts.

The night was passing. The princess from Chicago, who now turned out to be "Miss Halifax, Lady," was passing, act by act, from New York to London via the Cannibal Islands, and Grace found that, somehow, the Leycetts were being left out, that Mrs. Leycett was busying herself with her opera-glasses, detecting the ravages of time upon the faces of friends on the stage, and that Saunton was leaning towards her rather intent. He was a good-looking young man of about thirty, with very black hair and the bluest possible eyes. He smiled very little, and then purposefully. He looked, and knew he looked, a little like the sphinx. He was giving Grace his opinion of musical comedy: " an Irish stew without the meat, or more elegantly, the spice of ginger without the fruit."

" That's a nice little girl, that one, the one with the cast in her eye. . . . Rather handy thing, a cast in the eye, Mrs. Kinnersley, sort of permanent wink."

Grace laughed: " You'll be saying the glad eye is a natural deformity next."

" Oh, no, it's the eye that's not glad that's deformed. I say," he added confidentially, in a very serious voice, " she *is* a nice little girl, even though she's a bit thick in the leg."

" Yes," said Grace, seriously, " she is a bit thick in the leg." And then suddenly she wondered how she could allow Saunton to say such a thing to her, and why she was not shocked. She gave him a quick side-look, saw that he was not smiling. In that moment, as if she were now capable of new intuitions, she realised that Saunton was too much a man of the world to have spoken unguardedly. She felt that he was testing her, seeing what she would stand, and that if she seemed offended, he had ready for her a beautiful apology which would convict her of being a bourgeoise. Oh, she was not offended, her turmoil was too great. She laughed. She felt Saunton a little closer to her, his breath upon her hair . . . the play seemed very long and yet more incoherent . . . here was the princess again under the spreading chestnut tree, and Saunton a little closer: she could feel the warmth of his shoulder very light against hers. The blacksmith turned out to be the unrecognised son of a reigning duke. Saunton's shoulder pressed a little heavier upon hers . . . she dropped her programme and as, with her, he bent to pick it up, she felt her hair brush his cheek.

They were outside now, in the porch.

" I say," said Saunton, " you're not going to break up the little party like this? You'd better all come along to the Saxpence Club."

" Oh, do let's," said Mrs. Leycett, " you'll love it."

" A jolly little place," said Leycett. " It was only opened last week."

"And it'll be raided next," added Saunton, "so we'd better be quick."

"Kissing's compulsory," said Mrs. Leycett, "even if you're with your husband."

"Oh, no," murmured Grace, "I'd love to — but I can't — I must get back." A night-club! No, she really couldn't go to a night-club.

Saunton threw her a quick look. Once more he had tested her. A shoulder, yes, that was an accident. A club, no, that was intent. He had the measure of her.

"Well," he said, good-humouredly, "if you won't come to the Saxpence Club, we'd better go to the Savoy, or the Y. M. C. A."

XI

Grace told her husband that she had enjoyed her evening. He asked no questions, but supplied some information as to the way in which he had spent those hours himself. And Grace was telling the truth when she said that she had enjoyed herself. It was not "Miss Halifax, Lady," as a revolutionary sensation, nor Saunton, his handsomeness and his interest in her; it was as if at a bound she had cleared some encircling ropes. Not very high ropes, but yet ropes and, with her heart beating a little, she told herself that she was glad, for she was doing something.

She was one of that long line of women who grade indefinably from Brixton to Kensington Gore: wives of well-paid employees, of minor business men, wives of the professions and daughters of wealth; women who are not as the poor, laden with a household, nor taken up, as the women of the great houses, with social and political activities. They are desperately seeking something to do. A few, every day less in number, take up "good works," hating them, in a spirit half of mortification of the flesh, half of idleness. But the greater number wander from pleasure to pleasure, unsatisfied, greedily snatching at the new. They swell the audiences of the mystics, the theosophists, the Christian Scientists, the higher thought people; they are the buyers of Russian ballet dresses and of post-impressionist friezes; they are the golfers, the skaters; the winter sports women and the restaurant-diners; they, it is, dance first the Washington Post, later the Boston, the two-step, the one-step and the tango; it is they must dance at tea. It is they fill the Savoy and the Carlton, the Roman Catholic cathedral for midnight mass. And they who long to go to Premierland because boxing is in again and fighting a new sensation. Grace had joined them. She was one of the army of women who have conquered London streets. With them she now went, hard at work, affirming conquest. Oxford Street, Sloane Street, Bond Street and its vassals, the army has got them all. And hard at work in other places, in Westbourne Grove, in Clapham Road, Brixton Road and Holloway, others are thrilling, thrilling as buyers, as cheap hedonists, thrilling so as to be ready very soon, when their men rise in the world, to swell those other cohorts of women who occupy the West End . . .

She was awakened. She made no friend, but she whirled with other atoms such as herself, like fragments of glass in a kaleidoscope. Every now and then, when the instrument was shaken, the same combination of atoms formed and when the blue occurred next to the red, Grace, having met an acquaintance twice, thought she had met a friend.

She lunched out at the right place in Soho; people lunched with her; hors-d'œuvres appeared; she visited the picture galleries; she had a shot at golf; her mind was like a cave of dreams, full of the shadows of vague lusts, and yet she was restless, urgent, as if something in her were still hungry. Saunton had escorted her to the Grafton, but had gone too far in the cab as he drove her home. She had not scolded him, but without a word had withdrawn her hand. Thus also had she treated Major Mulben, who had fastened upon her at an at home and bluntly suggested that she should go back with him to his flat and see his Chinese curios. She was not angry, she was a little shocked. She wondered what it was in her had changed the attitude of men. She looked at herself in the glass: she had not altered. Here was still the high nose and high cheek-bones which she detested, the beautiful blend of rose and freckle, the value of which she did not know, and the warm glow in her autumn hair. She had not, she thought, become more beautiful. And then she wondered whether she were beautiful or whether that indefinable something in her that was faintly shadowing with mauve her lower eyelids affected the men who, still from a distance, were circling about her as moths about a lamp. For all men looked at her now, and even Lucien Cadoresse, so recently wedded to that pretty little girl, had the other day at the Raleighs' house thrown her a strange, deep look which, as it rested upon her, suddenly seemed heavy and purposeful. She shivered before the looking-glass, drawing her dressing-jacket about her neck as if the sight of her bare throat offended in her some obscure modesty. She was shocked, but thrilled.

XII

Almost before she could realise it, she was moving. It was as if she had sat down in a railway carriage, seen the platform edge away, snail-like, then, more rapidly, a wall of houses; glimpsed a bridge; and then, quite suddenly, had found that the train was roaring through the suburbs, faster and faster, towards the open country. It was incredible that she should be moving, just as it might have been incredible that the heavy train could ever pull out of the station. And now she could not stop.

The months had passed. Mrs. Westfield had had another birthday, Sir Henry had made a speech with the gravity of a new member who was becoming less new; there had been the summer recess and Edward to amuse in Cornwall, Edward telling boatmen how to sail their boats, teaching plus men how to play golf, and patting Grace's cheek when the idea came into his head; there had been Horace using longer words and gloating a little over the preparatory to which he would be sent; Susan determined to exploit her mother and everybody else for her own purposes. When Grace cast back her mind to these months and reconstructed family intercourse, it sounded something like this:

Grace: " Those dressmakers are beginning to press me. I don't know what I shall do; I say, Edward, do you like this pink sweater of mine? I — "

Edward: " I like being a country gentleman, but still I shall not be sorry to get back to the Temple. I wish I'd taken the Western Circuit. Talking about circuits, I — "

Horace: " I'm going to the preparatory soon; then I'm going to Winchester. I'm going to be a soldier, I am. I used to want to be a railway guard but that's common."

Susan: " I don't want to do any more lessons. I shall be a nun, and after that I — I shall have a carriage to myself, and the cook shall make me canary pudding every day, and I shall have indie if I like. I — "

And so on. It was exactly like a play by Tchekoff.

It never occurred to Grace that she had begun on a reminiscence of herself, that she had asked for interest in her own topics. She was willing enough to be interested in others, but a sort of sense of justice told her they ought to be interested in her.

As the winter came again, and the awful void of Christmas, with its compulsory rejoicings, its rough way of trying to pour wassail into champagne glasses, and good-will into the souls of the ratepayers, she began to touch the fringe of the intellectual circles of London, that is to say, she was drawn very slowly, as most rich young London women and all Americans are drawn, into the salons where the book of the day lives for a day, where the modern symphony has one echo, where the talk is of dancing when Society dances, and of sackcloth when it repents. At that time they were no longer discussing whether Shaw and Chesterton were sincere; mysticism was worn that season; *Howard's End,* and the gospel of mystic athleticism were the thing at lunch (especially on Sunday); ladies who usually scented themselves with amami developed a passion for Mr. Algernon Blackwood, held intimate conversations with the lilac bushes. The simple life was out but, on the other hand, anybody who had vision might meet a leprechaun on Chelsea Embankment. There was also the *New Machiavelli,* and a great slump in definite political opinions. Young women came down from Girton with the avowed intention of becoming the heroines of Parnell cases: in due course they married quite respectably and secured marriage settlements.

But out of all this welter something came to Grace. She read those books and managed to draw from them nobility, perhaps because there was nobility in her, just as her associates drew from them naught but futility because there was futility in themselves. She discovered the novel. She had been taught as a young girl that the novel was represented by Miss Edgworth, Miss L. T. Meade, and Miss Braddon; that there was nothing exactly wrong in reading novels but that no benefit could be expected from them; that novels did not improve one's mind and that it was exceedingly important to improve one's mind. Nobody had thought of providing her with a mind to improve as, in those days, everybody had a mind above six hundred a year. (That is, in the unmarried state; if one was married one began to have a mind at a thousand a year as it was obvious one got minds cheaper wholesale). But out of the echoes of that period of transition, when Socialism had been hoisted to prominence by Mr. Bernard Shaw, the Fabian Society and the Court Theatre, hoisted at such a pace that it became breathless, and recoiled as it encountered with a resounding shock of shields the champions of individualism, Grace drew a sense of ideas in conflict; quite suddenly she took the intellectual drama seriously; she followed the wild advice of the wild people, she ceased to go to Mudie's to ask for advice when the works of Mr. Anthony Hope were out. She ceased to read books and began to read. In the midst of her agitations, of telephone calls, of public feeding, of meetings with interesting persons who lasted as long as shooting stars, she began to dive back into literature; she read *The Golden Bowl* and *The Tragic Comedians* and felt sure they must be very clever because their style was so nebulous. A serious young man made her aware of Bebel's *Woman* and of *Sex and Character,* which annoyed her so much that she told herself that it must be very good for her. And then she discovered *Tono-Bungay,* which she read in a night with a fierce concentrated joy: it was as if in a nightmare she had been stifling under the blankets and somebody had suddenly come, pulled away the hateful hot weight, and she had seen, high above, the star-studded sky.

The Irish revival in full swing, the passionate rhythms of Synge . . . in an extraordinary confusion she seemed to be glimpsing the world for the first time, its incoherent commercialism, its empty ambitions, the desultoriness of the pursuits of the men and women that circled about her, who with one hand grasped at gold and with the other madly tried to capture the shadows which they called their souls.

She met people who talked about the divinity of spirituality, and the spirituality of divinity and the esoterics of digestion.

She did not know where she was going, nor what she wanted, nor what she meant; she believed in absolute liberty of action and in Christian resignation; she believed in barbaric luxury and in asceticism; a tag of Nietzsche and a tag of Marcus Aurelius made horrid confusions in her mind.

And there was nobody to help her out of chaos. Not Edward, who writhed in it with the other damned souls, but gleefully, as if the stress of the early years of the twentieth century had been designed to make a toy for him. Nor Mary, milk-white and content, nor Clara, who now seemed to near the threshold of her ambition, for she had united the four divisions of St. Panwich in a common association for housing propaganda. Sir Henry was not one of the young Tories who were so much more radical than the Liberals (when in opposition), but he was beginning to find it impossible to rein in his wife, that plunging mare whom he had hoped to train. Clara had intuitively touched the heart of politics, understood that an election is like a Dutch auction, that every vote must be bought at the lowest price in cash or passion for which it can be knocked down. She was urgent, perhaps she was happy. Ten years of a sterile marriage seemed to have been wiped away by the discovery that there is yet something a wife can do, something that can fill the gap in a life which passion does not occupy. Her nervous brightness was brighter, her clothes were more mannish; perhaps she neglected herself a little, or perhaps it was the new virility of her intellect which caused a few hairs to sprout from her chin.

Somehow the two sisters had drifted apart. As the one became more political, the other became more artistic. While Clara found out that the only thing she could do was to cut a straight path, and cut it straight, Grace discovered that what she had to do was to run as fast as she could along the first path that offered, then take the first to the left, then the first to the right, and then the first to Lord knows where. After all what did it matter! All roads lead to death.

XIII

One thing united the two sisters in their desultory or political energy: Mary. For Mary, in the midst of turmoil, was the permanent factor, the unchanging thing that could never change. She was that unconscious blind life that, bringing forth yet more life, maintains it. She was calm while they were uneasy, content while they were restless; she was living instead of enquiring. They ran, she stood. As she stood they hated her as they might hate the Albert Memorial because, like it, she meant the established, the certain, the permanent, while they knew they were impermanent, while at the back of their activities there always stalked a doubt. Always they were asking: what are we doing, and why do we do it? While Mary asked nothing, but simply lived. Both of them, they tried to think that she lived like some starfish, some jellyfish; and at other moments that she was rather as a beautiful, big, white flower that would become fruit.

So, while they hated her, they loved her. They tried to talk of dress and of societies, but always, as if they were linked with Mary by something thicker than blood, they had to talk of her, to revile her, to despise her. While they tried to thrust her out she thrust herself in. Always she was a spectre at their feast. For she was not uneasy. And it comforted them secretly to know that their sister figured in the system as a fixed star around which they zigzagged like comets. Eating, drinking, loving wisely, giving birth, preparing birth, sleeping, growing older gracefully, making ready to die gracefully, she was the expression of life, of the life which they were using or misusing.

Misusing? Preposterous! Mary was a fool and fat. They had got the real things, the things that were top-hole.

XIV

Grace's debts became pressing. Thirty-seven pounds ten for the June quarter had not sufficed to placate two accounts; the September money had been completely mortgaged for the summer outfit: the linen dresses, the new sweater, the unexpectedly necessary tweed coat and skirt, and a number of small but essential articles had created such a state of chaos in every account of the household that the clamour of these had to be stilled. There was a dentist's bill, long overdue. The doctor even had hinted that his expenses were heavy. She had not dared to soothe the Bond Street tradesmen, who were suspicious, not because she bought too much but because she bought too little, with further purchases. So that now, with an almost empty account, she found herself faced with several polite, but firm letters and one threat.

The debts were not much, only about seventy pounds, a sum which she knew she could have for the asking, but a debt was of itself repugnant to her: it was not for nothing that she was the daughter of Horace Westfield, the merchant, and the grand-daughter of John Elba Westfield, the merchant, the seed of a long line of hard, honourable men who thought infidelity undesirable and bankruptcy criminal. Sometimes she reviled herself for a bourgeoise, tried to acquire a little of the lightheartedness of the strange people whom she occasionally met, of those young men who founded weekly newspapers with twenty-five pounds in the bank, and of the couples who seemed to live happily upon half-crowns earned by palmistry or stray guineas for songs. In these moods she would swear not to care. But she cared: the Westfields had always paid their debts; the mysterious psychological processes of the bourgeoisie were working in her; she was of those who can have a hundred pounds in the bank and fifty pounds of debts, and yet feel uncomfortable, a little disgraced, because those debts are unpaid.

One evening she nearly opened to Edward. He had asked her how she was, thinking her face a little strained, and just as she was about to reply that she was bothered, so as to lead up to confession, he had added: "But I often feel like that. Of course it's quite natural, living at high pressure as I do. You wouldn't believe it, the amount of energy a case can take out of one. Why, that Puncheon case kept me at it for ten hours a day for four days. When I saw the solicitor — "

He told her about the solicitor, he told her about the case, he told her about his strain, and one of those cold rages with which she was becoming familiar rose in her, brought out all the harsh pride of her forbears, the merchants who could not ask a favour. She grated her teeth together and swore she wouldn't care.

It was in this frame of mind she had her first reaction. It happened quite suddenly, at a little at home at Mrs. Shapwick's, to which she had taken Clara on the plea that Shapwick might be useful to her, for he had recently rented a large house in Wilton Crescent. It was the usual indiscriminate affair, one of those at homes where the hunting set and the bridge set go to gaze at the long-hairs, in the vague hope that somebody will come in sandals, or clamour for proteid, while the long-hairs talk British sports, as if used to that conversation, quite determined to get good dinners and subscriptions for verse recitals out of the Philistines.

There was a lady who called her daughter "Daffodil."

There was a strange little old gentleman, in a blue frock-coat, who manœuvred his hands with faintly Jewish vivacity; he had formed quite a little ring, mainly of women, around him, and was explaining in a shrill whisper that if you wanted to find your soul you must practice silence.

"Silence!" he shouted under his breath, "thus only can you attain to the visualisation of the essential element of your entity."

Shouting under his breath was what the apostle actually did. One had a sense of enormous intensity; his tones were so low that they became noisy, as an excess of moderation ends in seeming violent. He was rather rosily bald, and here polished his head with his handkerchief with extraordinary energy.

"Silence," he murmured, "that is the key."

"Yes, yes . . . Oh, quite true," came in excited chorus from the women.

"But," whispered the old gentleman with absolutely epileptic restraint, "do not think that you will readily pass the threshold. No! mortification! maceration! retreat within your subjectivity! And these are but the preliminaries." (Polish.) "Come to my classes! there you will see all sorts and conditions of men, wonderful men . . . Americans . . . engineers, devoutly retreating in silence within their elemental cosmicity — "

It seemed that the classes, which took place in Bayswater, cost seven and six each, or four for a guinea.

"I should say he needs a little silence for a rest," remarked Clara, as the little old gentleman's shrill hiss threaded through the air of the drawing-room like a needle dipped in vinegar.

There was a lady who wore a dress of an obviously unobvious green. Grace liked green, as it "went with her hair," and realised that she was a bourgeoise, for her own green was always of an obviously obvious shade.

There was a couple, dressed in reeking brown tweed;

one was probably a woman who wore her hair short, and the other probably a man who wore his hair long. Both had curvilinear faces, chins and foreheads that receded so suitably as to make their heads into ovoids from which protruded long, thin and extremely inquiring noses. The probable man was introduced to Grace, and delivered to her a long lecture of which she remembered later that the only thing fit to eat was a nutton chop. The other ovoid was eloquently silent.

"Daffodil!" cried the lady who called her daughter "Daffodil."

Grace wandered with Clara among groups of colliding interests, of clubmen who were being addressed by earnest, rather hard, but very pretty girls, on the iniquity of the white slave traffic. The earnest young girls seemed very pleased with the interest the clubmen were taking in the subject, and were giving as many details as were required of them. Clearly the campaign for social purity was progressing.

There was a young girl with her hair pulled off her forehead who stated calmly that when the man she was waiting for appeared she would go to him and say: "Will you be the father of my child?"

There was a very dark young man who called himself a futurist; he created quite a sensation by sketching a lady's portrait on the spot, which looked rather like a kettle that had seen better days.

"Hallo," said Mrs. Cheddon, airily. "What's this?"

She was told.

"What a shame," she cried, "why did you tell us? We might have had such a nice little guessing game."

The young futurist became extremely angry and destroyed the masterpiece on the spot; he wreaked vengeance upon his neighbours by explaining at length the difference between kinetic values in Carra as opposed to static values in Sargent and that sort of person.

"The true poetry," he declared, "is the new spirit of Azrael. Do you know where it is? Not in your sodden fields, but in a dynamic, vengeful instrument significant of utility — in a municipal refuse destructor."

He became more and more violently dynamic and ended a breathless harangue by a string of exceedingly obscene words directed at the Post Impressionists. Fortunately he delivered these in French. When they came out, Grace and Clara walked in silence past St. George's Hospital. They did not at once communicate their feelings to each other, for this was not the custom of their family, but they were conscious, perhaps a little more clearly than usual, of having struggled in a sort of intellectual vortex. There still echoed in their ears the warring voices of all those people, struggling to express themselves in any way, providing it was a new way; the proclamations of the food movements, social movements, art movements. They thought of health, promoted by breathing fast or breathing slow (they did not quite know which), or by wearing cellular clothes, or having one's spine massaged; they felt the extraordinary contrast between the oddities and those men with the short-cut hair and the genial, suntanned faces who had come with their fashionable, hipless, breastless women to have a bit of a rag.

They were tired, they were reacting. It was the softening influence of the reaction made them talk openly.

"Good heavens!" said Clara, "those people have given me a headache, and I don't believe Mr. Shapwick will be any good to us. We want something more solid." But suddenly her tone changed. "Oh, bother politics. Perhaps it's because I'm tired, but somehow I ask myself what it's all for. Why am I doing this, G.?" she asked, more fiercely. "I'm running in a ring: meetings, schemes, sleep, then meetings and schemes again."

"Yes," said Grace, "it's something like that. But what else is there to do?"

"Oh," said Clara, impatiently, "I don't know. There ought to be something else."

"Yes, there ought to be. We didn't think it was going to be like this when we married, did we?"

"No," said Clara, and that word was spoken very softly.

It was without bitterness she added: "Those people, they think they have a salon. It isn't a salon, it's a vestibule."

Grace laughed. "Yes, you're right, Clara. They think they meet their friends, but you know they aren't really friends. You see, it was nonsense the things we used to talk about when we were at school. You know: about having somebody's name written on one's heart and all that sort of thing; we don't engrave the names of our friends upon our hearts; we keep an autograph book."

Clara did not reply for a long time, but then again she was in revolt. "I don't know what to do," she said, "and yet I always seem to be doing something. Do I want to do it? do you think?"

"How can I tell?" said Grace, dully, "I don't know myself."

"But," cried Clara, and there was despair in the high voice that was still girlish, "we always used to know what to do when we were girls."

"What we mainly wanted to do," said Grace, "was to have a good time and get married."

"Well," said Clara, "we got married."

"And now," murmured Grace, "we're having the good time."

XV

Grace had just left the little dressmaker in Earl's Court who was going to give that Belgian finish to the new lapels of her old coat. She stopped before the draper's looking-glass in the Earl's Court Road to see whether her hat was on straight. It was morning, and a soft, fresh wind made her cheeks rosy over the freckles. She smiled at herself and pouted lips which seemed a little redder than usual, as if she had used some salve.

"I look rather nice," she thought, and then a fear gripped her. Where was her brooch? It was a diamond brooch, Edward's first present, made up of one large diamond and two small ones. She knew that she had put it on when she left the house that morning, for she remembered pricking her finger. It was gone . . . lost. Somehow the idea pained her, created in her a sort of revolt: she was of the bourgeoisie, and she tended to blame herself for carelessness if anything happened, rather than to rail at fate. She looked at her feet to see whether it had just fallen, but the brooch was not there. There was nothing to be done, she reflected, but advertise or bear the loss.

Edward behaved charmingly. When he saw her woebegone face that evening, he laughed at her a little.

"Poor little Gracie-Bracie! has she lost the brooch her hubby gave her?" He fondled her arms. "Is she broken-hearted because she lost hubby's first present? Poor little girlie, she shall have another brooch, and hubby will put a nice big advertisement in all the papers."

She looked up at him, gratefully, while he fondled her, when at last he kissed her in that quick, detached way which made her think that he would kiss her like that if he met her while walking in his sleep. She even kissed him back, and yet in her sorrow she felt irritated, for she had touched in him a true sympathy, a true sweetness which she very rarely encountered, and it translated itself that evening in a continual pursuit of her, in clumsy caresses when she did not want them, when she was carrying a chair across the drawing-room, or when about to leave the room. And, later in the evening, she found a rage rising up in her against this man who continually tried to cheer her up by telling her interminable stories about his own occupations, and only became aware of her to caress her, to paw her in the unskilful, heavy and yet not powerful way of those who have never known how to give their senses full play, in whom the senses continually simmer without ever reaching boiling point.

The next morning the little woman in Earl's Court telephoned that the brooch was found. It had fallen under a heap of blouses and would be handed to her the next time she called.

"Isn't it lucky, Mrs. Kinnersley," said the little woman. "Such a beautiful brooch. I'm sure it's worth a hundred pounds."

"Yes, I suppose so," said Grace, "I'll reward the girl who found it."

"Just as you like, Mrs. Kinnersley," said the little woman. "I'm very glad we found it. Who knows? You might want a hundred pounds any day."

"Good-bye," said Grace, very quietly.

The idea thrust itself into her head.

Strangely enough it was no effort to go and sell the brooch. The Piccadilly jeweller was evidently quite accustomed to this sort of transaction with elegantly-gowned ladies. With one look he measured her, realised that this was no thief; too quietly and well-dressed. "Bridge," he remarked to himself, and then aloud: "Eighty pounds."

Grace came out of the shop, the money in fivers stuffed into her bag. In twenty minutes she had paid all her bills, and she walked, a new woman, free and yet enslaved. Only half of the Westfield tradition was satisfied; she was no longer in debt, but the other half of the tradition called out to her faintly from the graves of the dead merchants:

"You're not quite a liar, and you're not quite a thief, but, daughter, it's sharp practice, you know. It isn't quite the thing. We Westfields, we didn't do business like that."

Grace thrust back those scruples. She knew that to satisfy her own conscience she ought to have told Edward. She knew she ought to have told him that she owed money. She knew that she would feel horribly guilty later, when he happened to think of her and gave her a new brooch. But something in her was rebellious. "Damn," she said, "I'll do what I like."

And yet the dead Westfields dogged her, reproachful and sorry.

"Where are you going to, our daughter?" they asked. And it was almost as if to escape them she turned into St. James's Church. A wedding was proceeding, a large, fashionable wedding that filled the church. Unobtrusively she slid into one of the pews on the bride's side. She saw nothing clearly, she hardly looked; the service was just a noise; through her mind ran tumultuous thoughts. Why did I have to do this? Why did I have debts? Was it because I belonged to a man? Or was it because I didn't belong to him enough? Was it somehow because I was married?

And then, with sinister appropriateness, she heard the voice at the altar:

"Who giveth this Woman to be married to this Man?"

Who, indeed? She shuddered, and the rolling echoes of the darkened church seemed to thunder forth the question:

"Who giveth this Woman to be married to this Man?"

BOOK THE THIRD

GRACE

Whither, from the midst of the snares that beset me, shall I take my way once more? In what dark solitude shall I hide me from the all-seeing eye of Venus? What if I put on at length a man's courage, and yielding myself unto her as my mistress, soften by a humility not yet too late the fierceness of her purpose?

(PATER. — *Marius the Epicurean.*)

CHAPTER THE FIRST

THE SHADOW OF THE HAND

I

On the third of March, 1910, as the bells of St. Mary Abbot's were striking six, Grace was accosted by a man in Kensington High Street.

She had been aware of him for some minutes as she slowly walked along the High Street, stopping from time to time to look into a shop window. She had an impression of height, and of a long, blue coat contrasting with very light clothes. That was all. He had been one of the crowd, a figure that recurred rather frequently among the women who were walking in the same direction, sometimes outstripping her, then reappearing as the women stopped to shop-gaze. She had not noticed him much more than that, for she had, in her own phrase, a way of walking "with her nose in the air," thinking of her own concerns and of becoming very intent when something in a shop interested her. But at that moment she stopped to look at herself in a mirror and, as she so did, peering over her shoulder, there appeared a face. It startlingly blended strength and delicacy. Not handsome, for the eyes, which in the evening light seemed dark, were set in rather too large whites; they stared a little and seemed very keen. Under the rather broad felt hat the face seemed long, rather high in colour, and she noticed no more except, with surprise, the very slight smile of two beautifully-cut, clean-shaven lips. For a moment she did not move, nor did the face, which looked like a mask, for its smile did not vary; it seemed assured, faintly disdainful, and yet conscious of power, as if the creature behind the mask knew that its gaze, reflected in the mirror, was holding hers.

But quite as suddenly Grace felt awkward. Men often looked at her in the street, but the silence and the repose of this curious person made her uncomfortable. She turned away quickly and, as she so did, brushed with her shoulder against the rough, blue stuff of the now familiar overcoat. Head in the air, a little angry, faintly insulted by this commonplace attention, she walked away. She threaded as quickly as she could through the eddying crowd, becoming with every step a little angrier because she was jostled and delayed in her growing desire to get away from the figure which she felt followed her. As the big shops grew less, the crowd decreased and she walked quicker, but now she knew that the man followed her: she could distinguish behind her his steps which she already recognised. As she passed the station, quite suddenly the man drew abreast of her, threw her a look and passed on. She took in a sharp breath: gone at last! And then she found that she was faintly thrilled by the encounter. A few yards ahead she saw the man, tall, straight-backed, rather jaunty, and then there rose up in her a vague feeling of disappointment which quickly she crushed down. He was gone. But no, he stopped to look into a shop. This was ridiculous: the show-case was full of sewing-machines. And, as she angrily looked down to the pavement, every fibre of her knew that, as he stood before the sewing-machines, he turned his eyes towards her. Then, in another second, as she reached the corner of Young Street, he was by her side. With her he turned into the sudden darkness and quietude of the little street. She knew that he was going to speak, and a mixed feeling of wild anger, indignation and excitement filled her.

" Beautiful lady," he said, " your hair is like the autumn leaves. Why is there no sunshine to gild it? "

She did not answer. Perhaps she could not have replied had she wanted to, so hurried was the beating of her heart.

" Beautiful lady," said the man again, " why do you

not reply? I looked into your eyes a moment ago; they did not seem unkind."

Still she said nothing.

"Why do you go so fast?" said the man. "You're not afraid, are you?" He bent forward to look into her face and added again, as if taunting her: "Of course you're afraid, I can see you are."

A fierce impulse seized her. She wanted to cry out: "Of course I'm not afraid. Go away or I'll call a policeman."

But, for the first time in her life, she found herself subtle. She knew that he was taunting her to force her to speak. If she said a word she was lost. She clenched her teeth together and did not reply.

"No," murmured the man, as if musing, "of course you're not afraid. You'd talk if you were afraid, until we got to a place where you could threaten me but — " He laughed. "Fears and threatenings, this is hardly the way to begin. Is it?"

"No, sir," thought Grace, "you're clever, but I won't speak."

"You know," the man went on, "I really had to speak to you, you're so charming, and I do so wish you'd say you don't mind."

There was something a little pathetic in the man's voice, and Grace felt her mouth open. Again she controlled herself as she turned into Kensington Square but, at that moment, a dreadful embarrassment seized her. She was nearing her house. She must get rid of him now. She stopped and, contentedly, he stood in front of her. As she looked into his face, she was overwhelmed by a sense of repulsion and charm. She saw now that his forehead was very big and broad, his nose irregular, that over the prominent cheekbones the skin was burnt and glazed by the sun and rain. An outdoor man evidently, and, so far as she could judge from his clothes and voice, a gentleman. And his lips were beautifully chiselled, sensitive lips that seemed to ask for pity, while the large piercing eyes commanded.

"Look here," she said, bluntly, "don't be silly." Then, rather weakly: "I suppose you think you know me? You wouldn't dare to speak to me if you didn't think so."

"I'd dare anything for you," said the man.

In spite of herself, Grace stamped: "Go away," she said. "If there was a policeman about, I'd give you in charge."

"Oh, no," replied the man, smoothly, "you wouldn't. The eleventh commandment of a lady is that she shall keep out of the newspapers. Because we are what we are, I'll not kiss you under a lamp in Kensington Square, though it would be quite safe. I could kidnap you in a taxi," he said, reflectively. "Whatever happened, your relatives would beg the Home Secretary not to proceed against me. The question is what shall we do instead of indulging in such violence. Supposing we went and had dinner somewhere?"

"Go away," said Grace, feebly. She felt perfectly helpless; she wished that Edward would come home and rescue her, but then she was struck by the awful idea that there might be a fight in the square. Yes, the man was right, the eleventh commandment of a lady was indeed to keep out of the newspapers.

"Listen," she said, hurriedly, "you're making a mistake. I'm married; I live in this square. If you want to please me, you'll go away now."

The man threw her a quick look and seemed to think for a moment, then said: "All right, as you like, but you may as well know my name, Enoch Fenor. F-e-n-o-r, Fenor. It'll save you trouble . . . when we meet again."

He raised his hat to show a thick mass of close-cut, black hair, gave her once more the glance so queerly compounded of command and pleading, and quickly walked away. As soon as he was out of sight round the corner, Grace seized her skirt and, without looking back, ran home.

It was dark in the square, so she did not see a figure double back from Young Street, crouch and run swiftly along the area railings, watch her from a doorway.

II

Grace was disturbed. Disturbed for several reasons. It was not so much because she had been spoken to in the street, for several times in her life a man had done this; but there had been in this approach something so determined and assured that she felt as afraid as if she were being physically seized, and she guessed that this was but a prelude. Then she told herself that it was not a prelude, that the man had understood she wished to have nothing to do with him, and had gone away behaving, after all, very well. Contrariwise she also knew that she was not telling herself the truth: there had been something about him too dogged, almost sullen, something which frightened and yet not displeased her. As he said "when" we meet again and not "if" we meet again, she had been flooded by a realisation that he would see to it that they should meet again. It was frightening and it was delightful. A phrase which she had caught in one of the intellectual drawing-rooms: "Live dangerously," passed through her mind. This was not living dangerously, but still there was danger about. He did not know where she lived, she thought, but there had been something about him so determined that she suspected that he would find out. And then?

But what disturbed her perhaps more was the fact that she did not want to tell anybody what had happened. Years ago, when an elderly man had addressed her at the bottom of Campden Hill Road and asked her the way to London, she had laughed contemptuously and had told the story to all her girl friends, who also laughed. And, on another occasion, she had exchanged with Clara views on the outrageous behaviour of London men. But this time she said nothing. She knew she ought to feel insulted, that a lady did not allow men to talk to her in the street. Of course she had not allowed him to; he had merely insisted on doing so. And evidently she had to get rid of him to get home safely; she had been right, perfectly right. Nobody could have a word to say against her behaviour, but still she told nobody. And because she did not tell anybody, because she did not pour out what she felt, the feelings remained within her to ferment. A secret is no longer weighty when it has been told, but a secret that is kept secret becomes with every minute more portentous and yet more secret. At times she delighted in the incident. She knew very well that she must not take such a happening as a compliment paid to her beauty, for she held the view that men were indiscriminate creatures and that for most of them one woman was much the same as another. But still she was vain, and the fact remained that he had chosen her from among the crowd: she was not the favourite picking up the handkerchief thrown by the Sultan, but what was the favourite to do when the Sultan came to her and tied the handkerchief about her neck?

In other moments she hated him. She hated him because he had broken the social rule which edicts that no man shall speak to any woman in the street unless she belongs to a class inferior to his own, in which case he is doing something which is not quite nice, but which most men do and must therefore be accepted. She hated him because he compelled her to share a preoccupation and an interest. For she felt an interest. There had been about him something dare-devil, rakish, and yet good-mannered.

When he said: "Beautiful lady, your hair is like the autumn leaves —" she had felt some charm run through her anger. Nobody had ever said anything quite like that to her, and she pulled herself up angrily: This was nonsense; no wonder he was so glib, no doubt he did this sort of thing every day. She hated him. Perhaps he was not common, but he was vulgar, and that was worse, cruelly vulgar . . . trading upon a woman's defencelessness. But then she remembered how he had left her at last when she told him to go. No, in his fashion he had played the game. She remembered his voice, rather low-pitched, slow and melodious, a voice that seemed to caress her with every vowel. The memory of it thrilled her a little, but she despised herself as she realised that she would be glad to hear it again if they met once more. She shivered, for he had not said " if; " he had said " when."

III

Grace thought vaguely of another child. She remembered those long periods, seven and six years past, when childbearing had removed her from the turbulent current of life, and the two long years of recuperation during which she had seemed to do nothing and to want to do nothing, as if the birth of her two children had taken from her all her reserve of strength. In those days she had been so careless that she had been almost contented. Perhaps she had been contented: in those days it had been good when Edward came home from the Temple. Just like Mary. For the first time she began to see Mary clearly. Yes, Mary had found the anodyne: many children, many cares, and many satisfactions perhaps due to there being no time for dissatisfaction. Mary had found the way, Mary was drugged.

Drugged. Yes, that was it. She had found the recipe for sleep; already she was as dead, and in her sleep of death she dreamt her life. But something within Grace rebelled. Another child, months of continual discomfort, pain, danger, fear; then many more months of languor, of a sort of contented, vegetable existence. And then, little by little, strength returning, and with strength, emptiness, vague desire, unrest. And so on, and so on, until it was time for another dose of the drug, until it was too late to drug oneself. But, quite as suddenly, it came upon her that there was nothing in life to take except drugs: light pleasures, domestic duty, religion, politics, or art, more or less potent, more or less pleasant. To find the particular drug which was sweetest to one's palate, that was the thing to do. As the days went by, this feeling grew; she seemed to sink into a hopeless pessimism. What did it matter if kingdoms rose and fell, and chorus married coronet? The flame of patriotism or the flame of social ambition: were they not fires to make you comfortable and sleepy so that you might dream glad dreams?

But it would be a good thing, she suddenly thought, to dream glad dreams, for these dreams of hers which she called her life, they were not glad, and she saw the others dreaming too . . . other dreams. To her face she charged Clara with drugging herself, with cultivating illusion, for now Clara was dominant, and she seemed to have found in the hurry that filled her life something that satisfied her. Grace tried to explain what she felt, that all these movements and agitations were pastimes. Clara was indignant. She had quite forgotten her short-lived reaction. She was now engaged in organising what amounted to a regiment of St. Panwich women for the individual education of the electorate in the immortal principles of her party. And Grace had ill-chosen her moment for soul-examination, as Clara wanted to go down to her office to settle difficulties with Miss Lenzie who every five or ten minutes seemed to ring her up to ask for new instructions.

"I don't know what you're talking about," said Clara, at last. "I'm busy enough, Lord knows, without your coming along and talking metaphysics."

"But that's just it," said Grace, helplessly. "I don't know anything about metaphysics, but what I mean is . . . all this agitation of yours . . . it's only something . . . stuffed into your life."

"Well, you must stuff in something, as you elegantly put it," remarked Clara.

"Must you?" asked Grace.

"Oh, for heaven's sake, don't be lackadaisical."

No, Clara was not going to help her much. There was another person who might have helped her, and he, as it happened, did not do so. It was Mr. Sturry. The old man was fond of her. Indeed, when he was not tracing from the source coincidences which had resulted in certain Knights of the Plantagenet period having been buried in three separate churches, he would call at random on "One of the girls," as he called them, and sit with her very long, sipping tea, talking ecclesiastical lore, Thomas Browne, or Malory, or quite suddenly give vent to a pungent little view on the political or the fashionable lady of the day. Sometimes he induced " the girls " to talk at length about themselves, their occupations and their hopes. In reply he would sit and giggle in his character of an elderly faun, and thus keep his own counsel in the most eloquent way. Mr. Sturry was a sort of Monsieur Bergeret, who went about the world making notes and comments, but Grace always found that, though the notes were probably very many, the comments were very few.

One afternoon, as she left one of the queer parties in Chelsea, she met the old man on the Embankment. Though it was cold, the sun was brilliant. He leant over the parapet, looking at the river as if the silver glitter fascinated him. He did not see her coming and started as she laid her hand upon his arm. He said nothing, but smiled, and in that moment Grace felt impelled suddenly to cry out to him, as if something within her were trying to appeal to him:

" I say, do you know that a few nights ago a man spoke to me in Kensington High Street? " She smiled as she wondered what he would say. Almost mischievously, she determined to tell him in the hope of horrifying him, but at once the thick veil of her shyness and good-breeding seemed to swaddle her up. So she did not demur, when in a little while, after they had walked to Chelsea Bridge, the old man suggested that they should cross it and go into Battersea Park, where he would tell her the complete history of the Tetravi folio, which had just been discovered in the buried crypt of a Tudor princeling's private chapel.

He was talkative enough on his own subjects and as, rather slowly, they trod the moist, yielding, brown paths, Grace thought that she was interested in these technical details which she hardly understood.

" You see," said Mr. Sturry, " what's so wonderful about it is its state of preservation. They buried it in sand, some abbot, I suppose, and sealed it up in a soldered iron box; at least it looks like solder, though I'm not quite sure that they did any soldering about then. It may have been just beaten tin," he said, reflectively.

Grace found her mind wandering from the history of solder. But still, as they walked, she heard scraps of Sturry's conversation:

"Black letter . . . Whitechurch Canonicorum . . . probably St. Edmundsbury vellum —"

Then everything seemed to recede far away from her and, strangely enough, her mind did not fix on a precise idea. A sort of blankness fell upon her. She seemed to come out of herself and to see herself stopping, beside the old man, in front of a bed studded with purple hyacinths.

It was early afternoon, and in the light grey, watery heavens an immense number of fleecy white clouds, round as balloons, hung and gleamed a little yellow, here and there, where the sun touched them at their thinnest. A cold little wind sizzled through the trees, and there was a sharpness in the spring light that made every little green bud look like an emerald, definite in line and very hard. Vaguely she realised that Sturry was talking about the hyacinths, but she did not quite understand what he said. He said something about their looking like a regiment of soldiers in uniforms by Poiret . . . but she saw nothing of their details: they were like a rippling pool that the wind wrinkles, and purple only because in the blue depths some orange sunset was bathing. She turned to look at the old man who talked on, still smiling, but she interrupted him. Could it be she who spoke?

"Oh, Uncle Stull! Uncle Stull! Oh, Uncle Stull!" she cried, "I'm so unhappy."

He laid his hand upon her arm, did not reply. Her eyes were fixed on his, and she knew that they were calling for a word of pity that would loosen this terrible dumbness of hers, enable her to speak. But Mr. Sturry was still smiling, a little wearily, a little cynically, as if he had heard this phrase so often, as if, after despairing of a cure for human misery, he had at length begun to think human misery funny.

"Dear," he said, "what's the matter?"

" I don't know," said Grace.

" Then," said Mr. Sturry, " you're no longer happy with your husband."

" What d'you mean?" said Grace, rather angrily. " You needn't conclude that because a woman's unhappy, it's because she's not getting on with her husband. There are lots of other things. There's . . . there are . . . Anyhow, that's not everything . . . a woman's a human being . . . not just a sort of illustrated supplement to a man. I think you're very unkind, Uncle Stull."

" Is there anything else to be unhappy about?" said Mr. Sturry. " For a woman, I mean?"

Grace did not reply. She wondered whether there was.

" But," she cried, still trying to defend the indefensible, " how can one explain? One's just unhappy, just like that, until one dies."

" Yes," said Sturry, " that's right, Grace. When one ceases to be unhappy, one ceases to be alive, and then one dies."

" Is it worth it?" asked Grace, suddenly.

Mr. Sturry did not reply for a long time; then he pointed to the hyacinths.

" For every one of these hyacinths there once were two lovers. It was summer, and far from each other they loved. Then the time for mating came, and they went before the registrar (who was the wind), and the wind seized the pollen of their love and joined their hands. Bad botany perhaps, but still here are their children, all in a row, like soldiers dressed by Poiret."

" That was not pain," said Grace.

" No," murmured the old man. " But ask the hyacinths how long they lived underground in a choking bulb, and how hard, and cold, and wet was the soil as they forced up towards the light their little green heads. And ask them whether sometimes the wind did not sting them, the frost gnaw their purple blooms, the passer-by neglect their beauty — "

" Neglect their beauty!" said Grace. " Oh, Uncle Stull, is it worth the hyacinths' while?"

" There's no choice," said the old man. " I too, like every man, was born; I live and I shall die. Soon. My heart will not last long. But while from hour to hour I rot and rot, the others will ripe and ripe. To ripe, Grace, and to rot, it's the same thing. Living on the up-grade or living on the down-grade, it's all the same stuff. It's all life while it lasts."

" But it hurts! " Grace cried.

Mr. Sturry looked at her for a very long time and wondered whether he should tell her that but for her pain she would not realise pleasure; that pain is the necessary foil; that she too, one of the endless chain of hyacinths, must bloom again, and then again, until the blooming time was over. But the sight of this young and beautiful woman, unable to use life, rebelling against it and crying out, struck him as so usual, so commonplace; and she was so deadly serious about it. She seemed to think that nobody in the world felt like this, or could feel like this. Clearly she thought she had the monopoly of emotion. Doubtless that was how the world went on, thanks to the impulse of hundreds of millions of selfish wills, just as there would be no hyacinths to-day if there had not been an instinct in other hyacinths which told them nothing was as important as they. But, looking at all this from above and outside, as if he were Jove pillowed on those round clouds, it all seemed so small and far away that in his feeble old way he began to giggle; his little white beard twitched and, as Grace's face grew flushed and angry, he giggled more and more, irresistibly amused. She turned away, her head erect and her shoulders very straight, from the old and secretive faun.

IV

She shopped. She went to the play; she went to at homes and gave them; she ate lunches, gave lunches; she met men who thought her beautiful, two or three who told her so. It was the ordinary life, and sometimes she wondered whether it was the life everlasting. But there was some subtle difference in her; her memory sheltered something. Less than a fortnight had elapsed since her first meeting with Enoch Fenor — Enoch Fenor — She often thought of the name, a curious name, half romantic, half scriptural. She liked the two o's, the roughness of the Christian name. Sometimes, when she went to a rather crowded party, she would give a little start because she saw the back of some tall, black-haired man: to meet that man, that prowler, that low street adventurer, to be introduced to him, and to have to be civil, would be hateful, degrading. She would have to cut him on the spot. And yet, when the man turned towards her and it was not Fenor, she was very faintly disappointed; but she told herself that the sigh she heaved was a sigh of relief.

For they were not like Fenor, the others who sat out with her at dances, took her hand and tried to kiss her; nor were those who looked at her with hungry eyes and dared say nothing. One evening at the Shapwicks', a rather nice crammer's pup followed rather than led her to a balcony which gave out upon a garden, to look at the black sky where the stars shone like frosted diamonds. They stood a minute in silence, shivering a little in the cold air, and Grace, looking sideways, could see that the boy's eyes were intent upon her. He did not move. Still he said nothing. After the silence had lasted two minutes, she made a little movement as if to go. A desperate courage seemed to seize her escort. He put out a hand which was not quite daring enough to touch her arm.

"I say," he murmured, vaguely, "you look toppin', Mrs. Kinnersley."

"Do I?" she said, very softly, looking at him through her eyelashes.

"You've got such jolly hair, and . . . and . . ." He drew a little closer, murmured: "I say, I wonder whether you'd mind if I kissed you?"

Grace drew herself up very stiffly. "How can you talk such nonsense! of course I should mind."

The boy's face became very sorrowful. "Didn't think

you'd let me," he remarked, gloomily. "I'm a Jonah, that's what I am."

Grace laughed lightly as she led him back to the drawing-room. She had hurt him but she did not feel guilty. There was a rage in her, a rage, not against him and his clumsy, pathetic wooing, but a rage against herself because, as she looked at his smooth, fair face and his humble blue eyes, she had thought of another man and said to herself, almost said aloud:

"Enoch Fenor wouldn't have asked my leave."

V

It was not that she listened more intently than usual to Edward's conversation that night. He had annoyed her before dinner because he had no matches. Edward was the sort of man who never had matches and who somehow was surprised when other men hadn't got matches. And when she had found the matches for him, wooden ones, he had struck the first so hard as to break off its head, the second one so gingerly as to scrape off by degrees all the sulphur, while as he lit the third and put it to his cigarette, he talked so vigorously that he blew it out. Then he had gone up-stairs to dress and had announced the fact, being in a sportive mood, by saying:

"I vill vosh and clean myself."

And again, at dinner, he had persistently addressed her over the soup in bad French. He had referred to the salmon as "Soman."

One of those new rages was upon Grace. She hardly spoke to him; the buffoonery maddened her and when, a minute or two later, he at last noticed that she had not said a word since he came down, he leant over, took her hand and began to fondle it, fondle it in that awkward, soft, paternal way. She snatched her fingers away —

There was a long interval during which Gracie-Bracie was reprimanded. But yet not such a long interval, for, very soon, his preoccupation with his wife's temper slid into a greater preoccupation with his own work. For a long time she found she was not listening; she was sorry that she had snatched her hand away, and tried to accord her husband a restitution of his conjugal rights by throwing into the conversation, not one word of which she heard, some suitable "very likelys" and "how annoyings." She did not know whether they were suitable, but it did not matter much as Edward did not notice them. Edward was talking of his own affairs. He was not boasting exactly, but he was interested only in himself, and he needed her as an audience, he needed somebody to respond, to encourage him, more or less to say "hear! hear!"

But at last, quite suddenly, Grace found he was being interesting. Edward was not always uninteresting when he talked about his work. Like most men who do a thing well, he made his trade vital; it was only when he spoke not of his trade but of himself and his trade that he became intolerable. And suddenly Grace became aware that twice he had pronounced the word "Fenor." She had one of those sensations which mark a human being to the death. A sensation in which there was fear and delight. She felt like a slum woman courting her brute lover, kissing his lips immediately after he has struck her in the face.

"What's that? what's that?" she cried, excitedly. Then a prudence and a craftiness which she did not know herself to possess seemed to steal out of the depths of her femininity, and to whisper: "Hush! take care." It was like an instinct of self-preservation. With smooth face and languid voice, the virtuous wife almost yawned and said: "I beg your pardon, Edward, I didn't hear the beginning of that. D'you mind telling me again?"

"As I was saying —" replied Edward, who had not noticed the interruption any more than he had noticed her abstraction, but was fortunately beginning the story again at the beginning as he generally did — "He's a very queer chap. Why he picked me out, I don't know; he said he had heard of me."

"Who?"

“ Fenor, that man I've been telling you about.”

“ I don't quite understand,” said Grace, excited and crafty. “ It's so interesting, do explain.”

“ It's quite simple,” said Edward. “ It seems that ten days ago he was driving his car down Westbourne Grove and, I gather, at about fifteen miles an hour. He says he skidded or something. The next thing that happened was that he went right into a plate-glass window. How it was he didn't kill anybody as he leapt the pavement, I don't know but — ”

He smiled. “ If you knew Fenor, you might think he wouldn't care much if he had killed anybody. And he's as obstinate as a mule. He's quite in the wrong; he was on the right side of the road; he told the shopkeeper he wouldn't pay, and the case is coming on. He simply hasn't a ghost.”

“ But,” asked Grace, “ where d'you come in, Edward?”

“ Well, this chap, Fenor — ”

“ Fenor? That's a funny name; how do you spell it? F-e-n-n-e-r?” Grace marvelled at herself as she spelled the name. Would she have thought of such a subterfuge a year before?

“ No, Fenor, F-e-n-o-r. A queer name, Enoch Fenor. Sounds like a methodist preacher, doesn't it? But I assure you he's nothing like that.”

“ Go on,” said Grace. “ Tell me just how you got the case.”

“ I didn't *get* the case,” said Edward, a little acidly. “ Fenor's solicitor wrote to me, saying his client had heard a lot about me.” He drew himself up. “ Put in a lot of butter about his admiration for my abilities. . . . Made me quite blush.” Edward did not look as if he had blushed. “ And then, to clinch it, they marked the brief forty guineas. Simply absurd for a case like that, so I took it.”

“ Oh, well,” said Grace, airily, “ so much the better. But still,” she added languidly, “ it isn't what I should call an interesting case.”

VI

During the next few weeks Grace heard a great deal about the queer client. Enoch Fenor was extraordinarily queer. He broke all the rules of etiquette and apparently cared not in the least what his solicitor thought. He demanded several consultations; he behaved so abusively to the injured shopkeeper that an action for slander might very well mature, or perhaps one for assault. Edward was immensely amused, and Grace was informed almost every night of the extraordinary behaviour of the queer client.

"D'you know," said Edward, "I rather like that chap. He's an engineer. He seems to have been about everywhere, but he's not the sort of traveller who tells you all about it every time. I can't bear the man who can't keep off his own topics. He's keen on everything, even on the law; he came into my chambers this afternoon, and I should say he stayed an hour. I like the chap," Edward added, ruminatively. "I was telling him this afternoon about the Shepherd's Bush murder; you remember. He quite agreed with me. Yes, a very intelligent chap."

Two days later it seemed that Enoch Fenor had run into Edward as the latter came out of Middle Temple Lane. They had walked part of the way westwards together, for Fenor lived near Victoria Street.

Then Edward lunched at Fenor's club.

The case was coming on rather soon, it seemed, as the list was very light that session.

"He's a very interesting chap," said Edward. "I say, Grace, we haven't had a little dinner for a long time. I think I'll ask him; I'm sure you'll like the fellow."

VII

She was going to meet him again. And during the next fortnight Grace reproached herself several times a day because she had allowed this indignity to be put upon her without protest. She knew she ought to have told Edward the truth as soon as he pronounced the name. But in that queer whirl of repulsion and pleasure which had seized her when Edward first spoke of Fenor she had not spoken. At once it had become too late to speak; she had not forbidden the banns which Edward and Fenor were having called for the conclusion of their incredible friendship, and now she must for ever hold her peace.

"I was a fool," she told herself. "I ought at once to have cried out: "Fenor! Oh, Edward, I didn't like to tell you, but he's the man who — "

And then Grace sketched a beautiful picture of herself standing before her husband, the picture of the outraged matron proclaiming that she respected herself. She made a very fine speech; a moving speech, the sort of speech that ladies with a past successfully make in the third act of a play. After that Edward went out and thrashed Fenor — unless Fenor thrashed him. In novels and on the stage the hero always thrashed the villain, but life was a funny, upside-down thing. On the whole it was much more likely that Fenor would do the hitting —

Grace shivered. Yes, that was all very well, that speech. Only she hadn't delivered it. Far from it. She had fished for details, she had encouraged Edward to talk of his agreeable acquaintance. And she had said: "Very well, my dear," to the suggested invitation.

In the fortnight which separated the invitation from the dinner, Grace found that Edward was more interesting than usual. He talked of Fenor a great deal; apparently he was a man of great energy and decision who had shot several people, mainly black or brown, in the course of his career; who had been shipwrecked, laid up with yellow fever, held for ransom by brigands in Morocco, and had now determined to settle down respectably.

Grace was too interested to wonder whether Enoch Fenor had begun his attempt to enter respectability when he tackled her in Kensington High Street. Instead she tried to induce Edward to talk of him, and, as Edward readily responded, by a curious reflex process, as her husband interested her, she liked him better. She was gay, rallying; she could laugh now, and laugh with Edward so much that sometimes she wondered whether those eighteen months of unrest had not come from a little disorder of the body, whether after all she did not love her husband as always she had. Edward talked of Fenor and, as he talked, Grace began to think that she loved him.

But there were moments of reaction. What did this interest of hers amount to? After all, was some taste for low adventure in her? She did not know the man, she did not even like him. There was nothing between them or, if there was anything between them, it was something disgraceful and humiliating. Oh! if only she could tell the truth! But she knew that she could not tell, that it was too late. And then, if she pictured the result of the telling, the certainty of a breach, she knew that she was glad that she had not told. But this too was ignominious. Though glad that she had not told, she was sorry to be glad, for that meant that something in her that had seemed fine was not so fine. Then she would spurn her remorse, call herself prejudiced, foolish, and again despise herself because now she read as folly that which had seemed virtue. From day to day, and very much at night, she tossed in this uncertainty, hating herself for her own delight and enjoying her own humiliation until, as the day drew nearer, she found herself sleeping uneasily, until the word "Fenor" began to echo in her ears as she formed it for her pleasure and her mortification. In the early morning she thought and visualised so violently that it was almost an actual voice spoke in her brain, saying: "Beautiful lady, your hair is like the autumn leaves. Why is there no sun to gild it?"

It is not easy, ceasing to be a respectable woman.

The dinner itself turned out to be extraordinarily frightening and extraordinarily normal. It was, beforehand, wonderfully complex, for somehow Grace expended upon the menu more time than she usually did. Hers had been, for the first five or six years of her marriage, a bourgeois household which had of late, and little by little, with the growth of her taste for at homes and smart luncheon parties, become less so. She sought for some rarity such as swallow's nest soup, or terrapin. As these proved either uncookable or unprocurable in London, she had to content herself with the mildly *recherché* quality of river trout *meunière,* and later in the meal with some persimmons which turned out to be very nasty. And there had been reactions in the preparation of the menu: she had pulled herself up, told herself there was nothing extraordinary about this dinner, and that only by the conventions of Campden Hill Road had she been prevented from foisting upon her guests a steak and kidney pudding.

"Quite good enough for that sort of man," she remarked, and then wondered whether the entrée should be quails or larks.

It was a small dinner of eight. The Cheddons, the Marburys, for Marbury gave Edward a great deal of work in the course of the year, and, to balance Fenor, a creature aged between twenty-five and thirty-five, owning between a hundred and four hundred a year, with plenty of conversation of the metallically bright kind that makes a dinner go, whom they call an odd girl. As a rule the Kinnersleys dined at eight. On this occasion Grace suggested to Edward that eight o'clock was "out," so they began at eight-fifteen. Grace was taken in by Cheddon because Cheddon was dull. Fenor sat on her right. It had been easy to pair people at this dinner, as an odd girl is so handy to put anywhere. It was a solemn little dinner, not very successful perhaps, for Mrs. Cheddon wanted to talk dogs, and so did Mr. Marbury. But as Mrs. Cheddon was an expert, while Mr. Marbury was not, and as he felt himself entitled to lay down the law to her because after all he was a man, their intercourse was not quite harmonious. Edward was so successful in engaging simultaneously Mrs. Marbury and the odd girl that Grace found herself thrown back upon Cheddon, who was a small, sandy-haired, silent thing. It was said that his wife had married him because he looked like a ratting terrier. But, alas, he had not the brightness of his breed. "My wife likes dogs," he remarked at intervals. "Jolly good thing, dogs."

"Yes," said Grace. "Have you been to the opera lately?"

Cheddon contributed views on not going to the opera. She tried him on dances, but he didn't dance; she tried him on books, but he had views on not reading books; she even tried him on his digestion, but unfortunately he was in perfect health; so, for a long time, Fenor did not have any share in her conversation. She was just conscious of him beside her: very tall, rather heavy about the shoulders, and, in his silence, menacing. He had greeted her on arriving with the most perfect assumption of calm; that is, she tried to believe this, but felt there was nothing assumed about his calmness. He was not disturbed. And, while she hated him for this shamelessness, she delighted to feel him shameless. It was like going to the theatre and seeing the Sicilian players raving and weeping, despising them for their exaggeration, and yet wishing one could do it oneself. He had said: "Good evening, Mrs. Kinnersley, I'm delighted to make your acquaintance."

She had felt herself blush, and she knew that, as she blushed, the rose in her cheeks united the freckles with the white and assured her of her beauty.

Every now and then, as the dinner went on, she spoke to Fenor a little. He answered briefly, crisp things. He seemed to analyse or sum her up. She had the sensation that whenever he talked he meant something; it did not feel at all like a dinner party. She asked him how he liked London after his many travels. He became enthusiastic.

"It's a wonderful place, isn't it? So swollen, like some dreadful fungus, swamping the country, the fields."

"It doesn't sound very nice," said Grace.

"Well, it isn't at first, is it? to see the country turned into building-plots? and the poppy expelled by the sardine tin? But it's alive — like a heap of radium, you know."

"Oh, you see things too scientifically," said Grace, laughing. "Is that because you're an engineer?"

"Perhaps. Some of my friends say I don't see things scientifically enough."

Then Grace had to attend to Cheddon. It was only a little later that Fenor, who had been entertaining Mrs. Cheddon with a description of Dugdug, his yellow Somali hound, turned to her again. Grace had been listening while he talked; it had been quite easy, for her conversation with Cheddon needed no great mental effort. And she was amused, for she was a little suspicious. Fenor had been describing to Mrs. Cheddon some extraordinary creature that he called the Patagonian branquito and then, as this seemed to interest her, some Chinese dogs called, according to him, chooloos, that were half pekinese and half something else, probably cat. Mrs. Cheddon had listened very gravely to this traveller's tale told her with equal gravity, and a little streak of delight ran through Grace as she realised that Fenor was "pulling his neighbour's leg." But when she managed to turn to him in the later stages of the dinner, the burgundy had already followed upon the hock while champagne was in sight.

Marbury was engaged in a fierce argument with Mrs. Cheddon, for the latter had handed on to him Fenor's story of the chooloo dogs which were partly cats, while the odd girl, inspired by an unaccustomedly good dinner, had fastened upon Edward with a story of what they did to her when she was a ward in Chancery, as if she had quite forgotten that she was only the odd girl and Edward the host.

So Mrs. Marbury, a statuesque person with black hair who looked like an advertisement of an obesity cure "before," had taken Cheddon in hand and was slowly passing, in an interesting lecture, from ankylosis of the joints to fatty degeneration of the heart. Whenever Cheddon's mouth was not full he held it open, giving every sign of horror. In that moment of isolation there was so much noise that Grace found herself compelled to talk to Fenor of his motor accident.

"Was it a new car?" she asked.

"Yes, I'd only had it a couple of months."

" Did you damage it badly? "

" Yes, pretty badly, smashed the radiator and the bonnet. And as for the window — "

He laughed, and Grace joined in less easily. While he laughed, she considered him more carefully. No, he was not handsome. That broad lumpy forehead and that nose which she now saw was so irregular that it looked as if it had been broken, and that thick, hard chin, all that was not relieved by the red and brown, almost glazed and crackled surface of a skin burned by tropical suns. Nature had not been artistic, and the eyes, she found, with their large whites, more than ever disturbed her, and the quick, piercing quality of their grey pupils. Indeed, in that minute she thought him ugly; he looked strong, harsh, fierce perhaps, and quite beyond any ruling. That would not have mattered, but he looked coarse also. Then Fenor turned to look at her and as, without speaking for a moment, his eyes dwelt upon the beautiful forward curve of her throat, and upon the flush, half pink, half cream, which tinted her arms and breast, she suddenly realised that the mouth that smiled at her almost cried out to her. Yes, it was a delicate, pitiful mouth. Set there amid all the roughness of his features it was like a lost child.

She was impressed but she tried to be light.

" Rather hard lines for you, an accident like that after only two months."

Fenor paused. She saw him throw a glance round the table.

" Yes," he said, " rather hard lines if it was an accident."

For several seconds Grace did not see the table. She answered something to something Cheddon said, she didn't at all know what.

" If it was an accident? " The man upon her right had calmly said " if it was an accident." But what could his reason be?

Then suddenly a new creature seemed to rise up in Grace and to cry out to her: " Good heavens! stop this posturing to yourself. You know perfectly well that it wasn't an accident. You know perfectly well that he only did it to get hold of your husband and of you. Be honest, woman, just for once.''

She turned to Fenor and met his eyes bravely:

'' So you did it on purpose,'' she whispered.

The grey pupils were serious as he said:

'' Perhaps. An accident which I can bless, any way, whether it was an accident or not.''

She was not listening. '' But you might . . . but . . . but you might have hurt yourself or somebody else . . . splinters of glass — ''

He almost shrugged his shoulders.

'' All in the day's work, and — ''

'' It'll cost you a good deal, what with the car and the case you'll lose — ''

'' Oh, come Mrs. Kinnersley, don't give your husband away like that. I may not lose. Besides, if I do, a hundred and fifty will cover the lot.''

Again Grace was silent. It was not only that a hundred and fifty pounds was a good deal, but the idea of this car driven full-speed, leaping the pavement, dashing into plate-glass through flying splinters . . . just to allow that man to sit beside her at dinner. It was terrific. It was Quixote tilting at a windmill, and as she realised it she was stirred. She looked at him with something soft and humid in the green eyes which the lids half veiled. Before she knew what she was saying, she had murmured:

'' Was it worth it? ''

And he, imperturbable: '' Of course . . . and it is only the beginning.''

She turned so sharply that almost the whole of her back was towards him. She talked feverishly to Cheddon, but Fenor smiled for he could see the blush which was overrunning her neck and shoulders. His delicate mouth set close and, for a moment, was in harmony with the rest of his harsh features. His eyes narrowed, his black eyebrows came together until his dogged, relentless, assaulting air gave him the look of those monstrous dogs carved in brown stone out of the mountain, near the sources of the Nile.

CHAPTER THE SECOND

THE TOUCH

I

MARY was having an interval. That is, she had fully recovered from her last child and, as yet, no other child was coming. So she had given parties, for she was accustomed to give her parties when she could, to have what she thought little debauches of entertainment during those periods, always too short, when she could appear without blushing before the eyes of men. It had been a long interval for her, fifteen months, and, when she considered her nursery where now a nursery governess figured, because Rose was nearly seven, she wondered whether she would ever have another child. Sometimes, as she stood, calm rather than joyful, at the gate of her farm, she told herself that she wanted no more children, that these five were enough. But at the same time she reflected that here they were, Rose, Maud, Ella, Gladys, and baby Louise — all girls, only girls. Just now it angered her rather than hurt her to think that she should have no man-child. Tom had never reproached her, but sometimes it hurt her as he talked of the son who, he fervently believed, would yet be born to them. Once he had come in with a present for Rose: *Mr. Midshipman Easy.*

"Oh, Tom," she said, "Rosie won't read that, she couldn't. She may like boys' books by and by, as all nice girls do, but not *Midshipman Easy.*"

"Never mind," said Tom, his red face wonderfully jovial and optimistic, "it'll do for Jack."

Mary said nothing, but it hurt. That son to be born to them, they always called him Jack. And now, as she stood in her nursery and watched her five little girls, some having their hair plaited, others being told to keep still while their shoes were put on, while she heard the shrill voices of the two nurses and the advice to young ladies given by the nursery governess, she was overwhelmed by a sense of a world all female, which proceeded from her: five little girls and three women attendants, and she the mother. All women. She sighed.

There was something disgraceful, she felt, in this extraordinary dominance of the female principle which, she thought, or rather felt, ought to be slave and not master. What am I doing for the Stanleys? she reflected.

For Mary was wife more than mother. It was of the Stanleys she thought, not of her ancestral Westfields. Tom's people were her people, and she had no other. She might not have repined if Tom had put her away because she gave him no son. It would have been right so.

Still she had had too many children, too many satisfactions, too many periods of calm, and she had given too freely of her blood and her strength before her thirtieth year to have much of that nervous energy which made Grace and Clara tear at their own flesh. Indeed, though the idea of the son haunted her, it did not oppress her. Free from motherhood, she felt like a girl having a holiday, and she looked about her eagerly, wondering what she could do; she was excited like a child taken into a pastry-cook's shop, told to choose the cake which it liked best, and secretly anxious to eat them all.

During that winter there had been dinner-parties at Hammersmith Road. They had not been carefully selected political affairs like those of Clara, nor blends of commercial adventure with excursions into Bohemia, like Grace's. Mary's dinner-parties had not taken place at a quarter past eight, nor even at eight, but at half-past seven, and they had not been "little dinners;" nor had her guests been asked to dine "quietly." No, they had been long, bulky, sumptuous dinners, copied in spirit from the dinners of a livery company. There had been two of these banquets, each one of sixteen guests; there had been '38 Madeira, positively '38, plenty of good red and white wines; champagne had been tolerated. And it was characteristic that, somehow or other, a saddle of mutton had crept into the menu. Everybody had eaten a good deal, and the men had sat an hour over the port, while the women, in the big drawing-room, discussed their servants, their children, the advantages of Folkestone over Cromer, the immorality of the current fashions and the ailments of their aunts.

And there had been another kind of dinner now and then, the sort of dinner that Tom really loved, when, inspired by a sort of fury of entertaining, he would range round the Baltic and capture half a dozen of his old friends to come in just as they were. These functions were embarrassing, for they were rigged up at a day's notice, and Mary always found it a little difficult to cope with four or five women she had never seen before, who belonged to Hampstead tennis clubs, or Surbiton golf clubs of which she had never heard. The men sat together in groups, and one by one, rather shyly, pipes appeared; everybody talked Baltic, fluctuations of the provision market, freight rates, discounts —

Sometimes, at the very end of the evening, when most of the guests had caught their train, Tom would detain the last in the dining-room, send Mary to bed, saying they had some business matter to discuss. Mary would retire very respectfully, for she belonged to that section of society where the woman may talk of art, politics and even religion, but where she may lay no hands upon the sacred and imperial trade.

They were clumsy parties, and Tom always had rather bloodshot eyes and a smoker's cough next morning, but "He likes them," said Mary, and beamed as if her face were becoming larger with satisfaction. They were getting older, these two, but they did not know it. They were not illumined by any very clear ideal. Mainly, they were eating, drinking, sleeping, rearing children so that those might eat, drink, sleep, and also rear children. But right through this apparent coarseness there ran a few fine threads. Now and then, especially about half-past six in the evening, when Tom visited the nursery and stood silently at the door, his bull-dog pipe stuck in the corner of his mouth, his waistcoat rather prominent, by the side of his placid, white wife, he had a vision of his five little girls when they would be a little more grown up. They would all be dressed in white, and wear sashes. The tallest would stand on the right, the smallest on the left . . . they would go to children's parties, and they would be well brought up; they would not grab cakes, and they would not ask for the principal parts in private theatricals; they would dance well, without showing off, and when they left would, each in turn, tell the hostess that they thanked her for a pleasant afternoon. And later they would learn French; one of them would probably paint flowers, and it would do no harm if, just to vary the selection, one of them rode in the Row. Later they would marry nice, steady, young men with enough money to keep them in comfort, and enough prospects to keep them in cheerfulness. Then they would have nice little children: Tom Stanley saw rows and rows of nice little grandchildren. But none interested him so much as Jack's children. That unborn Jack would come by and by: already, inspired by his mistake about *Mr. Midshipman Easy,* he was very quietly getting together a library of Hentys and Ballantynes.

Nobody knew anything about this, not even Mary. He kept the books in the untidy, tumble-down room, behind the dining-room, in an old packing-case. Every now and then he would open it, have a look at the collection, and laugh at *Peter Simple* himself.

"I think Jack'll like that," he would murmur. And then he would look round guiltily, as if he were afraid of being caught practising some secret vice, hurriedly put on the lid and then make a mental note: "I think Jack'll like some Mayne Reid."

II

Early in April Mary gave an at home, for the Season was near, and vaguely, though she would not have expressed it in words, Mary liked to think that she had something to do with the Season. It had been a large, home-devastating affair. Now the guests of whom, between four and six, there had been a hundred, had gone, and the three sisters wandered from the drawing-room, littered with hired chairs, to the dining-room, where the big table, thrust up against the windows, was still covered with great bowls of claret cup, plates of little cakes and sandwiches. There was a desolation about the house, the desolation which clings to a ballroom in the morning, when all the apparel of merriment seems tired; even the chairs seem listless, as if they had been sat upon too much. They wandered because the familiar things of the house had been uprooted, because it was no longer a home, but a public place. Even Tom felt it and, with a muttered apology, went to his den, there to smoke a pipe for which a deep longing had developed in him during the whole of the afternoon. The three sisters remained together.

"Come into the drawing-room," said Mary, "let's be cosy in a corner."

"I must go," said Clara, vaguely.

"Are you doing anything to-night?" asked Grace.

"I must go," repeated Clara, in her preoccupied way. She had nothing special to do, still she felt that she must do it.

"Oh, don't go yet," said Mary. "We haven't had a word, you and I. How's Harry? I couldn't speak to him, he only dashed in for a moment. And Edward might have come, you know, G. It isn't often I ask him."

"He's gone to Bruges for a few days with a man," said Grace. "You forget this is the Easter vacation, Mary."

"Gone with a man?" said Mary. "I'd have thought you'd have gone with him, G."

"Oh, don't be goody," said Clara. "We aren't all of us Siamese Twins. Though he wanted her to go with him, didn't he, Grace?"

"Yes," said Grace, warily. "He said that I ought to come."

"Another honeymoon?" said Clara, vixenish.

"Oh, don't be silly," Grace snapped.

"Harry never takes me for a honeymoon," Clara went on, quite cheerful because she was being waspish. "I'm not the adored one like you, Grace. My story is the story of the little rhyme; you know it?"

"'Before they're married he takes her into the moonlight;
After they're married he leaves her at home with a cake of Sunlight.'"

Mary laughed so heartily that her big breasts and hips trembled, while an angry, red flush spread so deep over Grace's skin as to conceal the freckles.

"Going away, Mary?" she asked, rather stiffly, to change the conversation.

Yes, Mary was going away; the children needed a change in the spring; Tom had taken a house for them at Margate for three weeks and would come down for the week-ends.

"I can only hope it won't be too cold," she murmured, "but we want a bracing place."

"Skegness is so bracing," Clara, still frivolous, quoted from the railway posters.

"It's too far," said Mary, quite serious. "You see, Tom couldn't get down to Skegness for the week-ends."

"Oh, Mary," said Grace, a little acid, "how can you be so silly. Clara's only pulling your leg. But why are you worrying about Tom and his week-ends like that?"

"What else is there to worry about?" replied Mary. "And I don't call it worrying. Would it worry either of you if you were at the seaside and your husband came down for the week-end?"

"No, of course not," cried Clara, indignantly. "That's not what Grace means at all."

"One never knows what Grace does mean nowadays," said Mary. "I don't know what's come over her."

"Oh, she's been finding her soul," said Clara, flippant. "Finding one's soul's quite the thing this season. What are you going to do now you've found it, Grace? Ask your friends and have a one-soul show? or have a theosophist in to tint it mauve? That'd go nicely with a pink aura."

"I don't know what you're talking about," said Mary, stodgily. "Seems to me I must be living out of the world."

"Mary," asked Grace, "do you miss it? The world, I mean." And, as she spoke, wondered whether Mary were really living out of the world.

"Miss it?" said Mary, vaguely. "Well, in a sort of way. There's a whole lot of things I used to do: skating, hockey, and that sort of thing, you know."

"Gone," said Clara, cruelly. "You're too fat, Mary. Well, you mustn't complain, men have to give up football about twenty-five. You've taken up something else instead." She jerked her head towards the ceiling, indicating the nursery above.

"Yes, I know," said Mary. "I don't mind. Still, sometimes — "

"Sometimes you wish you were a girl again," said Grace, "with no encumbrances, as they say in the advertisements. Sorry," she added quickly, as Mary's face remained serious, "I don't want to make any jokes about it, old girl, but, still, it's giving up a lot, isn't it?"

"Yes," said Mary, "ye-s, it is. Still you always have to give up something for something, don't you?"

Grace did not speak; there was something in this elementary philosophy. But Clara protested:

"Oh, stuff, you never want to give up anything."

"How do you know?" asked Grace, puzzled.

"Well," Mary murmured, "I mean — "

Clara looked rather angrily at her fat sister, spoke at rather than to her:

"Why d'you make out that . . . that you're a mother of ten, and there you are; or a miniature painter, and there you are; and all that sort of thing. . . . Why, you can be lots of things. There's lots of room in life."

"Oh, no, there isn't," said Mary. "You can't eat your cake and have it."

"Yes, you can," said Clara.

"Got it?" asked Grace, suddenly.

"Oh, Grace, I wish you wouldn't ask silly questions. Ask yourself whether you've got it. Perhaps you have but—" and Clara suddenly became vicious: "are you sure you're eating it?"

"You can't have your cake and eat it," said Mary, with the enormous solemnity of one who, by repeating a platitude, imagines she is enunciating a profound truth. "Of course I haven't time to go to Prince's in the afternoon, I haven't even much time for reading. I've always got something to buy for the children, or trouble with one of the servants, or something."

"But, Mary," said Grace, "aren't you sorry sometimes? really sorry, I mean. You were talking about Prince's. I think you came and had tea there a month or two ago, didn't you?"

"Yes."

"Well, when you saw them dancing on the ice, weren't you a little bit sorry?"

"No," said Mary, gravely. "I've got other things."

"Better things?"

"I don't know, but I've got 'em, you see; I can't explain, but when one's got a thing really, one's sort of settled."

"Settled down," said Clara. "Settling down or settling up, that's the problem of modern civilisation, isn't it? You've settled down already, Mary—in the mud; no tide'll float you."

Grace listened to her sisters arguing, and thought mainly of Clara's metaphor. She was not so sure that Mary had settled down in the mud; perhaps she had reached anchorage. For one moment she wished too that she had reached anchorage, and then there rose up before her eyes an ugly face with a broken nose, large, piercing eyes, and a beautiful, tremulous mouth. She clenched her hands together, so intense was the vision. The idea of an anchorage receded in her mind, receded into nothingness. Enoch Fenor did not make her think of the sulky waters of a harbour, but rather of a racing frigate scudding under full sail. She was afraid, for she suspected that some queer flag was nailed to the mast, something like the Jolly Roger.

"No," Mary declared, ponderously. And her voice came from far away, just like that of the maid when she brings up the papers and the letters in the morning, and one is still half-dreaming. "No, I don't want to go to dances, or to spend week-ends with friends. I never did enjoy that sort of thing, it only kept me busy."

"Be busier," said Clara, with almost American eagerness. "Now, look here, there's one of our committees needs a really experienced mother — "

III

"What's wrong, old girl?" said Tom that night, turning upon the pillow a head which the whiteness of the linen threw out in violent relief of black and red-brown.

"Nothing."

"Well, you're not talking much." He had been reciting to her a few events of the day's business. Never very confidential, he spoke a little more freely in bed, where warmth, the softness, the feeling of freedom from clothes, caused him to relax.

"I don't know, Tom," said Mary, "only the girls came in this afternoon. They seem so bright and busy, Clara with her politics, and Grace with her clothes and her parties, and all her excitements."

Tom was silent for a moment. He felt this was a little unfair, that Mary was vaguely complaining, and that in three months they too had given several dinner-parties. Also that the at home had been a great success. Perhaps it had been too much of a success. Yes, that was it. He came a little closer, slipped his arm round Mary's shoulders, drew her towards him.

"I expect you're a bit tired," he said.

She smiled, and, responding to his movement, nestled closer to him. Perhaps he was right. Perhaps she was only a bit tired. And now, close held, his big, hard chest against hers, she had an extraordinary sense of solidity.

She did not think, but she felt the word "permanent." She looked into his eyes and thought their grey was very soft, that there was something gentle, almost humble, and very kind in this broad, hard man who held her within the crook of his thick arm as if telling her that there she might rest, that none should harm her, that if only she loved him it was enough for him.

"Penny," said Tom.

Very vaguely this offended her. But then Tom was like that. As he thus lay, with his placid, white wife in his arms, it was not such a phrase as: "Beautiful lady, your hair is as the autumn leaves," that came to his mind. What he felt was that, somehow, she was not quite happy, and that if she was not quite happy no more could he be.

"Cheer up," he said, careless after all of what she might think. And, as he drew her yet closer to him, something seemed to melt in her. She seemed to grow quite soft — fluid, and, as she impulsively threw round his neck her warm, plump arm, laid her cheek against his, she felt safe and contented like a very small cat that is being stroked by an enormous hand.

IV

It was midnight, and Clara lay in bed, blinding her wide-open eyes with the lights that were still fully turned on. She had been alone that evening as Sir Henry had left her at eight-thirty to go to the House. About her, on the coverlet, were scattered one or two books and the evening papers. She was restless, knew that she would not sleep well. It was as if something had excited her, something that made it impossible for her to fix her attention, and yet this did not result in her wanting to sweep out of her mind the ideas and the details which battled there. She reviewed her day and the list of many things she wished to do on the morrow. She thought of Mary, rather ignobly sunken in her content, of Grace and of her queer, half-artistic ways. She wondered what would become of them, what they would turn into, what they would look like, all three, when they were old. She thought of herself first, grey-haired, very much established and important. Harry would be in the Cabinet then, and there would be an awful lot of things to see to. It would be rather fun, entertaining everybody who was anybody. She made up a brilliant picture of a reception she would give in Downing Street; it would be very official and uniformed; the whole of the diplomatic corps would come simply constellated with orders . . . and she would write a letter appealing for funds for something, something big and charitable; it would be published in the *Times,* and be referred to in the leader as the Prime Minister's wife's appeal — and the Duchess of Saxe-Hohenheim had been very nice the other day: her visions became royal.

But with sudden weariness she felt that all that was very far away, that it would take a long time to get there, and she contrasted her position with the one that might be attained by Grace and Mary. Mary, she knew, would be very fat and very dowdy, and the red of her cheeks would by then include her nose, her forehead and her neck; she would be almost offensively jolly, and she would be frightfully interested in the households of her five daughters, or ten as might very well happen. Grace she was not so sure of. She felt that Grace would be the last to grow grey, ostensibly, that was. She suspected that Grace would always be elegant, absurdly so. "Yes," she murmured, "Grace'll be the one to dress mutton lamb fashion." She laughed as she thought her sister would later on pretend that Susan was not her daughter, but her niece. She could not imagine the Grace to be; rather *outré* clothes, no doubt, and new religions, and art movements — funny things —

But quickly her mind flew back to herself, for not long can one think of other people, so little do they exist by the side of one's own personality, that personality so large that the world can hardly hold it. Again she realised that it would be a long time before her hair was grey. Almost she wished it was so already. It was all too long and too tiring. She wished she had never tried so hard, and for so much. She could hear Sir Henry in his bedroom, for he had just come back. The walls of the flat were thin and she could hear his every movement. He was undressing rather quickly. She heard things being thrown down. There had been an all-night sitting the night before; he was tired, no doubt. And then a little impulse of tenderness seized her as she thought of her husband going to sleep, after two such very hard days during which she had had only glimpses of him, for two committees had coincided with the all-night sitting. He had not come into her room. Doubtless he did not want to disturb her. She felt she must speak to him.

For a minute or two after she had leaped out of bed and put on her dressing-gown, she hesitated, for she tacitly upheld the unwritten code of the modest wife who never enters her husband's room after dark and never locks her own door. Harry would think it odd; she thought it would make him awkward. She laughed: it would be rather fun to make Harry look awkward.

Boldly she entered her husband's room, mischievous now, rather than tender. He had not gone to bed yet. He stood in his pyjamas, drying his face and hands before the wash-stand. As she came in, he threw her a surprised look.

"Hallo! Clara." The tone of his voice showed that behind the two words lurked another two words: "Anything wrong?"

Clara felt it. She was curiously selfless that night.

"I only wanted to see you," she said, brightly. "I never see you now."

"No," said Sir Henry, as he meditatively dried his wrists. "We're both busy, aren't we?"

She came a little closer to him:

"We *are* busy," she said.

They looked at each other, those two, and, very vaguely, together thought it was a pity. Then Clara laughed uncertainly and put her thin hand upon his shoulder.

"Tired?" she said.

"Well," said Sir Henry, stretching his back, "a bit."

And carelessly he put his arm about her waist, which was soft and yielding towards him in the thin stuff of the dressing-gown.

"I say," he murmured, "it's rather decent of you to come and say good night to me." He bent down and good-temperedly kissed her upon the cheek.

But there was a nervousness, an exasperation, half-gay, half-unhappy in Clara that night. She pressed her cheek against his lips and then swiftly, as if the caress did not content her, threw her arm round his neck, drew his head down, kissed him upon the mouth. Her thin arms were too sinewy and nervous, as she clutched at the neck that was too high above her because her husband lacked all the feminine languor which makes of the male a lover, and did not bend down enough. An unusual excitement seized her as the thick, hard strands of his moustache interposed between their lips.

Though her husband lifted her from the ground and carried her across the room to the arm-chair where he seated himself with her across his knees, he was a little shocked and yet pleased. It was a compliment to be courted, even if it was not the thing for women to do the courting.

He loved her in his fashion, a rather stately, contented fashion, as if love and its accompaniment of caresses, its apparel of pretty words, were a thing to be proceeded with now and then, at the proper time and in the proper way, in virtue of the proper initiative.

When later, but not so much later as to cause her to find her bed cold, Clara lay down again with her face upon the pillow, she was soothed and yet not quite happy. It was perhaps not love she wanted, but something very like love, symbolical of it, because it was the only immortal thing. She had not really had love: she had asked a question and had an answer. But was it the true answer? In the dark her mind was clearer. She was capable of analysis. She was even capable of elucidating fact by a metaphor, for she suddenly seemed to remember an old riddle and to connect it with her life: "When is a door not a door?" said the riddle. "When it's ajar," replied everybody. "Not at all," said the sphinx, "but when it's an egress."

She had had but one answer to her riddle and there were two. Which was the right one? Or were both right or wrong?

She did not know why, for it came so slowly, but little by little her eyes began to sting and to blur and then, for a long time, she wept, though she did not know what made her sorry.

V

Across the empty bowl of Kensington Square the rain swept almost horizontally upon the wind which came swearing from the north through the gullet of Young Street. In interminable, brilliant needles, the water speared through the branches of the trees that were already flecked here and there with little, hard, green buds, and with young leaves that bent and curled before the storm. Grace stood at the drawing-room window watching the fury of April that was like the wantonness of winter raging because it knew that it must die and soon give place to summer, vowing that before it went to the cave of the dead years it would mark with yet another blow, while it had the strength, the face of the earth.

She drummed upon the window-pane. Her thoughts were not lucid and she was a little languid; she was not curious to know who had telephoned a minute before. The maid had not come up; wrong number, no doubt, as usual. She looked at the sky that was like a dirty, white plate, save in one corner where, in a rip between two clouds fleecy as a swan's rump, a brilliant blue streak zigzagged.

She watched the rain that now, caught upon the wind, was like burnished telegraph wires in a mad tangle. The window was open at the top, and though the blind was pulled down a little, now and then a few drops were flung into the room upon her face and hands. She could hear all the sounds of water: the swish upon the roofs, the quick decrepitation upon the pavements, and the dull, gurgling sound in the flooded pipes. It was a violent, valkyrian day, the sort of day which tied her to the house, for she was as a cat, hating even the little journey between her door and that of a cab; she hated the pavements running with black greasy water, the dripping umbrellas, the suggestion that every doorstep was laden with wet dirt. No, she would not go out.

A taxi stopped before the door, and at once she was filled with excitement. Somebody was coming to see her. She smiled in anticipation, glad that some one, any one, should keep her company. A man leaped out of the cab and, it seemed, in the same moment paid the driver. Running up her steps, he pulled the bell so hard that she could hear it echo through the house. She drew back from the window hurriedly, for in that second of time she had seen him, seen him though hardly better than does the hunter see the chamois as it jumps a cleft. It seemed very long, this interval, as do all short intervals when there is keenness in the expectation. She imagined him as removing endless garments — as brushing his rumpled hair or making some other interminable toilet, so long did it seem. She was alone, it was going to be dreadful. She would tell him to go. It was all very well his having forced himself into her house by a subterfuge, but he was not to imagine that he was going to settle there. No, she'd have nothing to do with a man like that. These proud thoughts made her feel taller, and she stood in the middle of the drawing-room, her hands behind her back in a prepared, dignified attitude, not realising at all that an attitude such as this, by its self-conscious rigidity, implied in her a tension of resistance that clamoured to be overcome. The door opened. "Mr. Fenor."

Grace came forward graciously. As the name resounded through the room, her prepared dignity and stiffness seemed to crumble, and, as Fenor took her hand, she was conscious of a new excitement in which was no desire that he should go.

She said: "You shouldn't, you know — "

"Shouldn't what?"

"Well, you shouldn't have come."

Fenor threw her a quick look, and it was for the first time she noticed, as he smiled, that he had very good, large teeth.

"Shouldn't have come?" he repeated. "I never bother about that sort of thing, Mrs. Kinnersley, I just come. Are you going to turn me out?"

"Don't be ridiculous," said Grace, laughing nervously, and then blushed as she released her hand, aware that Fenor had held it much longer than was usual in a conventional salutation. "Sit down," she said, indicating a chair. "You're in the nick of time, they're just going to bring up tea. How nice of you to come, and in such weather!"

Pause.

"And you must be so busy, what with your work, and London just beginning to wake up again —"

Pause.

"I suppose you're having a very interesting time? Do you go to the theatre much?" She stopped abruptly. She had attempted to cover her nervousness with a flow of commonplaces to which Fenor had not responded. He had not helped her, but remained standing, looking at her fixedly, with very serious eyes and a faint air of amusement about the corners of his mouth. For a moment they looked at each other in silence.

"Good," said Fenor, "I congratulate you on your small talk, Mrs. Kinnersley."

"What d'you mean?" she faltered. He was being rude, she knew, and she ought to be angry.

Fenor shrugged his shoulders. "You're not going to talk polite conversation to me," he announced. This was a command, not a prayer. "Are you glad to see me?"

"Oh . . . I . . . but, of course, I'm glad, Mr. Fenor. You put things so funnily."

"Straight, you mean. It's unusual, isn't it? Well, I'm glad you're pleased to see me. I'd have known, anyway, without asking. I knew you were in."

" How did you know I was in?" asked Grace.

" Oh, I just stopped the taxi round the corner, and telephoned and asked whether you were. You see, I didn't want to call and find you out, or I'd have had to wait a long time before I could call again. It's better to take no chances."

Grace did not reply. The truculence of this man! his audacity! And his craft, his way of thinking out everything in advance! She felt powerless. Strength and cunning, he had both and, as she looked into his eyes, she did not see that he had mercy. Rather distractedly she drew her hands across her forehead. " Oh, Mr. Fenor," she said, " do sit down and talk like a rising barrister or something."

He laughed rather harshly, and did not explain why he laughed, but it amused him to think that the first person whom she thought of as talking innocuously was one such as her own husband.

" Besides," added Grace, " the tea's coming up in a minute."

He laughed again, bent forward and said, in a slightly mischievous fashion: " Oh, oh, accomplices! We're getting on!"

Grace heard the clatter of tea-things outside, and it needed all her will-power to drive the crimson from her cheeks. But the serving of tea restored her self-possession. There is something disarming in the purely mechanical process of serving tea, sugar and milk, while the concentration necessary to give proper quantities helps out of tangles. And Fenor behaved exceedingly well. He talked more freely, first of the climate, which he contrasted unfavourably with that of Morocco; then of a musical play to which he had been the night before, and, at last, of the case which Edward was to conduct for him. Grace began to feel reassured, and as she grew reassured became disappointed: a tiger is a dreadful thing, but it is rather a pity when the tiger begins to eat out of your hand.

" I say," he remarked, " it's I who am making polite conversation. Don't I do it nicely?"

"You're behaving very well," said Grace, demurely. "I congratulate you."

"Don't," said Fenor, with humorous pathos. "With me it never lasts and I don't want it to, I always have the worst intentions. Fate plays into my hands. Why, think of the extraordinary good luck I'm having. If I hadn't happened to drive down Westbourne Grove and smash a plate-glass window, and if I hadn't happened to have heard of your husband as a smart man, I shouldn't be here." He smiled mysteriously. "Isn't it wonderful what accident will do?"

Grace wondered what she ought to answer to this. Fenor was playing with her; that she could see. At dinner he had not pretended that it was an accident, and now it pleased him to do so. Whichever way was she to take him? She deferred to his whim: "Yes," she said, "it was an annoying accident. Have you had the car repaired?"

"Yes," said Fenor. "Fortunately I was insured, but it seems rather a shame taking the company's money, considering I did it on purpose."

"Oh, Mr. Fenor," cried Grace, "I hardly know which way you mean it now: first you say it's an accident, and then that you did it on purpose. Why did you do it?"

Fenor did not reply. He did not intend to reveal to her the methods by which he conquered, his way of sowing uncertainty in a woman's mind, of stimulating doubt and curiosity, all creating in her brain a maze of which he became the centre. But, suddenly, he leant forward towards her, so close that she drew back, knowing that he was going to touch her. Then, in a very low voice, he said:

"You know—you know why I did it, and you're glad I did it, aren't you?"

And she found that she was not resisting as she felt about her hand and wrist the close, hard clasp of his fingers. For several seconds she felt powerless; his eyes were heavy upon her, and she did not struggle to free herself, as if she were fascinated by the brute strength and assurance of the man. She saw new details in him. One of them thrilled her: the thickness of his rather up-standing black hair, and the close setting of their roots into his burnt forehead. Half unconscious of the grasp upon her wrist she thought that Samson must have had hair like that. And a delicious shiver shot through her as she thought that Samson had had his beautiful Delilah.

But she had been well brought up and lived in Kensington. She repressed the impulse to lean forward suddenly and seize a handful of that thick black hair, to pull it as hard as she could, just for the delight of knowing that it was so thick and firmly rooted that no strength of hers could pull it out. Instead she stood up and freed her hand. It surprised her to find how easily she succeeded. Fenor did not attempt to hold her against her will; it seemed as if he divined her reaction against him, and as if at once he responded, as if there was something feminine, intuitive in him. She sat down again upon the sofa, a little further away. She was smiling, and her eyelashes were half-lowered so as to show only the half moon of green pupil, but she was not angry, only a little uncertain.

"You're an engineer, Mr. Fenor," she said, "it must be very interesting. Do tell me all about your work."

Strangely enough he obeyed. She seemed to control him just so long as she wanted to control him, and only to be subject to him when she wanted him to break her will.

"Oh, it's jolly work," he said, "I always wanted to do it."

"I suppose you mean you wanted to be a tram conductor when you were a little boy," said Grace, flippantly.

"Well, of course; every little boy wants to do that nowadays. Fifty years ago he wanted to be a soldier, and two hundred years ago he wanted to be a pirate; at least I suppose so. Nowadays he wants to be an engineer. But I knew it when I was at school, up North."

"Oh, you're North Country," said Grace, suddenly enlightened as to his directness and slight bluntness.

"Well, not exactly. I was born in Birmingham, but it might have been Cornwall if we'd been living there. My father was an engineer too, you see. He was Scotch, but like most Scotchmen he was always anywhere except Scotland. So I seem to have got my education in patches; at Rugby for a bit, and all sorts of places; at Lille, and some scraps of Latin from a friar in Catalonia. And then, to make the jumble complete, they sent me to Freiberg."

"You seem to have travelled a lot," said Grace. But she was of her class and had not noticed much except Rugby. She was glad he had been to a public school.

"Travelled?" said Fenor, thoughtful. "I never seem to have done anything else. My father used to pack me with his bag, I think, and then, when I'd taken my degree, I did the same; sort of family tradition. I'm a consulting engineer, you see. That means I've to go to every desolate mountain, and to every plague-stricken swamp, a thousand miles from any railway, if there's any metal there. It's a rotten life."

"You don't mean it," said Grace, demurely. "As you talk, I can see the idea greatly excites you. You love the work."

"Yes," said Fenor, "you're right, I do love the work. Oh, Mrs. Kinnersley, nobody'll ever make you see what it's like. Prospecting itself, hunting the golden slipper — half-breeds who tell you lies — and natives waiting for you to fall asleep to murder you and steal your rifle, and white men, the queer sort of white man that lives in a Brazilian port, or some way East of Suez where there ain't no Ten Commandments. The white man out there, that's the man."

She saw that he was labouring under violent excitement; his hands were clasped together and his mouth had set into a thin line: "The white man who's gone black, that sort, you know. He's left some wives behind him, and some debts, and a warrant or two perhaps. He keeps a store in a place like Sekondi, a bazaar for local lies. He'll sell you a plantation, or a girl, or a mine plan. He'd float hell as Good Intentions Limited. He runs the black women, and the yellow ones, and the brown ones, and he's the fellow who sells rotten beef to the ships. And now and then you meet him on the trail, looking for the colour in the rock, or putting it there to diddle the London engineer — ''

Grace was silent for a moment. Though he had not pronounced the word, Fenor seemed to fill the room with contest.

'' It must be very exciting,'' she murmured.

'' Exciting? '' He laughed. '' You bet it is. Hard life though,'' he murmured, thoughtfully. '' When I come back I find I've forgotten how to shave, I can't make out what the papers are about and I don't feel I want a bath any more. Why! three months in the bush and the smell of the place gets right into you. You stop being white, you've got too near the earth.'' His eyes became intent upon her, and yet it seemed as though he were looking beyond at other places. '' It's when you stop being white,'' he said, '' that life sort of begins. South America, with the pampas like a big, green carpet that's trying to unroll — grass, eight feet high, like green spears, thick and sharp at the point like a needle — and now and then when you're riding, perhaps just next to the track, a funny sort of ' S ' that goes moving in the grass keeping you company: just a boa-constrictor in the grass.''

'' Horrible! '' cried Grace.

'' No, it isn't horrible. Not even at night when the camp fires are alight and three little streams of smoke go straight up into the air because it's so heavy that nothing will stir it. Three little altars to the god of civilisation, just stuck out there with twenty days' march between you and the next saloon.''

'' Do you ever think of the saloons when you're travelling? ''

'' At first,'' replied Fenor, '' yes, when the rain's falling, six inches of it in an hour, and you feel your boots sinking so deep in the mud you think you'll never get them out again. Yes, then you do think of the saloon with its mud walls and its iron roof, and of half a dozen dagoes, a pot of drink on one side of them and a knife on the other, and some Scotchmen waiting for any fool to pay for their drinks, and an Englishman from the slums talking with some other Englishman with an Oxford voice who's got his reasons for letting his beard grow. Smoke, a nigger or two playing a thing with strings, some red stains upon the floor that may be wine or something else, and upon the stage at the end a girl, dancing, who looks like the *entente cordiale* of all the races in the world, making eyes, as she dances, at the local official and lifting up her French frock to show the dirty ragged lace of her petticoats — Yes, you think of all that when your boots are sticking in the mud. It is warm there anyhow, and so easy."

Grace did not reply for a long time. She hardly knew what to say, for Fenor carried with him some amazing suggestion of horror and romance; he seemed to have passed through every violence, hating and loving it as if, draining a cup of wine, he had sworn also to drink the dregs so that it should not be said he flinched. "But those are men," she murmured, hardly aware in her excitement of what she was saying. "Don't you look at the other things? the jungle and all that?"

"Funny ideas, sometimes," he said, still staring at her, but clearly not having heard her question. "One thinks of places in England, you know, not obvious places, just any place, a road between hedges and a bit of blue mist — a beech with its leaves turning orange, and one night, I remember, when the place was thick with mosquitoes, it was the miniature of a pretty girl, with her hair parted in the middle; it used to hang in the drawing-room of an uncle of mine. He's a vicar in Warwickshire. I couldn't sleep that night; too hot, perhaps; that miniature kept on looking at me, and some of the niggers were singing somewhere in a minor key, and she just went on smiling. You know, it seemed so far to all the old places, I felt I wanted to cry, like a new boy who's left his folk behind him."

A sharp little impulse of pity inclined Grace to put out her hands and touch him, but she was still well brought up, and she was just going to repeat her question when, suddenly, he replied to her previous one as if it had been recorded in his brain, and later only had he been able to answer it.

"The jungle," he muttered, "—black water, all thick and sticky with something, the blood of trees, you might call it, and insects, and things. Sort of life asleep and trying to wake up. Everything dark, and everything thick, and smelling of fungus and beasts. Other places too, where you find a city if you dig under a temple and, they say, still another city under that one—worlds on worlds."

He stopped and was silent for so long that Grace's mind wandered away from his words to him. He seemed in the thrall of an intoxication, as if the memories which he conjured up held him and were not travellers' tales told for her pleasure. His hands were close-gripped together, and there was sweat upon his forehead. His intensity thrilled her, and all this queer mixture of wild adventure, of pathos, bred in her an incomprehensible agitation. He spoke again, quite irrelevantly:

"I'd a dog once, something between a collie and a sheep-dog he was, an ugly brute with eyes like sherry—he wouldn't eat when I had fever, he loved me all right. Used him as a pillow now and then. Some 'gators got him at Chinde." There was something wild and longing in his eyes now, and a sorrow in his mouth.

An indignation rose up in Grace; it found form in impulsive words:

"Oh, tell me you . . . you . . . I mean, a man like you . . . doesn't go hunting women in the streets." She stopped. She found it quite impossible to express to him how incomprehensible it seemed that a romantic hero should descend to the practices of shop-boys on Hastings pier.

"Men like me?" he said, vaguely. Then he looked at her, a more habitual expression coming into his large eyes. "Oh, you mean the way in which we met when I tried to pick you up?"

Grace shrank away a little; she hated the expression.

"Yes," she said, with an effort, "that's what I mean. How can you do such things?"

"You don't understand," said Fenor, dully, and stopped as if he despaired of making her understand. Then his energy seemed to return, and her own anger to invade him. "You don't understand what we've got to stand, men like me, when we come what you call home. When we come back after so long, the men we used to know have gone somewhere, no one knows where, and the girls have got married, and everybody seems altered and duller, because it's so sudden. You see, if you stay, change doesn't matter; it's so slow; but if you come back after a time, it all seems so long ago. People get old in a couple of years when you haven't seen them."

"But," murmured Grace, "can't you go home?"

Fenor shook his head. "Haven't got one. My father's dead; one of my brothers is prospecting somewhere and we never meet unless we sort of coincide. And I've a sister, but she's married a Dutch judge in Java. All I've got is my mother; she lives near Birmingham where I was born; but when I go back there, it's worse. The place I used to know as a little boy, you see, it's all changed. Where I used to buy cakes, they're selling motor-cars now —and there's a new house-master at my house at Rugby —A strong gardener I used to be fond of, he's drawing his old-age pension. It's all just as it was, the place I mean, and yet it's all different after twenty years. Going back like that, it's going to a city of the dead."

"But surely you've friends?"

"Men like me don't make friends. As soon as we begin to like anybody, we go away and they forget us. When I come back to a flat that's never really mine, there's just nobody. I can't track addresses, and people have forgotten me; I don't get invitations to stick into my looking-glass. It's all right during the day, I'm busy; but about six o'clock I begin to know that here's another evening coming, a dinner all alone, and a club where they hardly know me, a long gap of an evening which I can fill up with a theatre all alone, and then, at last, a great big brute of a silent night.'' He made a helpless gesture with his hands. "What's a man to do? He can't live all alone like that.'' His tone became more resolute: "I've just got to talk to somebody, some woman, somebody gentle and pretty who understands, and who likes me a little — especially if she's not too happy or not too rich. Somebody who'll laugh with me a bit and cheer me up; or somebody who wants to cry and whom I can cheer up, which is still better. Or just somebody to make love to for, after all, there's nothing in the whole world better than that, is there?''

Grace did not reply; she did not trust herself to do so. This wild man speaking of his loneliness and asking for something to do, something to make him happy — He was pitifully like her, and she understood very well now how it was that he could be driven to cheap adventure, to the raffish pleasures of the streets, because like every creature in the world he needed pleasure.

Curiously the melancholy fell from Fenor.

"D'you know,'' he said excitedly, "it's fun too — splendid fun, chasing women, I mean. It's wonderful, one gets so clever, like a Red Indian.''

"I suppose you'd tackle anybody,'' said Grace, adopting his light mood.

"Oh, no,'' said Fenor, with the shocked air of an expert, "only at the beginning when one's clumsy. You see, it's an art.''

Grace laughed out loud. "An art! Mr. Fenor.''

"Yes, it is,'' he said, seriously. "There's a certain sort of woman — well, you know the sort I mean, they don't come in. One lets them alone. I mean, one doesn't hunt game that's looking for a trap to put its foot in. No, none but the respectable need apply.''

"Oh, surely,'' said Grace, becoming quite embarrassed, "if they're respectable, they'll not listen to you.''

Fenor's eyes twinkled. He thought: What am I doing here? and aren't you respectable? But he knew it was better to hold his tongue. "Oh, won't they?'' he said, lightly. "You don't seem to understand, Mrs. Kinnersley, what working-girls feel like. Just try and see; they're boxed up in a shop or office, sometimes from nine in the morning until seven; very often they don't even get out for lunch; and sometimes it's still worse, they're living in; they've got three hours freedom out of twenty-four. Why, when they come out, they're bursting with excitement; they want to play, to live, and to live quick, as much as they can. Just a little bit of happiness, anyhow, through anybody. It's natural enough, isn't it? Of course it doesn't always mean anything; it's flirtation; it's just like a kitten playing with a ball of wool. So you mustn't be surprised because they listen to any man who looks decent, for they know he's going to stop the awful treadmill business which is their life. I know what they're like, and I know what a lot of good it does them to tell me what a beast that telephone supervisor is, or the shop-walker: to be able to tell their grievances and to have a cup of chocolate and a kiss, it's paradise. Don't you understand?"

She did not reply, for she saw that he was not wrong.

"Yes," he went on, "they're quite respectable, most of them. It doesn't last, of course. Respectability is like firewood made to be cut down. That's pleasant, of course; virtue's a very necessary thing in the world; without virtue there'd be no vice and we'd lose all the fun."

Grace laughed, this cynicism amused her; then suddenly, she grew rigid, though she understood. But she thought it vulgar; she was still one of those who can understand without forgiving. That instinct in Fenor which linked him with women made him at once realise what she was feeling. He bent forward.

"You don't think it horrible, do you?" he said. "There's nothing else; even if I dine out, I'll never see again the woman I take in. There's no romance for me. You understand — Loneliness, I mean, the need for a little lightness, oh! the need — the need — "

There was such pleading in his eyes that Grace suddenly did more than understand, she forgave. A faded spinster or a crusty old bachelor may be lonely and unpitied of a woman, but not a young man. But she did not express her pity; she changed the conversation, for she had been taught to conceal her feelings and to talk of anything except that which at the moment lay nearest to her heart.

"But don't you do anything else?" she asked, "when you're at home, I mean, to amuse yourself."

"Oh, yes." Fenor's face suddenly became enthusiastic. "Apart from my work which I'm fond of, lots of things. I'm fonder of women than of anything, of course. In other places it isn't like that, but here, in your drab old country, women hold in their slim hands all the adventure and all the romance. They're the only things worth winning. And it may seem absurd, but one has a wonderful glow of success when some common, half-mercenary, hard, pretty little girl from a pickle factory has made you feel for a moment that you're a sort of prince, a power. In a way I like them better than women of my own class. I'm not wonderful to those."

"Peacock!" said Grace, for the first time familiar, and yet she was not sure that he was not wonderful in his simplicity overlaid with craft.

"No," he said, "the women of our class have been surfeited, they've got too much money, they've had too much trifling pleasure, too much attention, too many clothes. They can't get any pleasure out of a seat in the gallery at a costume play, they can't get it out of anything —"

Grace felt that this man was now beginning to pull at something intimate in her. With another effort she again tried to change the conversation. "But aren't you interested in anything else?" she asked again.

Fenor responded. It seemed that between his journeys he indulged in an orgy of the latest literature and that he managed to keep himself in touch with all the "movements." Every time he went abroad, there followed him a case of books, all the most recent works on economics and sociology, the poetry and the novels of the day. And odder things: the pamphlets issued by the socialist societies and the manifestoes of the " movements," vegetarian, artistic, or anti-anything.

" Yes," he said, dreamily, " it seems only the other day that I was looking through those Russian Ballet drawings. How that hut smelt when four of my niggers had sleeping sickness! "

There was a silence, and then again he seemed to be drawn to that subject uppermost in his thoughts:

" Women of your class," he repeated, " having had too much or having had too little, too much superficial pleasure and none of the real things . . . that's why they're sort of half-dying with boredom and with the sense of not having used their faculties, because half the time they haven't loved. A man can do without love and pull along somehow, but a woman can't. It's her only way, you see. We've got travel, politics, war, business, all the adventures ready; woman's only got the adventure of love." He smiled. " But fortunately it's a big one. That's what I felt when I saw you. I'd been looking at you without your knowing it; you looked so unhappy and so empty, as if you were looking for something."

Grace did not reply, her eyes were downcast. The man's voice grew lower and more muffled.

" I felt I'd got something that you wanted, and that you'd got something that I wanted. It was not only that you were beautiful; there's more than one beautiful woman in the town; it was a secret in you that called to me."

" Don't talk like that, Mr. Fenor," Grace whispered.

" I must, I must," he cried more urgently. Again he leaned forward, seized both her hands.

She felt herself struggling with him and yet knew that she was not struggling with all her strength. She heard him talking urgently, brokenly, pouring upon her words of love which he did not connect. She hardly knew what he was saying, and quite passively she let him hold her two hands, for she stood almost blinded by her realisation. There was a new feeling in her, a feeling almost indefinable. It was like being flooded with infinitely sweet, soft, warm sunshine. Or there was a growth in her, something developing. She was bathed in a terrible consciousness of a presence, and yet she was exultant, as if a creature within her were struggling for birth. She felt herself — flowering.

CHAPTER THE THIRD

HAND GRASPS HAND

I

" I'M a bad woman," murmured Grace.

It was just before dinner. She sat alone in her bedroom, looking into the fire that sputtered and crackled as if vowing that, though this was April, it would have its fling. She was staying with Edward for the week-end in this great house, near Epsom, where Sir John Churton, their host, was by degrees becoming a county magnate. She had exhausted the little unfamiliarities of the room, ceased to marvel at the intricate apparatus of town life transplanted into the country, at the peculiarly large and fleecy blankets, the cream pile carpet, the little library in costly bindings. All this extremity of quiet luxury, which six months before would have overwhelmed and pleased her, could not compete with the thought that dominated her brain.

It was four days since she had seen Fenor, and he had neither written nor telephoned, while Edward, no doubt because busy with some newer concern, had not alluded to him. She had been glad. She had hoped that Fenor was going to release her, realising that his suit was hopeless, though behind the hope stood the knowledge that he would do no such thing. But much more disturbing was the fact that, in this minute, as she sat alone, she resented his silence. Doubtless it was her vanity rather than her affections suffered, but she was not yet cynical enough to know that her pride might suffer and, therefore, she thought it must be her heart. She had allowed herself to slide into reverie, to wonder what Fenor was doing at this moment. She heard, very faintly, the carillon in the hall sweetly chiming a quarter to eight. He would have done work long ago; perhaps he was dining and then going to the theatre at half-past eight. A thought stung her: perhaps he might not go alone, perhaps even now — it was only a quarter to eight after all, and those hours, six to eight — perhaps they had not been unfruitful. A tiny, but sharp spasm of jealousy went through her as she thought of Fenor by the side of some vulgar girl, an acquaintance of one hour's standing. Perhaps he was holding her wrists with that hungry, wistful intensity that she had felt four days before. It was hateful, abominable, disloyal. She tried to control herself. "Well! what did it matter to her? He was nothing to her. A cheap adventurer! No better than the vulgar girls who listened to him. Vulgar, vulgar, vulgar," she murmured, angrily, as if this were an incantation with which to chase her pain away. "He was crude, coarse, insensitive; no wonder he was unhappy."

But this word "unhappy" changed her mood. It was as if a current of hot air were suddenly turned upon a block of ice. "Even if it was his own fault, he was unhappy, lonely; and it was because he was unloved that he was like this. If he loved, and was loved . . . no, no, not that." She shrank away from herself as the obviousness of her thought struck her. She didn't love him; it was absurd. How could a woman love a man she hardly knew? just because he talked eloquently about the jungle, and pulled wry faces over his loneliness, and behaved like a junior clerk in Oxford Street.

As if she had called to them to help her, a garrison of dead Westfields came and stood behind her: old Horace Westfield saying: "Damme, girl, what's this?" And grandfather, John Elba, wondering what things were coming to, and her father. But her father failed her: he seemed to think that she was doing wrong, yet very softly hinted that human beings were like that, and that, though he had given up painting for the sake of the oil-trade, he had never forgotten painting and had often made a little sketch upon his blotter. "Darling," said the dead voice, "life's not a cheerful thing, we must put into it what we can." He was almost an accomplice.

"Father," murmured Grace to the spirit, "may I go on?"

And it seemed as if Horace Westfield replied: "Little G., it's hard enough to manage one's own life without advising other people; one never knows what's good for them. You must do what you can, little G."

But again she swept away those dead and unhelpful spirits which seemed, as they lost their sturdy bodies, to have lost their solid merchant qualities: it was absurd, she would think of him no more. Why, she had to be amusing to-night, Sir John would expect it; and Hubert was coming back next week; she would be glad to see Hubert; and there was Edward. She'd been beastly to Edward for weeks, she knew it. Cold, hostile. When he had tried to caress her she had eluded him, said the telephone was ringing or something idiotic.

"I'm a bad woman," she said, aloud, and decided to be a better one.

But much more vigorous than the ghosts of the dead Westfields was the wraith of Fenor, who murmured in her ear:

"I'm very lonely, and so are you. Are you quite sure that you don't love me after all? if only because you're growing new again, because you're blooming again, and because you must love somebody. It's the only adventure for a woman, you know."

II

At dinner Edward was humorous. Though he was seated at some distance from her, Grace could hear him repeating some of the witticisms of Mr. Justice Sweetheart.

"I didn't know how funny that libel suit was until it came into court," he said. He quoted two of his Lordship's puns: "When he asked whether the defendant said that the plaintiff wore as little when she bathed as ladies wore in the streets, we simply screamed."

Grace lost the thread of the conversation. Then again she heard him:

"Oh, yes, he always plays libel suits like a screaming farce, but he's a good judge."

She could not bear to listen any more. For years every barrister she knew had, sooner or later, told her that Mr. Justice Sweetheart was a good judge. Besides, her neighbour, Lord Owen Wister, kept heavy upon her the gaze of his tired, but handsome eyes, and talked of the relation between the petals of flowers and the skin of women in a style which seemed impersonal, and yet every moment threatened to become so personal that Grace hardly knew what to say.

The elderly diplomatist was so diplomatic that she could not make out whether he was talking botany or erotics. Later only did she hear Edward again. Apparently he had taken in a *débutante* who had not learnt to fight a man's conversation down with the bridge-golf-theatre-Russian Ballet artillery. So he was enjoying himself, and the *débutante* was acquiring information which would doubtless be useful to her the next time the law took her in to dinner. She wondered how the *débutante* liked Mr. Justice Sweetheart's witticisms and how much she understood them. But then, *débutantes* had to go through the mill and it was very good that they should know something about the law, and art, and big game-shooting, and slums (for countesses). She let Wister talk. Mellifluous he flowed on. She ate carelessly, delicious things, and she drank what was given her. It was all very soft, and warm, and suave, and from the big bowl of fat French roses in front of her came a delicate scent. The footmen passed before her eyes like shadowy, black and white hop-poles. The butler was just a bulbous blob. Together she seemed to think of Fenor and of Edward. What was it in Edward that exasperated her so now? Why was he not as in the early days? It was only eight years ago. How good his stories had been then! as good as Sherlock Holmes. But some of them she had heard too often; she knew when they were coming, and when he told them to strangers she was angry because he might be telling them chestnuts. She told herself to be sensible; of course they were not chestnuts to strangers, but to her they were; she was all egotism.

How dared a husband not always be fresh to his wife? And yet once he had been fresh, and his gaiety had been charming; it had been exciting when he came to Campden Hill Road. His points of view had been so new, so original: eight years made originality very stale. But again she pulled herself up and turned to answer Wister, or rather to ask him to tell her how he liked Vienna, for she knew her part as a woman: to make men shine, because when they feel brilliant they like you. She reproached herself. Edward was kind and Edward loved her. All those little gallantries and fondlings of other women which he indulged in before her eyes, they were only triflings. To him she was the one woman, she was woman. Of course he was her lover still, so much so that, in her present mood, he was a nuisance. And he was glad when she was gay, when she wore fine clothes . . . but again a shadow passed over the picture: he liked her gay because that responded to his mood, and he liked her fine clothes when he noticed them, because they did him credit . . .

It was all chaotic and so painful. And the other man, that other man who seemed to think of her, not of himself, to understand her, to want to draw something out of her, to give as well as to take. What was he doing in her life? and what was he bringing there?

III

Alone the men were talking after dinner: motor-cars, guns, hunting, winter sports, and all the sports; politics and the progress of flying. And Edward on his trade, on his pleasures, on his projects; Edward on Edward.

This after-dinner talk of men, it has an immortal quality. A thousand years ago it was war, woman and the chase.

With passing centuries a new generation of priests and priest-politicians came to infuse into it something more mental. The king, the barons, the Pope and his cardinals, and the evilness of Jack Cade. Then again, time unrolling, the Stuart and all the graceful, half-debauched, half-pious arts of France and Spain; and much more talk of woman now, of Richelieu, of Charles XII, the Swede, of the length of ruffles and the price of wigs, and of the fashionableness of the King Charles dog. Other generations, and the ruffles all dusty; talk of taxes and of the Dutch. An interval of years. Port wine and the novels of Mr. Fielding (far less interesting than those of Mr. Smollett), talk of profits from John Company — and then Boney, the military value of Martello towers, the policy of Mr. Pitt, Mr. Brummel and his clothes — and then again, somehow, a leap: trouser straps, the restless common people, the factories; once again the Crimea and the wars, and iron expelling wood from the seas, steam —

It has always been the same thing: war tribal or war national, groats or cheques, the moot or the Parliament, the battle-axe or the torpedo, all unchanging as man —

In the dining-room, the women in flux, fumbling their way from the spinning-wheel and the harem towards the municipal offices and the universities. Two horses harnessed to the same chariot, one of them at a jog-trot and the other plunging because the driver will not let it gallop. "Wider fields!" cry the women, and the men: "The fields are wide enough."

IV

Clara was interested in the week-end at the Churtons. She had uses for the Churtons. "They're big people," she remarked. "And they're not *new* people. It wasn't Sir John made the money, but his father; that's much better. You see, those manufacturers, they have a way of remaining Liberals; it's a sort of habit from the days when they were working-men. Fortunately their sons get over it. Did you see Charlie Churton? They say he's going to stand."

"No," said Grace, "he wasn't there. They don't seem to have any children."

"Oh, yes, they have," said Clara. "The other boy's a snotty, and there's a girl, I think."

But quickly she wandered from these domestic and sterile topics into speculations as to what would happen soon. She was dissatisfied.

"It's a nuisance," she said, and her pretty face grew quite fierce. "Harry's so unreasonable, he won't go in with the die-hards. I keep on telling him that the Tory party's done for and that the only way is to go in with the young ones who are just the same as the Radicals and call themselves Unionists."

"Are they?" asked Grace, surprised, for her ignorance of politics was amazing.

"Yes, you know the people I mean; they used to be the Confederates."

"The Confederates?" asked Grace, puzzled. "Who are they?" Lady Govan grew very mysterious, shook her head.

"My dear," she whispered, "no one ever tells that, but a few of us know; it's like Free-masonry; they're still doing something quite quietly behind the scenes. Nobody quite knows what, but it's very, very important." She added, still more mysteriously: "B. M. G."

Grace was interested by this sort of secret society; she had never before heard of the Confederates, but whether Clara did not know or whether she was pledged to secrecy she could not find out; and she wanted to know what B. M. G. meant. But Clara had forgotten all about the Confederates and was now talking about the die-hards, Lord Algernon Cust and his friends in the Lords who were preparing to stand and fall in the "last ditch." The consequences had not yet been damned, but she was excited: the Parliament Bill was going to be a great big rag. She did not put it like that; for her the Parliament Bill was quite clearly the people *versus* American dollars.

She seemed to talk endlessly of the venal Irish, of that dreadful Welshman, of the possibility of creating six hundred peers. At last Grace interrupted her.

"I say, Clara," she asked, "what about Harry?"

"How do you mean?"

"Well, how are you getting on, you two?"

Clara looked at her with a shocked face; this was the first time in ten years that it had ever occurred to her to wonder how she was getting on with Sir Henry. She had completely forgotten that recent night when she had so long, and so unaccountably, wept into her pillow. Her forgetfulness saved her many an anxiety.

"Getting on?" she said. "What ever d'you mean, Grace? We're getting on all right, aren't we?"

"Well, d'you ever see each other?"

"Of course we do," replied Clara, rather hurt. "There's breakfast, isn't there? We're pretty busy, both of us, but it can't be helped." And then, as if indicating periods of immense, soul-satisfying intimacy: "There's recess too; you seem to forget that."

"Is it enough?" asked Grace.

"Of course it's enough. Good heavens! G., a husband and wife don't behave like a pair of love-birds after ten years."

"I know," said Grace, a little bitterly. "I wonder whether they can't."

"Oh, do stop wondering," said Clara, wearily. "You're always wondering about something. The amount of wondering you did about that Burne-Jones father bought gave me the fair sick, as they say in St. Panwich. What are you wondering about *now?*"

"I'm wondering," said Grace, slowly, "whether life's worth while if one's not in love."

"Oh, dear; oh, dear," murmured Clara, "this is dreadful. It's exactly like the intellectual drama: Ibsen and *The Walls of Jericho*, and all that. Why can't you let things alone? and have a good time, since that's your way? You know what I think. You'd be much happier if only you'd do something, but—"

" Do what?" asked Grace, suddenly. " Hang about St. Panwich and talk to the constituents' wives? and corrupt 'em with sacks of coal and blankets?"

" There's no corruption in it," replied Clara, loftily, " but I'm not going to argue that with you. Even if there were, it gives a woman something to do, something to care for."

" Oh!" cried Grace, pointing a finger at her in her excitement, " so you've said it, Clara, something to love. It's your career you're in love with; you think it's your husband's career, it's yours."

" I'm only thinking of Harry," cried Clara, suddenly defensive.

" Well, that's your way of loving Harry. One way's as good as another."

" Oh," said Clara, " you make me feel so tired." Then, as if appealing for mercy: " As if I hadn't got enough things to bother me. Why, when I hear you talk this sort of muddle about politics, and men, and loving something, I want to laugh. Men," she added, bitterly, " they're nothing but a nuisance. Why, last week —" Clara stopped abruptly, and by slow degrees became rosy.

" Clara! Clara!" cried Grace, excitedly, clapping her hands with delight, " Clara, you've got an affair."

" I haven't," said Clara, savagely, and her blush turned to crimson.

Grace leapt to her feet and gave three cheers for Clara's affair, while the victim sat, very rigid, her hands folded in her lap.

" Oh!" gasped Grace, as she relapsed into an armchair, " it's too funny."

" I don't see what there is funny in it," replied Clara. She turned her face away. Perhaps it was funny, but why should her sister think it so funny she should have an affair? It was hardly polite.

" Oh, *do* tell me all about it," entreated Grace.

" There's nothing to tell," replied Clara, still very staid.

" No, no, of course not," said Grace, " no man would dare — oh, well, tell me all about it."

There was not very much to tell, and it came out, little by little, in alternate bursts of amusement, pleasure, shame and surprise. A few nights before she had been to a meeting of the Union Jack Club, and had given a lift in her car to a really promising young man who lived in a Bermondsey settlement. They had hardly left the club, and she knew that she had given him no lead; she remembered exactly what she was talking about: it was about employing pensioned soldiers and sailors as local agents for wards, and then — was it credible? — the promising young man flung both arms round her and kissed her just as the car was passing through the New Cut.

"The New Cut!" screamed Grace. "Oh, Clara! you darling! bravo! it's the thing to do in the New Cut."

Clara drew herself up very stiffly. "I think you're very common. I suppose you'll be saying I encouraged him."

"Of course you did," said Grace, "anybody would be encouraged by those lobelia-coloured eyes of yours."

"Lobelia, pooh!" said Clara, but she was vaguely pleased.

Unfortunately there was nothing more to tell. She had talked very sternly to the young man all the way to Bermondsey, so sternly as to convict him in his own eyes of temporary insanity, and she had forgiven him because he was a promising young man. By the time they reached St. Saviour's Dock they had arranged the next meeting quite nicely —

"A meeting?" said Grace. "At Piccadilly Circus Tube?"

Clara did not reply to this vulgar suggestion. There was really nothing to tell, for the young man had not pursued her. He was like a seasoned mariner when an iceberg is floating towards him; he can feel the cold in the air and, if he is wise, changes his course.

Then, little by little, Grace, finding that the romantic adventure was not very romantic, brought Clara back to the subject uppermost in her own mind. Clara told her nothing, but she fulfilled that essential condition of conversation: she enabled Grace to express her own ideas.

"D'you remember," she asked, suddenly, "that experiment in a lecture on physics we went to when we were at the High School? the chestnut in the vacuum?"

"Chestnut?" asked Clara, blankly.

"Yes, don't you remember? He was demonstrating—atmospheric something—pressure, I think. I seem to understand it to-day; I didn't then. Don't you remember? He put the chestnut under a glass bell and pumped the air out, and the chestnut began to swell, and give off air bubbles and water—until it burst."

"Well?" asked Clara, puzzled.

"Don't you see? Oh, I've never seen it until to-day. The chestnut was full of air and water, and because there was nothing round it—no air—it swelled, and swelled out of its own vitality. Until it burst. That's you. That's you, the chestnut, and me."

"I don't see what you mean at all," said Clara.

"Oh, surely," said Grace, a little impatiently, "you must see that you and I, and nearly every married woman you know, are just like that, nothing to do. I mean, no real work. Love, or children, or something. They're all like that."

"They're not," said Clara. "Some are pretty busy, anyhow."

"Oh, busy!" said Grace. "Busy, like flies in a railway-carriage, buzzing about and not making an inch more or less progress than the train which carries them. Look at them. Look at Mrs. Cheddon and her dogs! Why, she might be an old maid; and Mrs. Shapwick, making just one more engagement every day than she can keep: no wonder she thinks she makes the train go. And Mrs. Leycett, returning to the stage. Why d'you think she's returning to the stage? She's got to go somewhere, poor thing! And look at you, your meetings and your agitations over a husband who only wishes you'd keep quiet, and me with enough money to pay somebody else to do everything for me. I've got to do that: it's the thing our sort does. Children who don't want me, and whom I can't force to want me because I'm not as good a nurse as the nurse, or as good a governess as the governess; and a husband sitting in the Temple all day, and dreaming of the Temple all night, a husband — "

She stopped, frightened by her own lucidity. At last the semi-conscious travail of eighteen months, following on years of inner working, was visible. And in that minute she realised with wild delight that the last six weeks had been more agitated, more revealing than all those years. It was as if she had been shut up in a little sphere and then as if, suddenly, the sphere had been pricked and a dazzling beam of light had pierced the darkness, coming from some brilliant star. It was a wonderful, terrible moment, just like that when the engineers of two nations, driving a tunnel towards one another through a mountain, have long listened to the others tapping, then suddenly see the last foot of earth crumble away and glimpse one another with delighted eyes.

But Clara did not respond. She did not understand, but she was impressed enough to know that Grace was not talking nonsense and that in her, as in all other women, some discontent was clamouring; so she was respectful as she asked:

" D'you mean it's because of marriage? "

" I think so," said Grace, less certainly, for now the light was dimmer. " Perhaps there's only one thing for us to do: to get a man; and when we've got him we're done, unless — "

" Unless what? " asked Clara.

" Well, perhaps unless we're poor and have to do some really necessary things: cooking, and washing the baby, cleaning the steps, all that."

Clara laughed.

" Oh, and nicer things too: decorating the house, and learning piano pieces, and reading the right things, and making pretty clothes."

" Well, you can do all that," said Clara, " if you want to."

Grace shook her head:

" No, we're not strong enough to cook and clean; it's

been bred out of us. And we never learnt the piano, or how to decorate. We were taught to strum and to daub. It's no good, Clara, we've just got to go and find something else."

"What else, then?" asked Clara. "Children, I suppose."

Grace started. Yes, there was something in that. There was Mary. She seemed happy. She did not seem to want new excitements. Perhaps her children were only a drug. Did the drug work? Mary was content and fat; for one moment she was about to answer: "Yes, that's it, we too must have children," but something secret in her said: "No, children are the best drug in the world for married women, but still only a drug. It's the real things, the real adventures we want. Something vivifying: colour, change, emotion. Yes, adventure while we're young; it's always too late to begin." But she said nothing of this, for her mind was in a turmoil as she remembered Fenor's words: "We men, we've got all the adventures: war, politics, business, but for a woman there's only the adventure of love."

It was Clara spoke.

"Mary — " she said, "she seems all right. She's expecting a new baby in December. I wonder whether it'll be a boy this time."

V

And yet, that night, she tried. She had not intended to do so, but Edward forced conflict upon her. She was reading and, as she read, he talked. He wanted to know what she was reading, whether it was interesting, who the author was. Curtly answered, he gave his views on the subject, on novels in general, on novels he had read. Then he took up the evening paper, and from time to time read selections in a loud voice, moving a hand rhythmically up and down. And, a little later, while Grace was reading a letter which the evening post had brought in, he amused himself by playing the newsboy with the headlines of the paper which he still held. At last Grace could bear it no more.

"Edward," she said, in a tone which she tried to make calm, "must you always talk?"

Her husband looked at her blankly; she had never said such a thing before.

"But—but—" he faltered, "I don't quite understand." Then, with sudden archness: "D'you mean hubby talks too much, Gracie-Bracie?"

"Don't call me Gracie-Bracie," Grace snapped. "How can you be so silly?"

He looked at her with astonished eyes, stood up, came to her and, taking her bare arm, fondled it. She tried to draw it away.

"Naughty temper," he remarked, still fondling the arm.

She leapt to her feet, tore herself from his grasp and then, with flaming face, she found that she had a great deal to say.

"Talk, talk," she gasped, "Edward, you never stop talking. I can't read a letter, and I can't read a book, and I can't sulk at breakfast, and I can't have a headache. You'll go on talking, making jokes when I've got the blues—you don't know I've got 'em, I suppose. You can't pass anything without talking about it. A dog mayn't wag his tail without your saying: 'The dog's wagging his tail.' Don't you remember the other day, at the Churtons', we went out in the afternoon? Don't you remember the flowers?—I'd forgotten until now—Why did you have to say: 'That's a ragged-robin,' or 'Look at the blue-bells?' I know." A strand of hair fell across her face; she pushed it away savagely. "You don't hear yourself talking, Edward. Don't you know I've caught you baaing to a sheep and whistling to the birds? And d'you know why it is? Because you never think of me, never look at me, never know I'm there except as a sort of ear. D'you know what clothes I wear? D'you know what I do with myself during the day? Have you ever listened? It's dreadful, it's cruel; I simply don't count except as somebody who's handy for you to talk to — " She stopped, out of breath. He was still looking at her, surprised.

" I say," he remarked, " what's wrong?" He was quite serious.

" Wrong?" said Grace, miserably. " Everything."

Fortunately in that minute he was not jocular, for she might have struck him. Instead he was humble.

" D'you think I talk too much?" he asked. " Perhaps I do, but nobody's ever told me."

Grace felt suddenly guilty. She ought to have told him long ago, but had she known? Does a woman know that her husband changes as certainly as her hair grows grey? She came closer.

" Sorry," she said, " I've got the jumps to-night."

But Edward was not to be put off. He was so egotistic as to be deeply interested in anybody's opinion of himself, even unfavourable, and he saw his wife so little as a separate person that her onslaught on him did not offend him. It was like his own consciousness working.

" I wonder whether I don't notice you enough," he said, musingly. Then, after a long pause: " Well, I'm very busy, you see — "

" But when you're not busy, Edward," cried Grace, despairing.

" Perhaps I'm always busy with my affairs," replied Edward. " It's a hard life, the bar, you know."

There came into his eyes a look which told Grace that once more his thoughts had flown back to himself. Still, she tried again.

" Edward," she said, gently, " don't you remember how it used to be before we were married? You wanted to know what I'd done then."

" Well, I still ask you," said Edward.

" Yes, but do you listen to the reply?"

There was a silence. Edward, cornered, became aggressive.

" It cuts both ways," he said. " You were keen enough to hear about me in the old days."

Grace did not reply, for it came to her painfully that in those days she had not been offended by his referring to himself as " hubby-to-be," or by his calling her Gracie-Bracie. She had called him " Brownie; " she had even called him, " little animal," because of his soft eyes. They had both pretended that he was a little furry animal with brown eyes. And she remembered what he had said about being happy like two pussies in one basket.

" Oh, it's different now," she said, vaguely, " one grows up."

" Getting old, Gracie-Bracie — " he began archly, but corrected himself to: " Getting old, Grace."

She threw him a quick look of thanks. He was trying, then; her heart melted. She saw him sorry. Faced with himself he was willing to try and remould himself to please her. She came up to him, put both hands upon his shoulders.

" Ned," she said, very seriously, " let's try again. Don't let's quarrel, only just try and see that I'm a woman with not much to do, that I want somebody to love me, to care for me, for what I do, for what I think. I never stop you when you talk about your profession, do I? "

" No, old girl," he said, drawing her close. " I know you're a brick. Only sometimes one forgets."

She kissed him gratefully; perhaps after all they could manage. But Edward was forgiven; he led her towards the mantelpiece. He smiled down at her.

" Well," he said, cheerily, " let's make a beginning. Perhaps little girlie-girlie will tell hubby all the little adventures she's had to-day? "

She smiled up at him sadly. No, it would never do. As she did not reply he did not pursue the subject any further; he searched his brain for something that might interest her.

" Oh, by the way," he began, " that case — "

She shivered: case, case, case again — but suddenly she hated herself because her interest had reared up like a flame. He had said:

"That Fenor case has been settled out of court. Of course he hadn't a leg to stand on."

She listened greedily to the tale of the case. She had heard it before, but it was still romantic, this idea of a man who for her sake drove a motor-car straight at a plate-glass window. She could figure him, head bent, under the shower of flying splinters. Yes, she could be interested in that case. It was not Edward's fault if he smiled because she was interested.

VI

Change and adventure. These things seemed now to Grace a condition of life. Vaguely she began to feel that where they ceased to exist so did life. And now the marriage adventure was over. Love had come to her eight years before, not on the flaming pinions that she imagined, but still it had been love. Love gentle, cosy, almost domestic. It had satisfied her, stilled her. But time had passed and she had become a different woman, while her husband grew into a different man. That which had been enough for them once upon a time was no longer what they wanted. The adventure of those days could not satisfy the changed persons. She remembered George Meredith's proposal for ten-year marriage leases. She smiled, but reflected that her time was nearly up. If, as Fenor said, love was the only adventure for a woman, then surely she must love again. But quickly, and still carrying upon her shoulders the Westfield tradition of strait cleanness, she thrust away the thought of illicit love. There were other things to do. There was still motherhood. Oh, not another child. She had two, and if they yielded her no solace she was not content to drone away her life in a sleep of pregnancy.

Again she tried to be a good mother. Hubert had come back from India, burnt red-brown where he was not liver yellow; he smoked abominable cheroots, talked endlessly of Rajahs, and the Taj, and the hills, and of the D. C., and the P. A., and various other initials. But he had the agreeable simple air of a man who has long been far from cities. Grace had enjoyed taking her brother to tea at the Savoy: somehow he seemed continually to be saying: "Bless my soul!" It made him young. So Hubert accompanied her to the Zoo to which she drove on Sunday afternoon with Horace and Susan. Hubert loved children; somehow he knew what to say to them. It was Hubert kept them both fascinated in the lion-house by telling them how a big tiger nearly ate him. It was a long story, but they listened to him as if he were Andersen and Ballantyne rolled into one. But as soon as he finished they burst into shrill questions:

"Do tigers eat little girls?"

"Shall I shoot tigers when I'm grown up?"

"What did the elephant say?"

Hubert laughed, assured them that the elephant said he was sleepy, promised to buy Horace a rifle that very day. The two children held him firmly, one by each hand. Their mother walked behind, for they ran, making their uncle walk very fast. They dragged him into the snake-house, and Grace found herself left out until she had to prevent Susan from giving cake to the crocodiles, upon which the little girl burst into tears and was soothed after a long time by Hubert. All that afternoon she knew she was out of it. She was there only to coerce and to forbid. She had nothing to give them. It was Hubert entered into a face-making competition with one of the monkeys; it was Hubert rode on the camel with a screaming child upon each knee, and all she could do was to call out:

"Take care, both of you! don't wriggle or you'll fall off."

And, at tea, there was more trouble, this time with Horace, because he insisted upon eating out of the common jam-spoon. Her children had too long been apart from her. They despised her for an amateur. Beyond the expert they knew nobody except perhaps Hubert, the adventurer. Yes, Hubert had had the adventures, Hubert was not rotting, he was a man. He was alive. She too could live through herself and not vicariously, have her adventures, even if for a woman there was nothing but the adventure of love.

VII

As Grace paid the driver a man stepped out of another taxi and, hurrying past her towards the doors of a big shop in Oxford Street, lost himself in the crowd of women who hung about the show-cases. Turning back, he came face to face with her, a perfectly well-assumed look of surprise in his eyes.

"You!" cried Grace. And, as she spoke, her freckles were drowned in a blush because she knew she had said "you" instead of "Mr. Fenor."

"Yes, I," said Fenor. "How curious! Shopping?"

"Yes," said Grace, "I'm just going in there."

"Oh!" said Fenor. "What a pity! I've just done. Still, are you going to be long?"

"No," said Grace, innocently, "I haven't much to buy."

"A toby frill, I suppose," said Fenor.

"How clever of you, Mr. Fenor. It's exactly what I'm going to buy. How *did* you know?"

"Oh, simple enough. You aren't wearing one, so I conclude you can't be happy until you do. But look here, let's be serious, dead in earnest. Go in and buy your frill; I'll wait, and then we can go and have tea somewhere."

"But—but—" Grace faltered, trying not to be glad, "but your work, you're busy. How is it you're here at this time?"

He smiled. "Yes, I'm busy but, you see, I'm practically on my own now. I can do my work when I like, so don't trouble about that. Go inside, buy your frill, and don't be long. We've only got one life, and I can't afford to lose ten minutes of you."

"You'll be dull," said Grace, without protesting, and

well knowing that she was happy to be so commanded. "Unless," she added, mischievously, "you look at the pretty girls. I—may not find you here when I come back."

"True," said the man, imperturbably. "It's the hazard of the die, Mrs. Kinnersley, so don't be long."

When she came back to him, after a quarter of an hour, she was already agitated for, in the shop, she had caught herself urging on the assistants almost rudely, in so great a hurry was she to keep the tryst. And then, having done this, she had told herself it was not politic to hurry; she had dawdled several minutes before things which she had no intention of buying. At last, here they were, together, publicly walking up Oxford Street. Fenor was silent, and she liked his repose as well as his hard, decisive way. It was warm, he wore no overcoat; his light, grey tweeds hung loose over his long limbs; there was an air of bravura about a soft felt hat he wore a little sideways, and something very manly, which thrilled her, in the thick reindeer gloves which were too large for him. As they walked side by side her hand brushed the heavy glove; she trembled.

"I say," he said, suddenly, "where are we going to?"

"I don't know," she replied. "Anywhere you like." She added: "You're in charge."

But this was hardly necessary; the tone of her first words had said as much. He thought for a little.

"All those little places in Bond Street," he said, "or the Carlton, there's such a crowd and we might—well, any of your friends—you see what I mean."

"Yes, yes," said Grace, hurriedly. She knew she ought to have snubbed him, but there was something exquisite in this complicity, in the idea that it was better they should not be seen. It turned the commonplace into the compromising.

Again he seemed to think: "Of course there are quiet places, like the Vienna Café. Nobody ever goes there, nobody you know. Oh, I've got it! Let's go to the Great Central."

" A hotel," murmured Grace. She was disturbed. Somehow a hotel was so much more compromising than a tearoom.

" Yes," cried Fenor, as if he had not heard her, " that's the place! Taxi! "

As if by magic, or as if it were true that fortune favours lovers, a taxi drew up in front of them. Grace felt that she wanted to protest, then found herself practically put into the cab, and it was all over. Swiftly the taxi was bearing them along Mandeville Place. Her heart was beating. Through her eyelashes she stole glances at the big, silent man by her side, and she was terrified when she remembered Clara's experience in the New Cut with the promising young man. She need not have feared. Fenor did not even take her hand; indeed he said nothing at all except once: " close shave," as they nearly went into a dray at the corner of Marylebone Road.

The lounge of the Great Central seemed enormous and very empty. There were a few solitary, elderly people busy with the evening papers; there was a large and noisy party, one member of whom revealed his origin by telling the waiter loudly that he would have a " boonn " with his tea; also, and that was more interesting, there were three couples, all of them much too quiet and much too smart to be travellers. They had settled, each one, in three corners of the great lounge, and had turned their backs as much as possible on the other guests. They were young, expressive backs whose very eloquent lines said: " We've come here to have tea and not to be looked at; so don't be nervous, we won't look at you."

As if guided by an instinct or by the obvious, Fenor steered Grace towards the fourth corner. And in a few seconds, to her delight and despair, she found that, quite instinctively, she had given her chair a twist as she sat down: doubtless her back also was eloquent.

At first the conversation did not go very well. Grace was shy. Fenor spoke jerkily, as if throwing off the oppression which had at first made him silent. And she, from time to time, looked at him without speaking, her eyes all moist with the glad, slave look of the woman who is about to conquer. As time went, she talked more freely, of the settlement of the motor-car case, of his work a little. But, as she became more responsive, she found him grow less so. Fenor let her speak, said very little except to prevent her from putting milk or sugar into his tea. He seemed only to want to look at her, and his eyes were tense as if he were filling them with her beauty. She knew that she was beautiful that day; there was a sparkle in her eyes, and the creamy flush of her skin had blended with the brown freckles into a uniform glowing colour. She was like a tea-rose. Little by little, they grew more silent and, as they grew more silent, more aware of each other. They seemed quite alone, for nearly half an hour had elapsed and the big party from the Midlands had dispersed, while the couples continued unobtrusive. Fenor bent forward:

"Russet," he said. "I've been calling you Russet in my dream. You know what I mean: it's your hair, like the autumn leaves and the bracken, and all that life-colour in you. It makes me think of beautiful, glowing specks of sunshine."

"My freckles, you mean," said Grace, trying to be flippant. "I hate 'em, I do everything I can to get rid of them, I — "

"Don't," said the man. "Don't you know that great ladies used to wear black patches to set off the whiteness of their skin? It's like that, those brown freckles in hundreds seem to have all blended together into beautiful uniform bistre patches; they make your forehead and your neck dazzling — so you'll let me call you Russet, won't you?"

Grace did not reply. Oh! craven heart! She knew she ought to have said: "Mr. Fenor, you must call me Mrs. Kinnersley." But she did not reply. Instead she let him speak endlessly of her beauty, recite what it meant to him, of her strong, capable white hands with the short fingers. Of her eyes, green to him like a shallow pool.

"When you walk," he said, "you sway a little, and

then you're a ship, all graceful curves, with a soft breeze filling her sails."

Still she was mute and did not protest. Never before, by husband or would-be lover, had she been appraised, detail on detail, by one who seemed to know the difference between a hand and a hand, to love a shadow under a chin, the set of an ear or the fine grain of the skin of a wrist. Epicureanism in love: never before had she met it.

"And it isn't only that," he said, quickly. "There's something so much more in you that no other woman ever had. A sort of silence that's like understanding, something very sweet and restful. I call you Russet, and yet somehow you're like the dew, so soft and fresh." He bent towards her: "And so very, very young, somehow, as if you'd never been married, and a mother and all that. You're like a young girl to me, and sometimes in my conceit I think it's only with me that you're a young girl, as if you were born again. You seem to know what I mean, what I've had to bear, and you seem sorry. Much more than that, I feel it sort of coming out of you: a sympathy, call it what you like, and perhaps something more. Just now I want to touch your hand, and I can't — we're in a public place, but I don't feel that if I did you would repulse me. I feel that you want it as badly as I do, just because you're unhappy, and I'm the first man who's known it. Isn't that true, Russet?"

She nodded. There was a long silence. Then Fenor said, his sharp eyes now as anxious as his anxious mouth:

"And aren't you happier now? Haven't you been happier these two months? I have, you know, ever since I saw you. Oh, of course I couldn't tell. Perhaps you might be angry with me, never speak to me again, but the idea of your just being there, so beautiful, my sweet, so radiant — It was like being in the night and knowing that the sun was there, on the other side of the earth perhaps, but there all the same, and bound to rise again. I'd always been hoping for it and, my beautiful, it's come."

She remained quite still, and though there was a contraction of resistance in her hand, she let him confront the dangers of a public place and, slowly bending forward, caress her wrist, then bury his fingers in her palm. For a long time they remained like this, linked by the warm contact of their hands. Suddenly, quite instinctive, she closed hers hard over the strong fingers . . .

They heard the clock in the bell-tower chime half-past five. Grace started to her feet:

"We must go," she cried. "I must go home quick, we're dining out to-night."

Fenor did not protest. He followed her out, hailed another taxi, and as soon as the cab had pulled out of the hotel-drive, sought for her hand. She laughed, for a parcel and a little bag had to be overcome. She tried to be light.

"I'm carrying too much luggage," she said. But her laugh was nervous, and she said no more when purposefully the big hand encased the whole of hers and Fenor's fingers rested hard against her wrist.

He leant towards her, looked at her intently. She saw him only in flashes, for the night was foggy and it was already dark. Every time the taxi passed a lamp-post she saw his face, determined and yet appealing, very close to hers. And she knew that he was going to kiss her. Instinctively she put out her hand against his shoulder.

"Mr. Fenor — " she murmured.

"No," he said, "you must call me Enoch. It's an absurd name, but — but what does it matter?"

"I don't think it's an absurd name," said Grace. "Oh, no — no, really you mustn't." She found herself struggling a little.

He held her close and, as she turned her head away, she could hear him murmur into her hair. A powerful excitement seized her as the man confessed his love for her, as in impossible hyperbole he described her beauty and his need of her.

"Russet," he murmured thickly into her hair, "I love you. Can you say that you don't love me?"

She did not speak, weakly tried to free herself. But still he held her. The lights of the street streamed into the cab, and she was terrified lest she should be seen. But still Fenor held her and tried to draw her towards him softly, firmly. The taxi had stopped in Praed Street, opposite a picture palace, for the traffic was held up at Paddington. An omnibus pulled up by their side and suddenly Grace felt degraded.

"Let me go," she murmured, angrily, and she succeeded in pushing him away.

He understood, but he was persistent. And in another minute, as the cab threaded through the dark silence of Craven Hill Gardens that is like a little oasis with a lover's tree, she was again in his arms. And now, no longer resisting, hardly knowing what she did, for the first time she felt his lips upon her neck, upon her cheek, and was quiescent while he dwelled upon his caresses as if they were infinitely precious, as if they filled his veins with that mellow current that was now beginning to flood hers. But, as his straying lips sought her own, her ancient prejudices reasserted themselves. She turned her head away, still murmuring: "You mustn't," and remained passive in his arms.

Just as they were reaching St. Mary Abbott's, Fenor released her.

"You're not angry with me?" he said.

Grace did not reply. She stood up, cautiously bending towards the door. She did not speak. He remained a second, holding her hand.

"Is it safe to write?" he asked.

She nodded.

"I'll write to you," said Fenor, quickly.

She gave him a long, slow smile, and one look of her humid green eyes.

VIII

Grace lay upon her back, her eyes wide open to the ceiling. She had just waked up and was still so quiescent that she noted almost with indifference the striking of the hour at St. Mary Abbott's. Three times it came. A quarter to eight, she mechanically recorded. She was just conscious of things about her, the weight of the blankets, rather too heavy for this warm weather, the ceiling which seemed so enormous and so white when one looked up at it, and Edward's breathing, a little stertorous in the companion bed. She was so inactive that she vaguely wondered whether she would go to sleep again. But then she heard something, some way off across the square: rattattat. The post.

All her senses leaped into activity. She felt her hands clenching, listened tensely to this sound coming nearer: the romance of the post winging towards her. But how slowly! There were endless pauses after some of the double knocks, pauses that thrilled her because they meant that the postman was passing doors. But here again it came, swiftly; she raged, he was not passing doors any more. It would be long, so long. Oh, here it was, quite near — and now a pause, a long, terrible pause. Could he have passed her door? And she did not trouble to ask herself why all her nerves were taut as piano wires. Only one thing was essential, that the postman should not pass her door.

The postman knocked. A thud in her heart served as an echo to the special double sound, sharp through the window and muffled through the house, which is made by a knock at one's own door. There were letters. Impulsively her hand went out towards the bell. No, it would never do. She could not ask the housemaid to come into the bedroom with her husband sleeping there; she had never done it before, and servants were so prudish. She must wait. But after two or three minutes a rage of impatience seized her. She would have to wait an hour. No, that was impossible. Ceding to impulse she jumped out of bed, and in slippers and dressing-gown ran down-stairs.

There were the letters upon the mahogany slab. She bent over them: three for Edward; for her two obvious bills, a coal advertisement, and an equally obvious invitation to dinner. That was all.

She went up-stairs again very slowly, leaving undisturbed the letters for which she had taken the risk of looking singular. Grace had many moods that day, moods of excitement when the postman's knock rang through the house, moods of tenseness as she came in in the afternoon having missed a post, moods of quiet, grey depression as she reflected that nothing would come. She was angry with Fenor. He had said he would write. He should have written at once. Surely there was much more he wanted to tell her than he had said, and she was unhappy. For as the hours passed she felt as a flower in dry, caked ground, that longs for water as every minute the sun shines more fiercely. The grey depression reasserted itself in the evening, which seemed to drag. It settled upon her still more the next day, when again nothing came, and to grow purposeful, massively crushing, on the third of those empty days. Then she reacted. It was better so. It was all very well talking of the adventure of love, but did she love him? She told herself "No." He disturbed her, but she did not love him. She had no passionate desire to see him, speak to him, touch him. That was all right. And she was not experienced enough in love to ask herself what it would feel like if she never saw, heard, or touched him again. It was all over, she reflected, if it had ever begun. He had played with her, amused himself with her, doubtless picked up some other woman five minutes after leaving her. Well, that was all right; she too had only amused herself with him. It had been very amusing, very nice. The thing to do now was to forget all about him and find something else to do. She had several engagements that day. She decided to buy a hat; there are very few sorrows in the world which are not assuaged by buying a really becoming hat. But Fenor hung behind her. He was not actual to her, but once or twice she thought of him precisely, and thought of him as Enoch. The name filled her, the name rather than the man. It was so hard, Northern, biblical. There was something about it like granite, or rather like the wood and steel, knotted together, with which engineers built bridges. So, when she bought the becoming hat, she hated herself for a second because she had caught herself thinking: "I wonder what Enoch would say to that?"

Then the letter came. It was quite short:

"SWEET RUSSET,

"I have thought of you for four days, and sleep has seemed waste because I am not of those who dream, and so I have lost some thirty or forty hours which nothing will give me back. I haven't written because I did not know what to say. It seemed I wanted to say so much or so little, and even now, as I write, I hardly know whether it is going to be very much or very little.

"I think it will be a very little because when I look at it again it is all I've got to say: I love you. ENOCH."

She read the letter eight or nine times. Then she fixed her eyes upon the last three words and read naught save them. She forgot them, because conscious only of the precipitate beating of her heart. She read the letter over again and was filled with a little ache of disappointment. It was so short, and it was not at all what she thought a love-letter ought to be. She grew colder; she remembered the published volumes of love-letters, passionate, lyrical, interminable love-letters, exhausting all the resources of hyperbole, glowing with metaphors, full of sumptuous adjectives. Those letters were long, passionate cries, or wistful weepings. And this letter, so short — it might have been a business note written upon a memorandum.

Then she abused herself. Fool that she was! Could she not see that the word was the word whether couched in a hundred pages or in one? He had not forgotten her, indeed he loved her. "Is that not," she asked herself, aloud, "Paradise enow?" And thought herself profoundly literary because she quoted Omar. She pulled herself up. No, she would not be literary. She would take this letter just as if she had been a cavalier, walking by some dark Venetian balcony, and as if some small hand coming between the blind had thrown her a rose to catch. She was alone; she looked about her anxiously, folded the letter up and thrust it through the front of her low-necked blouse. All that day she shivered whenever she felt it warm and crinkling against her breast.

But, as another day passed, a more positive desire came to her. He had written her this exquisite thing, but he had said nothing about seeing her again. This offended and yet excited her. Perhaps he did not want to see her again. That was nonsense: here was his letter, a thing surely "in the nature of evidence," as Edward would put it. Could he be playing with her, after all? A spasm of rage shook her, and then she felt herself become inert: if he wanted to play with her, he might. She was past struggling; she had wanted him too long, for many years before she saw him, she had been waiting for him all the time, all those years while, sacrificed too early, she clamoured that she must bloom again. She consulted no longer the ghosts of the dead Westfields: had they advised she could not have obeyed, for marriage and all it meant had run its course, and here was a new youth, a reawakening of desires, of hopes, a new craving to be a woman and to find expression in man. For can the bud repress the flower within its green sheath?

She was sinking into a sweet, languorous softness. In the streets she saw no ugly men and women, nor ragged children, and the skies were fair. All that was ugly she filmed with some rosiness of hope, or did not see. And it hastened her pulse to see the young couples go past hand in hand. She seemed to be all love. In the street she stopped to speak to the animals, to caress the cats, very long, with a delight in their warm furriness and the response of their supple bodies. The days passed and she seemed to want no more. Could this be enough? she wondered. Could she indeed be so warmed by a distant love? And only from time to time did she answer her own question and say: "I think it's enough now, but it will not be enough; I shall want more."

IX

Another letter came. This time it was long. It gave her a shock to see that it was dated from Moscow. Hurriedly she looked at the envelope: this was addressed to her in typewriting, and had been posted in London. She could not understand and, for a moment, could not read on. In Moscow! Could he — could he have left her? But purposefully, once more, she set to the reading. The letter covered three sheets of quarto paper. It began with a brief statement that business had taken him to Russia. Then, abruptly, it passed from him to her and, having reached her, did not leave her; it was her Song of Solomon. She read it from end to end, and then those last lines, so brief, so imperative, final. She was alone in her bedroom. She laid the letter down upon the dressing-table and looked at it much as she would have looked at a jewel, backing a little so as to see better. The languor had passed away from her and her blood went racing. In that minute she knew that she loved, for she had wanted this letter badly, and now that it had come it was not just a mild satisfaction, or even a complete satisfaction; it was that infinitely better thing, a new log thrown upon her flame.

She took up the letter again, read it through, then concentrated upon one passage which seemed to her to contain all the world in which she moved:

". . . I beg you, do not be offended because I praise your beauty, and all of you, all the sweetness and the response of you. Most men, I know, do not do these things. But if you are tempted to be offended, do know that I believe it is woman's first right to be worshipped. It is a churl refuses to applaud when the curtain falls on the perfect play; and it is a churl that doesn't tell a woman of her beauty when she has devoted art, labour and fine thought to making herself such as to go about the world shedding delight. For, after all, immortal beauty, immortal in our memory, is the only thing that endureth ever in our hearts as they grow old, and there are dusky cheeks, folds of silk, bendings in the stalks of flowers, that have for ever marked me, inoculated me with youth. And this too I feel in my own love of you, that woman hears these things not often enough, is not told by husband or lover that she stands in apotheosis as the triumph of the forces of life. She wants it . . . so badly. She craves, and vainly, for her Song of Songs — "

Abruptly, still all shaken, as if some cruelly strong hand had gripped at her most intimate fibres, she passed on to those last lines:

" I shall arrive in the early morning on the ninth of May. At four in the afternoon I shall come to you. Be alone."

The intervening days, of which there were five, passed away with miraculous swiftness. She could not understand this. Her first feeling had been: " Oh, how long it will be! " But time did not speed: it oozed away. She seemed to be busy with mechanical tasks: house, husband, child, fellow creature. There were things to be done and to be thought of: she did them and thought of them, but behind these activities was a consciousness of her own life unrolling, so purposeful, so natural, that she was no more conscious of time than of that process of disintegration of the body which slowly and inevitably leads man to death. And so, quite naturally, came the ninth of May. Quite naturally she decked herself for the feast, ordering the autumn bracken of her hair about her forehead so as to leave exposed the freckles that spattered the whiteness as bran might milk, the freckles now beloved of her because he loved them. With a touch of salve she enriched her lips. And she looked fondly at her manicured fingernails because they shone like coral. Of her clothing she hardly thought. Again quite naturally she chose a loose green gown that left her neck and forearms bare.

She stood in the drawing-room and was as a woodnymph, so slender in the straight folds of the green silk that moulded her soft curves. There was no fever in her hands, but an expectant quietude in the humid green of her eyes.

The clock struck four; the chimes blended with the tinkling of the bell. Almost at once he came, or rather appeared, and she felt herself smiling a little shyly as she stood before him, her hands clasped together, quite unable to give him a conventional salutation. As the door closed behind him, Fenor came towards her with quick steps and, unresisting, she felt his arms about her, his lips upon her cheek. She did not move, nor he, but almost unconsciously their close-pressed faces turned as they sought each other's lips. Their lips met, and they were fixed in their attitude as if they had fused together, blended.

She could not later remember much more of that afternoon. She knew that she had tried to be light, to ease the tension. She had asked him, among other trifles, how it was that the letter from Moscow had been posted in London. He had replied briefly that the Russian stamp would have aroused attention, and that the letter had been posted by a clerk in Victoria Street with thirteen others, addressed to non-existent persons so as to stifle the clerk's suspicions. The dead-letter office would deal with those thirteen others. She had laughed, and she had been glad when she thought that she had so wise a lover.

In the night she tried to explore herself. How could this be? so soon, and so easily? But then it had not been so soon, or so easily. It had been very long. She realised that she was ready and waiting. One thing only troubled her a little. Here were complexities coming, shiftings and secrecy, a double life. It was not the danger; that was nothing, for danger was life. But she suspected already there must be many ugly little stratagems and stolen meetings, hurried pleasures, hungers always unsatisfied. She would tread the roses on the path and the thorns too. Yet it thrilled her to think that she must tread thorns for his sake. Almost she fancied she would rather for him tread thorns than roses. As she sank into sleep, though, the regret was still with her: "Hide," she thought, "we must hide. It is cruel. Love ought to have been like the sunrise."

BOOK THE FOURTH

GRACE, CLARA, AND MARY

But who shall be drowsie at that howr which freed us from everlasting sleep? or have slumbering thoughts at that time when sleep itself must end, and as some conjecture all shall awake again.

(SIR THOMAS BROWNE.—*The Garden of Cyrus*.)

CHAPTER THE FIRST

JUNE

I

IT was not a merry, but a passionate month. The sky of day was hollow, like a pale blue vault, forsaken of English mists. From the illimitable depths came a radiance that seemed, as it touched them, to intoxicate the trees, to inspire every leaf with some fierce delight, with a desire to blend itself with the warm air that embraced it as a bridegroom. The flowers were . . . thundering; the geraniums in their boxes desperately strove to be yet redder, and the marguerites spread white wings; the water-lilies in the pond waxed fat and sumptuous like white, pampered sultanas upon rippling green couches; and as the reluctant sun left the heavens behind, he gilded the little clouds into innumerable shapes of lions and foxes, of legless flamingoes, into a wild pageantry of colour and heat where all things were rosy or scarlet, or blazing, as if copper fought gold for mastery.

As Grace set out to go to Fenor, she found that the violent energy of life about her, that seemed to fill all things, flowers and beasts already mated and content, men and women more urgent and still restless, demanding more of love and life because the sun was so high and so hot, its kiss upon their skins, was attuned to her. She was herself intimate with the earth, earth-conscious, and glad as if for many years she had allowed herself to abstain from trying to guess the riddle. She knew that she had not the meaning of life, and that no man hath, but still, that if it be a riddle there was virtue in facing the sphinx; for many years she had allowed the sphinx to set her riddles without attempting to answer, without even thinking it might be worth while to try and guess the riddle, even if failure meant that she would be devoured. As she went now, along a road to which she was becoming accustomed, she was content, though into her contentment there filtered something which had never come into the placid lives of the Marys of the world. She knew to what she was going and as she walked, slowly, conscious of the sun that burnt through her parasol and made her neck glow, she reviewed again the recent past. She remembered little things of Enoch: the first time she had been to his flat, the shrinking into the corner of the cab lest she should be seen, the attempts to be " sensible " when she told herself that, even if she were seen, there was no harm in riding alone in a taxi, and the delicious consciousness that one might be conscious of guilt — the block of flats, so familiar once upon a time when she passed it on the way to the Stores, now magical and threatening — the scurry up the stairs, past offices of colonial agents and societies, office-boys, girls from the typewriting agency who seemed so inquisitive, as if they knew — and the breathless interminable moment when, for the first time, she rang the bell. It seemed so long that in those seconds she could almost feel herself growing older — and then, just his arms round her, a veil before her eyes, and the world forgot.

She had been afraid, dreadfully afraid, she hardly knew of what. She tried not to be afraid, believing, so foolish and young was she in love, that fear, danger or villainy makes love less good. She had tried to tell herself that she was not doing wrong; she thought she would love better if she thought she was not doing wrong. Often, during those weeks, she had told herself that there was nothing to fear, that London was so vast; it had comforted her to find out that its population was greater than that of Belgium; somehow she felt better lost now she knew there were as many Londoners as there were men of a whole nation. And also she told herself that there was nothing to fear. She was still a bourgeoise, and it made her much stronger to know that she had a little money of her own. One is what one is. Grace tried, but even after the first kiss she could not forget that money counts; to know that she could stand alone gave her a strength that she could not otherwise have had, for she belonged to a society which has built itself on wealth and without wealth cannot stand. And so she was nobler in her courage than those others, Bohemians or workers, who could take all risks because they had nothing to risk; and yet, inconceivable paradox, she was less noble because she went into the struggle risking less, because nothing that she did could take from her her power to live.

Again she reviewed in advance what would happen. She knew: she would pass those offices more casually now, and she would not ring the bell, for she had a key; she would go into the sitting-room and find him there alone, his man dismissed. She could see the sitting-room without closing her eyes: the big, masculine leather chairs, the guns and spears upon the wall, the bronze group of a man throttling a panther. And, with a little thrill, she saw other things: the pipes upon the mantelpiece, the tumbled, untidy heaps of books, the big table littered with plans, where a specimen or two of ore gleamed golden or green. On a chair perhaps an old coat, the coat which he wore when he made a tracing: emotion blurred her eyes as she thought of the old tobacco-scented coat, worn into the shape of his shoulders and elbows. He would be waiting for her, he would say nothing, but just take her in his arms, and there she would stay awhile, as a ship after a long voyage moors lazily at the wharf —

There were many things she hated which she would not have hated had she not been what she still was: pure in mind and driven by a coalition of obscure forces. She hated the idea of secrecy, the careful working-out of safeguards, and the hint he had given her that, if she had a very dear friend, she should arrange with her a permanent alibi. She hated Fenor's carefulness, the way in which he took from her a railway or cloak-room ticket, a music-hall programme, so that nothing about her should ever reveal where she had been. She knew that it was necessary, but she hated it because it was too expert. Fiercely she wanted him to be clumsy, dangerous, young, so that, being the first woman in the world for him, she might feel the only one. For she loved him, and she was jealous of the past, though she had slain it. She hated those shadows of women who had passed through his life. Sometimes she could not understand her lover's almost ghoulish pleasure in deceiving society, his cynical vein.

"Don't you see?" he had said to her, "what fun it is? Here you are, Mrs. Kinnersley, a matron of Kensington, moving in the best society, well-housed, well-gowned, well-wedded, doing the right things with the right people — a sort of shell, beautifully painted, and under it — "

"A bad woman," she had suddenly replied.

He had held her closer. "No, no, not a bad woman. The most beautiful, the most beloved woman in the world, who has not been afraid to be happy." And then, murmuring into the warm bracken of her hair: "And it's just that that's so wonderful, that inside the painted coffin they call respectability, escaping now and then and exchanging its shroud for a garment of gold and purple, for a caress unknown to the mourners of Kensington, is the beautiful, living spirit that haunts me."

She had shuddered a little, though she was glad. She was still too young in love to understand it in its neurotic moods; she could not yet understand that a greater intensity might creep into passion if one knew it to be transient, that one might love more urgently, with a greater fierceness, if one knew that soon the body, temple of that love, would fade, wither, die, then decay — that haste to live made living more intense.

They could not go out together, except now and then, hiding in a box at a suburban theatre. One night, by separate conveyances, they went to Sadler's Wells. They took a box in which were four decrepit chairs, and they looked out, now and then, upon the shadowy auditorium where the people were dotted about on benches as sparsely as chessmen upon a board. They had seen a little of the play, laughed at the villain and at the comic servants but, mainly, they had pushed their chairs back so that they could not be seen save from the stage. All that evening Fenor's arm had been about her, holding her close, and she had let her head fall upon his shoulder until her hair was all tangled, and her face and neck marked and warm with his kisses — she was like a very small cat, stroked by an enormous hand. She had been without will, without desire, had been all yield and response. His voice, murmuring thickly into her ear, had been as a voice from some other world, distant yet familiar. She had tried to be light, shown him her hands all blackened with dust, for everything that they touched, the chairs, the velvet edge of the box and the hangings, was filthy.

"That's not very inviting," she said, holding them out. But Fenor had given a little gasp, bent forward and pressed his lips to the grimy palms, pressed her hands against his face with a sort of despair, as if an impulse bade him degrade himself before her, do things that were ugly, just to show her and again to show her that he loved her more than the ambient ugliness.

For he loved her. He had known many women and in many countries. He had loved often, that is, made love, and lightly. He had made love recklessly, without fear of the perils that follow upon recklessness. He had held his life cheap, and yet in the tendernesses, in the attractions of rosy lips, of quick wits, of the sudden softness, the sympathetic pities and the little motherly cares with which women make up that sumptuous feast of soul and body which is love, he had never found what he found in Grace. She filled a need which he hardly knew he had, though it was quite simple: to love and be loved. Some women had satisfied in him a fury of sense; others had wept because he was unhappy; others had been proud of him, afraid of him, or had dominated him by some elegance of mind, but not one had done all these things together. And Grace, without consciousness, without apprenticeship, did them. It was not only that he loved her as a woman, but as a human being, a creature mentally sentient, who understood not only his emotions, which is rare enough, but his ideas, his ambitions, who guessed, without knowing, that life for him was a romance. To him Grace seemed to realise all hopes.

And yet, even in that sumptuousness, there remained in Fenor the streak of cynicism which prevented him from rebelling against the secrecy, made him enjoy the evasions and the shifts. He had understood very well when Grace told him how she hated calling for her letters at the little tobacconist's in the Fulham Road.

"It's dreadful, Enoch!" she had murmured. "There's an old woman, very, very fat and very, very ill . . . her shop smells of tobacco and stale sweets . . . she's half-blind and she fumbles in a big box full of letters from a hundred other people who, like us, want to hide. Some of them are so dirty that they must have been there a long time, as if people to whom they were sent didn't call for them, didn't care any more." She threw him a quick, anxious look, and he understood, bent down to caress her. "And she fumbles," she went on, "fumbles and fumbles among old letters that have been there a year, letters from people who have forgotten — and when, at last, she finds mine, she gives it to me. And I give her a penny, she tells me it's a fine day, and then, I don't know whether it's because she's half blind, I believe she . . . winks at me. Oh, it's horrible."

"No, my sweet," said Fenor, "it isn't really horrible. Don't you see that if it weren't horrible, as you call it, nothing else in the world would be good? You wouldn't know what paradise is like if, now and again, you didn't go to hell."

It impaired his love a little, this knowledge, this expertness. He knew too exactly how to feel and how he would feel if he threw into his emotions some extraneous material fact. Yet he loved her. And he knew that he loved her when in the long hours they passed together, when she was quiescent in his arms, a soft allure of inertia which a word or a touch from him could quicken into response, he knew that a happiness had come to him that seemed more delicious than it was because he knew, with neurotic intensity, that it could never happen again. . . .

Once, suddenly impulsive, she wound about both their heads the long flowing masses of her hair, binding them together. He saw the light gleaming through the russet veil and there was a delicious sting at his heart, for he knew that this hair must fade. And so he drew her closer, yet with a fierce urgency, so that he might love her more while there was time. . . .

II

It was six o'clock. Grace, in the kimono of heavy, green silk that hung about her in rigid folds, stood at the tall narrow window, her hands resting against the sides so that the broad sleeves, falling sheer and immense, made of her a shimmering green moth all gilded with the sun about to set slowly over the empurpled roofs. From this high window she could see over Pimlico into the far haze of the south, pierced here and there by the sun-gilded spire of a church and the distant black rod of a smokestack. As she looked into the crimson which, she knew, would, as the hours went by, slowly fade into gentler colours, into yellow paler than the daffodil's, into green more tender than that of a flowing stream, she was happy. Still the memory of love was on her, and abstract, as if this man whom she could hear behind her, moving unseen, author of and partner in her delight, were but an incident separate from that delight. In this minute she knew that Enoch existed much as she knew that there were forces in nature, lightnings in those clouds which she could see slowly travelling in the sky, like ships with coppery sails; her lover was potential then rather than actual; more than a lover, he was love. Confusedly she seemed to understand for the first time that all this happiness upon which she had laid her hand was within her, with all the pains, had always been there, much as the evils, together with hope, had lain hidden in Pandora's chest. At his bidding she had opened the chest; the evils had flown out and hope had remained. It was like a revelation, the fact that she, her energy, her will to joy, were the explosive of which the man who loved her was naught save the detonator.

She heard his voice behind her and did not move, not even when he laid his hands upon her shoulders and drew them softly along her arms, lingeringly, as if every one of his fingers regretted to part, second by second, from the gracious surface they caressed. Then his voice:

"Aurora, they say, draws fingers of rose across the black heavens. See! your arm is all rosy with light." He bent down and almost reverently laid his lips to her arm just over the elbow. Passive, she submitted to the caress. As he held her closer, once more she had that strange sensation that she was all formless, fluid; as she lay, her head drooping upon his shoulder, the heavy bone of which she could feel through the thick veil of her unbound hair, and again as, bending down, she gave him her lips and closed her eyes to the blinding sun, she knew that she was flowering.

But soon he released her. He had been nervous that day, oppressed, as if he regretted a little their meeting. She was conscious of it, but not angry, for she thought he could not always be attuned to the greatest delight, and she was beginning to adopt his rather cynical philosophy which made her think that weariness was good; for without weariness there could be no zest. But, as she looked at him again, at the strong face with the irregular features, the mouth which seemed that day more tender, a little frightened, a pity invaded her. She was maternal; for she loved him; she was one of those women who take unto themselves a child when they take a lover.

"What is it, Enoch?" she asked. "There's something troubling you, isn't there?"

He laughed, unsteadily. "Well, Russet, yes. The fact is I've got to read a paper to-morrow night at the Institution."

"A paper!" cried Grace. "Do you mean a lecture or something?"

"Yes," said Fenor, gloomily, "I've got to read a paper

on The Eruptive Rocks of the Tarakan Range and the disturbances thus entailed upon the sedimentary beds of Northern Burmah."

"Heavens!" cried Grace, "what words! Whatever do they mean?"

He was still gloomy. "Oh, I don't think I'll start teaching you geology, Russet. It isn't exactly a bright topic, but what's worrying me is that I've got stage fright."

For a moment Grace looked at him in silence. That delicate mouth of his was drooping, rather childish now. It seemed absurd to her that this big man, who for so many years had fought, and starved, and loved, and somehow staggered into success and happiness, should be afraid of so little a thing. Impulsively she threw a soft, warm arm about his neck and, as swiftly she kissed his cheek, she laughed the beautiful, faltering laugh of a woman in love, that comes deep and hesitating, very low down in the throat, that beautiful laugh which rallies and caresses, and is uncertain because it holds no merriment, but is all nervous and thrilled.

"Silly boy," she said, "you must let me come and hear you. When is it?"

"To-morrow night, but don't think of coming — you won't understand it and you'll be bored stiff."

"Bored stiff!" cried Grace, indignantly. "How can you say that, Enoch? How could I be bored while you talked?"

He smiled, tolerantly, playing now with her fingers. "It's much more possible than you think," he said. "You see, I'll be talking geology, I shan't be talking about myself." He smiled more broadly. "I know you can stand a lot of that."

She gave him a playful dig with her elbow.

"Peacock!" she said. "I don't want to hear any more about your precious self. I'd much rather hear about geology; it'll improve my mind. So don't let's argue, I'm coming. I know where the Institution is."

"Oh, Russet," said Fenor, a little anxiously, "don't. I don't want to break down before you; it'll be bad enough to break down before three hundred people without your being one of them."

"No, my mind is made up. I'm coming to-morrow night, and if you don't give me an invitation card I'll go and see the president and—if I'm as nice as you say, he won't be so cruel."

There was a pause, then Fenor smiled.

"You do a fellow good, Russet. You haven't said anything about my doing the trick, but somehow you seem so sure that I will."

She took his head between her hands and looked at him for a moment. Then she said: "Of course you will. The man I love is invincible. Besides," she added, suddenly commonplace, as if instinct taught her the art of charming, "Edward's out to-morrow night and I shall be at home alone and bored. I'd better go to the Institution and be bored by you than by myself—" Again a swift, charming, instinctive change: "And you can drive me home after."

So the next evening, at half-past eight, Grace sat in the gallery of the Institution, a large building in Westminster, up the venerable marble stairs of which she had walked, causing great astonishment among the crowd of old and established engineers, and of callow students from the School of Mines who wondered whose wife she was or whether she were one of those queer Russian girls who had decided to emancipate their sex by invading the professions of men. They would have been more surprised if they had seen her better for, to avoid recognition, she had dressed her hair in a new fashion, well over her ears, and wrapped her head in an unusually thick veil which, with her simple tweed clothes, made her into a rigid and business-like figure. In the gallery the attendance was sparse. There were half a dozen young men, probably candidates for the associateship of the Institution, who sat all together, talking very busily in low voices, laughing very often at private jokes which she could not hear. They were rough-looking young men in soft hats, with very thick sticks and thick boots and a rather staring air, as if proclaiming that they were no popinjays, and that they could handle a pickaxe better than a teacup. A quite recognisable class, less bright-eyed and rowdy than the medical student, less well-dressed and frigid than the law student, and they had none of the obstreperous, loud pose of the undergraduate. They looked at Grace very hard, all of them, and when they caught her eye she was much embarrassed; the young mining men also looked away, much more embarrassed, though pretending to be most aloof. There was laughter in the group which she did not understand, rather thick, throaty laughter. Some silly, private joke, she thought.

Dotted about among the elder men, many of whom wore frock-coats in memoriam, and the rougher, red-brown people in tweeds who had dropped in on the way from Peru to Pekin, were only four women, one of them extraordinarily old, who calmly read a book on the subliminal consciousness, and was clearly in charge of an equally old husband whom she would have to wrap up and put to bed after the discussion; there were two faded, middle-aged women who had probably bought their clothes in St. Paul's Churchyard and were there, presumably having wedded Scotch engineers, because they were following their husbands as wives should. And there was a blushing young thing who seemed extraordinarily uncomfortable, if the continual shifting of her feet meant anything, doubtless the very recent bride of a member, come to see him do great things. She exchanged friendly glances with Grace, who covertly smiled at her, realising they had both come to admire their men; Grace felt maternal and sympathetic in that minute for, from time to time, she could see the girl's left shoulder grow quite rigid and slowly rise, as if she were keeping down some powerful, nervous excitement.

But soon the hall itself held her attention. It was built on the lines of an amphitheatre; the benches were already almost entirely occupied by members and associates, the usual assemblage of grey heads and bald heads; in the well, raised a little, was the platform, on which, as she looked, stepped the president and the council. She could not see Fenor and was anxious. She was afraid that stage-fright had been too much for him. If he did not come it would be dreadful, it would make him ridiculous; she felt a pang of anger at the idea that the man she loved might for a moment be ridiculous in the eyes of others. It did not matter if he were ridiculous in hers, for that made him only more lovable, but all others he must dominate if she were still to love him.

The president rose, made some announcements she could not catch. Then a little thin man, with protruding eyes and the most emaciated legs she had ever seen, read the report of current business, of meetings held, resolutions passed by the council, made incomprehensible allusions to the work of sub-committees. Her impatience grew. She hated the little man, his droning voice and all this futile talk about scholarships and silver medals, this farrago of technical words. She thought that the creature, the secretary no doubt, so small and so worried behind his eye-glasses, looked like an urgent, anxious little dog who had once known a good home and then been given away to the charwoman. She clenched her hands and looked at the blushing young wife; they exchanged a glance of sympathy which said: "Will they never have done? Won't it be His turn next?"

Then, quite suddenly, Fenor appeared: a tall and rather shrinking figure behind the backs of the seated council. He looked up to the gallery, and unerringly their eyes met; she made her smile broad so that he might see it well and be encouraged. He smiled back, a little mournfully, and, as he seated himself, Grace, throwing sidelong glances to the young wife, saw disappointment and envy in her eyes. They understood each other, those two. The secretary was still droning on, relating endless discussions on round shafts versus rectangular, on the applications of something that sounded like melinelonite to driving in decomposed rock. . . . A fury of impatience seized Grace. Would they never give him a chance? Then Fenor was on his feet, having been introduced in half a dozen words and greeted by applause which Grace thought disgracefully scanty. She had made herself quite ridiculous in the gallery by clapping Fenor as he stepped forward. And so had the young wife, for the subtle sympathy that united the two women had also made her clap Fenor hard, though, presumably, she did not know him. "You back my man and I'll back yours," the two women tacitly signalled to each other.

Fenor disappointed her. Was this rambling, lame statement that basalt and porphyry were the chief components —

Grace lost herself. And then an endless, incomprehensible argument as to the relation of the upthrust with a fault located some twenty miles away. Could this be the magic speech she was awaiting? Fenor read badly; he hesitated, he stumbled; three times he failed to pronounce clearly "oligocene." For a second Grace hated him, and she found herself whispering to herself: "He must do it better, he must." Even his voice had changed. The beautiful soft tones that came low from his throat and like honey, had become harsh, grating. She guessed that his throat was dry with excitement, and across the space she passionately willed that he should drink a gulp of water, but he did not; his voice still came hard and toneless; his audience was bored. The members below lay back rather listless on the benches; in the gallery the young men had again begun to whisper. Then the very old lady suddenly dropped the book on the subliminal consciousness, with a bang that made Grace start and grow hot.

But what was this? Here was a change, a change even in the voice, which deepened, began to vibrate like a caressed violin string. And what was this he was saying that she could understand? Was this geology?

". . . and then we struck camp and loaded the stores upon the waggons. It was three hours before dawn, for we wanted to break the back of our journey before the heat of the day. High in the heavens sat the moon, that was flat and orange-red as if she were blushing — we had four waggons drawn by oxen that were, all of them, white as snow, and that night in the beams of the moon, bathed in silver and in gold. We had left the range behind us, and the convoy trailed ahead of me, the shadows of the oxen black upon the white sand as if painted in China ink. At the head of each team walked a coolie cast in golden bronze — "

What was this? He was no longer reading from his notes, but speaking, and his eyes, fixed upon the glass vault over Grace's head, seemed to see the stars.

". . . We seemed to go so slowly, as if there was no such thing as haste and as if we didn't care whether we reached that other range which I could see upon the sky-line, cut out sharp like black lace against a heaven that was bluer than the deepest sea. Upon the sand the oxen trod soundless, and not even a cart creaked. We were as a procession of ghosts making for some immaterial goal. I seemed to think just then that it didn't matter whether we passed from the silence we were leaving into some other silence, for there are not two silences in the East, not three, but one silence where all life revolves as if bound to a wheel ever returning to the same point — I didn't think about geology just then, with the silver and the gold gleaming upon the oxen's flanks, and in my nostrils the wind — the wind of the night all soaked with the soft, sweet smell of the flowers of the tamarinds — "

Grace felt within her something swell, as if tears were near, for Fenor, his eyes still fixed above him, was speaking dreamily, almost as if he were speaking to himself and as if suddenly seized by a languor, by some incomprehensible memory of a softness and a sweetness. Round her the others had gone tense: the very old lady, who had picked up her book, had let it fall into her lap; the chattering young men had ceased to chatter, or even to look at her and at the young woman, who bent forward fascinated, her lips a little parted. Then Fenor broke the charm.

"The feldspaths of the Tarakan Range," he began again, harshly, "disappointed me in their alumina contents. You will have concluded from the statements I made as to local metamorphic formations that not less than four per cent. of anhydrous silicate was to be expected, given that igneous action. . . ."

They listened contentedly enough, for clearly it was a good paper, if ill-delivered, but the charm had vanished. Grace, looking into the well, could see several men making copious notes while the president, from time to time, nodded gravely, so that his long white beard swayed, while the extraordinarily fat man by his side worked himself into some state of excitement and continually whispered to him with an air of indignation. Half an hour had elapsed and the paper was nearly at an end. Fenor was describing some old workings where the formation he was expecting had been exposed, and it seemed as if there the paper would end, adequate, competent, and dull. But the workings were very old, Fenor said, perhaps aboriginal. He stopped, looked at the paper of which he held the last sheet; evidently the paper was done, but he hesitated, laid the sheet upon the table and said:

"I don't know why I thought of them just then, that band of primitive engineers, just eight or ten black men, with their loins bound up in white, standing round a fire of wood that reared its flame into the night like a torch, smelting the ore, and watching the metal appear more clearly with a sort of wonder — a long time before the days of Krishna, Siva and Vishnu perhaps. That metal being born of fire — it was a god or a god's gift — to a dozen black men, stumbling upon truth, and standing round the work of their own hands, wondering whether it was god or demon who had made those hands assured — "

Grace did not remember much of the discussion, which was hot, involved and to her incomprehensible but, a little later, as Fenor drove her back and she lay in his arms in the cab, she could hardly answer when he asked her whether she had been bored. She nestled closer and said: "No, no, it was wonderful."

"I was in a blue funk," said Fenor.

She stroked his cheek. "Only when you weren't being yourself."

"I don't know what you mean," said Fenor. He did not realise that the poet in him had dominated the engineer. She loved him for that obtuseness and she felt boastful as she thought that after all her man had justified himself. It would have been a reflection upon her if he had not, and it troubled her not at all to think that this bold man suffered from timidity. For was it not splendid that with her he should not be timid?

III

Enoch Fenor, Grace began to perceive, was the triumph of environment over heredity. During those first weeks he had often talked of himself, of his early life and the first influences that made it. They had loved and made love, and he had talked — enormously. She had curiosities of his youth; she had often pried into that childhood near Birmingham and into his memories of Rugby, but he was not very responsive. It was as if those early years, those times of school and university which matter so much to the ordinary man, did not matter to him, doubtless because the ordinary man does not grow up and sees still as epic the footer, the practical joke and the boat-race night of his youth. Nor was he very much more talkative when she wanted to know what he had done with his early manhood in so many countries. It looked as if nothing existed for Fenor save the moment, and as if his one desire were to find a moment to which he could say: "*Verweile doch, du bist so schön;*" every day he buried his dead past and he had an answer to all oppositions, to all suggestions that something might be dangerous or might be unwise:

"Why not?" he would say, "in another ten minutes we may be dead." And that indeed was reason enough; more than a reason: it was a stimulant. "Enjoy!" was his cry, "for as we speak, we die." It was not only "let us eat, drink, and be merry, for to-morrow —" It was much more. It was "let us eat, drink, and be merry, let our souls flame, let our minds and our brains soar into fierce activity, for as we speak some strength ebbs from us, these eyes grow dim and this strength waxes faint. As we think in our greatest power, our reserve power grows less and the body, which is as a flower, with every second decays."

"It's a race," he said, sometimes, "a race between pleasure and death, and we're bound to be licked, you know, in the end. But, by God, I'll have a good run for my money."

When he said such things as these, Grace shuddered. She was still one of those people who could not view life wholly, who could not with any actuality see herself lying waxen and in her shroud; despair of life could not for her enhance the joy of life; she could not see that it is death makes life vital. She did not connect youth and age: age, disease, death, those were things that happened to other people and which should be pushed away from the sort of somnambulistic dream which still she called life. She was soft, sentimental, she was tender, she was all those things which make up a human being, unguided. And so, sometimes, she failed to rise to an understanding of the man who seemed to have with both hands seized his own life and steered it as he would, where he would. But though she could not understand, she could sympathise, for she loved enough to be able to love those things which passed her understanding.

There were many such mysteries in Fenor's temperament, for he was the very opposite of the men she was accustomed to; he was not consistent.

"To call a man consistent," he said, "is another way of calling him a damned fool. The most consistent thing in the world is a needle-making machine; you can always back it to turn out its goods to sample, but, thanks, I'd rather be a sort of Vesuvius whirling Lord knows what into the air."

Such ideas fired him, for he was compounded of two strands: in his attitude towards life he inclined to realism, yet turned, by a not unnatural antithesis, towards violent romanticism, a romanticism sometimes unconvincingly exuberant, and yet true to his actual self. More than anything he was a lyrical person, and often in speech he was word-drunk: he might have bound himself down to any view if he could embody it in a happy, but beautiful phrase. Certain things, mainly passionate, some colours, some scents, music such as that of the bagpipes, and ideas which he did not really hold himself, such as freedom for Poland, a world church, art for the democracy, or the aristocrat as despot, all these could inflame him, merely because they were large and dominating. He was an epicurean, even in matters of intellect; he loved all things that gave him satisfaction and none others. He had never argued with himself about right and wrong: the question had not interested him. He had not even condescended to justify himself by adopting a philosophical theory based on the agreeable. When Grace asked him whether he sometimes did not think that he had done wrong in approaching her, he said:

"There are two ways of living in the world; one of them is never to do anything of which you can be ashamed, and the other is of never being ashamed of what you do. I prefer the second way."

"Oh!" cried Grace, who remained a Puritan and who would always remain a Puritan, whatever she did, "surely you can't govern your sense of shame?"

"No," said Fenor, "I don't govern it, I merely don't feel shame. Why should I?"

Grace had been a little shocked by this attitude; she felt that Fenor could commit every crime, and that though he might perhaps feel fear, shame he could not, for he seemed to have taken all the moralities and thrown them behind him.

"They talk very glibly," he said, "of the respect we ought to have for life, and how dreadful murder is. But is it? We kill the ox and the sheep, why not man? We hang man legally, that is to say in virtue of the will of the majority through the minority, and the majority is always wrong; so why should not we, each one of us a minority, exercise our own discrimination to execute those whom we think evil? We kill men in war without even the excuse that they have done us some harm, and in all nature something kills something: a Sikh told me once, in India, that the tiger eats the leopard, that eats the panther, that eats the wildcat. There are only two kinds of people, you see: the weak ones who make faces and the strong ones who bite. 'Cats and monkeys,' as Henry James says, 'monkeys and cats: the whole of life is there.'"

They were then standing together against a white wall, near Denham, that was blazing in the sunshine as a tablecloth under electric lights.

"Enoch!" said Grace. "—Don't you think anything wrong? I see what you mean about murder, and of course one can excuse it sometimes, but other things, like stealing and lying, and—and what we're doing."

"Stealing," said Fenor, reflectively, "it's only wrong if property is right, and if property has value. Perhaps it hasn't, you see. How much better off are you for having six frocks and only one body?"

Grace laughed. "But somebody might steal the frock I wore!"

"What for?" asked Fenor. "If that other person has a frock too, she can't wear them both together. Don't you see that it is only because we want to possess more than we need that some of us steal?"

"But some people steal to eat," cried Grace.

"Why shouldn't they?" said Fenor. "If human life is as sacred as the suicide law makes out, then surely a man ought not to be sent to gaol for stealing to maintain life; he ought to be given a medal by the Royal Humane Society."

She laughed. She liked his paradoxes, which sometimes were hollow, but yet all of them sprang from something truthful in his nature, from the consciousness that there was no truth. For him life was an experience, and he inclined to think with Peter Pan that death too would be a very great adventure. And yet he was cynical. He seemed assured that charity was another name for remorse or patronage; that sacrifice was a voluptuous indulgence in pain; that the fulfilment of one's duty was a way of getting out of thinking out what one ought to do; that the love of man and woman was hostile, based on a desire mutually to dominate each other, to use each other for satisfactions, physical, mental, monetary. It was not base, this creed, and it was not bitter; it was serene.

"Why analyse a pleasure," he said, "if you are so fortunate as to feel it? Why make of some rosy illusion a drab reality? It's no use, for when you've soiled your illusion into drabness, even then you won't be sure it's reality. Anything you think, you see, is nothing but the dream of a giant asleep in a planet, a giant who is your self and for whose pleasure you're dreaming; but while you are he, you create him and the world that amuses him, yes, him, while you dream — "

She did not always understand him. She could not reconcile with the rest of him the efficiency which she guessed was in his work, his punctual keepings of appointments, his cunning, his readiness to lie, his shifts and evasions to shield her or himself, his taste for accurate accounts and the ease with which he could so quickly switch his thoughts from love to trains which should be caught. She could not reconcile all that with the bursting rhetoric which came from him quite truthfully, nor his sudden, passionate rages with his equally sudden wistfulness, almost Teutonically sentimental, before a flower with light blue petals or the golden hair of a child, nor again with the sombreness that seized him when he loved her, urgently, gloomily, desperately, conscious of the sweep over his head of the wings of the angel of death, always drawing nearer and bidding him hasten to enjoy, for the time was not long —

His life, the adventurousness of it, all the fighting and seeking, the loneliness, the drinkings, and the roisterings, and the black moments of fever and pain, all this, it made of his mind something like a kaleidoscope: any touch shook it into a new shape, every moment becoming laden with a significance that made it adventurous. That day, at Denham, quite suddenly he stopped as they crossed a ploughed field, seized Grace's hand, raised it to his eyes. He played with the short, capable, white fingers and solemnly laid a kiss upon every one.

"Beautiful hand," he murmured, "beautiful hand, wonderful."

Grace laughed nervously. "One might think you'd never seen it before, Enoch," she said.

"I haven't," he said, "never with the eyes with which I see it now, for, if I did see it some moments ago, have I not changed in those moments? and are my eyes not new? Oh, don't you understand? as we grow older, second by second, we see things with different eyes, and everything that we have seen already, when we see it again, becomes a new adventure because we are, each one of us, become a new adventurer."

She understood. She was a little afraid of him, of this violent impulsiveness and fantasy. He had spoken of Vesuvius, a little time before, throwing Lord knows what into the air, and as she went with him it was like walking over the lava under which you can hear rumblings and crashes, which lets out, here and there, little spirals of steam. But she knew that never before had she found in another man so powerful an excitement, that while he frightened he dominated her, because he seemed to hold up before her eyes a revolving mirror such as that which dazzles a lark. Sometimes she asked herself whether she loved him, whether he was not the man of a moment in her life and whether he was the man of all time. But she was too tired, perhaps too happy, perhaps too torn, to judge him sanely, and in the end she found herself thinking:

"Whether I love him or not, what does it matter? I think I do. And if illusion seems real, it is reality — "

She stopped, shivering, for she had a horrid sensation that phrases such as these could never have been framed by her three months before; much more secure than the capture of her passions was this capture of her intellect.

IV

They had gone to Denham that day by separate trains, and there had been something guilty and charming about their meeting outside the station, when they arrived, after the draper's traveller, the big farmer, the labourers had gone, and the governess cart had loaded up a tweedy girl and her golf-clubs. Grace was still afraid that she might be known, and found in her distracted mind no excuse for her presence. Much worse, she feared that, carried away by remorse and having confessed, she would find herself too weak to face the consequences of her deed.

But all that afternoon the sun streamed upon them, a pagan sun, proclaiming through every ray that his warmth was life and justified all things that were in life. And now they had returned to an inn that hid shyly at the end of the High Street, behind a little front garden where the blue of the lupin fought that of the larkspur. Against the white wall stretched the purple hands of the clematis. They sat together, at first silent, in the parlour which they occupied alone, an old inn parlour furnished with Windsor chairs, a Welsh dresser, some willow-pattern plates; there were some rough colour-prints of hunting scenes; on one wall was a collection of brightly burnished warming-pans. Upon the table was a large album in which Americans wrote the emotions inspired by Denham or appropriate quotations from Emerson. Fenor read one of the original contributions: "Social unity is inherent in the harmony of the cosmos." "Vurry int'restin'," he remarked, "it only wants a few more words, words I seem to miss, like mental, elemental, and an allusion to the bird of freedom and the star-spangled banner, with an advertisement saying that Hoskin's pickles are the goods, to have a truly — cosmic picture of America."

Grace laughed. "You don't seem to like Americans, Enoch."

"Like 'em?" he said. "I love 'em; they manage their lives as if they were acting for the cinema. People laugh at the Americans; they are quite wrong. They may be excited, but they are frightfully hard at work trying to enjoy themselves while England is hard at work seeing to it that she is properly and piously bored. They're active, anyhow, the Americans, and now and then they make me laugh, but the English — they make me yawn."

She smiled, not knowing whether she should take him seriously. She never knew, because a paradox or an epigrammatic turn of phrase was unusual to her, and as she came from the respectable classes, she found it hard to realise that a thing said unusually might truly be meant. But she did not long ponder the American character, for she was absorbed in the ritual of serving tea. She felt that this was not just serving tea, that there were grades in the ceremony; that there was tea-obvious, with one's husband; tea-formal, when one had a few friends; tea-domestic, in the nursery; and no tea at all at a really successful at home. This was tea-romantic and, in an incomprehensible way, tea-adventurous, illicit, and, much more incomprehensible, tea-intimate, wifely. It is one thing to exchange kisses and another to do with one whom one has caressed the little commonplace things which seem at first to have no place in love until love makes them vital. She was thrilled as she reflected that she knew now that he took no sugar: to know that implies great other knowledge. As she smiled at him across the table, she liked to look at him; she was pleased to find a little green in the grey of his eyes, for were not her own eyes green? Desperately she wanted community with him; she wished he had had her hair, just as she tried to adopt his thoughts. She tried to phrase to herself the thought that union is not always love, but that love must be union. The thought troubled her and she wanted to question him, but suddenly she was too shy: sitting with him like this in an inn-parlour, it was like a honeymoon, and she was tremulous as a bride, afraid to say the wrong thing, anxious to be polite and entertaining. So, her social instinct guiding her, quite instinctively she drew him out. One can always talk to a man about his subject.

"What have you been reading?" she asked.

"Not much lately," he said. Then, tenderly: "I've had other things to think of — but still, just a little, a queer thing by Stirner, *The Ego and His Own.*"

"Whatever's that?" asked Grace.

"Individualism, more or less, a sort of revolt against socialism. Interesting you know — as true as anything else, which is not much, perhaps — an illusion of truth, the nearest thing to which man can get."

"What's it about?" asked Grace, practically, for abstractions puzzled her and tended to annoy her.

"It's rather hard to explain," said Fenor. "Perhaps it's just a glorified selfishness, an idea that we've got to struggle against the state and society, against all the machinery that is trying, with schools and arms, and drawing-rooms and fashions, to turn us out all alike, — I to be number 159,672 and you, Russet, to be 159,673, and so on. It's a reagent, a demonstration that if there is a duty, it is the duty to develop oneself, to live for oneself, to lead in the race if one wants to, and the Fabian Society take the hindmost."

She smiled, he smiled back. What else could a man, talking, want?

"Of course," he said, "it's not enough as an ideal, but one wants an ideal of some kind. Anything will do, a woman or the Empire, or the Empire Promenade, it doesn't matter what it is. It's the ideal is ideal to you."

For some time Fenor went on talking, reflectively, to himself as much as to her. She soon lost herself, found that she was thinking of him, not of his views. So it should be, for love is not interest. And then, later, silence fell upon him. For a very long time he sat smoking his pipe, softly blowing into shapes that pleased him the opal smoke. She thought of herself first and of the change so soon wrought in her. Here she was, a married, respectable woman, mother of two alleged charming children, young, beautiful, popular, with money in her purse — compromised with a man who, if questioned, would have called himself an adventurer. Quite calmly she reflected that this was an ignoble position, and, as calmly, that she was delighted to be in that position. "I suppose it had to be," she thought. "My life seems to have struggled along without my guiding it until I got to this. I suppose it had to be whether I liked it or not; it had to take some form." But at once the question came to her: "yes, but what next?" At once her mind replied: "You love him, he loves you; what more do you want?" She replied: "I want it for ever." But a secret cynicism in her laughed and said: "You fool! it won't last for ever. It can't last — not like this."

As that thought came to her she despised herself, hated herself, for she had been taught as a child and as a young girl that one loves but once and loves for ever; at least, that is what respectable people do. One marries (one loves: that is synonymous), and one goes on loving for ever. But Grace had developed; she faced the situation and thought: "No, one does not love for ever. There are moments in one's life when another creature can creep quite close. Then one changes, one grows up. The creature that had crept so close no longer gives warmth, and it is over." She had a sharp little pain as she realised that which Fenor seemed to know so well, that nothing is permanent, that life indeed is a great wheel, revolving, that it always seems to return to the same point, but does not. It turns, true enough, but the axis slowly travels, so that never does it pass again through the wheel-mark of old. Everything struggled in her to make her say: "This is for ever." But she knew it was not, and suddenly she grew ten years older as she thought: "Nothing is permanent, and it is well so, for the thing that is fixed is dead, nothing is worth while save the impermanent, the temporary. The permanent is never intense, never vital, the permanent is like an obelisk, thousands of years old and dead; the temporary is like the apple-tree that clothes itself each year in new blossoms. If life endured for ever, life would be death." She had a moment of exultation: to think such thoughts as these was indeed to pierce the mystery of life.

"What are you thinking of?" asked Fenor, suddenly taking his pipe from his mouth.

She blushed and forced herself to speak: "I was thinking," she said, "that if life endured for ever it would be death."

He looked at her a little surprised. He guessed that she was learning, but he was too tactful to say so. "Socrates," he said, "said that life and death were the same thing. That was the reason he gave for not committing suicide, but he drank the hemlock in the end."

There was a pause and he broke the tension. "Let's go out," he said.

They went out silently into the hay-field where the hay was flowering, and every little bending head was passionately breathing. It had rained heavily the day before, and there were smells of earth, rich, clayey smells and pungent smells of bark. They sat down upon the tree-trunk that made a rough bridge across the ditch; there was honeysuckle in the hedge, and it too seemed to strain towards them with wilful delight. It was earth breathing. Disjointedly they found themselves speaking of love. It was because Grace had said:

"I seem to know you so well now, Enoch."

"You don't," he replied, swiftly, "or you wouldn't love me. Love between the sexes is based on mutual ignorance or, if not, it would have to be transcendental — Paolo and Francesca, Abelard and Heloise. If one knew one another well, it would be hard to love one another."

"But surely," cried Grace, "that's what one wants; to know everything the other feels and — and wants, and hopes. One wants to guess before the other speaks."

"Yes, Russet," said Fenor, gloomily, "one does want to do that, to take all the mystery out, to kill the thing one loves. But then that's life: killing to live. Our emotions are strengthened by the destruction of another emotion, just as in the Indian proverb I told you the panther is strengthened by the blood of the wildcat. But it doesn't matter," he added, and became thoughtful. Then, after a pause: "It doesn't matter, you see, if you do it freely, consciously. That's why I want women to be free, not only to have votes and all that sort of stuff, but the freedom that is going to come out of the use they will make of that vote. To-day they are lawless because they have never had any share in making the law. I don't want them to be tied up by the law any more than I want them locked up in the harem. I want them to keep the law if they think it's a good one, just as I want them to stay in the harem — with the door open."

Grace had picked up only one phrase: "Do you think us really lawless?" she said.

"Yes," he said, "they say there are three anarchists: love, birth, and death. Those are abstract anarchists, but the material anarchist is woman. You see, woman's never understood why she should not do as she liked; that's why she's always done it in the end, that's why she's trying to be free while most men are willing to be slaves, and that's why no man was ever any good in the arts who had not a lot of woman in him. For there are no men, you see, and no women, there are only majorities."

For a long time Grace did not speak. All this audacious, hardly understood talk charmed her, perhaps because it was striking, certainly because it was novel. She loved it just as an Englishman, fallen into Spain, suddenly discovers woman's beauty for the first time because he gazes into stranger eyes. It was love-making, but of a peculiar kind, the kind that came in with Newnham and the intellectual drama: love without rouge. But yet at once her thoughts took a personal application; he was man and general, she was woman and particular. Without intention, she found herself speaking of her marriage, trying to tell him how it had come about, just like that, without her knowing it, as one may fall asleep or wake up. She told him that it had been good and then, somehow, always the same thing, while she grew up and became different and then, she couldn't tell why it was all different.

He asked a question.

"Well, yes, of course — Edward became a little dull;

he talked about himself all the time, he — " She pulled herself up: " Oh, I'm beastly, I mustn't talk like this. He's kind to me, he's fond of me, you see. I oughtn't to tell you these things."

Fenor did not reply, did not question her. He was too tactful to abuse her husband, had he wished to do so; he did not want by attack to enlist her loyalty on her husband's side. On the contrary, sometimes he would speak well of him, knowing that he slew him more truly by praise, because to praise the one who held the thing he loved invested him with so extraordinary a generosity. But, on the other hand, he knew that he must help her to say the thing she wanted, oppose her gently, so as to give her stimulus, something to shove off from.

" But your children," he said.

" Oh, they — " said Grace, " they're growing up; they've done with me just as we're done with everything as we grow up."

" The child," said Fenor, " yes, we exaggerate the child. People think a woman who's a mother stops being a woman when she's a mother, but they'll know one day that the child is only a by-product of love, that love's a bigger thing than maternity, for maternity's only the race, a thing perhaps not worth keeping up, while love is certainly worth while."

" But, Enoch," asked Grace, urgently, " is not the child worth while when love grows less? "

" Oh, yes, it's an endowment insurance policy, but it isn't everything. It isn't enough to make you forgive."

" Forgive? " asked Grace.

" Yes," said Fenor. " You see, when you marry a man you give him a glorious wedding garment; his new morning coat and the orchid in his buttonhole, they aren't in it by the side of that garment, and he can't go round to some heavenly tailor and order another. It just gets older and dustier and more bedraggled, and he can't even take it off; you've got to see him in his old wedding-garment, all stained with tears and blood, stained where the acid of angry words has fallen, and crumpled in the places which ought to have been unfolded now and then, but haven't been touched for years. You can't forgive that, you know. You can't forgive marriage because the early rapture has gone out of it, nor Eros, who used to sweep above your head, deafening you with the beating of his wings; you can't forgive him when his wings begin to moult. You never believe that his feathers will grow again, and you're right, for they don't."

Grace felt tears in her eyes. This was one of his moods of gloom, and it had a horrible application to their own relation, six weeks old! That was a long time. Could it be a feather from the wings of Eros which she could see very slowly falling before her eyes across the faint blue haze that filled the brilliant sky? But she fought down the impulse, brought him back to actual things.

"But then, Enoch," she said, "what you're saying—it amounts to saying that marriage won't work?"

"It can't," said Fenor. "Not as we run it, with people living together without privacy, without a bedroom, sometimes without a bed to themselves. You know I'm right; I'm not talking of the very rich, but of the commonplace middle-class millions whom you always forget. People who've quarrelled half an hour before sleep by each other's side because they dare not do anything so revolutionary as to part. It's vile—it's immoral."

Grace laughed.

"You laugh; I know it sounds like a paradox, but it's true. Loving or hating, they dare not be separate for a moment. They'd rather defile their relation than dare to loosen it. They're tied together like coupled fowls sent to market, that tear at each other to get free. They must take their meals together, each one eat food the other likes, and call that self-sacrifice. I call it mutual oppression. And they do hideous things, things that kill love by killing mystery; they watch each other putting on their boots, or cleaning their teeth, or worse; they get dull, they wear their oldest and ugliest clothes in each other's presence because each one has got to stand it. They see each other unwashed, unshaven or with untidy hair, unbeautiful— And yet they must go on; they must go out together on Sunday morning, willing or unwilling; they must take their summer holidays together, whether both like the place or not; they hardly dare to go out alone with one of the other sex, and other people can't ask them to dinner separately. So their friends go in for mean little subterfuges: they ask the wife on her husband's Masonic night, or the husband on the mother-in-law's evening. They try to get a little liberty, a little air into that awful, stifling room where two people are gasping for breath and out of which they can't break— "

Grace was silent for a while. She was shaken. She knew that he was right, that marriage with its right to dictate movements could become hell. She knew the anxiety which could seize the married when they felt they would be late for dinner and would be asked: "Where have you been?" But she knew that he exaggerated.

"I don't say you're wrong," she replied. "I know one's never alone, that one loses all the honeymoon illusions, and all that. And I know that one wants now and then to go away, to sleep anywhere, just to be alone. Still, some marriages are happy."

"Of course there are some," said Fenor. "The union of a man and woman, cleaving to each other, can be the wonder of life. To be as in one, you and I, joined by love, separate in interests, that is happiness. Please, please believe that men and women are not united by the man's work and the woman's servant problem; they are joined by the love which inflames the lives they lead separately. Love, like literature, makes life vital. They can have a few interests together, indeed they want to, but they must be interests in art, in ideas, in pleasures, not in business deals and cooking-ranges. Business and the household merely maintain life; love makes it worth while. I don't believe in promiscuity; I believe in monogamy, but I don't want to live in a kennel for two. In days to come, men and women will love as now, but live separate, meet only when they want to—and silk ladders will be let down from balconies to the sons of men who to-day enter the home like process-servers."

Grace did not reply. She shrank a little. She did not like to say the idea of common living pleased her, that she did not rebel. She would have liked to say that she wanted to hear about his business and that it would have been thrilling, because intimate, to see him put his boots on. But she was too shy. She remained general.

"I see why you never married," she murmured.

"You don't quite. For I think I am one of the few who can take the risk. You see, I'm an adventurer, like the artist; people like that can marry with just a ghost of a chance of success because they don't respect the bond. By despising it they slacken it. We aren't like the clerks, the professional men, whose morals are censored; we can manage to live freely, to stand divorce and even irregular alliance; but even for us, sometimes, the bond may be too strong. For the ordinary salary-slave or fee-grubber it's made of steel."

Grace was still thoughtful. Her idea of adventure was more domestic: romance and a house in Queen's Gate—well, they ought to be compatible.

"It sounds as if you were right—" She smiled. "As usual. But I feel that marriage ought to work all the same."

"It hardly ever can nowadays. It did work once upon a time, in a rough sort of way, when woman was a slave and thought it all right, and it does work now, sort of, in Turkey, and China and India, though even there, I hear, the women are a bit upset. Even men find it uncomfortable."

"Oh, men," said Grace, scornfully. "They're always all right. Nobody cares what they do, even when they are married."

Fenor shook his head. "You're prejudiced, you're being unfair, you're not taking into account all sorts of things: men's muddled sense of duty and their conventions; they're much more conventional than you women, really; and their desire to have homes, stodgy, sleepy, comfortable sorts of places, and their liking for children whom they can boss and make as like themselves as they can, and a whole lot of very sweet affection they have for you, a way of loving women as if they were flowers."

"But we're not flowers!" cried Grace, half angrily.

Fenor laughed. "There you are! There's the whole of the sex-war in that reply. That's why marriage won't work. You're all saying: 'I'm a human being, though a woman,' and we men, most of us, haven't grasped that yet. It's not men who are breaking marriage up, it's women, and it's our fault; we've done idiotic things from the masculine point of view. First of all, we made you work for wages instead of making you work under the lash; as soon as you got more economic freedom, you began to look us in the eyes in a very aggressive way. We let you own property while we pretended that you, yourselves, were property and so, of course, the thirty bob a week coal-heaver hadn't a chance against the maiden lady with five hundred a year for whom he heaved coal. If we'd been sensible, we shouldn't have allowed women to inherit, we'd have kept up the Mosaic ways, a woman being thrown into the estate when her lord died — with the cattle."

"Don't be horrid," said Grace, not knowing whether she was irritated or amused.

Fenor perceived her tone. "You see, it makes you angry, what I say: sex-war again. If we hadn't educated you, you wouldn't be angry; what I say would seem natural to you. You'd think all you had to do in life was to play the tambourine until I told you to shut up, but you don't. We've opened universities to you and let you be chartered accountants, and police-women, and doctors and all sorts of things. We've done worse; we've actually let you be teachers and inspectors, to sit on borough councils — actually to make by-laws for *Us* and then, when we've done all that, we've got the cheek to say that you ought to know your place. Why, you haven't got any place of your own since we took your old place from you, the place under, you know, and we won't let you sit next to us. Russet, it'll end badly; women will get so exasperated that they won't be content with the place next to us, they'll want the place over — and if they play their sex-cards properly they'll get it."

"But marriage, marriage," cried Grace, bewildered by this speculation.

"Oh, marriage, it's the best institution in the world, just like the gold and silver Italian clock in South Kensington Museum; only they don't work, either of them. It can't work until it's contracted on equal terms, that is to say, until every woman has the right to be taught to work, the right to work, the right to her earnings in the home as well as out. That is so long as there is a home, which I hope isn't for ever. Property in her children without the responsibility of them, freedom to break the tie for fair reasons if she wants to — home rule within the rule of the home, that's about it."

"Don't you think," said Grace, "that if we were all so free, marriages would be broken up all the time?"

"Let them be broken up," said Fenor. "It isn't an argument to say that marriage must be maintained because it was entered into. If you send a man to gaol for seven years, you don't keep him there fourteen; far from it, you let him off two years earlier if he behaves. Besides," he added, more gravely, "one can't be too free, because the freer one is, the more freedom one has, the less one wants to use it. It's tyranny makes you kick, not liberty; if women could break the tie more easily, they wouldn't want to break it at all. They'd stay in the harem all right if the door was open."

There was a long silence and as, little by little, the deep breath of the earth about them came rising, laden with the scents of the flowering hay and of the honeysuckle, conscious of something else, much larger than the mechanical conduct of their lives and the organisation of the society in which they happened to live, Fenor looked away towards the horizon, saw nothing save the immense billow of the green field, ending sharp in a wavering crest on the light blue haze of the sky. So placed, they could see nothing but each other and the billow of the field. For a moment he looked at Grace and thought how her green dress and the bracken of her hair accorded with the grass and the purple leaves of a beech-tree that hung above them. He bent forward.

"Elf," he murmured, "elf of the woods." Then, more sportive: "Nymph — clad in Sloane Street."

She threw him a soft, sidelong, humid glance, the love-glance that is as the love-voice, veiled like a meadow when the dew rises. He snatched her hands, drew her closer and, as a bending bough seized by the wind, she abandoned herself to his grasp, rejoicing in her power to make him wish to have power over her. She felt his lips in her hair and upon her neck, and as if from very far away came that hoarse, thrilled voice that through her hair murmured into her ear:

"I adore you . . . I adore you."

CHAPTER THE SECOND

SOUTHERN SEAS

I

GRACE stood at the edge of the cliff, among the pine-trees. Her slim, tall body in its green linen gown was straight as those trunks about her, as if by some mimicry she attuned herself to their spirit, or, as Fenor would have said, she were for the nonce a hamadryad. She was happy. She looked out over the North Sea, that was like a roof of plate-glass, at the little ship with brown sails that the sun made crimson.

It was August and she had changed, though not changed.

The thinness that had come into her face in those days when she went alone had vanished, and her cheek-bones seemed less high; she had changed only in becoming once more what she had been. And yet there was about her something new. Now she had deep eyes, graciously zoned, and a gay, defiant mouth, and a smooth radiance — as if all things were well with her. She went with lifted head, as a spirited palfrey contemptuous of the bit. And her clothes, the audacious red spots of her green sash, marked in her a taste for adventure and a gaiety, a fine secure courage of colour and line. She stood blinding her eyes with light, until that light grew so intense in her pupils as to become a darkness in which the little ship that flickered on the sky-line was like a red lamp in the gloaming. In that moment she was not thinking, but feeling, as if every one of the pores of her skin had not one, but five senses, all of which coalesced to tell her: "You are loved and you love. Don't dwell on it with that vile thing, your brain, but let it come to you from outside as does the wind or the breath of the magnolia in your garden.''

It was later, in the garden, that Fenor's voice seemed to ring in her ears. She did not know what he said, and wondered whether happiness could make mad those whom it would raise up, for she was conscious of his voice, the voice that always seemed to penetrate in her some unexplored depth, that soft, low voice, all of the throat, that came as a sweet narcotic, as velvet, that seemed to twine itself about her as the breath wound itself in and out among the words, a voice like wine, drugged wine—

The words that formed at last embodied not his but her thoughts: "I'm like a shoot that blooms, that once bloomed and, neglected, died; now I bloom again and I'm all drunken with my own perfume, the perfume of my new bloom, of my second blooming." A horror ran through the delight: once more she was blooming, fast blooming in that little dream called life that for a moment illumines the sleep of death that begins before birth and after death resumes. It was as if the soft distant voice, river of milk and honey, were whispering too that even this bloom, so new, must wither soon. In her agony she clenched her hands together and saw her finger-nails whiten as she pressed them into her palm. She was there, all alone, just a little human creature in rebellion against the originating will, vowing that she could not die, that love itself must be eternal. In that minute she hated her body, because it could not for ever be fair, the molten glass of the sea, because her eyes must one day be closed to it, and love itself, because it could pass but once, as it passed that day, through the sky like a shooting-star. But still the voice came whispering, more tender, reassuring now. "Why trouble myself?" she thought, "love passes; and why should I ask what the herons do when they have entered other skies, even if my eyes cannot follow them? For high fly the herons, and beautiful is the curve they make as they fly." An immense exultation seized her. Her body was bathed in the heat of the sun, and all her brain seemed to be melting as if indeed she were a flower opening in a passionate embrace its petals to the sun. She raised her arms, gripping the air as if to embrace it too, the red heat of it and its blueness, as if she too were a flower incredulous in its second blooming.

II

The Kinnersleys had taken for six weeks a house upon the cliff that overhangs Kingsdown. It was the development into a modern villa of an old cottage which, augmented by wings and a rose-grown porch, was now called "Southern Seas." It had, little by little, become quite incoherent in design, for the bedrooms were very small and the living-rooms, conceived in the late nineteenth century, were better fitted for entertaining than for habitation; there was an unpleasant contrast between the centre of the house, with its low ceilings and its sunken beams, and the wings with their bay-windows. But the beauty of "Southern Seas" lay in its garden, a sloping bit of down, crudely levelled here and there to make a flower-bed, which suddenly threw itself into the arms of a little pine wood. The wood grew so close that it managed to be mysterious and dark, and it clung to the edge of the cliff as if it so loved the soil that it could not forego an inch of it, as if it were ready to fight the sea for its possession. It was in the wood Grace spent most of the time that was left her by other occupations, while Edward, when not muscularly engaged on the golf-links or benevolently telling the fishermen how to fish, preferred the garden. He liked to lie in a deck-chair reading the *Spectator* or, with greater ostentation, the most blatant of the little penny weeklies. He never threw their covers away, as do more modest people in the Tube. "I like 'em," he said. "Keeps you in touch with the people — one mustn't get too high-browed, eh, Gracie-Bracie?"

Edward liked to outrage one convention out of say a hundred: that made deference to the other ninety-nine look like a sane choice. Also, in the deck-chair, he got sunburnt. "Come back lookin' like a bloomin' explorer; that's what the seaside's for."

Edward was not very troublesome that year, for the modern spirit had invaded him (three or four years late) and he was leading the simple life, which consisted in elaborate bathing, golf, walking ("The best exercise in the world"), some light reading, and repose in the bosom of his family subject to the laws of the annual honeymoon during the summer recess; he lighted St. John's fires with a bundle of briefs.

More exacting were the Westfields, a generic term which included other people, for Mrs. Westfield, who was now and then disappointed, thought that her daughters should have a reunion about her at the seaside, as, unfortunately, they could not all live in the same house in London. So she had established between Kingsdown and Walmer, in a large hired house, something that felt like an assembly, a clot, a coagulation of Westfields: Tom Stanley and Mary, their five little girls, were housed by her; Sir Henry and Clara had been half-dragooned, half-shamed into settling within sound of the five children's voices. Even Spot, more affectionate than ever, was of the party: Mrs. Westfield on this occasion would not hand over to a coachman the care of a Westfield dog. And Mr. Sturry had appeared, ostensibly to have another look at Canterbury, but in reality to show that he was a naturalised Westfield. They were rather troublesome, Grace thought; they involved picnics, sitting on things that were not good for her clothes, getting blown and wet and lank-haired, all sorts of things she disliked because coquetry was for her a duty. Horace and Susan were bad enough, but when Mary's children and their attendants were collected and Grace had to enter Deal, heading, with Mary, a procession of seven children or so and three or four nurses, it felt altogether too matronly. There were the three men too, pretending to enjoy themselves hugely, at bottom very bored because Parliament, the Temple and the City were so far away, and not quite sure that these institutions could get on without them. The men became annoyingly energetic: golf, sailing, bathing were not enough, so they smoked too much, ate and drank too much, became irritable and developed livers, refused to go for country walks except accompanied by a woman who didn't want to walk and couldn't walk in her thin shoes, and wanted tea, which the men always forgot.

It was a regular holiday.

In the evening the men had to be amused, which was difficult, as they had done no work during the day. Bridge had to be organised by women who couldn't play bridge, and didn't want to learn, and had to learn instead of sitting together and discussing their own subject: people they knew. There was a dreadful night when a touring company came down and three husbands went with three wives and one mother, and everybody had to applaud very hard a silly play played by a bad company because, as Edward said, in August one must make allowances. Yes, it was a regular holiday.

Grace had thought to counteract these diversions of a united family by entertaining a few guests at "Southern Seas." She was so exasperated as to ponder the queer people whom she had met at Mrs. Shapwick's and others. Only she did not know them well enough, and she was afraid of complications. To feed them was probably as difficult as to find out exactly the proper diet for a mongoose or a mandrill; or they might want to sleep in hammocks hung from the pine-trees, or to bathe clad in moonlight and no more. Besides, her one attempt, when she suggested Mrs. Cheddon because she was doggy, and Edward, not being doggy, would presumably think he liked a doggy woman, failed.

"Oh, no," said Edward, and yawned prodigiously, stretching himself to show that he was having a holiday and was therefore relaxing. "Oh, no, Gracie-Bracie, let's keep ourselves to ourselves. Me and my old Dutch" (slight East End interlude), "we're 'avin' a bloomin' day aht."

Evidently the Cheddons would be *de trop* on the annual honeymoon. But later Edward did something quite horrid; he actually suggested that they should ask Fenor down for a week-end. His fancy for the man had abated a little after the settlement of the case, for Fenor had ceased to search him out and had therefore been forgotten. But Edward had accidentally met him the day before, having gone up to town for the day, and heard from him that he was going abroad some time. He had then found it necessary to persuade him that Kingsdown was much pleasanter than any place abroad. He had inferred that the place he, Edward, had selected must be the best place; Fenor had said nothing precise. Something seemed to revolt in Grace when Edward made this suggestion. For a moment she stood with knitted brows; secretly she was shocked. The idea that her husband should so trustfully ask to his house the man who had betrayed him — it was an impossible idea. Though her heart gave a leap at the idea that if she said the word there would be whole days when she would see Enoch, speak to him, she thought: "no, it really won't do," and said:

"Well, Edward, after all I think you're right — we see so many people, we'd better not have anybody down."

And Edward, who was already thinking of something else, took no notice; as he never organised anything, but expected others to do it for him, nothing was done. Grace tried to analyse her feelings and failed; she merely did not want Fenor under her own roof. To the end she never found out that her traditions had spoken for her, that she would not have thought it decent, that, do what she would, she remained a respectable woman. The respectable find reform much more difficult than the vicious.

Besides, there was a new fact in her life, due perhaps to her not having seen Fenor for a fortnight. She had suddenly become aware of Edward, who, for nearly three months, had been to her a phantom, something hardly more significant than the furniture. She had talked to him, entertained and been entertained with him; she had in the ordinary, normal way, been a wife to him, but there had been in that a quality so mechanical that she was hardly aware of its existence. It had been the love-making of Svengali and Trilby in a trance. And now suddenly she realised him again, realised him in the little exasperations of his presence, his way of displaying boisterousness upon the beach, his stone-throwing matches with the children, his habitual strokings of Clara's and Mary's arms, while praising Providence for the invention of the short sleeve, his rather shocked delight at a few bathing-dresses on the beach which, he declared, gave quite a Parisian touch to the scenery. But it was not only that. Horrible to think, there was something else in Edward, the something from which sprang the qualities which had, after all, charmed her and for a while held her. She could not help seeing his pleasure in the country; even if he did point to an elm and tell everybody it was a beech, still he did love the tree, and he loved, in a crude, pious fashion, the children, the pretty girls in the village, the burnt, canny fishermen, and all the animals. He was stumbling, clumsy; yet, under all his silliness, was a fine, generous softness of heart; when he bored people he really wanted to entertain them, to please them; he wanted to be popular because it flattered his self-esteem, but he also liked to be loved. Edward did not want to be cruel, and was not; he wanted to be kind: only he did it badly. Every now and then it faintly came into his head that he wasn't as popular as he'd like to be, and that made him unhappy: it was because he was fond of his fellow man that he wanted his fellow man to be fond of him, and that made him still more clumsy, made him talk too much to people who liked silence, made him do pathetic, awkward little things like forcing them to let him pay their fare on the Walmer motor-bus. He would so much have liked them to be pleased.

He was no fool: in his chambers in the Temple no man was keener than he, quicker or a more obstinate fighter in a bad case. There he was a shrewd, steady man, a man at his work, a noble thing in its way. His intellect, his views on politics, on the drama, on men and their character, — at bottom all these things were sound. Sometimes Grace found him interesting: but the bungling of his words, humorous or boisterous, seemed to spoil everything; he was like a man who, bidden by a woman to bring her a rose, brought her the whole bush, with a great lump of clay sticking to the roots, and the flower itself much tumbled during the exhausting process of digging up: it was pathetic, this contrast which sometimes grew agonising. Grace had a sharp pang one morning when she went down to the sea with several of her family, for she had complained of the dingy little hut from which she had to bathe, because the boards were rotten and smelled of tar and fish: in the night a beautiful, spacious hut, bearing the label of a well-known London maker, had sprung up. It had two little rooms with glazed windows and pretty chintz curtains, a ribbed floor which would be nice and dry, and a large oil-stove which would supply hot water to the white porcelain footbaths if you felt chilled. And absurd, agreeable fittings: a little library, a swivel-mirror, a row of scent-bottles.

"But Edward!" cried Grace, "what a surprise! and how sweet of you."

He nudged her playfully with his elbow.

"Hubby's bright idea," he declared. "Gracie-Bracie'll turn out like Venus from the waves in future, with her hair curled just like the Royal Academy." He giggled. "Mind the curtains, though, there'll be many a peeping Tom about to watch my girlie."

It was maddening. Grace found herself wishing that she had quite another kind of husband, some drunken brute who beat her now and then. Then she would know where she was, but this kindness, this sweetness and generosity, mixed up with all this intolerable lack of stimulating power, racked her nerves, and at the same time it was so well-meant, so gentle that it made her feel guilty.

Guilty! For three days she found herself struggling with remorse —

She had been educated in the belief that though there might be seven cardinal sins there were no cardinal virtues. That is, somehow, her morality, as her faith, had been constructed on abstentions; on things which she might not do, rather than on things she should do. And she had not done them until lately. When it came upon her suddenly that she was deceiving her husband, she suffered because she was doing something active. One can allow one's husband to die, and that is only omission, but one can tell him a convenient lie, and that is commission; that is much more serious. So it was not wonderful that the knowledge of this activity of evil which proceeded from her should begin to follow her and to poison her. As if with a cruel intention, Edward seemed every day to become more amiable, more admiring, perhaps because she had grown more beautiful, and kinder, more generous. Just as, once upon a time, everything that he had done and meant kindly had been tainted by the exasperation which he bred in her, now, in her revulsion, everything that he did without any kindly intent became a deadly reproach. He came in from Deal, bearing a great bunch of tea-roses. "Tea-roses for the little girlie-girlie," he remarked, laying them down on the tablecloth. Grace ought to have been irritated for, clumsy as usual, he had not had them wrapped up, and a big stain of water was forming on the clean cloth. This was the sort of thing that angered Grace: a soiled tablecloth marked her imagination much more than an earthquake. Still she was not irritated, she was grateful.

"This man," she thought, "whom I'm deceiving, betraying, this man who has loved me, and whom I love, yes, whom I do love," she asserted angrily to herself, "to whom I'm a bad wife — he brings me roses as if he were a lover. It's almost — cruel of him."

The sense of this incongruous condition began to run through every moment of Grace's life. She became anxious to please him. For three days, every now and then, she even put to him hypothetical points of law, and she listened to the answers. She availed herself of a liver-attack which Edward had developed to play with him the role of sick nurse, to read to him aloud, though he would much rather have got up and gone out. Grace kept him in bed and offered herself up on the altar of repentance.

She was bored, the reaction was passing away; yet she persisted in telling herself, more or less: "I've brought you to the bedside of your sick husband, and repent you shall, even if you do enjoy it." It was horrible and it was delightful. For the first time in her life Grace realised the colossal hoax that has made the Christian martyrs, the daughters devoted to their cross old fathers, the patient wives of brutal husbands, and all those people; she found something voluptuous in self-sacrifice.

And, as soon as she realised this, she was shocked; she was always a little shocked at the idea of enjoying herself in any way, having been taught that on the whole anything agreeable must be more or less sinful, but the idea of drawing pleasure from the immolation of self and from the atonement for a sin: it was abominable, it was—Continental. And so the fit was brief. Little by little, from the consideration of the sin she passed on to the details of her intrigue, its hole and corner quality. The days were passing now and, in that week, the weight of the Westfields was less heavy, for Mr. Sturry had gone to Canterbury while Sir Henry, unable to stand any longer having his arm taken or his knee patted by Edward, was cruising along the coast in a small yacht. Mary, who was preparing for the trials of December, was not so well that week and kept her mother busy providing her with comforts and asking her a great many times a day how she felt now, which had the effect, little by little, of making Mary quite hysterical and imagine before the evening that she was going to be very ill. So Grace had plenty of time to think. She passed out of the remorseful stage. She first wondered how it was that she could pass out of it. It was not normal; she ought to feel remorse, she thought, for was she not after all doing that which was forbidden to all wives? being false to vows which she had taken freely? She could not understand herself. She wondered whether she had changed, whether, little by little, there had grown up in her a new consciousness which might be a new morality, rather than merely a revolt against the old. Why did she not maintain her repentance and follow it up to its logical conclusion, that she would give up Enoch Fenor? It seemed almost insoluble. Logically she could not together repent and retain her lover. Not for a moment did she think of giving him up, and nothing could have been more significant of her development than that. A year before, had she been so placed, Grace would have plucked from its socket the eye that offended her. Now she began to wonder whether the eye offended her at all. Then she remembered. They were Fenor's words, like seeds carried by a chance wind into unexpected soil, that flower:

"One thing I never understand," he had said, "is this sort of insanity about monogamy and monandry. Here we are, men and women, growing people, vital most of us, and we've the folly to think that we can see only one beautiful thing at a time, appreciate but one charm, hold but one love. Good heavens, you might as well say that you cannot love Italy and Norway at the same time, or care for Italy at all because you preferred Norway once upon a time. It's just nonsense. There's so much in all of us of what we call love, which is really anything between faint liking, via friendship, to consuming passion, that one might almost love all the world together — differently. And then, when people come along and tell me that a husband suffers because another man has stolen his wife, I want to laugh."

"But surely," Grace had said, "she can't love her husband any more."

"Russet," replied Fenor, "you're a bourgeoise. If I wanted to be cynical, I'd tell you she might love him all the more by contrast. There's nothing like a holiday to make you like home. But it's much more than that, it's the whole idea of human relations. If one wanted to secure each other against the attractions of people who have no legal property in one, people'd have to be forbidden to meet except in public, and that wouldn't be safe. They couldn't dance, and they couldn't shake hands, and they couldn't talk lest some dangerously agreeable things might please. We'd have to lock each other up in private gaols — and even then I don't think one could trust the warders. No, Russet, all this exclusion idea, love and marriage strictly preserved, trespassers will be prosecuted, it's all rot and for one reason only, that it can't be enforced."

Grace remembered every word of that conversation. Fenor saw the world upside down; that was why at first she had thought that he wanted to turn it upside down (there is only one right way in the world and that is one's own). And now she too was seeing it as he did. She loved Edward, if she loved him at all, not less than before. Indeed, because her emotions had been satisfied, she loved him better, for he exasperated her less; she was not always clamouring for a satisfaction he could not give her. She thought of Fenor and what he would have said, something like: "Well then, I've done him a good turn." She shivered. Cynicism still made her afraid.

The realisation that Edward did not suffer from the "stain upon his honour" which would exist only if he knew of its existence, seemed suddenly to explain to Grace other matters that were a little dark in her relation. At first she had suffered in the arrangement of assignations, hated the concealment, the appointments, specific and therefore lacking in spontaneity. She had hated the secret and the illicit. That feeling which she had had the first day in her own drawing-room: "oh, why can't love be like the sunrise?" which involved that she should be at all times beside the man she loved, was still with her. A phrase, read in some book, passed through her brain: a clean bolt.

Yes, that was all very well, a clean bolt, but it wasn't done in her world. The funny people whom the Shapwicks knew, they went in for clean bolts; but then they lived on poetry recitals and borrowed half crowns. They didn't have children, most of them, and houses on seven-year leases, and accounts with tradesmen (for, of course, they couldn't be trusted); they were not inextricably mixed up with servants, and gas contracts, and electricity contracts, and library subscription, and settlements, and furniture — all the paraphernalia which makes life run very easy when you've got over the complications. When they went in for a clean bolt they didn't come in, Grace reflected, for the appalling smash that she would have to face. Husbands weren't moral in that world, but Edward was moral, and therefore he would suffer deeply: he would suffer because he lost her, and he would suffer because he would publicly appear as the husband of a bad woman. He would carry his injury and the shame of the injury she had done him. The children too. In the Shapwick world children just happened when one wasn't looking, and they were handed over to the caretaker, with the cat, until they were old enough to be dressed in hygienic or æsthetic clothes. Nobody wanted to know who the parents of the Shapwick type of child had been: the mothers of the bourgeoisie brought their children up to be respectable, the Shapwick mothers brought them up to "find themselves," or began at the age of two to direct them towards the career of playwright. And then they found themselves, or not, and wrote plays or something. That was all right, but the Westfield kind of child wasn't treated like that: when it grew up it went to a public-school, and it didn't like it if the other children's parents said they couldn't accept the holiday invitation from "that house;" if it was a girl people merely said: "her mother — well, you know — so sad."

No, it wouldn't do, she couldn't bolt. Dimly, she was conscious that she herself wouldn't be happy if she bolted, for she knew that all those conventions were strong in her blood. If she went into what some people call freedom she would merely be burgling a gaol. Besides, and this stung her a little, Fenor had never suggested to her that they should bolt. But she understood him. She knew him for the brilliant rake he was. He rejoiced in a queer, rhapsodical, lyrical way, in things that other people thought ugly, but which he thought beautiful because he looked at them from the other end of the telescope. He loved the secret and the illicit; it was his way of revenging himself upon a society that cramped him. If he had wanted a religion he would have adopted devil-worship, and Grace was half-converted to his view that love has nothing to do with marriage, that it can occur in marriage, with luck, and be maintained in marriage if you have a nice, sleepy brain. But what surprised her a little was that he did not seem jealous; she did not expect him to be remorseful, she knew too well that if ever he felt remorse he washed it out with a new sin: that was all right, philosophical, logical, the way an intellectual man would think,—but jealousy, that was quite another thing, a primitive feeling, not a view. She wondered how he could tolerate the idea that another man might claim anything from her. It ought to cause blood to surge in his head; then she remembered what she had discovered in herself, her own mechanical attitude. She understood him a little better. Yes, Fenor was right, it was not the things one did that mattered, it was what one thought and what one felt as one did them. A fact was not a fact unless one knew it was a fact. That was it. He saw the truth too well, he was not as are nearly all men, swindled by appearances. He knew that woman's surrender may be her act of conquest, and conversely that a man may be the father of a woman's children when she has never given him a thought, been no nearer to him in soul than if they had lived out their lives in two hemispheres.

He was sure of her, he was right.

III

Grace was surprised now and then because she did not miss Enoch Fenor. It struck her as faintly wrong that she should not miss him, for she was enough of a bourgeoise to apply conventions to her departures from the conventions. If one was so bad a woman as to have a lover, one had to be obsessed by the idea of that lover, and it worried her a little to find that she was not. Now and then she seriously asked herself whether she really loved him, and it was only by conjuring up the possibility of losing him that she could assure herself she did. But then Grace Kinnersley was very much a woman: the certainty of love mattered to her more than love itself; it would have meant more to her to receive every Saturday through the South African mail a love-letter from a man whom she never saw than to be the toy day by day of a man who did not love her as a lover should. It was the romantic in her that spoke, bridging absence, gilding words, the romantic that creates the thing which the romantic makes lovable. And, besides, her quickening mind had extended from introspection to a closer observation of her fellow creatures, notably her sisters and, much more notably, Clara. Never before had Lady Govan so well justified her dead father's joke about "Clara, Clara, burning bright." She was at Kingsdown indulging in the politician's wife's holiday; while recovering from the last session she was preparing for the next. It was going to be an enormous, a terrific session. Sir Henry had made his maiden speech and created a great impression because, advised by her and letting alone the Lords and all those things that everybody was fed up with, he had introduced an intricate little bill dealing with patents. The House had yawned and listened very respectfully because, on the whole, it did not understand the speech, which had been carefully worked up by a patent agent; it then decided that Sir Henry was a good man who would certainly make his way. But Clara's activities were going further than preventing her husband from trying to make jokes which made one popular in the halfpenny papers and suspected at Westminster. Her schemes had at last expanded; that dream of hers, of schemes national, schemes imperial, was coming true. She had in the early summer laid the basis of the Education League; it really had a much more complicated name than that, the words "Imperial," "British" and "Democracy" having been introduced at suitable places, but it was already mentioned in the papers as the Education League and no more; that was success. No society succeeds until it acquires a pet name. The Education League was a wonderful idea; it was supposed to combine with the inculcation of sound Conservative principles lectures on subjects which would improve the mind of the electorate. There were lectures on Dante, on Jefferies and George Borrow, lectures on "How to Become an Engineer for a Penny a Week," and practical classes where it was demonstrated that soap-boxes, brown paper and sardine tins could be used to beautify the home. Tariff reform and "How to Make a Refrigerator!" It was an immense success. Already there were branches in nineteen counties and Clara, like a hysterical hen, seemed to go about dropping in unexpected places the eggs of further ideas. Futurism, she thought, must not remain foreign to Bury St. Edmunds. "And you know," she said, excitedly, on the long and abominable walk through miles of slushy lanes where she had dragged Grace, protesting, on a rainy day, because exercise would do her good, "we're getting Wales; think of that! The other day we got the Strathpeffer branch on its legs; I could have danced. They're a hard lot in Scotland," she added, reflectively, "but now we've actually got a Welsh branch. I'd never have thought it." She smiled viciously. "That'll make the chapels sit up." She grew eloquent: "We'll have to alter it a bit for Wales; we might — we might have some history classes to show how much more civilised Wales was than England before the nonconformists came in."

"Was it more civilised?" asked Grace, indifferently, for a quantity of puddle-water had flooded one of her boots.

"I don't know," said Clara, "but what does it matter?"

True, it didn't matter; after all, this was politics. For a long time they walked side by side while Clara feverishly expounded her scheme. This was not dull, though she expounded it every day, for the Education League was a growing organism and every time varied a little. It had a diabolical acuteness of conception: every history class or lecture was tinted pink, so that the moderate folk might not be frightened, while the bolder ones could swear that the pink led up to painting in red the map of the world; the improving lectures were bound to hold out an irresistible appeal to clerks who wanted to be farmers, to farmers' sons who wanted to be shop-keepers, to shopkeepers' daughters who wanted to go on the stage, as it was apparently in the nature of man to want to do anything except what he was doing; and intermingled with the activities of the league and its branches, there seemed to be a network of coal clubs, blanket clubs, burial clubs.

"Pity we can't have maternity benefit," said Clara, gloomily. "Lloyd-George did us out of that. It would have been great," she added. "Fancy what it would have meant for the league if every member could have had, say two pounds to stand treat with at the Red Lion every time his wife got a baby. Votes! They'd never have got us out. Still, there's plenty of other things one can do — "

Clara was quite prepared to do the other things. The Education League was nothing but a marvellously cunning engine of local corruption. How a penny a week could produce a ton of coal, nothing but the central office of the Education League could say, and blankets dropped as if from heaven into such cottages as were loyal to the Cause while, of course, the members of the middle-class, those people who, as Mr. Shaw said, could be recognised because they did not accept a tip less than five pounds, could go and hear about Shakespeare's heroines and the case for the House of Lords.

Somehow Grace seemed to perceive the Education League as an embodiment of Clara's state of mind. Clara was excited and yet content in her excitement. It was as if she were doing something that corresponded faithfully with her mentality; it was as if she were realising herself, as if somehow, by expanding from narrow interests into broader ones, she were satisfying a need that she had felt for a long time. There was in her movement a greater quality of action. She had a purpose, she was achieving something, and though still nervous there was now in her something glad. "She is happier," Grace thought, and for a moment wondered whether that funny little adventure of Clara's, when she had been kissed by the young man encountered at the Union Jack Club, had had any results. But at once she smiled. No, of course not, Clara was not the sort to do anything like that, but then — suddenly Grace seemed flooded with lucidity. Yes, here it was, the Education League of course. This was the thing which Clara had found with which to inflame her life: on one side husband, lover, child; on the other society, or art, or politics — one drug or another, one way or another of making something of an empty life, of giving it purpose. During the budding, Clara, just as she herself, had suffered and wanted because this thing that could for a moment inflame her had not yet come; now Clara, with a live thing in her hand, this growing, spreading, energetic organisation that was like a healthy baby grabbing at everything it saw, Clara had an object and a satisfaction. She was becoming the centre of an abstract life which depended upon her. She was the soul of which the League was the body. She was giving it her labour, her enthusiasm, and because she was giving it so much, she loved it. It stood above her, a big, greedy thing, its appetite made up of a thousand little lusts, and it was taking from her her flying minutes of life, taking her pleasures, her sensations, taking her entirely, little by little devouring her. She was giving herself to the League much as Grace had given herself to Fenor, and as she gave she glowed, for the thing which she fed, which preyed upon her, became dependent on her; because it became dependent it became charming.

Yes, Clara was blooming, she too. And it did not matter much whether the flower that she brought forth was of the same colour or fashion as the one which was born of Grace. She too had been married and then, little by little, been forgotten. She had known loneliness and emptiness and seen her youth turn into a maturity on which nothing made claims. Her energy and love power had crept back until, having to give, she gave to that silly political association which made her as happy as might have some querulous, deformed little child, or some man, surly, hateful, vicious, cruel, who might either of them have been noble in her eyes because by love made noble. She too in her fashion was once more blooming.

The new quality in Grace carried her to Mary, who was daily becoming more sluggish, more content to lie up in the picturesque attitudes of motherhood. Often Grace looked at her, but with less envy than formerly when she herself had had nothing and Mary had seemed to have everything because wanting nothing. What struck her most was that Mary had changed so little in all the years she had known her. She seemed hardly older; she thought the things she thought ten years before. She was content except in one thing: "I hope it'll be a boy this time," she said; "Tom'd be disappointed if it was another girl." And her face grew sorrowful; it seemed to mean a lot to her that Tom should not be disappointed, and then it flashed upon Grace that the phenomenon of Mary was not comparable with her own or Clara's. If there had never been any urgency in Mary, listlessness, obvious suffering, if she had just gone on from year to year, living, bearing children and content, it seemed that she had found yet another drug with which to dull life. The child, the husband, the home, — yes, that was it. As Grace looked at her sister, very large, very white, rather beautiful upon the sofa, and unruffled by a desire save perhaps for a gift to her husband, a son, she saw no difference in Mary, none of the tempestuousness which seemed to have invaded her own life and that of Clara: Mary was not again blooming; from the very first day Mary had bloomed.

IV

Fenor came. He had wanted in his carelessness and his impetuousness to come before for several days, to settle in some forgotten little inn on the road to Walmer where she could visit him; then they had hesitated, feared, and yet they had dallied with the idea just as one plays with a cat which one knows will scratch one if one goes on long enough. It was Grace who had forbidden him to do this dangerous thing, and yet it was she who had wanted him to do it, because, at bottom, being woman, she recognised no law, because her desire was greater than her fear. And, strange paradox, while he strove to convince her that he might safely come he, so very much man, was still being reasonable and wise and full of doubts as to the excellent case which he presented. In the end he did not come, but it had been agreed that when at last he could finish the report on a smelting plant which had so uncomfortably fallen upon him in August, he would go to the Continent for a short time and snatch a day as he passed through Dover to meet her near Martin Mill.

She went trembling, as self-conscious after three weeks as if she were about to meet a stranger, wondering whether she would still be as beautiful to him, whether he still loved her or whether some fairer creature had seized upon him and whether, therefore, he came only out of that stupid, delightful, quixotic sense of duty that men feel for a while towards women whom they no longer love. A sort of shame, as if they were in debt, as if they knew they had taken more than they had given, and thought they must redress the balance by a few words or a few caresses which they no longer wanted to give; those were hideous thoughts that held her. She waited near the station towards which she had strolled as carelessly as she could after a hurried, scared drive from Kingsdown, cunningly arranged with a job-master in Walmer chosen because the family did not patronise him. She could see the twin snakes of the railway-line winding away brilliantly in the sun, and for a second she hated them as men lost in jungles hate nature, because she could not control the thing they might bring any more than man could cope with those peculiar scents and heats, with the heavy gloom of the hanging trees. Her heart gave a sudden, convulsive leap and began to beat so fast that she could hardly breathe: it was just a signal that had come down with a sharp clatter —

She was following him as he walked through the village, stopping as he now and then stopped to look with affected interest at the ugly new villas. They went out of the village upon the high road, and it was as if the road conspired with the sun, for their footsteps seemed so loud and their shadows so intimate. She followed, and so great was her excitement, though the sun was not hot, that she found her hands and brow quite moist. She followed; the houses grew more scattered and hedges replaced the palings; it seemed endless, this following. They turned up a lane, a little rutted path it was, with mauve flowers the name of which she did not know growing in the ditches. A bend in the lane hid from her the tall figure, clad in grey flannel that she followed as if ready to follow it for ever; she found that she walked faster, as if she could not bear that the hedges should conceal him. And then, quite suddenly, under an old, heavy oak, before she knew that he was waiting for her, she was in his arms, inarticulate, almost weeping, unable to do anything save grip him closer, press her face against his breast. They were motionless, close-clasped, these two, too tense in their excitement to relax enough to caress each other. As if in the grasp of an external force they held to each other, trembling.

It was much later only that they found civilisation reasserting itself over the primitive impulse of union which had thrown them silent and without will into an embrace. In that embrace they had given each other "news"—as if there were any news, as if anything could ever be new save a love that will endure. But still they were civilised people and they talked; they talked even of commonplaces while their eyes were greedy.

"I'm going to Dover to-night, and then to Ostend. I'm just going to stray about Belgium for a bit." He paused. "I've always wanted to see Bruges and Ypres—"

"We're not going back to town until the middle of next month," said Grace. "Mother likes having us all round her."

"Yes, I suppose so," said Fenor. There was a pause,

and they knew they were lying to each other, that all the time, while they said these things, they were casting towards each other the powerful effluvium of their passion, that they hardly knew what they were saying, so drunk were they with their other message. After a time they found they had nothing more to say, and very slowly they walked on along the little path that broke into the fields, meandered through stiles and up and down the hollows that were all green with pasture; they walked, arms round waists, close-linked and silent, stopping now and then to draw closer and kiss with a fierce, mute energy. It seemed as if during those three weeks of absence a need had accumulated in them that demanded satisfaction, a need so large that thought or deed could not satisfy it, and that they sought some means of communication more subtle, more intimate than word or caress.

And yet, after an hour, they found they had slipped back into their old relation. Fenor began to talk, no longer of his work and his plans, little things of no account, but of those things which made up the raw stuff of his personal life. Without any transition he had turned to politics, was talking of monarchy and what it meant. As she listened, Grace had once more her old feelings of mixed delight and disappointment. She always hated it a little when he spoke or thought of anything but herself, yet she was always glad when he laid before her the treasure of a mind which she thought so sumptuous. But in this minute she was thrilled, because once more he was being as he had been, and that seemed to mean he would so be again.

"The kings," said Fenor, disjointedly, "we haven't got any kings left, not real kings; they're too solemn now, too different, too like the presidents of republics. Democracy's become the fashion among the royal families of to-day, or rather no: it's bourgeoisie's become the fashion, the whole lot of them, czars and emperors, and so forth. And it's not the bourgeoisie of the bourgeois, it's a sort of super-middle-class idea, doing as little as possible lest those who don't do it may not like it."

"But surely, Enoch," said Grace, "kings are still men?"

Fenor shook his head sadly. "No," he said, "if they were I wouldn't object to them. It would be splendid to get hold of royal power and — harness it to the things that are worth while, as they used to do. You don't see what I mean, I suppose. I mean the old kind, Medicis, and Louis XIV, all those people. They weren't afraid of mixing with their subjects, of making love to them — and their queens weren't afraid. They were human and they could afford to take the risk of making themselves cheap because they were so high up that nothing could really make them cheap. We've only got one sort of king now, and that's the squire in his village; he isn't afraid of passing the time of the day with the blacksmith; he can't lose caste, you see. Well, they were just like that and they could enjoy themselves; they could afford to take up the arts which the people didn't like because it didn't matter what the people didn't like. They could even afford charming vices."

Grace laughed. "You'd better write that out, Enoch," she said, "and send it to the Kaiser for him to read it to his sons and try and make the household less good. They say," she added, womanlike with her lover, picking out a woman for attack, "that his empress is a good needlewoman."

Fenor gave a short, vicious laugh. "Yes," he said, "goodness, that's it; they just stew in goodness by order of King People. Good Lord, what a chance missed! Think of what they might do, people like that. They could lead all the arts, and all the philosophies, and all the sciences, if they liked. If I were a king, I'd have Bernard Shaw to lunch, if he'd come; and get a futurist to decorate my palace; I'd ride in busses and go to music halls. I'd still be the man behind the throne. I'd give money to everything that was new, and the more absurd it was the more money I'd give it, just because it was new, active, alive. Dancers should wear my crown-jewels — and dance with me at the Artists' Revel."

Grace laughed. "There'd be a revolution," she said.

"There might," said Fenor, "in fact it might be rather fun to lead it. Fancy a king joining the I. L. P.! The papers would love it. But it's no good, no good at all. It's much easier to stay inside, look at things officially and prohibit the bunny-hug."

It seemed much later, and the transition had been imperceptible when they took up once more the tale of their passion. They had walked back along a by-road, the hedges of which were thick with blackberry bushes dotted with glistening, red-brown berries. They had stopped for a long time to look at a bank where straggled the pale yellow flowers of the St. John's wort, and then again before a cottage where, behind tall stooping hollyhocks, upon the white wall the clematis spread violent purple hands. It was warm now, though the sun was slowly slanting towards the western lands, for the wind had fallen. They had become more silent and a little anxious, though they did not tell each other so, for they knew that half an hour only remained, that soon they must part, and she rejoin the carriage that would be waiting for her at Martin Mill. They stood near a bridge of rough planks that spanned a brook, crushing under their feet a thick, fragrant bed of bending grass. They looked into each other's faces as if anxious to carry away every detail of their features, and they did not smile but were tense and sorrowful, for this evening that was falling upon them was falling also upon the brief delight of their two hours. Quite involuntarily Grace found herself clutching at his coat, drawing closer to him.

"We've got to say good-by," she said. "Oh, I can't, it's too soon."

He folded his arms about her. "Yes," he said, "it's too soon, it's always too soon — but if it doesn't feel too soon it's too late. It hurts me to say good-by to you, but it's good. If it didn't hurt me it would mean I didn't love you."

She looked up at him seriously. "It hurts me too," she said, "but see, I can still speak — I can bear to part with you after all. Does that mean I don't love you enough?"

He smiled, pushed back from the forehead some of the heavy hair, and laid soft, slow kisses upon the massed freckles. "No, my darling," he said, "there's a limit, you see. It's dreadful to think of it, but our bodies are dull, poor things — they want to live, just of themselves — and they can't feel quite enough, not as much as the spark inside." He laughed. "We're like the lizards who part with their tails to save the rest."

She was still serious as she drew down his head and very gently pressed her lips to his. There is no passion in partings; there is something tender, maternal; it is all giving, not taking as in passion. As she clasped him close, she thought that she wanted to be to him as a mantle that he could wear, to give him all the emotion that was in her so that he could walk in an aura made of her soul. Then, womanlike, she wanted reassurance.

"Enoch," she murmured, "it's for ever, isn't it?"

For a long time he did not reply. He kissed her lips again, almost sadly.

"Little Russet," he said, "are you still asking those questions when so much is given to you? Oh, not me," he added, hurriedly, "I wouldn't be so fatuous. But the delight of loving anybody — anything will do. Titania was happy in the possession of Bottom and there you are asking me whether it's for ever, as if I knew. There's no to-morrow so long as there's a to-day, and if you've to-day it's ungrateful to ask for more."

She looked at him still silent and uncheered.

"Would you reproach the apple-tree in December," he said, "because it carries no longer the blossom of May? It'll bloom again before it dies. So in May stand under the apple-tree and capture its blossom so that it may jewel your hair; in December look up at its bare branches and tell yourself that it will bloom again."

She flung her arms about his neck in a nervous clasp.

"Oh, yes," she whispered, "it will bloom again, and again, and again, until the end."

V

" Please, mum," said the maid, " I've found some newspapers in Mr. Kinnersley's bed."

" Newspapers ? " asked Grace, " what ever do you mean ? "

" Yes, mum, between the blankets. There was the *Times* and the *Telegraph,* mum, spread out quite nicely all over the bed. I found 'em yesterday morning and I took 'em out and folded 'em up, but I found 'em there again this morning."

Grace received this queer information vacuously; another man was in her thoughts, but later in the evening it occurred to her to ask Edward why he put newspapers in his bed. It appeared that he had been cold in the night and that he had heard that newspapers were almost as good as an extra blanket.

" But why didn't you ask me for another ? "

" Oh, well," said Edward, " you seemed worried having to entertain your mother, and there's a lot to do away from one's own house, isn't there ? " Then, irrepressibly, with the complacent Edwardian smile: " A good hubby must look after his missus and see she's not worried."

Later in the night she reflected that this little incident was inexpressibly tender. He had thought of her in his clumsy, unreasonable way. His hesitation to do a quite obvious thing that would give nobody trouble had somehow expressed his odd tenderness for her. It was silly and charming. Was he beginning to think of her ? and was it too late ? For a moment tears filled her eyes and, though her veins were still flooded with the warm joy that had been hers that day, she wished it could have been otherwise, that the old Edward could rise from the dead; she thought of that ridiculous, wonderful day when he had said to her that they would be happy like two pussies in one basket. She smiled in the darkness at the absurd phrase, but the smile was sad, for she knew it was no good. He had thought of her as often before he had thought of her — during vacation. Her eyes were wet with tears as she sank into sleep, and in the half-dream which precedes sleep itself, she felt bending over her an unseen face. Unutterably longing she tried to stretch out her arms towards it, but already sleep was upon her, gently pressing down her body and hugging it to its soft, warm breast.

CHAPTER THE THIRD

ENOCH, HENRY AND JACK

I

THE Education League was booming, for this was November, and the general election which had been imminent since Lord Algernon Cust led his gallants to die in the last ditch, whence they emerged in time for the grouse, was upon the country. Lady Govan was taking her full share in the education of her masters, and as it was a cold winter the characters of Dickens and sacks of coal were in great demand. There was something cheery and democratic about Dickens, something that warmed the great heart of the people; the coal also did a little warming; a great many votes seemed all right. The banner of the League — a nice little thing, red, blue and orange because the party could never make up its mind whether it was red or blue, and because the only part of Ireland that counted had somehow to be included — was no longer floating merely over English fields but over others, where the thistle, the shamrock and the leek bent their shamed heads. There were now forty county branches, and there was even one in Galway.

"It's a jolly branch we've got there," said Clara to Mary, "even though they did have a little trouble the other day."

That was putting it mildly, for three-fourths of the audience had risen and sung:

Oh! the French are on the say,
    Says the Shan Van Vocht;
The French are on the say,
    Says the Shan Van Vocht;

Oh! the French are in the Bay,
They'll be here without delay,
And the Orange will decay,
Says the Shan Van Vocht. . . .

After a while the audience had turned its attention to "The Night Before Larry Was Stretched" and at last to "The Wearin' o' the Green." Later it had broken the League's educational furniture. The Irish Cerberus had not yet swallowed the coal.

"Never mind," said Clara, briskly, "keeps things going — prevents the Bulletin from getting dull."

For the League had now a bulletin with accounts of branch meetings, weekly appeals and letters from indignant retired colonels (indignant with the Government and in general). In these days Clara led a strenuous, delightful life; she seemed to have been born for it, and because of this predestination she was succeeding; she had found the work that was made for her and was making it the work of her life. She was successful: a Cabinet Minister had played golf with Sir Henry; an ex-Cabinet Minister's wife had called and received a call; Clara's portrait had appeared in the *Sketch* as "one of our brilliant young political hostesses." And one day Clara's cup was filled to overflowing, for she was cut dead by a leading Primrose Leaguer: this meant that her organisation had made good. She was making enemies: that was success. A few more, a quasi-unanimity of dislike, it would be victory. One morning she received an anonymous letter threatening to expose the inwardness of the Dante and blanket business. She looked into the mirror at her pretty, tight, rosy features, and brightly remarked to herself: "You're a dangerous young woman, that's what you are!"

And, meanwhile, Sir Henry in the House maintained the respectability of the affair by dissociating himself from it. He did not like the League, which he thought vulgar, but fortunately he did not understand it. If he had known — but he did not. What he did was to attend regularly, to vote regularly, to speak only when he was wanted and never at great length, to check his references, to avoid Latin and personalities, to play the game. Briefly, he behaved like a gentleman, while Clara — ran the League.

Lady Govan was not quite clear-eyed enough to know how all this would end, but she had enough intuition to suspect that it could end only in one way: that the League would become so powerful, so disgraceful, so dangerous, that it would have to be bought out by the party and that, when the time came, Sir Henry, having behaved perfectly well, would be the person who could safely be promoted as a compensation for the stoppage of the League's activities. Clara, ignorant of Benavente, emulated Crispin, was impudent so that Sir Henry might afford to be modest. But she did not read; she preferred to act: she arranged for cooking-classes, hired teachers of deportment, and wondered whether the cry of: "We want eight," ought not to be made into: "We want sixteen."

II

Mary lay upon the sofa, rather pale and weak that day, as if already she feared that recurrent trial of body and nerves which she knew so well and yet was always to her an adventure because, after all, maternity was the one adventure of her life. Grace had come to sit with her and found her silent, depressed. Outside the yellow mist hung over the Hammersmith Road, the motor-busses went by in procession, their noises muffled by the shroud of thick, moist air, and as they passed, dully tooting, there was a little movement in the oily shroud about the bare branches of the acacia tree. Grace, having exhausted the gossip which she thought might interest Mary, her mother's chronic servant troubles, the latest remark of Horace, and the cost of furs, found herself grow silent as night came on swiftly. Mary lay motionless on the sofa, firelit, and in her abundance beautiful as Ceres. Sometimes she moved her hand to fan her flushed face with a magazine.

"Are you feeling all right?" asked Grace, suddenly.

"Pretty fair," said Mary, "considering it's so soon." She became confidential. Then: "I do hope it'll be all right."

Grace laughed. "Good heavens! Mary, you're not frightened, are you?"

"No, of course not," said Mary. "I'm an experienced mother, as Clara says. It isn't that I mean. Only here I am — with five little girls and Tom wanting a boy. I too of course —"

Grace was a little annoyed by this, "I too." The phrase was somehow so subservient.

"Would you mind so much if it was a girl?" she asked.

"Very much," said Mary. "You see, I've found something out. Tom never says much, it's a sort of joke when he talks of Jack, but the other day, I was looking for a silly book I'm rather fond of, I won't tell you the title or you'd laugh, but anyhow I wanted to find it. So I rooted about in Tom's study and, opening an old box, I found a whole lot of boys' books."

"Well," said Grace, "what if Tom likes to keep his old books?"

Mary shook her head: "Oh, no, they're not his. There was Henty, and Marryat, and Ballantyne, and a whole lot of new people whom I don't know, with funny titles like *The Indian Trail* and even *Captains Courageous* — enough to amuse a boy until he was fifteen. And some bound volumes of the *Boy's Own Paper.*"

Grace understood. "You mean," she said, "that already —"

"Yes," said Mary, "he's been thinking about it for years. There was a bill in one of the books, five years old, and he never said much about it. It wasn't my fault and I suppose he didn't want me to think it was."

There was another long silence during which each sister thought of her own man and of men in general. Both of them were moved by this delicate sentimentality, by the idea of this burly, rather stupid man, stopping perhaps before a book-shop in a City street, disregarding the books that men really like, the W. W. Jacobses, the Nat

Goulds and the Edward Coopers, considering other titles: *Brooke of the Sixth Form,* and *Ungava.* They had a vision of something very tender and shamefaced, something much more delicate than could grow in the more sensual, the hotter soil of a woman's soul. Something very wistful and Northern. Tom, hiding these books for his unborn son, was doing it guiltily, tenderly, as if he were afraid of being caught in the office reading Andersen's fairy tales.

The room lit up as Tom suddenly opened the door, for the lights were on in the hall.

"Hallo," he said, cheerfully, "what are you plotting in the dark, you two?" Coming over to Mary, he kissed her, enquired in low tones how she felt; then he put a large box on the little table by her side and, a little exultantly, like a boy opening a school hamper, broke the string. They were big, black grapes.

"Oh, Tom," said Mary, "how sweet of you!"

"That's all right," he said, roughly. Thanks made him awkward. "Must have a wash now, see you again in a minute, old girl."

He did not come back at once however, not until Grace had gone, and somehow the atmosphere had grown tenser for they had said nothing, but slowly and one by one eaten a few of the grapes; it was as if a fear hung over them, as if in that minute both of them were living only for the satisfaction of this big, kind man, and were afraid that once more he might be disappointed, might have to continue in this long dream of his to buy year by year, for half another generation, boys' books as they came out.

III

Grace was impelled to tell Fenor this little incident, for now, after six months, she wanted to bind him closer to her by making him familiar with the daily events of her life and with the characters of those who figured in it. In the early days of her passion, passion had been enough. Hours had not been too much to solve such questions as:

"Do you love me?" "Why do you love me?" "How do you love me?" and "When did you begin to love me?" Then came another period when Fenor's ideas mattered as much as the love he bore her. He knew a great deal about the Govans and the Stanleys, about Mrs. Westfield, her servants and her reading, and sometimes he would generalise about those people who were almost strangers to him. He had not met them very often, though he had again dined at Kensington Square and formally called just in time to meet Lady Govan, who had pronounced him to be rough, interesting, but no good. This meant that he had flatly refused to give the Education League a lecture on mining, illustrating the need for closer union of the Empire. Grace did not mind, for Fenor never attacked her relatives; he knew that bourgeois blood is thick. But he liked to talk about them, he came to know them through the medium of Grace, for she was accurate if unimaginative. She supplied the facts and he the distortion; between them they made all those people very human. When she told him the story of Tom and his store of books, they were standing together on the crest on Primrose Hill, all alone, one afternoon in November. Below them lay an immense bowl, stretching far across the river towards Denmark Hill, in the white mist of which London lay buried and breathing hard. They leaned against the railings, looking into the south-east, shoulders touching, very conscious of each other in this solitude, for Primrose Hill in a fog is like a desert island where no Man Friday ever lands.

"It's charming," said Fenor, at length, "and, Russet, it's just what I've told you always: that sort of thing shows how unfair you are to men; you don't like 'em, you know."

"What!" cried Grace. "Well, I should have thought you'd be the last — "

Fenor laughed. "You don't understand at all; loving and hating's almost the same thing. Hate is the desire to crush, love is the desire to conquer; crushing and conquering are very much alike. They talk of women giving themselves to men — it's bunkum. They don't do it any more than men give themselves to women. It's not even exchange, nothing so just; it's contest, conquest, hostility, combatant caresses; that's all it is — and the only thing worth while in the world."

Grace pressed his arm. "You're being silly, Enoch," she said, "a battle can't be the most beautiful thing in the world."

"Oh, can't it?" said the man. "There's nothing so fine. Contest, that's life; peace, that's death; so long as we want to dominate we know we are strong. We must grow like trees even if blood must feed our roots. If we cease to grow we begin to decay; we must fight for life and for love because nobody's going to give us life or love for nothing. There's not enough to go round, you see. It's taking we've got to do and the taking justifies us because none save the strong have the right to live. Poverty, weakness, self-sacrifice, these are the crimes, these are the soft spots of the strong, the things that overcome them in the end. We're like crabs in a bucket, all anxious to get to the top and the noblest are not those who lie at the bottom, for they'd gladly be at the top." He drew in a heavy breath. "My God, I'll go gladly singing into battle."

They were silent for a long time, and Grace said:

"But Tom doesn't fight all the time. Can't you think of him stopping in Leadenhall Street and just picking off a bookstall a peace-offering to his ideal?"

Fenor nodded. "Yes, it's charming, and like all charming things it's a little foolish. If he wants a son as badly as that and Mary can't give him one, he should cast her off. The old Mosaic law was not wrong in that, any more than any other Jewish theory. They're strong people, the Jews; nothing can crush them, for they know that though there may be a spiritual world, there's a material one; they're the only true religious agnostics." He pursued his train of thought, consciously drawing Grace closer, as if holding her to him he fed upon her vigour, and by so preying became more lucid. "A belief in the hidden things,'' he said, '' that's the ticket. A belief that there's an illimitable field beyond the things we know, that's immortality, but also a belief that the field with limits which we call life is well worth our tilling. There's an inner life and there are hidden things, secret mysteries, desires and powers in us; some of us capture a flicker of them and there's genius; and others go along paying their rates. If you have anything of the gleam then nothing is below you — if you can bear all things then you can dare all things — you can be secret — and criminal and lying and vile, and yet be so big in your knowledge that all these things slide off you as drops of water from the polar bear's coat. You've got to be a hero to afford to be heroic; none save a bird can fly over abysses, but he that dares to fly over abysses can sometimes become a bird.''

In the long silence that followed, as the fog took them upon its soft, cold bosom and stroked their faces with ghostly, clammy hands, Grace felt herself completely remote from the encircling world: it was as if they had been marooned. Uneasily her head moved upon the man's shoulder; she drew closer, softly kissed his passive cheek. This man who held her, who seemed the only warm, actual thing in the world, and he casually holding her, thinking his own thoughts, caring little in that minute what it was he held, he was Olympian on Primrose Hill. She took his face between her hands, looked long into the sharp, grey eyes with the big whites, playfully ruffled the thick hair that fell under the soft hat. But, no, her movement was not playful, it was caressing and admiring.

'' Knight,'' she said, '' what would you do for your lady? ''

He looked at her seriously. '' So long as she's my lady, everything.''

Grace's heart froze. '' And when she's no longer your lady? ''

He did not hear her. '' Heroism is the only justification for love. To be ready to bear and to dare, that alone can make it justifiable.'' He looked at her more intently.

"I have you and I want you, no man shall take you from me, nothing shall take me from you."

She pressed closer and insisted: "So long as I am your lady."

He smiled as he bent to kiss her. "You are my lady," he said.

IV

For the first time in her life perhaps, as Clara occupied the chair, she was conscious of things outside herself. She felt lost in the enormous emptiness of Albert Hall, though it was packed in every seat, though even the sacred stalls of the freeholders were filled, and though in the galleries she could see faces, bunched and piled, row behind row, forming solid masses that had, by their blending, lost the character of separate humanity. She might have been suspended by a thread, so individual was this eddying of heads, men's heads, many of them grey or bald, and women's heads, feathered or aigretted or, which was still more complimentary, roughly shawled or surmounted by a man's cap. The aristocracy was there, and that was good; the democracy was there and that was better; and she in the middle, the god in the car rather than the god in the machine. Not even the people closer to her, the row of reporters busy with the agenda at the long table at her feet, nor the packed orchestra, nor her neighbour, the Countess, nor the others, members of Parliament, presidents of country branches, nor the bishop, nor the Conservative Wesleyan, had any relation with her. They were nothing, all of them, but the gorgeous setting in the midst of which her life chose to manifest itself.

For a moment, while the Countess, who was in the chair, spoke, Clara felt extraordinarily lucid. She realised her disconnection: it was like the disconnection between a mother and her child. Mother and child, organiser and League, close things both, and yet separate, wonderfully separate, growing. In that minute she loved the League that she had made out of her own energy as if it were a growing boy that had sprung from her body. And, behold! here it was more and more like a noisy child, clapping as the Countess finished, and cheering and cheering. She swiftly returned to the world as a worldly preoccupation seized her. After the M. P. she would have to speak. She had a little pang of fear. She had often spoken before; she spoke well if without inspiration, but this place — it seemed so large, made one believe against all experience that one would need a very powerful voice. And it was so full, so anxious to approve that to disappoint it would be terrible. Then she lost that queer feeling of union by a thread, of not hearing very well, of not seeing clearly, of being aware of nothing but the beating of one's heart and of one's eyes trying to come out of their sockets, which is what they call stage-fright. For the member of Parliament was droning on successfully. At first she had heard nothing but the traditional words: "Government by faction" (Cheers) — "A united empire" (More cheers) — "Pettifogging Welsh Attorney" (A crashing roar of cheers) — Yes, it was going well. Clara grew more lucid, saw expressions upon the faces of the platform: the Countess apparently rather bored and evidently doing it because somebody had to do it — the bishop in his "Punch" attitude, hands clasped over his stomach — other faces, some of them quite excited (they came from the country) — and yet others, very conscious of being looked at, a little rigid, the women showing their profiles and the men as if before a camera, trying to look stern and brave.

A burst of cheering and clapping told Clara that the M. P. had sat down and that now her turn was coming. Curiously, she felt cooler, more lucid than at the beginning. She heard her name announced by the Countess who, looking more bored than ever, insulted Clara by looking at the agenda very carefully and inserting a pause between the words "Lady" and "Govan," just enough to show that she wasn't quite sure who Lady Govan was. As Clara got on her feet she threw the Countess an angry glance, determined to be even with her one day, if it took her a generation. She put the flicker of anger away in the little museum of hatreds that most of us store in our brain and out of which, some time or other, some of us extract enough, when our adversary is down and out, to send him a loan collection.

She was speaking. At once she knew that she was speaking well, recounting the early struggles of the League and how it was born, just of itself, to bring culture within the reach of the homes of the British democracy. Sentimental touch: "Think of it as a little League" (Great emotion) — "The hard spade-work, conversion of people of influence" (Face turned away from the Countess) — "the slow-spreading activities over the country — enlightenment, culture, deportment and — and culture. . . ." Humorous touch: "The map of the British Isles upon the office-wall and the little flags planted in county after county." Clara's childish delight in sticking them in — Short interval for dutiful merriment. Then the triumph of the League: "Fourteen hundred meetings a week — two million four hundred and twenty-three thousand leaflets — a hundred and forty-two touring-vans — Education League pierrots on Margate sands — Education League aeroplane at Hendon, actress included — "

Clara spoke now in broken sentences interrupted by laughter, clapping and cheers, for the activity of her slender body seemed to radiate upon the vast audience, to excite, to inflame it and so, when suddenly she abandoned her baby and attacked the general problem of the political situation, her hearers were in a mood attuned to hers. She did not waste time on the intricacies of what the Radicals intended to do with the House of Lords. Glancing every now and then at the ruling phrases typed on the slip of paper she held, Clara let herself go: "Ladies and gentlemen!" she shouted, "we must not forget what it is we have come together for. It is not enough that we should have an association destined to further the spread of literature and the arts — No, ours is a yet more sacred and more earnest mission: to uphold with the faith of our fathers the principles of justice and of equity which have made this great Empire what it is." (Socialist protest: "Yes, look at it," ignored.) "In these days when all things are menaced, when our trade decays before our eyes, when the unity of these islands is endangered by Irish conspirators and American gold, when the House of Lords which has stood — four square in the breach to defend the people is to be cast down so that the buttress of our constitution may fall away and we be delivered, hands bound, into the power of party politicians — the time has come for us to rise in our thousands and our millions, and say —" (Slight hesitation over Miss Lenzie's typing) — "this shall not be, for Britons never, never —"

A roar of cheers drowned her last words. At once half the hall was on its feet, taking up the cue of this brilliant peroration. As if by a prearranged signal the organ let forth — two lieutenants of some devoted stage-manager stood up in the orchestra and together began to sing. Already the audience was singing:

> Rule Britannia! Britannia rules the waves!
> Britons never shall be slaves. . . .

Trembling, her colour high, Clara sat down. Behind her was Sir Henry, a little rigid, still not liking it very much, and by his side, Grace, excited almost as Clara, because the tense effluvium of the audience worked upon her already stimulated mind. Clara threw her husband a glance so delighted that it was almost loving. He smiled back, then leant forward and said into her ear, speaking aloud to dominate the roaring strains of "Rule Britannia:" "I say, I saw the Whip a minute ago, I'm to have the Central Office — they're reorganising it."

Clara felt her face grow hot with a rush of blood. "Organiser!" she whispered. Then, to Sir Henry: "Oh, Harry, then that means — Under Secretary of something — when we come in."

The big man smiled at her good-humouredly. "Well," he said, "perhaps it does." And then, as if he could not bear to leave unsatisfied her girlish glee: "It might even mean a little more, I'm told; not quite the Cabinet, of course, not at once."

"Oh, Harry!" cried Clara, clasping her hands together.

"We're not in yet," said Sir Henry, laughing.

V

Grace was told the news. She knew that Sir Henry was not a man to speak rashly. If he had said that, it was certain. Under-Secretary of State at least! the Cabinet perhaps. So Clara had won. A great delight seized her; she was glad, violently glad that Clara had somehow justified herself, had managed to snatch out of life, that hard affair, something that made her joyous. Yes, Clara too, after years of waiting, she too had come to bloom, to the second blooming.

Grace moved restlessly in Fenor's arms, for she was thinking these thoughts in the taxi where she had joined him. Edward had not been able to come to the meeting and now, swiftly, the taxi was taking her to Kensington from Albert Hall, via Regent's Park. Fenor had refused to talk about the meeting, though it had delighted and amused him, even excited him: he loved "Rule Britannia" quite as well as "The Red Flag." But another feeling, that feeling which inflamed Grace, had passed into him and made him careless of material things such as meetings and successes. As he held her and from time to time pressed kisses upon her neck, she felt that this night was not as other nights, that time had led them still a little further, still a little higher, that they were, both of them, on the crest of their wave. They had nothing to say, as if all things had been said, as if now love needed no explanation, but only beatitude. He took her face between his hands and for a long time looked into her half-veiled eyes; she smiled up at him, passive, secure and conquering because assured that she was conquered. At last only did he say in that hoarse, soft voice that she so loved, that came to him only in these moments: " I adore you, I adore you." And then her smile was killed in a kiss, and her fingers upon his neck grew rigid, each one of them animate with her triumphant love.

VI

Upon the hall-table in Kensington Square lay a telephone message scribbled upon the block: " Mrs. Stanley gave birth to a son at half-past nine." For a long time Grace looked at the message. A son! Mary too! And for the first time, as she thought together of Mary, to whom a son was given, of Clara climbing the dizzy heights which led to power, of herself rich at last in the possession of a love-filled life, she knew what the commonplace phrase meant that delight can be almost unendurable. All three of them then — on the same night triumphant.

BOOK THE FIFTH

MARY

He that hath the ashes of a friend hath an everlasting treasure.
(Sir Thomas Browne. — *Hydriotaphia.*)

Plaisir d'amour ne dure qu'un instant,
Plaisir d'amour dure toute la vie . . .
(A garbled but, in its paradoxic form,
truer version than the usual.)

CHAPTER THE FIRST

THE THREE SISTERS

I

It was half-past three, a brisk January day with the wind about the corners, dust and paper on its wings. As Clara stood upon the refuge at Oxford Circus she was irritable again, as if something of the cold, quick sting of the wind had got into her blood. She felt irritated with the traffic which moved slothfully before her, cutting her off from the northern pavement. Those motor-busses, taxis, those crawling horse vehicles; would the ribbon never end? So slow. She stamped, and the old, military-looking gentleman who shared the refuge with her and two large women laden with parcels, smiled at her childish impatience. The old man was a psychologist in his way, having nothing better to do between the hours he spent at his club, for he was on the retired list. "Nice girl," he thought. "What a devil of a hurry she's in. I suppose she's meeting her boy round the corner. Perhaps she can see him now and then between the busses. Hero and Leander, Romeo and Juliet, all that sort of thing — Poor kid."

Lady Govan might have been annoyed if she had been a thought-reader, but she had no idea how young she looked, though this was 1913 and she thirty-five. It was her nervous energy kept her young. But Clara was not thinking of the old gentleman; she just stamped. The old gentleman smiled.

"Lord! " he sighed, half-humorous, half-sad, "I wonder whether my little Betty ever stamps like that when she's got a rehearsal the day she ought to meet me. Don't suppose she does," he added, philosophically. "And I'm too old to do much stamping. Hallo! What's this? "

There was enough to arouse his attention, for quite suddenly all signs of impatience had fled from the wind-stung rosiness of Clara's face. Her eyes had grown large, her mouth fallen open, and she stared with extraordinary intentness. Taxis passed, and motor-busses, and still she stared. There was a gap in the traffic, quite a long gap, and she did not cross the road. The old gentleman was so interested that he too forgot to cross but just went on watching the pretty woman who looked strange. She looked so strange that, after a hesitation, he came to her side with the air, part chivalrous, part friendly, part insolent, that comes to men who are fond of women.

"I beg your pardon," he began, "but could I do anything for you?"

Clara looked him full in the face and then, suddenly, without replying, crossed the road.

"Offended," muttered the old gentleman. "Well, well, perhaps I didn't say the right thing, one doesn't always."

He was wrong. Clara had no idea of what he had said, and now, having leapt into a taxi that had mysteriously drawn up at her feet, as if guessing her need, she had forgotten all about him, was concentrated upon only one thought and its significance. She drew no clear conclusions from that thought. She was just conscious, as the taxi turned into Park Lane and then along the Park made for Hammersmith, that she was doing something quite instinctive, obeying a command. She was not happy, unhappy, or excited; rather she was numb and excited together. Outwardly calm, she was like an ordinary brick house inside which a murder is happening.

II

Mary was at home. She generally was, never having quarrelled with woman's sphere. She sat in the drawing-room upon the settee, doing some fancy-work. She was alone, for the nurses had led out the members of her rabbit warren to take the air. Face down upon the sofa lay one of Tom's absurd, idealistic, charming little traces: *The Public Schools' Year Book.* For Jack was two now, and Tom was gravely considering at which school he should have him put down. He even discussed Oxford and Cambridge now and then. Mary smiled up at Clara and remarked:

"How nice of you to come, Clara. What have you been doing with yourself since last week?"

"What d'you say?" asked Clara, and as she spoke she felt dimly offended because Mary greeted her with a commonplace. Mary ought to have known, she thought. But then, tact was never Mary's strong point; too fat, she supposed. "Look here, Mary," she began, briskly, "I've come to talk to you. Something's happened, something dreadful."

A fear leapt into Mary's eyes. "Is Harry ill?"

"Oh, dear," cried Clara, "I wish you wouldn't think there's nothing except people's health — or their stomach, or something. No, it's much worse than that. It's about Grace. For heaven's sake don't look at me as if I was going to tell you Grace has had a fit. Grace is perfectly all right in health. It's something else."

"Something else?"

"Yes," said Clara. Then, hurriedly: "Grace is unfaithful to her husband. She has a lover or she is going to have one, and I know him. It's Fenor; you know the man I mean."

There was a long silence, for Mary looked at her as if she hardly understood.

"Grace —" she said, at last, "and Fenor! Oh, Clara, this is dreadful, but — but are you sure? How d'you know? Can you be sure?"

"I've seen them," said Clara.

"Where? How?"

Clara looked away from her sister and began to speak as if she were reciting a lesson: "I was standing on a refuge in Oxford Street and the traffic was slow. Just for a second a taxi pulled up in front of me and I saw them together — they were kissing."

"Good heavens!" said Mary.

There was a pause. Then Clara became impatient. "How dare they!" she snarled. "It's abominable. I never thought Grace was that sort of woman. Here we are, sisters, known each other all our lives — and only find it out now."

"Well," said Mary, comfortably, "you didn't expect her to advertise, did you?"

"Don't be funny. It only takes you about once in five years and this isn't the moment. Don't you see that this sort of thing can't go on? Not only it mustn't go on, but it can't. It'll come out. There'll be a scandal. Oh, I can't bear it, I can't bear it. Mary, it's dreadful! It's abominable!"

"Of course, of course," said Mary, soothingly, employing the tone which she used to Ella, who was often peevish. "Keep cool, Clara; perhaps it isn't as bad as you think."

Clara laughed rather harshly. "Oh, no, Mary, it's no good. If they had only met a month ago, I don't say — but she has known him a long time, three or four years, isn't it? It's much more than just a flirtation — you've got to make up your mind to that. G.'s a funny girl, you see; I've never quite understood her. But every now and then I've thought she was different, the last few years."

"She used to be steady enough," said Mary. "She never used to want to go out much or anything."

"That's true, but I seem to remember a sort of change. I can't say what it was exactly. Don't you remember when she began wearing all those funny clothes?"

"No, I can't say I do," said Mary. She had noticed even less than Clara. "If you ask me, she seems to have been steadier and happier the last few years than ever she was before."

"There you are!" cried Clara, pointing a triumphant finger at her. "I hadn't thought of it myself. You can't pretend now that something didn't happen in her life."

There was a long pause during which the two sisters grew quite convinced that they knew the truth. Mary's state of mind was in that minute complex. She blamed Grace. Grace had done a dreadful, abominable thing. She was a bad woman, she'd disgraced herself — and yet — and yet. Mary struggled to find out what this was that dictated in her mind: "and yet." Edward had something to do with it. And Grace's last visit, when she had been so gay in her repose, so lovely with the last freckles of summer slowly melting into the rose of her cheeks. But as Mary softened, Clara hardened.

"Look here," she said, as briskly as if giving instructions to a billposter, "we can't let this go on; it's got to be stopped at once. We can't have a scandal, it would — " She paused, feeling a little ashamed to say just then that she feared the effect of the scandal on her husband's career. "It would — break mother's heart," she substituted.

Clara melted a little at the thought, for she was quite genuine. She wanted to spare both her husband's career and her mother's heart. And at the bottom of her soul was a warped, Puritanical, bitter little envy, a sort of rage of the dyspeptic in presence of a banquet. She did not know that. "Anyhow," she ended up, "it's got to be stopped. We must see Grace and tell her so — we must have it out. What d'you say, Mary?"

"Oh, well," said Mary, vaguely, "of course." She knew very well that Clara was not consulting, but instructing her.

"What shall we do?" asked Clara. Replying to her own question: "I'll telephone her now."

She ran out of the room. Almost at once, it seemed, Mary heard her sister's voice in the hall: "Mrs. Kinnersley — not at home — oh, of course not — I forgot. I'm Lady Govan." A pause. "Well, tell Mrs. Kinnersley to ring up Mrs. Stanley as soon as she comes in. It's very important."

The receiver rattled and, as Mary listened to Clara's

quick step upon the stairs, the odd melancholy seized her again. "Poor little G.," she thought, "what trouble she's in for." She pulled herself up. "Serve her right, she oughtn't to have behaved like that. It's abominable, that's what it is."

Clara came in. "Of course I ought to have remembered they're still out together."

Mary found herself thinking: "Poor little G., what trouble she's in for!"

"Don't expect she'll be in for an hour or two," said Clara. "The maid said she had somebody to tea at half-past four. But people get delayed when they're like that."

Mary smiled faintly. "You seem to know a lot about it, Clara."

"Don't be silly. It's precious little one doesn't find out about that sort of thing in St. Panwich."

"Well," said Mary, at length, "there's nothing we can do, is there? Don't let's think about it, not until she comes. Let's talk of something else."

For a while they did talk of something else and, quite naturally, it seemed to be of Henry's, or rather Clara's career. Those two years had been eventful. Sir Henry had proved himself at the Central Office and had been chosen to move the amendment to the address; he had acted as a sort of supernumerary whip, and his cheerful urbanity made it possible that he would become Chief Whip in the course of the coming session if, as seemed very likely, the tenant of the office retired from Parliament. Yes, Sir Henry was a success, or was it Clara? The Education League was still in being, still powerful, but it absorbed less of Clara's energy, for steady pressure had been applied to her from certain sources and, little by little, the League had become respectable. The coal and blanket idea had slowly been suppressed, had disappeared from the field of the League's activities and been transferred to a few individuals who were at the same time charitable and political. The League was still going in for culture: indeed it had become a serious competitor of the "Everyman," and "T. P.'s Weekly" circles. It was perhaps not quite as powerful as it had been, but other business had come to Clara, more important, more soul-satisfying.

"I wish she'd come," Clara fumed at last. "It's half-past four now. She ought to be home, and I must get off soon — I've got that dinner to-night."

"What dinner?" asked Mary.

"Oh, the Southern Counties," cried Clara, petulantly. "Don't you ever read the paper, Mary?" She remained silent and raging for a while, unable now to think of her political dinner, concentrated upon the horrid tragedy of her sister's life and what it might entail. Disaster of some kind, that was sure, unless it could be smothered at once. Then the telephone bell rang. Clara leapt to her feet.

"Let me go," said Mary, "you see, it may be somebody else."

Something instinctive, deep inside her, told her who it was. She felt she wanted to spare Grace the sharpness of Clara's words.

"Yes," she said, in reply to Grace's voice, "it's me, Mary. No, there's nothing wrong, exactly wrong — "

"But what d'you want?" asked Grace.

"Well, I want you to come here at once."

"But why?" cried the voice. "There must be something wrong!"

"Well, yes," said Mary, reluctantly. "Yes, there's something wrong — You'd better come at once."

"But I've got somebody coming. Oh, do tell me."

"No, not now," said Mary, softly. "Clara's here too — it's serious — you must come."

Grace's voice grew shrill with excitement: "Mary, please — "

"No," said Mary, putting down the receiver, and, very softly: "not now."

As she went back into the drawing-room, she thought: "Poor little G., she doesn't know yet. Let her still be happy for ten minutes."

III

Grace closed the door behind her and instinctively stood almost against it. In that minute, as she looked at her two sisters, Clara standing up and Mary almost presidential in a large armchair, though she knew nothing she suspected everything and, figuratively, she stood with her back to the wall. It looked queer, this quasi-court of justice. Its solemnity clashed with its appurtenances, the cerise curtains and the family photographs in silver frames that suddenly seemed so large. Yes, she knew, and it was a tribute she paid to her own fine courage that in the coming of that knowledge she squared her broad shoulders and suddenly looked bigger in the heavy sables that climbed up her cheeks, mingling with her hair until her face seemed quite small and all the softness of her cheek and neck gone. There was nothing of her to see save her over-red mouth, her high nose, her anxious, defiant eyes.

Her sisters watched her warily, very like boxers about to strike, afraid to move lest they first might be struck. They knew that the first word would open up between them and their sister an unbridgeable chasm, and they were afraid. Even Clara, who was angry, was afraid; Mary was afraid and sorry. They were never to forget the tension of that moment when all three knew that the irremediable was to be spoken and that it was irremediable it should be spoken. But it did not last, for the grade of its intensity was too high, and it was Grace who broke the silence, less because she was impatient than because these two and a half years of association with a man to whom courage was a policy had given her something of the desire which drives the regiments, running, towards the cannon's mouth.

"Well?" she said, harshly. This was not her usual voice; all the tender hesitation had gone; this was a woman now, and fighting.

"You want to know—" said Mary, then hesitated. "You will be wondering why we — you see, G. — "

"Oh, shut up, Mary!" cried Clara, suddenly, "if that's all you can say. Look here, G., it's like this. We know all about it, about you and Mr. Fenor — it's got to stop."

Grace drew back a step so that her back touched the door. She had not expected it to come like this, peremptory. But, as the solidity of the wood touched her, courage seemed to flow into her. "They're hitting my man," she thought. "Now then, no surrender!" And aloud, in a quiet voice: "You know? And pray what do you know?" They did not reply, and she went on: "You know that Mr. Fenor comes to my house sometimes. Well, what next?"

The two sisters looked at each other, rather frightened. They had expected anger or tears, not this calm evasion. But Clara returned to the charge: to return to the charge was the only thing she could do in life, and she had found by experience that it always worked. "It's no use talking like that, G.," she said, more amiably. "Of course I'm very sorry for you. It's no use pretending; I saw you, you see."

"Saw me?" asked Grace. And as she spoke there was a little ooze in her courage. What had Clara seen? There was so much she might have seen, so much that was tender and sacred, and which, by being seen, became vile. But Clara was talking, almost gabbling in her excitement:

"I saw you in Oxford Street, and him — in a taxi — an hour ago and he was kissing you." She drew in her breath and stopped as if it had cost her an effort to bring out the fact. "And it's no use your telling me it doesn't mean anything, because I know it does, and because you know that I know it. It's no use pretending — you and he — Oh, don't make me say these things." She clenched her hands together nervously. "But it's got to be stopped — it can't go on. It's — it's wrong."

"Is it?" asked Grace. And it seemed to her as if a soft, throaty, melodious voice had prompted her reply.

Clara had not heard or had not chosen to hear. Already she was on ground more important than the moralities.

"Don't you see," she cried, "what it all means? It can't go on because it's got to come out; it can't be kept quiet. I don't say it ought to be," she added, with a renewed access of moral rigidity. "But, anyhow, it can't be kept quiet. I've seen you; perhaps somebody else has seen you, or will to-morrow or in a month. And they'll talk and talk, and it'll spread until you're just in the middle of hundreds of people, all talking about you. Oh, G., you must stop it while there's time."

"Why?" asked Grace. She was still on her defence, but now she was no longer denying.

"But Grace, my dear," said Mary, softly, "you can't let things go like that. Don't you see what it'll mean. It'll get to Edward's ears, and then what will you do? You've got to think of him and your children."

"Oh, my children," said Grace, impatiently, "they're all right."

"Yes," cried Clara, rather trenchant, "that's not the question at all, Mary; it's the scandal. We simply can't have a scandal; there's never been one in our family."

"Then," said Grace, "according to the law of probabilities, it's about time we had one!" And she thought: "Who said that? Enoch or I?"

"Don't be silly," said Clara. "We simply can't afford a scandal. You're only thinking of yourself. Mary's right, in a way, about Edward and your children. I repeat that's not the only question, but it comes in. There are other things: your position in society and your—connections."

"Connections?" asked Grace, "I don't quite understand."

"Well," said Clara, "have you ever thought what it'll mean for all of us?"

"I can't say I have," said Grace. "I suppose I ought to," she added, reflectively. Then, suddenly biting: "You're quite sure you're thinking about me, aren't you, Clara? You say I was only thinking about myself; you're quite sure that it doesn't apply to you too? No, of course not," she murmured, before Clara could reply, "it wouldn't matter to you."

"Oh, wouldn't it!" cried Clara, stung. "There's all sorts of things you don't know of. Do you think it would be nice for me? — in my political position — ? In politics it simply won't do. And Mary and — her friends — they're not so tolerant as you think — about here."

Mary looked angry. She did not quite like this suggestion of suburban intolerance among her friends. "Don't bother about my friends," she said to Clara.

But Grace had not noticed. "Oh," she said, "is that it, Clara? I'm sorry, I hadn't grasped. You mean the House would expect you to live down to me — is that what you mean?"

Clara stamped. "No, of course not, it's bad enough your having behaved like this without your being cheaply smart about it. I'd have thought you'd have a sense of shame."

Grace was still hard, still fighting. "Sense of shame!" she said. "Why should I be ashamed? There are two ways of living, Clara. One of them is never to do anything of which you're ashamed, the other is never to be ashamed of anything you do and — " She stopped suddenly, for her eyes filled with tears as she remembered who it was had first said that. Clara shrugged her shoulders.

"Well," she said, "if you're going to talk like a society play you may as well be stopped and be done with, for what I've got to say's plain enough, and that is that you can't go on with this sort of thing. Everything's against you. Isn't that so, Mary?" Mary nodded. "Everything's against you," Clara began again, "the opinion of society, your responsibility to your husband and your children, to the rest of your family and their interests. Good heavens! it looks as if you were willing to let everything go just for a passing fancy of yours. I'll tell you what it is: you haven't got any natural feelings and, what's more, you don't try to acquire any."

Grace laughed at the Irish bull, but behind the laugh

was an angry gasp. "Whose interests were they thinking of, all of them? Were hers considered?" Suddenly anger took her. "And I?" she cried, "And I? Where do I come in? Are you forgetting all about me? It's a case of charity beginning at home! Why should I be the last to be considered? Haven't I a life to make worth while, if I can? You think it's all plain sailing, or you pretend to think it's all plain sailing for me. You think I got married eleven years ago, and was happy ever after. Were you? I'd like to know. And if you think I've been happy all these eleven years, why can't you let me go on being happy? why are you trying to do me out of my happiness? And if you think I was unhappy all the time, again I want to know why you're trying to do me out of this little bit of happiness? But I'm not going to argue that, don't be afraid. I'm not going to argue out whether it's envy's moving you, Clara, or where you come in, Mary. It doesn't matter, after all; the only thing that matters is the truth about me."

"You might as well tell it while you're about it," said Clara.

"Tell it!" cried Grace. "D'you think I'm going to hide? I've been hiding up to now because I had to, because the world can't bear the idea of two people loving each other; it's a sort of jealousy. You all want other people to be more miserable than yourselves because it cheers you up in your own unhappiness. It would be nice, Clara, wouldn't it? if you were the only woman in the world without a wooden leg?"

"Oh, don't be idiotic."

"People who tell the truth are always called idiotic for a while. I'm going to tell it all the same. Yes, I'm in love with Enoch Fenor, and I have been for nearly three years and — you may as well have the whole truth — there's nothing that he can claim from me as a lover that I have refused him." There was a silence. "Well? aren't you going to answer? Aren't you going to tell me what you think of me? What have you had me up for? To tell me I was a bad woman, or an immoral woman

— isn't that right? Come, Clara, don't let me say it on your behalf. What would you like to call me?"

Clara looked up to the ceiling and sighed. "I don't know what's happened to you, G. — the way you talk, there's something wild about you, I've seen it coming on for a year or two. You say the sort of thing people don't say. You've changed."

"Ah!" cried Grace, exultantly, "you're right, Clara, I've changed. I've come to life, you see, instead of just walking about like you, dressed in the latest thing in shrouds. I've found out that the only thing worth while is not to be afraid of taking happiness when it comes — it doesn't come very often, just once or twice perhaps and, for us women, very much in the same way. Love is the dream that comes in the sleep of death." But suddenly her fancy, less winged than that of the man who was inspiring her words, fell to the ground. "And I am not going to give him up. I don't care what you all say or what you all do. You can tell Edward, you can tell mother; you can go and shout it outside if you like. I don't care, I've got him and I'll keep him. D'you think I'm going back to what I've had to stand? a husband who didn't care for me — well, he cared for me like he did for the Welsh dresser — he'd bought us both. Oh, I'm not saying anything against him really; Edward's no worse than the rest, rather better in many ways; awfully sweet sometimes, and generous, and kind, when it occurs to him, and the children are all right. They're fond of me in their way, I suppose. Just as you all are, just as a lot of my friends are. But it isn't enough, it's like being in a crowd, just squashed among people you don't know. It's only by loving somebody that you can know. D'you think I'm going back to that loneliness with nothing to do that matters? Too much money to have any work worth doing — just doing nothing over and over again. No, I won't give in; do what you like and say what you like, and I won't give in, and it's no use asking me to have any pity for the Education League, Clara, though that's what you mean."

A hot flush rushed into Clara's cheeks, but before she could speak Mary had intervened.

"G.," she murmured, "don't talk like that, please. Don't talk like that, you sound so hard."

"I've got to, you're against me."

Mary went up to her sister, took her hand. "Dear," she said, "I'm not against you; do try and understand. I'm not going to say a word against you or against him, only, you see, it'll have to end some time. Won't you end it before it begins giving pain to all of us? You're fond of us too, aren't you?" Grace kept down a sob. So long as they were hard to her she felt well, she almost enjoyed herself, but sympathy seemed to melt her. She shook off Mary, but her sister persisted. "I don't want to say anything about it, about — whether you were wrong. Of course you know what I think: a woman's got her husband and her children, she ought not to want anything else."

"Oh, ought! ought!" cried Grace, impatiently.

"Yes, I know. It's hard sometimes to do what one ought, but one has to all the same; isn't that true?"

"Mary," said Grace, suddenly, "do you want me to give him up? D'you want me to give up the only man I've cared for just because there's a risk of a little trouble? of silly people talking? D'you want me to give up the only thing that's been worth while and to go back — well, to what? What d'you offer me, Mary? I'm thirty-four, I've got a long time to live, probably. What are you going to give me?"

Mary was silent for a moment. Then, uncertainly, she said: "You really ought to give him up, Grace. You can't deny it."

Grace Kinnersley did not reply, but looked long into the sad blue eyes. They understood each other, those two; they had lived together half a lifetime and never before had they come at all close. Now, in two sentences, they had taken the measure of each other. Mary understood the impetuous longing that had formed under her sister's calm and wistful exterior, while Grace received a hint of embryonic discontents in Mary, of something that had never developed, that still cried out very faintly now and then for a chance to live, knowing that it would never live, not quite, that it would just appear like this to weaken a purpose dictated to Mary by her conventions and her habits. As they looked into each other's eyes they became accomplices.

Suddenly Clara spoke. "Well," she said, "I don't know what I'm doing here. Anyhow I'm not doing much good. I've got to go—I've got to go to the dinner." She pushed past them, and as she so did added: "But I mean it, G., it's got to stop, even if I've to take a hand in it."

They hardly noticed her, for still they were looking at each other shyly, like a very young boy and girl who suddenly suspect love in each other. Yet they did not speak much. Grace refused to sit down; she felt stronger standing up; to walk about the room enabled her to keep up an energy which dominated imminent tears.

Soon, too, she said: "I must go."

Mary followed her along the hall. There they stopped for a moment, and Mary put both hands upon her sister's shoulders, looking up into her face and finding her that day very tall, very fine. "G.," she said again, "can't you? It would be much better."

Grace shook her head. "No, I can't, Mary. Not so long as he wants me, I can't."

Mary did not reply directly, but she drew down her sister's head and kissed her mouth and cheek. Then she murmured into her ear: "Try, dear. But, still, if you're unhappy, or in trouble or anything, well, you know—"

Grace impulsively threw her arms round the massive shoulders. "Yes," she murmured, vaguely, as she kissed her sister, "I know."

The door closed behind her and she stood for a moment upon the steps. It was almost dark now and the wind was tearing at the bare branches of the plane trees, but she did not feel alone. She was followed by a soft radiance of almost understanding pity.

IV

For a long time Mary sat alone in the drawing-room. She had mechanically switched on the lights, and now remained with her hands folded in her lap, looking into the fire. For the first time in her life thoughts began to formulate themselves clearly to her. It was Grace at first occupied her. Why had this happened? Grace was not unhappy in her marriage, as marriages went. Perhaps not so happy as she herself was with Tom. Then the thought turned to herself. "Was she happy with Tom?" She pulled herself up, reproachfully. Of course she was happy, and she knew that it was true that she was happy, that she loved him, those five little girls and Jack, but still — but still, somehow, nothing seemed to happen. For a long time she searched her mind, but did not find the phrase which would have expressed what it was she wanted: the adventure of love. "Nothing seems to happen," she said aloud. "I wonder whether this is marriage. It's different from what one thought — in the love-stories and the books, and yet it's got to go on. One can't live without marriage, but then what's it for?" Unused to introspection she struggled with the idea that marriage was perhaps only a way of living, of bringing up children properly, and she had a glimmering that love was quite a separate thing, that it might exist with marriage, or that it might not.

And then, very vaguely, she found envy creeping over her. She envied both her sisters, Clara, who seemed to have work that interested her, work with a meaning, and Grace who had love, all the danger and the excitement and the delight of it. "And I?" she thought, "what have I got?" She knew that she had a great deal in the husband who loved her and whom she loved, but, still, Tom seemed so tangled up with the household and the children. She was fond of all of them, of everything in the house, and of all it meant, even of its furniture, and yet, somehow, there was something indefinably inadequate about it all.

"Poor little G.," she said, aloud, "it's wrong of me, I know, but I hardly know whether I can be hard upon her after all."

Her senses woke into action. Far above her head she heard a long, faint cry. She listened; it was not one of the girl children; it was Jack's little voice. Mechanical and quick, she went to the door, climbed the stairs. As she went, all other thoughts expelled and all unrests stilled, the whole of her, body and soul, seemed to be filled with the long, faint cry of her infant son.

CHAPTER THE SECOND

THE TWO SISTERS

I

THE struggle had begun. Clara and Mary had not realised, when they stood as accusers before Grace, that a subtle antagonism had arisen between them; that there was a cleavage in the party which, automatically, two wives who had respected the marriage bond formed against a third who had not. They had thought, or rather assumed, that they could both together throw stones at Magdalen. But they were wrong: when one throws stones the other tends to sicken of the sport, and there were other reasons too, hardly definable. Little differences of temperament had parted them: jealousies, old as the nursery; rivalries still unsettled, and unreasonable angers which affected money, social status, clothes, those things which preoccupy sisters and are, so long as possible, thrust into the background, which are snubbed when they obtrude themselves and yet persist, creep out as villainous little allies, base camp followers when a true difference arises. And yet, paradoxical enough, never in their lives had Clara, Mary and Grace been so intimately concerned with each other's affairs; never had they been so united as now in their disunion. This formal family love which they had for one another seemed to wax fiercer as hatred crept in to stain it, for it was acquiring the hostile quality of the love of the sexes. The man, central object of the debate, obtruded himself as a ghost in their counsels, and the shadow of love imparted to these an intimate quality which made the contest other than any other contest, social or financial, could ever have been. For even frigid women cannot be frigid to love.

Clara and Mary did not realise what had happened until a day or two after the event which Fenor, speaking to Grace, called the police court proceedings followed by a remand. To take up his metaphor, they had met to decide in the prisoner's absence whether she ought to be committed for trial. They had met at Harrod's, and there was at first some uncertainty in their conversation because Mary had thought in the bus of a few things she had to order and had not put down on her list. Perhaps that was why she let Clara do the talking.

"What I can't make out," said Clara, "is her attitude. She didn't seem to be a bit ashamed of herself; she stood there as if she was defying us."

"Yes, I suppose she did," said Mary, abstractedly. "Perhaps it was because you tackled her so hard, Clara."

"I didn't tackle her any harder than I ought to. It's no use mincing matters. I suppose you're not going to argue about whether a married woman ought to behave like that?"

"Oh, no, of course not," said Mary. "Would you mind if we went into the drugs for a moment? I've just remembered that we've run out of cod liver oil."

Clara followed her into the drugs, still talking.

"Yes," she said, "it really rather puzzles me. I'd have thought she'd either have cried or asked us to keep it dark, or that she'd have been ashamed of herself or something, but what I can't make out is why she didn't seem to care whether we knew or didn't. I suppose she does care," she added, reflectively, "but if she does it's hardly the way to make us keep quiet, her way of throwing the glove down."

"Well, you're going to keep quiet," said Mary.

Clara thought for some time. They were walking towards the lift, and she was so preoccupied that she bumped into several people without seeming to realise it.

"Keep quiet," she said at last. "Yes — I suppose so."

"Then — " Mary stopped.

"Then what?"

"You're not going to give her away, are you?"

They stood face to face in the furniture department, where there were very few people then, and Clara noticed, without quite understanding it, a sudden flush in Mary's cheeks.

"No," she said, decisively, "of course I'm not going to give her away, though somehow I feel I ought to. It's not only the moral side," and her voice suddenly became political as she added: "though the well-to-do classes are responsible to the people for their ethical behaviour. No, it isn't that. Of course I think like you do, that it's very wrong, that she's behaved disgracefully, but I don't quite see what we can do, except perhaps — well, what I mean's this: we won't give her away but somebody will. I mean, they're so imprudent; anybody might have seen what I saw, and when a thing like that begins it doesn't stop. Then it'll get to Edward's ears, and I know he won't stand it — I don't say he ought to," she added quickly, "but anyhow — Edward's rather too full of himself to stand it, don't you think, Mary? It would break his heart, but it's not only that. Somehow I feel that Edward would look upon it as an insult as well as an injury."

Lady Govan was unusually penetrating in that minute.

"That's what makes it so difficult," she began again. "Oh," she protested, anxious to clear her moral outlook: "I do want you to see, Mary, that I don't think he ought to stand it if it came out, only — if he didn't there'd be trouble, a divorce, all that, an awful business and, heaven knows, it's hard enough in politics without having complications in one's own family. People say — oh, you've no idea how beastly they are in the House. It's bad enough in the constituencies where they don't read anything except the Sunday papers — but in the House! Unless you've got all the way it's six hundred and sixty-nine pairs of eyes watching every man for a speck on his great-grandmother. We're a moral people; I suppose that's why. Somebody was talking to me about that a little time ago. He said that we believe that the best man ought to win, but that the best doesn't mean the best at his job. You see what I mean, Mary, don't you?"

"Quite," said Mary, rather curt.

They entered the lift, and Clara realised that Mary had not expressed any opinion, had said nothing much more than the words necessary to help on the enunciation of Clara's views. This exasperated her. It was like playing tennis with a player so bad that not a single ball came back; she didn't want every ball to come back untakable, but still just a few now and then, to give an interest to the game and a meaning.

"You aren't saying much," she remarked, after Mary had placed a long order for children's hats and clothes, and spent what seemed much too much time on a woollen jersey for Jack.

"What is there to say?" asked Mary. "We aren't going to give her away. We can talk to her again, of course, though I don't see much use in that. Seems to me the best thing we can do is to help her to keep it quiet and hope for the best."

"Mary!" cried Clara. She was really shocked. "You really can't mean *that*. Don't you see — but you're talking as if you were backing her up!"

"I'm not backing her up," said Mary, quietly, "but what are we to do?"

"Do?" cried Lady Govan, and an animation came into her voice as if the word "do" stirred something deep in her active nature. "Why, there's lots of things we can do. We can write to her and to him, and we can try to make them see that it simply can't go on. We've got to stop it and it's no use sitting down and — and —" She nearly said: "doing fancy-work," but was able to stop in time as it would not do to offend a possible ally, "and mope," she ended up. "Anyhow, I'm not going to. I'm going to telephone him and he shall come and see me, and by the time we've had it out — well, we'll see."

"Clara," said Mary, after a time, "it seems rather

hard. I know they've done wrong, I'm not arguing about that but — well, G.'s been so different these two years. I hardly knew it until now. I mean, she seems to enjoy all sorts of things: pictures and theatres, and all sorts of things I don't care much for, but I suppose they mean something to her. I hardly knew it, but I see it now — she's so happy. And even if it's wrong, well — it does seem rather hard."

"Hard!" said Clara, angrily. "You wouldn't think it was hard if you weren't soft. Mary, you make me sick. One might think you had no morals at all."

"Oh, yes, I have," said Mary. "I wouldn't do a thing like that, but still it's rather hard."

Lady Govan brought her thin hands together. "Rather hard, rather hard," she repeated, "you seem to be thinking of nothing else except that it's rather hard. But haven't we all got to stand things that are rather hard?"

"Yes," said Mary, "but I'm just wondering now whether we do stand things when they're really hard. Don't you think that we only call things very hard and that they aren't? and that we wouldn't stand them if they were too hard for us?"

"In other words," said Clara, "you mean that Grace is justified?"

"I mean nothing of the kind," said Mary, at last a little nettled. "Only we don't know what brought her to it."

"No more would a common jury," said Clara, with a high little laugh, as if she relished the idea as much as she feared it.

Mary said nothing, though the words excited her too: no human creature can avoid excitement at the idea of a scandal in the family.

"Anyhow," Clara summed up, as they reached the exit, "take it from me, I'm not going to let it drop."

"You really are going to see him?" asked Mary.

"Certainly."

"Oh, well — " said Mary.

As she walked away along the old Brompton Road, she

was conscious of infinite pity for Grace. She wondered whether it was very wrong of her almost to dislike Clara.

II

The interview between Fenor and Lady Govan was not the success she had anticipated. He was not entirely surprised when summoned. Tenaciously sticking to his own metaphor, he said that he was to be put into the witness-box. He had just passed through a difficult two hours with Grace in which she had told him what had happened and what she had said. He had had nothing much to reply, for the situation was too undefined for him to take a line. He was not at all afraid that the sisters would create a scandal.

"You needn't bother about that, Russet," he said, cheerfully. "If I was a poor man and wanted to do a little blackmailing this would be the time: the more they knew the worse off they'd be. In fact, if you want to close their mouths completely I'd better give them the full history of my most undesirable career. The more unsatisfactory person I turned out to be the worse would the scandal be which an exposure would entail."

Grace had laughed as she always did when he took a cynical line, but she had laughed with very sad eyes. Though he held her as he spoke and though within the shelter of his arm she felt safe, she knew that things could never again be as they had been, that the essence of her love was secrecy, a sort of kingdom for two, and that now, when she was open to reproach and to argument, she could no longer bask in the sunshine of her passion: always there would be watchers, far away perhaps, but still watching. She threw her arms about his neck, drew him close, but as she so did she knew that with the beloved body she embraced the shadows.

Later, when she had gone, Fenor tried to define his own attitude. He still loved Grace. There was no change in him, though habit and time had modified the urgent, tempestuous quality of their first coming together. They had passed in each other's company not more than hours or days, but the sum-total of this snatched time made a large account, and there had been letters. Moreover, when they were together they had talked enormously, they had been anxious to tell each other everything that they had ever done, wanted, felt, known. They had wanted to tear off their bodies and show each other their souls. They had not been quite successful, for they had suffered the common tragedy of love: that it is impossible for two human creatures ever quite to understand each other. But they had managed to tell each other so much that now, after two and a half years, it was rare they came upon some unexplored patch in each other's temperament, and Fenor, who was not consciously seeking for an adventure of the soul, was accepting rather than welcoming the fact that Grace could no longer give him adventure. They had lapsed into a relation which slowly from irregular grew regular. It was not marriage, but it was in the nature of marriage. She had done wifely things for him: chosen the patterns of his suits, found him upholsterers and cleaners, copied out library lists; now and then, when she came to see him, she had even run an errand for him. Love and domestic economy. It was very like marriage after all.

He asked himself whether it was not very delightful, and he told himself it was; that he still loved her and needed her, that he was not afraid of scandal or anything of that sort, that he was going to stand by her, not because it was his duty, for that sort of thing didn't matter, but because he still wanted to. And then came another more characteristic thought: "I wonder whether those sisters of hers are going to kick up a dust. If they do it'll be rather fun."

And so he was not surprised when, on coming home later in the day, and having been told that a lady who had refused to give her name had telephoned him three times, he was once more rung up by Lady Govan and told that she hadn't seen him for a long time, and would he come next day to tea at half-past five. He said he would be very pleased. He had met Lady Govan three times altogether, and the invitation might have surprised him if he had not known what it portended. Clara on her part realised also, guessing that Grace must have told him, why it was that he showed no surprise. But that evening and during the next day he was haunted by a delightful sensation that there really was going to be some fun after all. There was something youthfully pugnacious, schoolboyish about him, which did not interfere with his true feeling for Grace: he loved her and he wanted to keep her. But he wanted to fight for her, not only because that was probably the way to keep her, but because he loved a row.

At half-past five he sat at Lady Govan's tea-table, and she was telling him, while he reflected that she was very pretty and that it was extraordinary how she differed from Grace, what exactly he ought to feel about Home Rule. For a while the conversation was purely political.

"I don't disagree," said Fenor at last, after having put the Home Rule case. "You see, it's only chess, these pure politics; they'll do quite as shocking things under the green flag as under the orange. Those things don't matter; there are only five things that matter, you see: love, birth, death, beauty and sunshine."

Clara did not reply at once. The opinion did not stimulate her, and she felt that this swift passage from political party conversation to a philosophical idea meant that Fenor was challenging her. The way in which he had pronounced the word "love," and the seriousness of the face she thought ugly though powerful, were quite enough to make his meaning clear. Yet for another second, hesitating before the struggle, she tried to escape.

"Surely," she said, "there are other things that matter, like progress and politics."

The man seemed unmoved, resolute in his inertia. "No," he said, "and most of the time there's only one of the five things that matters and that's love."

Clara drew in a quick breath, but she was no coward; she came out:

"I'm glad you think that," she said, "it's love I wanted to talk to you about. You know what I mean?"

"Perfectly," said Fenor. "Will you begin or shall I?"

"What?" asked Clara, incredulously.

"Well, *tirez les premiers, messieurs les Anglais!*"

Lady Govan flushed with anger, for his heavy determination had slipped from him. He was actually lounging, spoke almost flippantly. This made her rough.

"I don't quite know what you mean," she said, "but, apparently, you know what I've got to say so I needn't explain in detail. My sister and I know of your — of — of what has happened between you and Mrs. Kinnersley."

"Yes," said Fenor.

"I don't want to pry into your affairs or to enquire how this has happened; besides it's not very important."

"Not at all important," replied Fenor.

"Oh," said Clara, acidly, "I should have thought that you would have thought it important. It seems to me you're taking it very lightly."

"Why shouldn't I? Nothing has happened that matters."

"D'you mean to say," said Clara, a little hurriedly, "that this exposure — this scandal doesn't matter?"

"No, not a bit. I'm sure you don't think any the worse of me for it, do you?"

"Yes, I do," said Clara, rather trenchant.

"I'm glad of that. It shows I was wrong in thinking you disliked me thoroughly."

"Well, so I did," said Clara, suddenly.

"Then things can't be any worse," replied Fenor, with maddening suavity.

Clara cut a new channel. "Mr. Fenor, I haven't asked you to come here to discuss your character or the way in which it affects me. I'm not in this at all."

"I'm sorry. Judging by appearances I thought you were."

"I mean to say that all I'm doing is — is for Grace's sake."

"Ah! she asked you to send for me?"

"No, of course she didn't."

"Oh, it was on your own initiative? I perceive you want to be kind to us, Lady Govan, but tell me exactly what you want to do."

"I don't want to do anything. It's you who've got to do something and that is, you've got to give her up."

Fenor thought for a moment, and Clara felt from within her a hatred of this man who seemed so calmly to ponder whether or not he should give up her sister, and she realised, with disgust at her own self, that if he did give her up she would hate him still more, which, morally speaking, was preposterous. But apparently that was not what he was debating.

"Now, you know," he said, "that's a very interesting idea of yours, Lady Govan, that I should give up your sister when I don't want to and when she doesn't want me to."

"Mr. Fenor!" cried Clara, "I hardly follow you. You say that as if you were — as if you were entitled to behave like this."

"Well, I am, am I not?"

"But," cried Clara again, "surely you realise that a married woman — that the law and — and all customs — that everything forbids it."

"Yes, I know all that. Only I don't obey."

Clara stamped. She had expected protests, perhaps rhetoric, perhaps even more rebellion against moral laws, for men were like that, but that he should treat those moral laws as if they simply didn't exist! Why, she hardly knew what to say. Still she tried.

"Look here, Mr. Fenor," she said, briskly, "I know you're very clever and all that sort of thing and that you can talk and — and make a case, but it's no use pretending that you're entitled to — to get my sister into this compromising position."

"You're quite right," said Fenor, feelingly, "we shan't drive about in taxis again. It was very, very careless, and I promise you I won't do it again."

Clara seized her teaspoon and rattled it violently in the saucer. "How dare you talk like that! You know perfectly well what I mean."

Fenor looked at her rather wickedly without replying. He was enjoying himself hugely, and still more when Clara returned to the charge, this time practical.

"Don't you see what it can end in? what it must end in? Don't you see it's bound to be found out? and then there'll be a scandal, probably a divorce. It wouldn't be very nice for you, Mr. Fenor."

"No, it wouldn't," said Fenor, flippantly. And then, suddenly, his voice became very gentle, so gentle that Clara just heard the words, which were: "but it would be worth it."

"Worth it?" she cried impatiently. "Oh, don't talk nonsense, Mr. Fenor. You give half a dozen people endless pain, you compromise your own career, you wreck a home and then you say that it's worth it!"

"I might change my mind later," said Fenor, "but at present, I do think it worth it, and might I point out that, so far, none of those dreadful things have happened."

"But they will happen."

"They won't. I'll see to it that they don't."

For a second Clara was shaken, for his tone was firm; he carried conviction, but the situation was too anomalous for her to accept it. "And what if they do happen?" she said.

He shrugged his shoulders. "When they happen it'll be time enough to think about them, but if you really insist on knowing I'll tell you that if they do happen tomorrow I'll stick to her. It's not my habit to make up my mind much in advance, and I'm telling you this just to please you."

"To please me!" Clara screamed. "But if you think, Mr. Fenor, that this is the way to please me—"

"I'm doing what I can," said Fenor. "I don't want to do anything."

"Except," cried Clara, who was now losing her head, "go on with your immoral behaviour."

"Ah," said Fenor, cheerfully, "this is getting more and more interesting. Do give me an idea of what is moral behaviour."

"Mind you, I'm not being Puritanical."

"Oh, not at all," said Fenor, "please go on."

"But there's nothing more to say!" cried Clara. "You've got to give her up because a married woman has to be faithful to her husband, and because if she's not you expose her to risks."

"That's all right," said Fenor. "She's willing to take the risks; so am I. Therefore the reason for giving her up, on your own showing, falls to the ground."

Clara searched her mind for some reason in abstract morality. It did not come so she took up her catch-word: "You've got to obey the law."

"Have I?" said Fenor. "It's jolly awkward, you know, having to obey the law. There are such lots of laws. If Grace and I happened to be on board ship, what law ought we to obey?" Clara stared, not understanding. "Ought we to obey the law of every port as we touch? to behave like the English in England and, let us say, the Turks in Turkey? or would it be all right if in Japan Grace were to sell herself to increase your mother's fortune? Or there are other places where she could have six husbands if she liked, while there are much pleasanter ones where I could have six wives."

He understood Clara to mutter something about the white man's code.

"Oh, yes," he said, "the white man's code, a wonderful thing! I've seen the white man's code at work in South Africa, in South America and in Burmah. Jolly thing, the white man's code, a beautiful, comfortable, flexible thing, as tractable as the average conscience. And let me spare you some trouble, Lady Govan, all the religious part which you'll have to talk to me in a minute, because it's the thing to do, though you don't believe in it. Do you want me to obey the law of Brahma or the law of Buddha? or that of Mohammed? Pretty good things, all of them, you know, and supported by the best reasons."

"Don't talk nonsense," said Clara, "you aren't in South Africa and you aren't a Buddhist or whatever it is. You're in England and you've got to obey the English law."

"I've already explained that I don't obey, but I'll let that pass. I confess it was rather cheap, what I said about Japan and the other places. Let's face things squarely."

"Yes, do let's," said Clara, ironic.

"I'd like to make you a speech on the white man's law," said Fenor. He smiled. "But I'll let you off. I'll only say that the law is merely funny. At least it would be if it weren't mischievous. This marriage business, for instance, that's the cause of infidelity. We tie each other up and lock each other in until we just hate the relation, until we're sick of the sight of one another and have got to break out to have some air; we make a law compelling us to live together and fining us in alimony if we can't bear it; we make another compelling us to be unfaithful when we don't want to if we want to get free; we make another in divorce to give the children to what we call the innocent party, who may not want them, and take them away from the guilty one who adores them." He laughed. "The law is a miscarriage of justice, Lady Govan."

"That doesn't concern me," said Clara, stiffly, "the law is the law."

"True and pity 'tis 'tis true. All the more when we consider the horror and hatred with which the State views marriage."

"What?"

"Well, if the State doesn't hate marriage tell me why women inspectors, teachers, civil servants may not marry?"

"The reason's obvious," said Clara, loftily, "and we need not discuss — "

"We need not, especially as the conversation is fast growing indelicate." Fenor smiled mischievously. "But however indelicate it may be, let me remind you that the obvious reason does not prevent women from working in factories.''

Clara was silent for some time. She saw that Fenor was talking round the question.

'' Look here,'' she said, '' we may as well stop if you can't stick to the point.''

'' I am sticking to it. I'm trying to make you see that the whole idea of State marriage is sham; that the State absolutely discourages marriage; leaving aside those who don't marry, tell me why old couples whom you call respectable get seven and six pension, while those who live in sin get ten shillings? and why two people with three hundred and twenty a year between them are exempt from income-tax if only they will do without a ceremony? And tell me why — ''

'' We must uphold the sanctity of the marriage bond,'' said Clara, the phrase coming out naturally.

'' Alas, Lady Govan, the sanctity's gone. The Church will re-marry a divorced person now, or join a man with his deceased wife's sister. It's a purely social contract, a way of living. One has to love very deeply to stand marriage. Love is outside it because love's too big to stay inside.'' His voice suddenly grew soft, and so melodious that Clara felt drawn to him. '' Love,'' he murmured, '' don't you see that of itself it carries the one sanctity that may exist between men and women? That it cannot be bound because it is as light airs, imponderable. So fierce that all things it touches it burns. So sweet that whosoever hath drunk shall ever more be thirsty.''

For a moment Clara, shaken, did not speak. Then she tried to be rigid, tried to make her voice harsh, but it came softer than she intended.

'' I only want you to obey the instincts of an ordinary, decent man.''

'' Decency, I regret to say, is entirely foreign to my nature.'' He was flippant as if reacting from his moment of exaltation. At once Clara hardened.

'' Yes, so I observe,'' she said.

"I'm glad we're beginning to know each other."

There was a long silence during which she wondered how to get hold of this slippery person, but she could not think of anything new to say, so suddenly she tried to work upon his feelings. "Mr. Fenor," she murmured, a little breathless, "you don't seem to have any heart. You don't seem to understand how we all feel about it. Our sister whom we're all so fond of — and the dreadful things that may happen to her."

Fenor looked at her more gently. "If you really felt like that," he replied, "it might move me a little, though it wouldn't make me do what you want. You see, I've got to think of Grace first, and until she has said she wants to give me up I won't let her go. If she does I shan't say a word. She came to me freely, and if she wants to go she can go freely. But it's no use trying to influence her against me," he added, and his voice became hard. "She shall go freely if she likes, but she shan't be kidnapped."

III

"A lady to see you, sir."

Fenor looked up from his desk. "Lady —? what?" he said.

Before him lay the blue prints of the lower workings of the Natchez mine, and he was as if hemmed-in by stacks of assay plans, residue statements and prospectors' reports. *Hatch and Chalmers* lay open before him, and it needed an effort to break through his concentration, to take and to open the envelope which the clerk handed him.

"Mrs. T. H. Stanley," he read half aloud, "Hammersmith Road. Who the deuce —? Oh —"

He remembered, and as he remembered he smiled. Then he felt annoyed. This work was tricky, and it would never do to make a mistake. He was disturbed, but still — if any mischief had been done it had been done already, and the idea of having an interview with Grace's younger sister amused him. "That's number two," he thought.

"Lucky Russet's father wasn't a curate." Then to the clerk: "Show her in."

He had met Mary once at dinner at Edward Kinnersley's, and he had not then taken very much notice of her, for she lived in Hammersmith and seemed to have bought her clothes a little further west. He vaguely remembered splendid shoulders and a placid, blue gaze, but he did not remember having talked much to her after dinner; Grace had spoken of her from time to time, but she never seemed to have of her sister a very clear impression. It was as if something in Mary escaped analysis, so that it was a stranger he was now to see. But, given the peculiar circumstances, it was a wonderfully intimate stranger, a stranger who knew a lot about him and had an interest in his affairs: it would be ambiguous, like taking one's own wife to dine in a private room.

Mary came in, and at once Fenor was impressed by her solidity. It was not only that she was shorter than her two sisters and more buxom, for that might be due to the heavy black velvet and furs in which she was wrapped; it was something more, a steadiness, as if she knew her place in the world and liked it. They shook hands quite naturally, and Fenor indicated the big chair which he generally used for clients with whom he was going to drive a hard bargain. Mary took it with the air of one who was accustomed to big chairs, and she did not indicate how wildly her heart was fluttering. Indeed she spoke first.

"I hope you don't mind my disturbing you at your office, Mr. Fenor," she said. "We know each other so little — I was afraid you might think it rude."

"Not at all," said Fenor. "I quite understand. You'd have found it a little — difficult to get hold of me otherwise."

"Exactly," said Mary. She did not seem offended by his bluntness, nor did she seem hostile. So Fenor determined to let her talk instead of attacking her. There was a long pause during which Mary inspected with evident interest the Mercator map, a glass-case full of specimens of ore, and the other glass-case containing the mysterious fragments of the core of a borehole. Then she said, as if casually:

"You know what I've come about, Mr. Fenor— It's about Grace." Then very gently: "It's a sad business."

He was on the point of replying flippantly, something like: "Is it a sad business?" But Mary did not invite flippancy. Instead he said: "Perhaps, Mrs. Stanley. What's to be done?"

"I hardly know," said Mary, "and yet I feel something ought to be done, for it can't go on just like this. You see, when nobody knew, when it was just you two, it was different, wasn't it?"

"Yes," he said, "it was different." And he sighed. "But still, even if it is different it's still there."

"I know," said Mary, "only, you see, now there are four of us who know instead of two. Still—" She looked for words, not being used to express ideas of this kind. "We—we get responsible, we get responsible for all sorts of things: Grace's happiness and that of her husband and her children." Fenor stiffened and opened his mouth to speak. "And your happiness," added Mary, very softly.

The man did not at once reply. For a moment he wondered how he should handle this woman, and thus realised that he did not want to handle her, that he just wanted to speak with her quite openly about the twist in the strand of his life which seemed every minute to grow closer and nearer to a tangle.

"My happiness!" he said. "Oh, that can take care of itself, I'm all right. It's Grace that matters."

"And the others," said Mary, "don't forget the others, Mr. Fenor. Just because you two, you've managed to make yourselves happy for a while, don't forget the rest, people who don't seem to matter but who do. I'm not talking about myself, I'm thinking of those who depend upon Grace, they've got their rights too, you see."

"Oh, rights!" cried Fenor, impatiently.

"Yes, rights, but I'm not going to argue with you."

She smiled faintly. "Grace has told me that it isn't worth while, that you always get the best of it even if you're quite wrong. I just want you to see things as I do for a moment, even if I'm silly and sentimental. Now here you are, you two, who've behaved very badly, the world would say, and mind you, I'm not on your side; I think so too. I think you've done very wrong, both of you, but still, there it is — There may be a good many reasons for doing wrong and it isn't always the worst people who do. But you've been very happy, haven't you?"

"Very," murmured Fenor, "I never knew what it was like before."

"And now —" said Mary, suddenly bending forward. Fenor stared at her. What did she mean? Could she actually be penetrating enough to observe a change in him and in his relation with Grace? Could she actually know the effect of time, of habit, and now of exposure? of things that he hardly acknowledged to himself? For a second he wondered whether some time or other Mary too had been through what Grace was now enduring. Then he threw aside the preposterous suggestion: he knew enough about Mary to see that could not be but he did not know enough to realise the change that had come over her, very slowly as she matured, rather late, as she began to think of her sisters and the way in which they managed their lives, a little to understand the recent revelation.

"Now?" he said, vaguely, "well — well, I don't see that anything's changed much, Mrs. Stanley."

"No?"

"Of course not. You don't want to do Grace any harm, any more than Lady Govan does."

"We don't. But aren't things different?"

"I don't say it doesn't alter things." He sighed, and for a while thought; then went on: "I don't say it doesn't alter things, but then I can't expect it always to be easy. It's a pity, but we must just go on."

"Mr. Fenor," said Mary, "can't you give her up? Hasn't it lasted long enough? Oh, don't mistake me," she added, quickly, as she saw his face set, "I don't mean to say that you don't care for her any more, it's not that at all, only nothing lasts for ever. You change, you—well, how shall I put it? You grow up and things that used to be valuable, well, they're still valuable, but not quite in the same way. I know it would be hard for you, very hard, just as it would for Grace. Only you've been so happy, you two, and they say you've got to pay for everything in life. I don't want Grace to pay, at least not too much. Pay in some way I suppose she will. She'll be sorry she did it, but I don't want her to be ruined by it; you understand?"

"Yes," said Fenor, "I see what you mean. You mean I'm not worth a scandal and a divorce case."

"I don't mean that at all," said Mary, without anger. "I'm not judging you, Mr. Fenor. I'm sure you've made her very happy and that you matter a lot to her, only don't be too sure that you'll matter for ever. She's a young woman, still beautiful, she's got many years before her. If there's trouble, are you going to be enough for her?" The man looked puzzled. "I mean, supposing you're found out, and you will be, you know, sooner or later; supposing there's a divorce and you marry her after? She'll have lost her children and her social position; it'll be awkward. Are you quite sure you'll be enough? that you'll love her enough? and that you'll go on?"

He did not reply, and for a little Mary thought not of Grace, but of herself. She was a little surprised by her own lucidity, by her own suggestion that nothing matters save the permanent. She was very conscious at that moment of the strong roots, husband and children, which bound her to the soil. Yes, she had developed during that week. Then Fenor spoke suddenly:

"It's no good, Mrs. Stanley. Even if I didn't want to go on I'd have to. I'm responsible to her quite as much as to the others, and she still cares for me. I see that you aren't entirely wrong, but there's nothing to be done; it must go on until the end."

Mary looked at him a little sadly. She liked him, she liked his obstinacy and the sort of gloomy courage that he exuded as he said: "until the end." He was like a soldier holding an outpost against an enemy which he knew must overcome him, and yet would stay until the last moment, perhaps longer.

"I see," she said. "Nothing can be done, then; I don't think Grace will give in, and you won't, so just let me ask of you one thing: if you must do this try not to hurt anybody. I know you think me weak and sentimental — "

"Far from it," said Fenor.

"Oh, yes, you do. You men, you're used to struggles and to hurting things; we aren't. So what I want to ask is for you to try not to go on any longer than you must; everything has an end, you know. Don't go on, don't take the risk of hurting so many other people when that time comes."

He hesitated: "All right, Mrs. Stanley, I'll promise you that much; it's not difficult for me because I think as you do about it."

Mary rose to go. They shook hands, and for a moment she held his hand, looking up into his face with a little smile and sorrowful eyes: "I wish I could be more angry with you, Mr. Fenor, but when I think of Grace these last few years — I never knew until now how much happier she is — But don't make me say these things, I'm weak, I'm hateful — There, good-bye — Try and be happy somehow. I seem to feel it's the only thing."

IV

No day passed now without Grace receiving a letter from Clara. It was always the same kind of letter, not very long, evidently written between two engagements, upbraiding her, sometimes on moral lines, for having broken her marriage vow, but much more often hinting at ingratitude, at callousness.

"You don't care what anybody thinks," said one of

the letters. "If mother knew, it would break her heart and you wouldn't care." In one form or another that phrase recurred in every letter, and every time it seemed to cut deeper into Grace's heart for, though she had never had for her mother a passionate love, she was now beginning to develop such a love merely because it was suggested that she did not feel it. Much more often, however, Clara begged of her to consider the probable consequences of her behaviour. She openly spoke of divorce, asked her how she would like to be the subject of an evening-paper placard outside Middle Temple Lane. In the same sentence she suggested that Grace could not care for her children, and then went on to ask how she would like to lose them, to have them taken away from her. And, continually, through the letters ran Clara's preoccupation with all that would be said, with the difficulties a scandal would create among mutual friends, with the careful way in which people would in future avoid mentioning Mrs. Kinnersley, just as if she were dead and they were afraid of hurting her relatives by mentioning her.

When the fourth letter came Grace, who had not answered, lost her temper and wrote to Clara begging her to mind her own business. This resulted in a rather abusive telephone call: Clara announced that she would come that afternoon to see Grace and force her to be reasonable.

"I'll be out," said Grace, defiantly.

"No, you won't," said Clara. "You'll be in or I'll know the reason why."

Grace slammed the receiver down, went to a call-office and telephoned Fenor to be at his flat at four. That afternoon Clara called in vain and, after waiting for an hour, vented her fury by writing to Grace, in her own dining-room, a four-page letter in which she said, with growing virulence, everything she had said before. She ended up with a veiled threat that she would give her away if she went on. While she was writing the letter Grace was waiting alone at Victoria Street, for Fenor did not come till a quarter to five. He had been detained, and it had been materially impossible for him to keep the appointment. When at last he came Grace, who had nervously been pacing up and down the little drawing-room, felt a stream of reproach rise to her lips, but there was in his face and in the worried lines on his forehead something that suddenly melted her, made her throw herself into his arms, shaking while she tried to speak, and at last just lie close-pressed against him, slowly weeping, weeping as if she would never stop. They sat like that, saying nothing at all, for over half an hour. Fenor had taken her across his knees and was holding her against him, rocking her softly as if she were a child, now and then pressing gentle kisses upon her forehead. He loved her then more than perhaps he had ever loved her for, broken and pitiful, she made to him a new appeal. And, though he had come to her exasperated, he too having received from Clara long, biting letters, in the face of her sorrow his irritation seemed to vanish. Unhappy as she and tears near his eyes, all he could do and wanted to do was just what she wanted too: to hold her close and, burying his eyes in the ruddy foam of her hair, to try, thus holding her, to make their two miseries into one happiness.

They did not speak until at last, her hair ordered, her eyes still red but dry, she powdered herself lightly before putting on her veil.

"I'm a fool, Enoch," she said, "don't mind me."

He came behind her, putting his hands upon her shoulders:

"No," he said, "of course you're excited; so am I, but it'll all come right."

She tied on her veil, turned to look at him again before she went. "Enoch," she whispered, "you —" Her voice became urgent, "you still love me?"

For answer he drew her softly into his arms and, very long, very tenderly, kissed her through the veil. Hands linked, they looked at each other for a second. Then, with a nervous laugh, she closed the door behind her, comforted a little and yet conscious that the quality of this parting was not as that of other partings. For all those other times when they said good-bye had been naught save the preludes of other meetings; now there would be other meetings, just as there had been other partings, but they would be different: when they had been, just they two, without serpents in Eden, their partings had been as the fall of night, night forerunner of the dawn. Now the parting was defiant. It was like the setting forth of a forlorn hope that might or might not return.

As she sat in the Underground that carried her towards Kensington High Street, her unhappiness grew. Something within her began to clamour that this was cruel, that this was wrong, that there was no reason why she should suffer so. She cast behind her all those moral ideas according to which, having sinned, she must suffer; she had ceased to think that she had sinned, and she knew only that she suffered. She grew hot. A little knot of furrows formed between her eyes. Everything about her, the young man who stared, the fat woman with the parcels, they were hateful, ugly, gross; they represented the world around her that was prying and censorious, that envied her and would slay her happiness if it could, because it was not happy itself and could not bear that a woman should be happy. Never had she felt more separate from the world. She was outlawed, not yet publicly, but in fact because now she was aware of the opinion of the world as represented by Clara's anger, by Mary's sorrow, by Fenor's hesitating pity. All against her, then. Or if not against her then not with her. She clenched her teeth together; she was wounded, angry. " I've got my back to the wall," she thought. Yes, she had become an outlaw.

That evening, as if Fate were anxious to pile ridiculous irritation upon horror's head, she had a wrangle with Edward. It was she invited it, not he. A week before she had as usual given him the quarter's bills. He had not checked them any more carefully than was his habit, but as he gave her a cheque he managed to insult her.

" Two hundred and seventeen pounds, eight and four pence," he remarked. " I've made it two hundred and twenty." He smiled. " That leaves about two and a half guineas for Gracie-Bracie to buy herself a ribbon with."

Before she could think she had flared up. "Ribbons!" she cried, "I don't want any ribbons, Edward. I wish you wouldn't be so idiotic." He stared at her. It would have been better if he had spoken, even been jocular. His surprise irritated her, for it seemed to her stupid. She went on in an unusually high voice: "Why can't you give me what the house costs? and nothing more. Good heavens, Edward, I'm not asking you for a tip."

"I didn't mean —"

"But why then d'you do things you don't mean? Don't you see it's irritating to have you suggest —? You suggest I try to make something out of the weekly bills for my dress-allowance."

Edward looked at her still more surprised. This indeed was a monstrous accusation. As she spoke Grace knew that she was talking nonsense. She grew ashamed.

"I didn't mean that exactly; please forgive me, I'm being silly."

His face cleared. "Girlie-girlie mustn't get excited. She shall give hubby change. There!"

Grace stamped. "Oh, don't." But as she weakened he had grown rallying and thrown an arm about her shoulder.

"Poor little thing," he murmured, with mock sympathy, "poor little spiteful, spitting cat! No, she's a great big fine independent woman who mustn't be tipped."

"Don't, Edward."

"Mustn't be tipped; mayn't even be kissed perhaps." He bent down, kissed her clumsily, as usual, half on the lips, half on the cheeks. Her impulse was to struggle. Then she gave way. She felt weak. What was the use of struggling? After all, if she did struggle all that she could do was to be unjust.

V

Clara's plans were not maturing. A month had elapsed since the discovery of Grace's relation, and every moment, during the first week of the session, Lady Govan had been too busy to think much about her sister. She had had other things to think of. It was not Sir Henry's career that troubled her; that was well enough, for her husband had taken an unexpectedly leading part in the debate on the address and, having been so fortunate as to secure first place in the ballot, had introduced on a Friday afternoon a small amending education bill which was so moderate, so well-balanced and so intelligent that the Government half-pledged itself to give it facilities. For a member of the Opposition this was a triumph, and it was whispered in the lobbies that Sir Henry was certainly marked out for office, less perhaps because of his general ability than because of his peculiar ability for doing just enough, not too much, and doing it nicely. But, taken separately from her husband's, Clara's affairs were not flourishing. A few nights before, on a political occasion deemed to be non-party, Clara was conscious of the very faintest coldness shown her by a person whose position placed her above and yet within politics. It had been charmingly done. She had just been told when suggesting a little bluntly that she would have a word with a certain Cabinet Minister, that "it would be a pity if she troubled herself with so trifling a matter." That had been all; the august person had smiled and Clara had understood very well that she was, without any doubt, snubbed. And she had had to smile and to bow to hide a blush, to pass on, exchange small talk, with something stinging and bitter in her soul, some consciousness that her country did not recognise her merits.

There had been other things too. Perhaps because the Education League had become respectable people seemed less willing to subscribe to its funds; there was not exactly a short-fall in the income, but the increase had not been commensurate with the growth in the number of branches. There was as much money as ever, but there was less money a head; it was therefore clear that there would have to be fewer meetings; the pamphlets would have to be husbanded; the best speakers could perhaps not be entertained because local magnates seemed less willing to extend them hospitality. Nothing exactly wrong, but a general discomfort; it was not a smash, it was perhaps something more depressing because less exciting, a sort of quiet decay, as if the Education League were getting old: it seemed that honesty (unwilling, it is true) had not been the best policy. And, to make the trouble complete, a letter which Lady Govan wrote to the *Times*, stating the objects of the League and pointing out that more money would further those objects, was politely returned with a note from the Editor, beginning: "Dear Lady Govan," and stating that the letter was too long for insertion. Clara knew what that meant, and was just tactful enough not to cut her letter down and send it in again. But it was wrong, wrong, all wrong somehow. Everything stood much as it had stood, but less firmly; while Sir Henry's career steadily progressed hers seemed arrested. She was sorry — for Harry's sake. She knew she could be so useful to him in his career; she did not consider whether she meant Sir Henry's career or her own. All she knew was that a new exasperation had come into her life. She did not yet realise that the slow pressure of events was placing her once more in the position out of which she had fought herself: her husband's dependent and appendage. But Clara was very much a woman; she was man a little in her feverish and restless activity, but she was very much more woman in so far as she bore better than a man disappointments and insults. She had in a sense a double courage, the courage to do and the courage to withstand. Already she was struggling with the new bonds before they fastened upon her, plotting, hatching new schemes, but the process was irritating and, naturally enough, just as disease flies to the weakest organ in a body, her irritation turned back upon her sister. She could not connect Grace with her disappointments, but, quite unconsciously, she was making her the scapegoat.

They had had several more interviews in February, though Grace did everything she could to elude her active accuser, and they had been interviews similar to the first, angry, reproachful, almost vulgar. She had, with all her dogged energy, set herself to the breaking of Grace's relation; she had almost ceased to know why she wanted to break it: she only knew that she did want to break it. Now that, slowly, she began to realise that Mary did not sympathise with her, almost suspected that Mary was against her, she was proving her fine courage by redoubling her efforts, for she had two enemies instead of one. Even on those occasions when she met Grace on neutral ground she did not spare her. She did not want to hurt her but she could not help it; it was as if an outside force animated her, bade her crush out this thing because it was disorderly, unsocial. Clara was one of the ring that makes the law: she wanted others to obey it. So deep did the preoccupation become that, one afternoon, at an at home which Grace attended, though her husband was not in politics, because the most promising people of Kensington had many months before been listed by the giver of the at home, Clara broke out.

It was the usual kind of political at home. The local member was there with the members for neighbouring constituencies; there were many smart, helpful young wives, loudly talking nonsense about the poor; older wives who had been through six general elections, and liked it; large, semitic ladies who were getting into Society via party politics. Here and there promising young men leading to the buffet, under the instructions of the party stage-manager, those ladies whose husbands could be useful. A sprinkling of young couples who found the at home very convenient for quiet flirtations because everybody else was so busy self-advertising. Mixed in with all these, a number of real people who had made politics their business and their faith, hard, sturdy stuff, happily devoid of imagination. Grace for a while listened to one of these. He was talking about the federation of the Empire: "We'll have to come to it," he said, "now we've got to swallow Home Rule. It'll be a jolly difficult business though, if we're to prevent Government A from serving out all the subjects of Government B who happen to live under Government A's flag. Yes, it'll need all our common sense, or it'll be bad for trade." Grace looked at him admiringly. He was a large, ponderous man whose eyes, set very, very far apart, gave him an air of immense, if ovine reflectiveness. "It'll be all right," he pronounced. And somehow Grace felt that it would be all right. Vaguely he refreshed her after Fenor and his volcanic political theories. She was talking not to a man, but to something that thought comfortably, thought in by-laws, to the god of common sense in human form, a sort of Billiken, the God of It Will Be All Right. "Only," he said, "we mustn't have fanciful ideas: national flags, all that sort of nonsense. In those things one's got to be hard-headed."

He was, Grace thought, hard-headed. His head looked as if it would be as difficult to get ideas out of it as it would be to get any in. She was preparing for a longer conversation with the pioneer of Empire and four per cent. debentures, when Clara joined her with one of the promising young men. He was a nice, brown-eyed creature with a brisk, friendly air which, had he been born in a lower class, would have marked him out for an estate agent. Clara was virulently talking politics to him. It seemed that Sir Henry had refused to put his sword at the service of Ulster; it was horribly disappointing. What was disappointing too was that the pioneer of Empire, who inferred that he had interests in Belfast shipping, did not at all like this idea of swords. It is true that he had no interest in armaments; besides, his wife, who with another woman joined the group, was only what Clara privately described as a little bit of fluff. Clara found herself in the middle of the group, the sole champion of constitutional revolution. It irritated her; she never enjoyed being in a minority unless she was quite sure that she was going to turn it into a majority, and, to complete her exasperation, the promising young man seemed to succumb at once to the little bit of fluff. He completely abandoned the task for which he had evidently been born. To Clara's annoyance he dropped Ulster and talked plays;

the pioneer of Empire became painfully arch about the French Revue at the Middlesex. Within thirty seconds the conversation had completely degenerated. This might have been quite an ordinary at home where people nearly enjoyed themselves, if not quite. And Grace! Why she was actually talking to the promising young man, and quite flippantly, just as if she had nothing upon her mind. Clara did not express to herself that Grace ought to be wearing sackcloth, or a scarlet letter or something, but that was what she felt. Then she had another shock: while she stood, silent and mechanically smiling, these people actually discussed a society scandal. It happened quite suddenly.

"Yes," said the promising young man, "it's come at last; it's been coming on for years and everybody knew all about it. But of course Sir John, when he found out — well, he simply had to take steps. If you ask me I don't believe he wanted to."

There was a shocked murmur from the little bit of fluff and her friend.

"Oh, no, he didn't," said the promising young man, smoothly, "he'd much rather have let things alone; but public opinion's too much for him."

"What a nuisance for him," said Grace, calmly, "if he was fond of her all the same."

Clara grated her teeth together. Really, this was too much. Grace had said nothing cynical, nothing offensive, but how dare she speak about those things at all!

"Oh," said the large man, thoughtfully, "we're not free agents, any of us, you see."

The remark was received respectfully except by the promising young man, who was congenitally disrespectful.

"I don't know that we aren't," he said, generally, "but still — when a thing like that comes out — Fortunately," he laughed, "they don't come out, most of them."

Almost before she knew that she had done it Clara had spoken.

"Oh, don't they? It's only a question of time, and

serve them right. People have no right to do these things."

"Quite so, quite so," said the large man, soothing.

But Clara was not looking at him; she had looked full into Grace's eyes as she almost publicly flung down the challenge, and it afforded her cruel pleasure to see just for a second a blush drown the freckles on her sister's cheeks, and another pleasure when her own bright, blue eyes met a hard gleam that was almost one of hatred in Grace's green ones. She did not speak to Grace again that afternoon. She went home feeling together guilty and righteous. She had been justified in hitting her sister, though perhaps she had hit her rather hard. "Never mind," she thought, "it serves her right and it can't go on." All that evening the thing that had happened seemed to follow her. It was almost as if she had parted in anger from one about to die, but the thought did not soften her. Any disturbance in Clara's brain always turned her acid; she wanted not to weep but to quarrel, and that evening, quite easily at dinner, she managed to quarrel with Sir Henry. It was neither Empire nor activity brought on that quarrel. It was just an absurd, hateful little domestic wrangle: Sir Henry was wearing a shirt with only one gold stud. Clara remarked that everybody was wearing two studs. Sir Henry said that he had always worn one stud. Clara said, a little louder, that people who were careful in their dress wore two studs. Sir Henry spoke very gently and said he didn't care. Clara said it was a pity he didn't. Sir Henry said nothing. Nor did Clara. This happened at the entrée, and mutual sulks were well in progress when the savoury appeared. When they were alone and Sir Henry began his glass of port Clara suddenly let fly:

"You don't care a bit what I say, or what I think. It's just as if I didn't exist — you don't consult me about anything. You never ask me what I want, or how things are, or anything."

"Studs," said Sir Henry, maliciously.

"Yes, studs!" Clara screamed, suddenly deflected

from her general wrong to the particular. " It's only a little thing, but it's just like the rest; you don't care what I think, you don't care, you don't care."

Sir Henry looked at her rather puzzled. She was exhausted. He concluded she was going to cry: according to his standards that was what women should do in those cases.

" My dear," he said, " don't begin to cry for a thing like that."

" Cry! " Clara screamed, " I'm much more likely to swear."

" You mustn't talk like that," he said, stiffly. " I expect you've been doing too much, as usual."

Clara shrugged her shoulders. " Oh," she sighed, " I don't know what's the matter."

The scene was not renewed; indeed, little by little, their good humour returned. They laughed at their own wrangle; they kissed before Sir Henry went to the House, and yet, when Clara was alone, later in the evening, for she was not due at the political party of the day until half-past ten, she reflected gloomily that something very like this had happened to her three or four years before. Indeed everything seemed to be returning to the state in which it had been: her own activities were shrinking, Grace was struggling to maintain upon her lover a hold which enabled her to make her life different. Mary only seemed unchanged, or rather continuing. For a moment Clara envied Mary. Then she grew savage. " She's on Grace's side," she thought. " Well, we'll see."

VI

Mary had a relapse. It did not come, as properly dramatic relapses should come, in the middle of the night while the moonlight streamed upon her bed, and she lay tossing and wakeful, etc. It came on a Sunday night when she was alone with Tom, who lay in the large armchair, half-asleep, half-reading a magazine, while she sat at her writing-table in the corner. She had drawn up most of the menus for the week with the help of three cookery-books; her conscience bidding her to be economical, she had looked through *How to Live On Ten Shillings a Week,* and had regretfully decided that with appetites like Tom's and Ella's, let alone the nurses, and Jack's chicken-broth diet, it simply couldn't be done. She wondered why one could not live on ten shillings a week. This led her to wonder why one never seemed able to do what one liked. She thought of Grace, who had somehow managed to do what she liked. But would it go on? Mary rested upon her plump, white hand which, as it happened, had short capable fingers like her sister's, the beautiful, white chin under which was forming a visible second, and perhaps, very faintly, a third. Her blue eyes were big and very clear; the rose of her cheek was only beginning to show the very faint lines of what would one day be rosacia, and her hair, heavily banded over her ears (by being out of fashion it had got to be in the fashion of the day) crowned her with a heavy diadem that in the light shone as the hazel leaf in autumn. She was beautiful, peaceful; she was Demeter, the fruitful, with eyes pitiful and wondering. As she thought of her sister she was sorry. Yes, Grace had managed somehow to snatch out of a life founded upon some undefinable error a delight, transient perhaps, but yet a delight. Again, as without turning round Mary listened to Tom's heavy breathing, a regret seized her, the very faint regret that comes sometimes to the happy when they wonder why they should be conscious of their happiness, and therefore not quite sure that it is happiness. For the eupeptic do not know that they have a digestion; he who knows that he has a digestion must at once realise that something is a little wrong. But was there anything wrong? At once she blamed herself. What was this new mood that had come upon her during the last month? Could Grace have stirred in her a hope that lay dormant? made her realise that there were other dreams? She scolded herself: ridiculous! how could she be so absurd! Here she was, with a husband who loved her and whom she loved;

with her little son — and she strained to hear whether by any chance he could be crying above her head; and the little girls, of course. She thought of her little girls as she had seen them the day before, all in white at a children's party: one of them in a red sash, and one of them in a blue sash, and one of them in a green sash. She laughed. She had forgotten the sashes of the other two. She laughed again as she wondered whether, as time passed, her family might not exhaust the stock of the solar spectrum. She sighed rather comfortably. "Well, yes, there might be some more," but she hoped they would be boys, at least the next. She had not yet discussed the education of Jack; she had merely let Tom talk, but privately she thought that it would be rather nice to have one in the army and one in the navy, and of course, if the gods were kind, there were other professions.

But Grace! Grace! The thought came intruding again. Why should she feel so sorry for one who was so happy? Mary knew it was because it could not last and, because she knew, felt rather than knew that the only scrap of Swinburne she had ever learnt: ". . . Sighs, and with eyes forgetful, weeps that no loves endure," was true enough. "Well," she thought, with sudden sharpness, "no more it ought to." She became quite hard. What was she doing, after all? sympathising with her sister. There was no pretending: Grace had done wrong; she had done a thing no respectable woman ought to do, and she was actually brazening it out as if she didn't care. For a moment Mary was seized by a hot indignation, quite comparable in quality with that felt by Clara. She suddenly saw Grace as outlawed and outcast, and she blamed herself for having tacitly been her accomplice. True, she had done nothing to help her, but she had not attacked her, she had not thrown in her influence with Clara's to stop this disorder. "Yes," she said, half-aloud, "I've done wrong." Suddenly she determined to enlist against Grace, to try and force her to make an end to this before it was too late. She at least, which Clara could not, might talk of children and their rights; she had more authority when defending the fireside. She would do it. As soon as she had determined upon action all the melancholic quality seemed to go out of her. As she sat at her writing-table her mind was brisk. "I'll do it," she said again. And then, still inspired by this new energy, she returned to her work. She took up the copybook in which she had pasted cuttings of "The Best Way," collected from the woman's paper which every week gave a half-crown prize for the best household hint. Then, with meticulous care, she sketched out the children's teas and the servants' suppers. She frowned at the weekly books, made up rough accounts, blamed the fishmonger whose bill was not in; she roughly estimated the fish orders for the past week, added them to the total. About twelve pounds, fifteen. She frowned: fifteen shillings over the estimate again! Really there must be some waste somewhere; she determined to have it out with the cook next morning, put away the books. Then again Grace intruded upon her. She looked round: Tom was quite happy now. He lay back, his hands clasping the magazine and folded over his waistcoat. She thought he looked rather heavy as he slept with his mouth a little open, but at the same time he seemed so solid: she had a vision of Tom incorporated into the armchair, into the whole of the furniture, the house, the servants—a sort of cosmic domestic machine and she in the middle of it: Mary Stanley, engineer. She laughed at the vision, gave Tom a fond thought and began to write to Grace.

Grace was faintly surprised when she received that letter. She had assumed, without much warrant, that Mary was on her side. Accustomed to the rather brutal handling which Clara gave her upon every opportunity, she had assumed that Mary's acquiescence in the state of things meant that she almost approved. This had not struck her as curious; for one moment she wondered why Mary, happily married and a good mother, should not stand before her as an outraged champion of the moralities, but her own troubles lay too heavy for her to give much consideration to the mental attitude of anybody else.

She had dismissed the puzzle, glad only not to be hurt, and now came this letter, cold, almost harsh, telling her that, on thinking things over, Mary was against her, reciting the whole case about husband and children, and society. It was exasperating, and it was getting rather dull, but it hurt too. With Mary friendly, or at least not actively unfriendly, Grace had not felt quite alone in the world. That day in the Underground, she had felt outlawed, but that had been a mood at the back of her mind; she knew quite well then that she was an outlaw like Robin Hood, with a price upon her head but beloved of the people. Now things had changed; there was nobody left except Enoch. They stood, they two, just they two. She shivered. A month ago they stood just like that, all alone in a sort of wilderness, and wilderness paradise enow. But now it was different, for dreadful things watched, hidden in the grass.

She telephoned Mary, asking whether she might come to see her, and she was surprised because Mary's voice was soft. A night had passed: once more Mary had changed. She felt that she had been too hard; she found it so difficult to be hard for long.

"You'd better come and talk it over with me," said Mary.

"All right," said Grace, soothed already by the gentleness of the voice, "when shall I come?"

"Oh, when you like, come to-morrow afternoon."

"To-morrow," said Grace, "that'll do."

"And —" Mary seemed to hesitate, "if you like — well, we'd better talk things over properly — tell him, if you like."

Grace did not reply. She put down the receiver, her heart suddenly beating: she was to tell Enoch; she was practically invited to bring him to Mary's house. Oh, she mustn't be silly; of course Mary only meant to put the two prisoners in the dock together. But still, all this soft sympathy implied in a few sentences, was it all for her? or could it not be that it included a little pity of the man and his relation with her?

Fenor met her on the doorstep. He was smiling defiantly as usual. Though Mary had left upon him an agreeable impression which he could not quite analyse, he had to be defiant in a case like this. They just had time in the drawing-room to exchange one kiss, which was long and anxious, before Mary came. She seemed quite normal. She talked the usual tea conversation and, indeed, by the time she had done with the merits of Beerbohm Tree, Fenor began to grow slightly bored. To have come for a battle and to be put off with a tea-fight, well, really — he felt inclined to hurry on the conflict by asking Mary what she meant by it. But he hesitated: there was about Mary something so moderate, so established; it seemed a pity to disturb her; it would be like digging up Edward the Confessor. So it was much later, only when the conversation had dwindled because the topics that could be discussed safely had all been exhausted, because Grace and Fenor had not helped much, they came on personal ground. Mary opened quite suddenly, like all nervous people.

"It can't go on," she declared.

Fenor opened his mouth to reply: "Why not?" but his tongue seemed independent, and he said, quite gravely: "It must."

Mary looked at him a little unhappily. Yes, this was exactly what she feared. As she looked at them, unconsciously Grace shifted her chair nearer to Fenor's. It was as if she felt stronger by his side.

Still Mary tried. "Oh, no," she said, "it need not, you know quite well it need not. Supposing one of you were to die it would stop, wouldn't it?" They did not reply and Mary made a big effort, determined to be cruel: "Besides," she added, "you know quite well these things don't go on for ever."

"Some of them do," said Grace, defiantly.

Then, for the first time in her life, Mary had an inspiration. "No," she said, "they don't. Look at the people who get married for love, and look at them after."

There was a long, heavy silence, and the lovers knew that this time Mary had struck them a hard blow, that their relation, having now lasted nearly three years, had become so like marriage that it had few of its merits while it had to face most of its perils, but still they struggled.

"Never mind," said Fenor, "you may be right, though I don't think you are. But still we must go on; we can't help it, you see."

Mary leaned forward to look at him and, with a little spasm of self-reproach, told herself that she liked him, his uncouth face and brilliant grey eyes, and the unexpected turn of his speech.

"Well, if you can't," she said, weakly, "then — "

"Dogberry," said Fenor, laughing.

Mary had not heard him, nor would she have understood. She was walking about the room wondering what she should do or say. She was facing things with which she could not cope, and now she wondered whether she wanted to cope with them. She was filled with melancholic pleasure; she knew now why it had always made her a little glad, if a little ashamed, to see couples kissing in the Park. It was love, and she could not avoid being interested in or charmed by love. These two people, after all, guilty people, yes — they loved each other. Mary gloomily wished that they were all living abroad where love was supposed to excuse everything; that made life so much simpler. But then they were not living abroad and they had to make the best of it. That thought was a protest against morality and convention; it was as far as Mary could get, but it served. She looked at them both, side by side, and she wished that Fenor would take Grace's hand before her. As the thought of the love flame, so near her, began to warm her, she quite unashamedly wished to hear them tell each other that they loved, to watch them embrace. Something of the radiance she had herself vaguely looked for invaded her, though she knew herself to be removed from all hope of romance.

"Well," she said, at length, "I suppose it's no good. I suppose I must accept it."

"You have, Mrs. Stanley, long ago," said Fenor. "You've accepted it before you knew it, every time you yourself weren't quite happy and wished things could be different."

"I suppose I did," said Mary. "All right, I do. Do your best, do the best you can."

"All good women are immoral," said Fenor, jauntily; but his voice was husky as he added: "Thank you."

Grace went up to Mary, put both arms round her shoulders. "You're just like father," she said, smiling. "A long time ago, before this began, I thought of him. I tried to make him speak to me, tried to believe that spirits could speak, and he almost did, you know. He said: 'Life's very hard, little G., we must do the best we can.'"

Mary kissed her, then drew away, looked at them both almost fondly. "Do you know," she said, "it's very wrong of me, but somehow I can't help feeling — Oh, I mustn't say these things — well, almost glad." Fenor was watching her; she turned to him. "I don't know you," she said, "but you've managed to make her happy. It's all wrong, I suppose, but I suppose it's all right."

He smiled. He did not know that Mary could make a paradox, but he was stirred and at once gave up this consideration while Mary went on talking, exuding now a sort of motherly tenderness as if she were very, very old, and this were her daughter's young suitor. She was kind, but as she spoke a peculiar sensation invaded Fenor. Mary was going further than she meant. "So if I'm on your side I suppose I must do what I can. I'll try and keep Clara off; I can't quite, you know, she's slippery, but I think I — well, I might manage to make her see things a bit differently."

"Thank you," said Fenor, "I wish you would. I had another letter this morning."

"I'll try," cried Mary, and she seemed to grow excited. "I — I know I'm doing wrong, but it's no good, I'll do all I can. If you have any trouble about writing to each other or seeing each other — Oh, no, no, I mustn't."

Fenor went up to her, took her hand. "I'll help you," she said, and, putting her hand upon his shoulder, she looked into his face. He drew back. There had been a look in her eyes as if she were about to kiss him, to kiss him uncomfortably upon the cheek, almost as a sister. It made him uneasy. He suddenly saw Mary as a danger to his peace greater still than the irritable and angry Clara; he had a vision of an accomplice who forced herself upon the criminals, who in this case was too tender, too motherly, too loving; who, wanting to help too much, displaying too great zeal, might sicken by unnecessary enthusiasm those whom she would help. Mary was not sensitive enough to feel his recoil. Melting in her own gentleness, she said, clumsily:

"Oh, I've got something to do in the nursery. I'll soon be back. I shan't be more than five minutes."

She was gone, and for several moments Grace and Fenor sat separate, looking at each other. Mary had left them, inferring that they wanted to be left and that she would help them. It was too much, it was just that excess of graciousness which created discomfort. Grace tried to speak but Mary had thrown over them a blanket that stifled them.

CHAPTER THE THIRD

FLIGHT

I

For a whole day, during which Grace did not leave the house, she was tempted. For the first time in three years she made a self-examination, a sort of balance-sheet. On one side she saw complications, peril for the future, an inimical family; her social position, not very valuable while she had it, would seem precious if she drifted into outlawry. On the other side was Enoch. And then, to her horror, she found that she considered, just for a fleeting second, but yet for a fatal second, whether there was as much on one side as on the other. She did not consider this directly: woman-like, she arrived at her feelings through her suspicion of another's feelings. What she asked herself was not: "Do I love him?" but "Does he love me?" In that moment by doubting his love of her she ceased to love him. She did not know that. She was as a mariner whom his ship carries towards the love who waits for him in port. His mistress has aged; she has forgotten the things that were close to him; perhaps she loves him no more and has given herself to another, but he does not know that. Buoyant still he lets his ship carry him towards the inevitable end.

She wondered whether by an act of her will she could make all things to be as they had been. She looked about her, considered the human beings that affected her life, and now she seemed to see them, after a lapse of time, changed. Here was Edward, more than ever engrossed in his work and the changes of work which he called pleasure; Susan, no longer a child but a little girl, precocious, pretty, vaguely attached to a small boy of eleven called Reginald; Horace, at the preparatory and talking grandly of what he would do at Winchester when he followed in his father's footsteps: already, now and then, when Edward thought of Horace, he was warning him against "tother school notions." They had all changed, and it seemed quite sudden because she had not looked at them for three years. It was like visiting, after many years, the place where you were born. Yes, Fenor was right: where you once bought cakes they now sell motor-cars; the postman has been superannuated; the place where you saw *Hamlet* for the first time now bears a picture palace. And yet it is all horribly like what it used to be, only different, a city of ghosts.

No, there was no going back, there was only going on, in the dark, towards the dreams that might come, or the awakening. For a moment Grace tried to face the future, but she was not strong enough, she had not yet suffered enough to learn how to live without needing happiness. Casting away all thought of return, she looked for some drug with which quick to assuage this suffering, with which to fill in her being the void of which she had suddenly become aware. She did not review those things which are called pleasures, any more than she had tarried long over possible duties, for at once her mind flew to the only drug which she could take, to the man, to him who had given her so much happiness that she could not believe him incapable of giving her all the happiness she wanted. She had become such that there was no pleasure left for her save in love; it was love alone could cause her cheek to flush, and love alone could cool it with a soft breath, and love brought peaceful sleep and shining days. There was nothing else, for whosoever hath drunk shall ever more be thirsty.

She flung herself back upon the man who had loved her and therefore must love her still. She was no longer now a soft, almost shrinking bride, but rather a grasping, urgent harpy, demanding of him that he should love her more because she needed him more. It was she now telephoned Fenor, wrote to him. It was she who, half-invited, waited for him at his flat when he returned, perhaps tired, perhaps cross, unwilling to lay upon a neck burdened with business a yoke which, though soft, was heavy. He was afraid a little. There was a new quality in this urgency of Grace's passion; her arms about him were now no longer soft and responsive: they were fierce, they were anxious. She held him now all the time, even when he was alone, in a clasp which implied: "I must hold you, for they are trying to tear me away from you and I mustn't let go."

Once, in those days when they were together, sitting before the fire, she had slid to his knees and there pillowed her head, holding his coat with both hands. For a long time he had let her lie like that, thinking with calm æstheticism of the glow that the flames made in her hair. He was viewing her impersonally as a beautiful picture and, at the same time, consciously, as a collector looks at the beautiful picture which is his. Then he realised her, sitting like that, as abased before him, too much his creature, and suddenly he felt ashamed. He still loved her too much to bear the thought that she might not adopt with him an attitude of equality. He took her by the arms, tried to raise her to him, but her hands clung. She did not know what he wanted and she did not seem to care. She resisted him; she clenched her hands when he tried to open her fingers. She did not reply when he spoke, she seemed to know only one thing: that she must cling lest something should bear her away. At last he lost patience. Rather brutally he tore her hands open, seated her across his knees.

"What's the matter?" he asked.

She looked at him with frightened eyes.

"What is it?" he asked again.

As if she did not hear him she went on looking at him, and she was unmoved as she realised that in the last weeks he had grown paler, thinner, that in his cynicism was something weak which seemed to have been hurt. She saw lines of anxiety which she had not noticed before, and she did not care. She thought of him as hers now, not of herself as his. She needed him, she was selfish.

"Oh," she cried at last, "I don't know." Then, suddenly clasping him round the neck and burying her face against his shoulder, "I don't know — only love me, Enoch, love me enough."

He held her close, and soon there was nothing but the soft murmur of his voice in her hair as he consoled her, as he dedicated himself to her.

But this was only the prelude of other scenes. They did not seem able to meet normally. In every embrace they embraced shadows, the shadows of those who knew and, perhaps still more abominable, yet another shadow, the shadow of a creature which had been immaterial and had been their love. They could see it now, that thing of which they had been conscious only when it was in them. They could see it now. Did that mean it had left them? passed out of them? and now was with them only as a phantom? They did not know, and yet there was in them an exasperation, a rebellion. They were like flies, touched by just one thread of a spider's web, struggling with an invisible that entangled them, which they could not shake off, which every moment seemed to tighten, something that paralysed them and grew more paralysing.

They did not turn upon the obstacle because it was intangible, but upon each other. Once even Grace charged Enoch with no longer loving her.

"You don't love me," she said. "I know. I don't say it's your fault."

"My dear!" cried Fenor, holding out his hands. His gentleness did not soften, but it angered her. In that moment she hated him for being gentle; she hated him because she had hurt him, and therefore she wanted to hurt him more.

"It's all over," she cried, "and you're only pretending. You think it's the thing to do, don't you? You've given up loving me and you're only going on — well — in your own phrase, because you won me like a man, and you want to drop me like a gentleman." She stood up, clasping her hands together as if to avoid striking him. "You're only pretending because it'll be easier to make me give you up than for you to do it yourself. Oh, you're clever — I know — That's what I used to love in you and now I'm going to hate it." He took her by the arm. She tore it away. "Let me go! How dare you touch me? It's hypocrisy now, an insult."

Fenor stepped back. For a moment he was frightened. These eyes into which he had looked and thought how starry were their depths, — whence came the hysterical glitter that was in them? And this beautiful, amber hair — why should it fall across the freckled forehead in so mad a wave? He was afraid but he was not a coward. "She's going mad," he thought. "Well." He leapt forward, seized her in his arms, and his fear gave him a thrill of extraordinary joy, for he loved to conquer this terror, to caress the woman from whom he shrank. In his own eyes his courage glorified him, and it was a new spice somehow, this love with a touch of Bedlam. She did not resist him. Quite suddenly her fury fell; she wept on his breast:

"Forgive me, forgive me," she murmured, "I'm mad, I don't know what I'm saying, it's they — it's their fault."

Softly he caressed her hair. "Yes, my sweet," he said, "I understand."

But at the sound of his voice her grasp became harder, more possessive. "Oh," she muttered, hoarsely, "only love me, love me enough."

II

In swift alternations they passed on from moments when they were reasonable and had no fear to others when they were lucid and analytical and thought there was nothing to fear, that nothing could touch them and that they were fools to worry; to others when the quasi-innocence of their early love seemed to sport in them; and yet to other furious moments of reproach and hatred when their relation seemed to subsist only by that hatred. Now and then it was as if they could not let each other go because they wanted to torture each other.

There was an interval. Unexplainably their spirits seemed to settle. They were for some days as they once had been. They found themselves able to do the ordinary things which had been so charming: to lunch together at the railway hotels where nobody ever went except travellers; they even took in amity a long, cold, wind-swept walk over Oxshott Common. In spite of moments of tension that was a wonderful day. The sky was as a pearl; they did not talk very much, but they were glad because easy again. Many years later Grace was to remember that day and the man who did not speak to her but sang as he went:

> "I saw a ship a-sailing, a-sailing, a-sailing,
> With emeralds and rubies and sapphires in her hold;
> And a bo'sun in a blue coat bawling at the railing
> Piping through a silver call that had a chain of gold;
> The summer wind was failing and the tall ship rolled."

Everything seemed to be as it had been; the feverish glitter had left Grace's eyes while Fenor every day seemed to become more normal, more himself, able to be cynical and gay. But underneath was not peace. There was worse than excitement: lethargy. Instead of caring too much they were ceasing to care at all. Both of them in the morning woke up weary for the round of the day, and they went through that round mechanically, as if they realised that there was nothing else to do. It seemed to Grace as if it was now as in the beginning: round and round, and round and round, and round and round again, until the end and perhaps after: the curve of life bending back upon itself.

She did not care. She had accepted a long time before an invitation to a dance. Edward went with her, and after booking three of her dances, cut two of them, having either forgotten all about them or mixed up the numbers, or done something equally Edwardian. She danced, for she liked dancing, but she was slightly annoyed because she had not learnt the tango. It exasperated her to feel she would be at least three or four months late. The irritation passed. What did it matter after all? The lethargy of her spirit did not lend itself to a long regret. Besides she was now dancing with Patrick Saunton whom she had not seen for a long time. She had only met him once or twice since that evening when she had been to the theatre with him and the Leycetts. She remembered that first act of revolt. He had not changed; he was still the elegant, paradoxical young man with the blackest head, the bluest eyes and the most dangerous air. He danced with her, talking well. He took her to the buffet to get her lemonade and by mistake brought her champagne.

"Are you tired?" he asked.

She did not know she was, but he had suggested it so cleverly.

"Yes," she said, "rather."

"Well," said Saunton, "let's sit out the next. I'm pretty rotten myself."

Thanks to a sort of professional instinct, Saunton found for her a seat on the leads behind the tall palms. He sat by her side for a long time without speaking, watching her, allowing her to sink for a moment into a contemplation of the star-spangled sky. Bending forward, "You're cold," he said. He adjusted her wrap about her shoulders and, as he so did, she could feel his finger-tips lightly brush her neck. She did not move, she felt so quiescent, and this man who talked so little seemed to know that she did not want to talk. He guessed that she was tired, that she was cold. It was all very comfortable and easy. She closed her eyes and she did not open them or move a finger as Saunton bent over her and boldly kissed her upon the lips, boldly and yet gently, as if implying by his caress that he had in him all that was strong and all that was tender. She opened her eyes and looked at him without anger, without pleasure. Then, very slowly, she pushed him aside.

"We must go down again," she said. "It's cold."

Her hand upon his arm and her lips faintly smiling, she went down again where they were dancing to the tune of the maxixe, punctuated now and then by hoarse cries from the band —

She felt no remorse in the night. But the next day when she met Fenor, quite calmly she decided to tell him. She could not feel remorse just then, that was too vigorous an emotion. She felt that she had to tell him and that was all. She did it quite simply. And then, as if more anxious to clear herself than to tell the truth, she added: "It isn't that I don't love you any more, Enoch, it isn't that — but everything seems so queer nowadays. I didn't do anything. I just couldn't resist — It was like something happening, as if I weren't living, as if something else was living my life for me."

"I understand," said Fenor. He had not interrupted her while she talked. There had been no reproaches; indeed he had sat unaccountably silent, head down and his hands clasped over his knees. "I understand," he said, hoarsely, "of course you know — well — I too — I hate telling you and yet somehow it's better, isn't it? These last weeks, oh! it's been so difficult and somehow so lonely because it was so complicated. I just spoke to her, here in Victoria Street, outsides the Stores. Well, you know — the usual kind of thing — quite innocent, just an evening. We went to the Victoria Palace — Oh, I hate telling you. It was nothing, just the usual way of passing two or three hours. I almost wish it hadn't been innocent, it wouldn't seem so contemptible, so trifling, after a woman like you. Only it was so simple, you see, and it's all so complicated, you and me, so difficult just now."

For nearly a minute Grace did not speak. This confession shook her, for she told herself that where she had been passive Fenor had been active. There are degrees of disloyalty. Had she been the woman she was five years before she would have turned upon him, either furious or cold. But, dimly, she realised that woman is not always passive when she seems passive, that man's activity is not the only form of aggression.

"Yes," she said, "I too understand. Besides, what does it matter?"

They looked at each other sadly, took each other's hands.

"We must begin all over again," said Fenor, "it's that or break."

A flush came into her cheeks. "Oh, no, we won't break," she whispered, "we can't. No, Enoch, we must begin all over again. It'll be fine, won't it?"

Some of her fervour seemed to gain him. "Yes," he murmured, "all over again. It'll be fine." He became thoughtful, then suddenly said: "D'you know, I've an idea I'm going away at the end of the month."

"Going away!" she repeated, frightened. He smiled as he kissed her, so forlorn was her face.

"Not for ever, you goose," he said. "I've got a mine to inspect in Northern Spain. I've given up nearly all that work, as you know, but now and then I've got to do it, and this is a case. Now I only want five or six days, but I can take an extra week off which we can pass upon the coast. Come with me!"

"Come with you?" murmured Grace, "but, Enoch, how?"

He smiled. "Is it possible a woman can have a wish and not know how to gratify it? If you say 'how,' Russet, I'll believe you don't want to come."

"Don't say that," she said, "it hurts me. Tell me how, rather. I'm stupid, you know, nowadays."

He took her face between his hands, looked her in the eyes as if trying to infuse strength into her.

"It's so simple," he said, "you make me laugh. You aren't looking very well, you know. But don't be afraid I'm telling you you're looking ugly; I know women always think you mean that when you tell them they're not looking well. It suits you."

"Don't be silly."

"I'm always silly about you, but listen. Go to your doctor, tell him you're not very well. He'll examine you and find nothing the matter; then he'll say you're run down; all doctors do that when they don't understand a case. He'll say you want a tonic. You'll ask what tonic, and he will say either iron or strychnine. Then you'll say you can't take iron because it affects your digestion, and that you can't take strychnine because it makes you feel as if you wanted to leap into the air and your nerves won't stand it. Then in despair he'll say you've got to go away. It'll either be the South Coast or the Riviera, and you'll say you hate the South Coast, so it'll be the Riviera."

Grace smiled at this skilful plan.

"But," she said, "you forget Edward. He might want to come with me to the Riviera. Besides —"

"Don't worry. You're going to be sufficiently ill to have to go at once; and your husband can't get away just before the Easter recess. It can't be done, so you shall go to the Riviera alone. You can fence if they want to send anybody with you. You can tell anybody you like that you need to be alone so as to find your soul. It doesn't mean anything, but everybody pretends to understand. It's quite modern."

She laughed. "I don't see how much better off I shall be on the Riviera, Enoch, with you in Spain."

"You won't go," he said, smoothly. "You'll take your ticket for the Riviera, but you'll change at Tarascon and the train will carry you straight to Barcelona. And leave the rest to me."

Grace looked at him, smiling no longer. He was right, she thought. Perhaps in the sunshine wounds might be healed. And he seemed so decisive, so sure of himself. She had something to lean upon again; besides she could not resist him: she was not strong enough.

"All right," she said, humbly.

III

Grace's mood of lethargic humility found no stimulus in the following days. Everything seemed to happen too easily, as if a vast conspiracy were at work of which she was the unsuspecting object. The doctor did not even prescribe tonics; he said: "Go away for a change." When she said: "Where?" without any prompting he replied: "To the south of France." And Edward raised no difficulties; indeed he was enthusiastic, regretted only that he could not get away with her. Her sisters were equally quiescent; they seemed to think that this was the beginning of the end. Clara almost said so to her.

"What are you going to do there all alone?" she asked.

"I want to be alone. I want to find myself," said Grace, "find my soul." She remembered Fenor's instructions.

"Oh, yes," said Clara, with a satisfied air, "it's quite an idea."

Finding one's soul was so fashionable that even Clara was infected, though she was still too busy to have a shot at it herself.

"I think it's all right," she said to Mary. "She's going to think it over and wants to be alone for a bit. Of course it can only end in one way."

Clara did not dwell upon the subject; she was not well; her eyes shone too blue, and she was thinner than ever. It seemed as if some internal fire consumed her, as if the energy within her were shattering a body overstrained by its tasks. She complained vaguely of nerves. Recent events, snubs, difficulties were telling on her; she was aimless and yet there was nothing for her to do save pursue her aimless quest. Mary did not help her. She made hardly any comment upon Grace's journey; she received the news thoughtfully.

"All alone?" she said. Then, still more thoughtfully: "Perhaps it's as well."

Clara talked of something else; just then her mind did not respond to the inflections of voices.

Meanwhile a brief interview with Fenor prior to his departure for Spain allowed Grace to see that on that side too a conspiracy was at work to smooth her road. She never knew the exact details of the arrangements, but she gathered that Fenor would buy an accomplice at the Hotel des Etrangers, at Cajus, for he had made her pick out one of the quiet little places which Britons and Americans do not reach because there is no motor road. Apparently her letters were to be received and forwarded to Spain, and her own to be provided for by an abundant supply of stolen hotel note-paper. Fenor hinted that in due course she would be supplied with picture post-cards of Cajus, with tourist guides and a few humorous stories about picturesque fishermen which would fill her letters with local colour. It was all easy, disgracefully easy; wrong somehow. Grace felt that this formidable adventure ought to have been a matter of extraordinary duplicity or of extraordinary daring. But Fenor was unwilling to dare too much. He refused to join her at Cajus.

"No," he said, "it wouldn't do to be seen together and, so long as we aren't, it doesn't matter what you do and whether you disappear. You're finding your soul, you see, and people who are in society always do eccentric things at that time; only they must do them in a lonely way."

There was no risk; except that Edward might suddenly take it into his head to come to her; very unlikely, and the only element that made the thing thrilling.

In those few days which elapsed before her departure, as Fenor had already gone south, Grace had time to think. It shocked her a little not to be excited, and she did not quite understand that she had been overstrained, that this new adventure, after so many scenes, should give her not stimulation, but content. She reviewed her relation and sometimes she wondered why it had come to this point without resolving itself, why, quite simply, both of them, they had not made a clean bolt in the face of the world. That was Fenor's fault, she knew. Oh, it was not that he did not want her, but he realised too well of what elements their love was made: of secrecy, of difficulties, of irregularity; their love was a protest against the moral law, and if it managed through legal formalities to struggle back into the acknowledged and the respectable, so many feathers would drop from the wings of Eros that he could not soar again. Without danger, no passion.

She knew that if it came to it, if discovery overtook them, he would not fail her; even if he wanted to fail her he would not do so: to fail her would not be elegant. But so long as it did not come to that, he felt that a clean bolt would merely mean something like marriage over again, that he would kill the beautiful adventure, become her husband and, in due course, become what all husbands become.

So she asked herself now and then whether, if she had the power, she would snatch up her lover, bear him away, marry him, live with him, be interested in engineering after having been interested in the bar — ceased to be interested in engineering as she had ceased to be interested in the bar —

What did they know of each other after all? in spite of all this loving, and this talking, and again this loving? Did they know how long they could make each other happy? Whether a new relation might arise and last another day, another month, or a life? They were different and separate people, parted by barriers of habit and way of living, by views and absence of views. They knew much of each other's temperament, but they had loved too much to show the fiery tempers, the sulkiness, the meannesses, all the little beastly things they hid from each other as they courted: the vanity, the selfishness; and they had not even seen the whole of the other side, their sweet modesties and self-deprecations, their generosities or their capacities for self-sacrifice, nor the courage they had too, both of them. They had had glimpses only of all these things, but not more than glimpses, for they had, both of them, paid the penalty of love: they knew that in the closest clasp two people are still two people.

IV

Swiftly, as if borne upon a magic carpet, she was at Albacin. There had been no incidents on the journey. She was bored for two hours at Tarascon as she waited for the Barcelona train in a station which disappointed her because it was so like any other station when it ought to have had something of the heroic spirit of Tartarin. She had watched the land unrolling, fat Languedoc, the lagoons on the coast, and the blue wash of the Mediterranean very near, Roussillon, and the little white hills like sugar-loaves studded with sticks that would bear grapes. Then another country that made her heart beat a little, because, among those quiet, harsh, dark people, Enoch waited for her. She thought of him as slowly Cataluña unrolled before her, black and arid and fierce.

Gerona. High above a pyramid of white rock and yellow sand, the old city, walls and roof all black, blushing here and there to red. The hungry slopes caving below walls that bellied out full of fissures, eaten by moss, as if the slopes were treacherously receding so that the earth might suck in the impious works of man. And in the midst of all, near the old red castle, scorched, dazzling as a jewel, the church spire, so long and so thin, glowing so golden, proudly protecting the town as a shepherd his flock, straining towards heaven without humility as if it would challenge God to injure so true and so proud a servant — he was waiting for her. As the train steamed in, so slow, she could see him, tall in his white flannels, so different from those others, nearly all dressed in sober black. He seemed so fair, suddenly, in comparison, so English. She was often to think of him again in after years, and it was just like this: a man who seemed immensely tall in his white clothing, sharply outlined against the prior impression of the town, black, red and gold on a pyramid.

Everything now seemed to come so swiftly, so easily. She had fallen into his arms simply before all those people whom her effusion did not seem to surprise. Then there had been more travelling, a junction and yet another wait. She had laughed, had remarked that the further south she came the more travelling seemed to consist in waiting, and as the junction afforded neither coffee nor tea, she had drunk some crude red wine which at once got into her head — At first they talked a great deal of things which had not the slightest importance, as the local train bore them away towards the coast through an endless desert of rock, broken here and there by a tiny cultivated patch which seemed to hang upon the mountain side by means of some little natural grappling apparatus, and now and then over an iron bridge that spanned the ridiculous, foaming rage of a yellow torrent so shallow that rocks stuck out from its blustering water. Then, little by little, silence fell, and as they sat, hand in hand, more conscious every minute that they were entering a new land that would be theirs alone, they grew serious. Indeed not a word was said until suddenly the country changed, turned into a wilderness of pink-white ground strewn everywhere with vivid red boulders and small stones. Not a tree, and not a stream, but just this prospect of apocalyptic horror, of land so dry and so bitter that not even an insect could live on it, and yet sublime in its beauty for the sake of which it repulsed man, proudly refused to feed him; all red and torn, erupting everywhere into small rock-piled crags, the desert was virginal. Alone and high above, a flight of crows was speeding towards the sea, as if knowing that even crows would find no hospitality in this land.

The train slowed up. Fenor looked out. Then, turning towards Grace, he said: "Albacin."

V

Grace was disappointed in the Spaniards. She could not speak a word of their language, but she had expected to communicate easily with a light, southern people who would indulge with her in excited pantomime. This bourgeoisie, almost uniformly clad in black, these quiet, dark faces, rather sullen, very hard; these fishermen, devoid of a red sash or even of a picturesque cap, quiet, avaricious of words, and these women with the black shawls tied close round their ugly faces, all this was not Spain, was not the country of the Moor, the bolero, the bull-fight, of blood and sand. They were handsome, some of the men, and walked with an air that was not haughty (another disappointment), but merely self-possessed and indifferent. They seemed to live each within himself and often, when some tall, superior creature with high cheekbones and large melancholy eyes passed by, aloof as a cat, Grace thought this was not what Edward called the sunny south, but rather Scotland.

Albacin itself was not what it should have been: it ought to have had white walls, green shutters; there ought to have been many open cafés, full of shrieking crowds drinking sweet drinks. It was not that. Albacin was a little fishing port upon two hills. Upon the northern hill was a clot of small houses built in grey stone, relieved here and there by a wooden roof with an eastern-looking tower painted white. The houses seemed to tumble down the hill on either side of a winding alley, lined with small dark shops, some of them open to the street. The alley called itself Calle Mayor, which was an insufferable piece of arrogance on its part. The port was nothing but a long pier, along which slumbered half a hundred fishermen's barks and a ridiculous little tug with an enormous flag and a captain who, when he took his ship out to do nothing whatever, looked with his stomach and his gold lace cruelly too heavy for her. Sometimes only, when the sun hung in the sky at a peculiar angle, the white roofs came glowing up like silver, and then Albacin was transformed: the church, next to the old black ruin that had once been a palace and now housed the Government, glowed yellow as a topaz; in those moments the town was all black, silver and gold, and it seemed as if from such sights the makers of the old armour had taken the gold and silver frosting which they laid upon the blackened iron.

Upon the southern hill stood the inn, the Fonda de la Perla, a squat white building devoid of all beauty, its eight windows without decoration save red-brown blinds. Upon the lower slopes some villas, deserted until the summer, and the melancholic casino destined for the Barcelonians who would visit it later on.

But from the windows of their rooms they could see the sea that washed down to the foot of the hill so close that one could have dropped a stone into the splashing water far below. Often, during the first days, Grace stood looking out of that window, in the grip of a horrible fascination, watching the water that was so blue as in its depths to seem moving, crushing itself savagely against the wall of rock and there breaking into a thousand scintillating sapphires under the haze of air that already was light with heat.

But very soon Grace knew why it was Fenor had brought her to Albacin. Not for the little town, so busy with its tiny activities, nor even for the sea that far away was like a blue lake and near by so brutal and so strong. It was for quite another country, for that harsh, desolate endlessness of red rock which the train passed through. When he took her out on the first morning and made her climb the slope behind the Fonda, she understood. Half a mile away, upon the edge of the plateau, stood three palms, close together, their green leaves erect and fit to make a wild head-dress for some monstrous Indian chief. The last trees — and beyond the red rock where nothing could live, where a man and woman, standing side by side, were alone. Her heart beat as she looked at the three palms where civilisation ended. She was conscious that all her life had slowly been directing towards the moment when she would stand by the side of those last outposts — and perhaps go beyond.

VI

Grace realised that a renascence was working in her. They sat at breakfast in the long, narrow dining-room that was white and cool; they were almost alone in the hotel for, besides themselves, there were only a very old couple who seemed to live there permanently and to pass their time looking at the sea and waiting for meals until the moment came for them to die, and a commercial traveller who took no notice of them, for he had littered his table with catalogues. They had rashly ordered chocolate *à la Español,* deriding the idea of chocolate *à la Française,* and Grace had struggled quite despairingly with the unsweetened drink, the hard, dry loaf and the extraordinary cylinder of blown white sugar which seemed of no use save as an Easter offering to a small boy. Fenor showed her how to use the implement, to stir up the chocolate with it until the sweetness was perfect, but he failed to make her like the dry loaf.

" It's no good," she said, laughing. " I'm English, quite English, you know. You've taken me too far south! "

He looked at her softly. " Not really? You wouldn't rather be having eggs and bacon with me at Brighton, would you? "

She looked almost shy. " Oh, anywhere," she murmured.

They did not speak for a while but looked at each other with a love so intense and yet so gentle that it was almost melancholic. Then Grace broke the silence.

" I do like your tie," she said.

He laughed. He knew that it was an ordinary tie, just knitted blue and white silk, but his heart was touched because he knew so well what this meant: that a woman loving must admire the clothing of the beloved. He stretched himself, sat sidewise at the table: he knew he would draw her further, and yet he was sincere. He succeeded.

" And those boots," she added. " I like you all in white, and a man ought always to wear buckskin."

Still he smiled and gently touched her hand. He was inducing her to flatter him because flattery from her was sweet, and also a little because to make her flatter him made her rejoice in her possession, made her happy.

There was emotion in the air, and for a while it impeded their conversation. On Grace's part it was retrospective. She wanted to know whether he really loved his work.

"Oh, yes," he said, "you know I do, Russet, I mean so far as one can love work, so far as one can love work when one knows it's not the thing that matters most."

She threw him a grateful glance. She knew what he meant, but still she had to make him say it.

"Oh, you don't mean that surely," she said, "everybody knows that a man's work matters more than anything."

"No, we only pretend; only love matters. Work for a man in love is only a drug or a bridge." His eyes upon her were eloquent.

"Well," she said, "that seems to mean only that you haven't got the work you really ought to have done."

"Don't see what else I could have done."

"Oh, lots of things. I'm sure you could have been a barrister, you're so specious."

"Thanks for the compliment."

"Oh, yes, you are, and yet, Enoch, there is something so — direct about you even when you're talking crooked. Something soldierly."

He smiled. "I've never wanted to be a soldier, exactly."

Grace's mind took a leap. "Enoch! have you ever killed a man?"

He shook his head and replied with mock gloom: "No, it's been a narrow shave once or twice. I tried once, but he nearly killed me instead. Awfully sorry: I'm not a bit exciting in that way."

"Don't be absurd! As if I wanted you to have killed a man! Only I'm sure you could."

"I continue to be sorry. I fear I've not got the temperament of the soldier or of the murderer. I can't satisfy you in that way, Russet."

She was brooding. "Yes, there are lots of things — thoughtful things, I mean. Not only active ones like engineering or being a soldier. D'you know, I think of you sometimes as very old, doing research work with a lot of crucibles and funny glass things with tubes sticking out of them, and lots of papers and books — logatrims — "

"Logarithms! you ignoramus," he cried. "Dear me, Russet, you seem to think I can do everything."

She did not reply but remained looking at him and faintly smiling. Yes, that morning, that was about what she meant, and she was very proud to think he was her conquest.

That day they went out behind the Fonda, along the plateau towards the three palms. They stood awhile looking down the slope where a bush of bitter aloes served as a transition between the three palms and the desert of red rock. It lay, Grace could now see, like an immense bowl which some miles away ended at ridges that in the sun stood out as scarlet lace. It was broken here and there by little winding paths of pinkish pebbles, the beds of torrents now dry. Cut off from Albacin, they could hear no sound behind them, and in front was a silence yet more purposeful, for it was true silence. Whereas behind them lay a quietude in which mixed, though they could not distinguish them from one another, the breaking of the sea, footsteps and the sounds of industry, in front of them lay the interminable rock above which there did not even buzz a bee.

"You see," said Fenor, at last, "emptiness. I came here ten years ago and never forgot it. Here one is alone." He took her hand. "Will you come into the wilderness with me alone?"

She did not reply but pressed his fingers, and very carefully he led her down the slope along one of the torrential beds, the pebbles rolling and giving way under their feet. The sun was high but not very hot, for this was April and there was no greater sting in the rays than in an English July. Through their thin clothing, as they walked, the reflected warmth from the red stones came caressing — They seemed to walk for a very long time, and Grace did not know exactly what she thought. She was hardly thinking: rather she was feeling, had a composite sensation of small round stones under her feet, warmth all about her, air coloured pink, and strong fingers entwined with hers. They stopped by the side of a tall boulder, cradled in sand, its edges almost rounded. It was like the egg of a roc. She touched it. It was smooth, so smooth and so warm that she shuddered a little as she fancied that she could feel some life pulsing in the stone. It was as if she caressed earth's breast. But the man drew her to the other side of the boulder where there was shade and, strangely enough, a flatness of soft, pink sand. Half conscious now of what she did, she let Fenor draw her down by his side; through half-closed eyes she could see before her the emptiness rolling away towards the fierce, scarlet hills. They merged with her dream as he held her close, and then closer; through the dream came his voice, softer, more narcotic than ever she had known it, singing this time her Song of Songs with the joy of one who had never thought again to sing it. She lay abandoned in his arms with the sun burning her eyelids. Idly her hand played with the warm sand and she was conscious of naught save him.

VII

A letter came from Clara, redirected from Cajus. It was a queer thing, written on Education League notepaper. The style was even jerkier than usual: most of the sentences were made up of seven or eight words, though it held nothing tense. Clara spoke of worries, vaguely, of the difficulties she had with Sir Henry, who was inclined to compromise on Ulster. Also she was going to buy a new car. To Grace it all seemed foreign and extraordinary; it was like fiction, frightfully like life and yet not quite. Politics, cars — As she read the letter again Grace wondered at herself; she seemed to have been reincarnated and to remember something of the old life but yet to find it strange by the side of the actual life. One part only in the letter seemed real: "I hope you are all right and feeling better. I can't say I'm the same. I've got the jumps. Can't sleep and all that sort of thing. Doctor says I must slack. Shan't."

Illness and suffering! Well, yes, those things were always real even when you were reincarnated. But at once the sadness fled from Grace. Suffering was true, but so was the sunlight. She glowed as she thought of the new life which had come to her, wiping away the old. She was sure of it now: once more she was blooming.

And indeed she was, for the bitterness and chafing of the past months had gone, was forgotten. It was not that all the time she touched the passionate point which she had attained in the shadow of the great red rock; it was much more. It was that Enoch, having forgotten the fear and the exasperation bred in him by watchful eyes, was returning to her as he had been, not only lover but companion, returning humorous and worldly, speculative. On the second evening, as the twilight fell and the rim of the sea was dyed pale green and tender yellow, they stood at the edge of the hotel garden, watching a long line of bullock carts that wound from the north into Albacin. The bullocks came very slowly, each one swaying a little and the whole line swaying with their movement, two by two, pale cream and glowing in the rays of the fading sun, like rosy flesh. By their side walked black figures under broad, dark hats, foreshortened so as to look like toadstools. All of it so far away that no sound could be heard and the whole line was as an arabesque of little men walking by little bullocks, which now and then they jabbed with a tiny goad.

"Look," said Grace.

He nodded. "Yes," he said, "I've seen something like that before." At once Grace remembered the night at the Institution, three years past.

"It's beautiful," he said, "and yet it's true." He grew excited. "To see life as it is and to see it beautiful! What a discovery! It's not many people have made it." He grew thoughtful. "All those people who have tried to sketch life for us, they've seen it so wrong — all the corpses and the dunghills and none of the other things. Oh, yes, I know, there's more in life that's ugly than there's beautiful. But still, there's the beautiful too and so much of it, and it's so easy to be blind to the hideous, if you like.''

"Literature, you mean,'' said Grace.

"Well, yes, literature among other things — It was not all bad in a way, that ugliness — Zola and the realists, and Gissing and all that. It was honest enough; we had to react from the romantic 'thirties and the sentimental 'sixties, from all that rot about noble Arabs and pure English maidens and Polish heroes like Thaddeus of Warsaw. We couldn't go on for ever with young ladies writing poems in morocco books, entitled *Mes Larmes,* and pressing little blue flowers between the sheets. In course of time the little blue flowers began to smell nasty and that is where the trouble came in. Instead of throwing them away, the little blue flowers, because they smelled, thousands of people started saying: Behold! they smell! let us tell everybody. And they did. We got a brand new literature: instead of the love pangs of the aristocratic Englishman in Turkey, who ate yataghans, or sat under the flowering yashmak, or some nonsense of that sort, we got — well, Whiteley's catalogue. We had to, but we've got to get out of it into something finer.''

"I suppose we will,'' said Grace, thinking of the psychological and mystic books that she had read.

"We will, yes; nowadays realism is psychological, it's almost romantic. We're not content with describing a dynamo; we make it romantic and by Jove! it is romantic, if you're able to feel that it is. I suppose it was Kipling taught us that the man who made the bridge, or the man behind the gun was a hero of romance. We're going further nowadays; it's the gun and the bridge themselves which hold the romance. Latently, you know, just like — well, just like that big round rock like an egg, under which we sat. An egg a million years old — perhaps it'll hatch.'' She laughed, but he went on. "It's the egg of Time,'' he said, "with the sun keeping it warm, and new life inside. Pooh! I'm talking nonsense; but, never mind, it's a stirring time we live in, and isn't it good, except — '' Melancholy seized him and he was silent.

"Yes, I know," Grace murmured, "I know quite well what you're thinking. Stirring times, Enoch, but not for long."

He had turned away, and now his eyes were fixed upon the western horizon, the fusing together of the crimson rock with the opal fire of the night. But he dragged himself back:

"Oh," he said, "I don't want to go on like this. Good heavens, let's be intellectual and dry."

"You can't," said Grace, pressing his arm.

He hardened. The words "you can't" always seemed to breed in Fenor a pugnacious madness:

"Oh, can't I?" he said. "You seem to think that intellect is intellect, and emotion emotion. Bunkum! There are not three incomprehensibles, or two, but one incomprehensible. It's all intellect, even what you feel. Art, politics, religion, patriotism, social reform and love, it's all made of the same stuff and you turn it into one form or into another, just as you like. You direct it if you're strong enough or something else does if you're not. You direct your life, you make of it what you choose. Give me intellect and let me twist it, let me take it through the furnace of passion, and here is Casanova. Put it into the laboratory, let it live on the differential calculus, and that's Röntgen; or give it colours and a passion, a dream of sound, even if it's deaf, and there's Beethoven, or Rubens — it's all the same stuff, only twisted. Perhaps I'm wrong in saying: 'give it to me to twist in my laboratory or my studio.' It's not quite like that. It's something else, perhaps some essential spirit, supreme being if you like, that twists the stuff just for its own fun in its own laboratory."

They were silent for a long time and now, as night began to fall and the shy stars to grow brilliant, the existence of a supreme being fashioning their lives, as it had fashioned the great boulder, seemed so assured that it ceased to be surprising. In the enormity of nature God is obvious and, strangely enough, Grace did not feel that in His immense and all-seeing eyes she was doing wrong. Could indeed anything be wrong that He allowed? Could anything be such that it did not fit in with His gigantic purpose? She was not afraid. He would not strike her down: a lion does not strike at an ant. Beaten now, rather than afraid, she pressed closer to the man, but he was not stirred by those primary emotions; he was still thinking, not feeling, continuing his speculation.

"We don't understand these things," he said. "We make ourselves slaves to what we call feeling because we don't want to believe that we don't feel, but think. It's the same thing really: one thing in two forms; only we don't understand. We're not civilised, you see . . . not really. We've lost all the old freedoms of savagery, we haven't yet got the new freedoms of civilisation. We're in transition." He grew excited: "By Jove, though, it's wonderful to see it happening."

Then he realised her close against him, her eyes shut, and his thought took another turn, a turn so sharp that suddenly he was shaken, asked himself, half-ashamed as if he were a traitor to his own theories: "Is it true? Is this not emotion after all? something different from just thinking?" As he bent down to caress her he was yet more uncertain; his kiss was half an abdication.

VIII

Sometimes, before beginning the climb up to the hotel, which was rather steep, they stopped at the Eusebio Bar, a little wine-shop which had set precarious roots in the slope of the northern hill. They would sit there for an hour at a time under the striped white and green blind, and Grace always felt that she was doing something disreputable when drinking in the open air. It was delightful. And one day she had had absinthe which Fenor taught her to prepare in the professional way. Absinthe! This was the abyss. It always seemed extraordinarily peaceful near the wharf where nothing ever seemed to happen and where, Fenor declared, the crane was probably rusting through unemployment. Along the rough cobbles, now and then, passed a team of bullocks, white or the colour of amber, harnessed to a cart made of long planks balanced on two wheels. Or two men met, gravely saluted, engaged in conversation and apparently went on for ever talking in the middle of the street. Once they saw a team of mules, all gay with red chenilles and jingling their bells as they defiantly trotted, throwing to the right and left sulky, proud looks from the loveliest eyes in the world. It was all peace and ease and rest, the calm expectation of a to-morrow which next day would be postponed to a morrow, making action not worth while. It was just alive enough not to be dead; it was not asleep. Somehow it was too self-assured for that, too stately.

It was on the fourth day, a Saturday, as they sat under the green and white awning drinking a disgusting concoction, supposed to be tea, because something John Bullish had come out in Grace and made her demand it, that a man drew near, rather furtively, and, doffing his hat to Fenor, mumbled a few words. Fenor made him repeat them, for he spoke Castilian, while the Catalonian brogue lay heavy over this man's speech. The man explained again, every now and then throwing at Grace a glance of admiration which she did not misinterpret. She wondered while the conversation went on; it seemed interminable. At last she noted words that recurred all the time: "*aficion*" and "*aficionado.*" Every time the stranger said these words he looked more obsequious, but Fenor merely grinned.

"What does he want?" said Grace at last.

"He wants to sell us tickets for the bull-fight to-morrow at Barcelona. He says I'm an *aficionado,* a sportsman that is, but we haven't come here to see bull-fights, have we?"

"A bull-fight!" said Grace in a low voice.

The idea seemed to stir her. Indeed her heart suddenly began to beat as she had a vision of blood.

"You want to go," said Fenor, at once understanding her.

"I don't," she said, rather hotly. "I think they're cruel, disgusting things."

The Spaniard bent forward and murmured something which made Fenor laugh.

"What does he say?"

"Oh, he says that the lady's eyes are so beautiful that she must wear a veil lest the manhood should go out of the matador."

Grace blushed. "How dare he say things like that!"

Fenor again began to laugh. "That's the Spanish way, but he doesn't mean it."

"Oh, doesn't he? you rude man! If I could speak Spanish I'd soon find out but—of course they're dreadful things, Enoch—but I've never seen one."

"Well," said Fenor, tolerantly, "just to please you, and besides, if you want to know, I want to go myself, badly. You're sure you want to go, aren't you?"

"Yes," said Grace, looking rather ashamed.

Fenor held out a twenty pesetas note.

"Shade tickets," he said, "we're in luck. And now, Russet, you've done it. Until you've seen a horse gored you haven't seen much, and until you've seen a white one gored you haven't seen anything."

She shuddered but did not reply, and Fenor was puzzled and interested. It looked as if she had become more primitive, had been completely rooted out of England and her class.

It was a curious journey to Barcelona. They caught the Gerona train where, at this point, even in the first-class carriages, there was only standing-room, for this was the first fight of the season and Bombita was billed to appear. It was only an hour's journey, and yet it seemed intolerably long, for at every station the train stopped, and yet more people came in; clerks and their wives in black, peasants under immense hats, and spare, dark soldiers with uniforms that were too small for them. Every now and then the two *guardias civiles* pounded along the platform, looking into each carriage to make sure that nobody wanted to fight. Along the platforms passed men with bellying skins full of wine, out of which they filled cups for a copper coin —

And then Barcelona seized them. The train seemed to be only one of a dozen simultaneously entering the Estacion de Francia. They were as if gripped and sucked in by the crowd which bore them on as a wave, roaring as if the Spaniards, throwing off their hard reserve, were already shaking with excitement at the thought of what was coming. The crowd flowed on, irresistible, through broad streets where the modern Moorish fronts of stone glowed in the sun, like white zinc roofs, and through the young palms of the Plaza de Cataluña where every leaf blazed in the sun like polished jade, past the high new hotels crowned with minarets. It was like a wild dream, this modern city with its tramways and the big boulevards she could see sloping away, for an hour in the hands of a wild mob come to see bloodshed, yet not without dignity. It was not European, it was African. The dark, handsome faces with the soft, black eyes and now an air of excitement and lust, the new fever in the hands, these people were African.

And then the Plaza, behind a corridor where she was deafened by the screams: "*Perra gorda! perra gorda!*" of the hawkers who wanted to sell her a cushion for the copper coin known as a "big dog." The Plaza, a circle, broad and harmonious as the horizon, tiers of undulating bodies — Much black and white, and here and there a patch of colour; dark heads, a very few under mantillas and very many under the crudest French hats — The sand, pale yellow as a daffodil, and the sky above now pure and deep, brilliant like a vault painted in copper salts.

She saw a procession which she hardly understood: the *chulos* with their red capes, the *banderilleros,* carrying long goads festooned with flowers; the *picadores,* clumsy in their armour as fourteenth-century men-at-arms, on horses that staggered on to their doom; and the *matadores* at last, each behind his *cuadrilla,* blazing in gold and jewels, curled, oiled, not condescending even to smile, smug as a cleric and proud as a knight, like a murderous human humming-bird.

Curiously she watched the President throw down to the marshal the key of the *toril,* saw the first bull come out and then stand, not yet angry but inquiring and disgusted, as if some one had played him an annoying practical joke. She had borne with the *banderillas:* somehow, as the bull twirled round himself like an enormous top, trying to bite the goads that stuck in his rump, she had not been able to realise that he suffered. But then the *picadores* came in; one of them detached himself, trotted towards the bull: for a second, they made a group: the man bending down a little, his lance directed towards the place where he would strike. It was a tense, quiet moment. There was a cry, a hoarse, low murmur rather, but already Grace had fallen against Fenor, half-fainting for, before the cry came, she had had time to hear a sound, a sound new to her, something like "prrrroff. . . ." It was the sound of the horn piercing the horse's side, rather like the noise tarpaulin makes as it rips. She closed her eyes; she had not seen the by-play, the delightful skill of the *chulos* as they drew off the bull from the fallen man, nor had she seen the gored horse wildly careering round and round the arena at an incredible pace, dropping every yard something of its vital organs, nor had she seen it at last fall, kicking, and its coat turn almost entirely from white to vivid red. Fenor held her close. "Don't look," he said, "it's rather hard on you that the first should have been a white one."

She lay like this for a long time; every now and then a roar told her that something terrible had happened.

"Look," said Fenor to her, "don't be afraid, look; they're not hurting anything just now. They've got a new bull. It's quite wonderful!"

She opened her eyes, and indeed it was wonderful: before the bull, which was dark and rather small, stood a man flapping a cape into its eyes and every time eluding the rush of the brute by what looked like an inch. It seemed to go on indefinitely, for all the time Grace expected the man to be caught and tossed into the air, but he was not, and it was so exciting that suddenly she forgot the horses. But still she looked away when the *picadores* came in, shrank small and cold as the horses were gored, and she had to keep down nausea when the fire-*banderillas* exploded in the bull's rump and she could smell the roasting flesh.

Suddenly the arena was empty.

"Now," said Fenor, "you've got to go through with it, Russet. They're going to kill that bull; don't be afraid."

She seized his arm with both hands. "Oh, no, no," she cried, "take me away."

He shook his head. "Can't be done; we couldn't get out."

She looked round, despairing. It was quite true. The arena was packed with a mob so close and so intent that, had she fainted on the spot, she could not have been taken out. Against her shoulder she felt the heavy pressure of another woman's arm. They were wedged in; all she could do was to make the best of it.

"All right," she said, weakly.

She was surprised when it was over. It seemed too swift; for a few seconds just a picture of a little man in front of the black bull, then a change in the man's attitude, and a glitter from his sword. One movement, extraordinarily swift, and a black shapeless mass, heaving and blood-flecked, for a moment feebly kicking and then still. A great roar went up round her: it was a wonderful stroke and she was aware of objects being flung into the arena, cushions, hats, fans. She sat breathing rather hard as if she had been hit over the heart. It was horrible and yet wonderful. Then she looked at Fenor, and, without knowing why, she hated herself for loving him, for his free hand was clenched upon his knee, and there was in his eyes a fire she had never seen before. He was in the grip of some powerful excitement and in that minute she realised the gulf which lies between the civilised man and his woman. How much nearer he is in brutality of action to the primitive patriarch who, a myriad years ago, stole wives from foreign settlements. A good, bold stroke: that was still man's creed.

But other revelations were to come to her that afternoon. For a moment she thought she would be overcome with sickness; her cheeks and forehead had grown cold and wet, but it passed. She found herself watching quietly the play of the next bull and, even at the end, when he gored a horse, she did not flinch. And, a little later in the afternoon, she was able to look at the fourth bull carrying for a while a horse which he had speared upon both horns. She was able to watch those who thrust back into their place the lungs that hung as a pink nosegay, sewed up the ripped side, set the tortured beast upon its legs. — Able! No, much more than that, she was excited, she was thrilled; she was cold no longer now, for from the purple vault the sun struck the yellow sand and radiated over her a heat which carried a scent she had never smelled before, a curious scent that made one think of hides, with something pungent, ammoniacal in it. It was the first time she had smelled that scent. This she told Fenor after a while. He smiled.

"Of course," he said, "you wouldn't know that smell, but once I was on a Mexican battlefield — and bar gunpowder — "

"You mean — " she said.

"Well, yes," he replied, "that's what you smell."

She shuddered, hesitating to pronounce the word, when somebody else did it for her. Three or four seats away, in the row below them, sat a very small, very young man, who had thrown off his hat. She could see his black hair dancing on his head as he quivered up and down with a regular, horrible movement that made her think of a man having a fit. His body was shaken all over by a convulsive, continuous tremor and with it came a steady, hoarse refrain. She heard the word: "*Sangre.*" It must have been that her perceptions were keener now than they had ever been, for she did not have to be told that it was merely: "Blood! Blood! Blood!" this little creature, in the grasp of temporary madness, was monotonously chanting to himself. For a moment she looked at him, half-frozen, but then she looked again into the arena into which there had just come the fifth bull, very large this one, the colour of olives, but nimble and mischievous as a tiger cat. She did not again look at the little man or his shaking hair; she fixed her eyes upon the bull the colour of olives, and she felt a hot flush rise from her breast up to her head. She did not even ask herself what new creature had been poured into her body as she realised that she wanted to see this bull slain.

They slew it and, close-pressed between Fenor and the woman, she was transformed by the savage aphrodisiac of blood. She had broken away from polished restraints, was a woman before all other things now, and with an exultation in which was no understanding she let herself feel that the outer world would never recapture her.

IX

When they came back it was very late, and when Grace was alone in her room she found herself suddenly overcome by a leaden weariness. She tried to think again of what she had seen. For a moment the horrid memory of the horse she had seen thrown on its side, its lungs protruding like a nosegay, haunted her. But it did not outrage her. She was too tired. There had been in that day too great a violence of colour and of excitement; she had found in herself as primitive an emotion as she had found in Enoch: while he as a man enjoyed the bold, brave stroke, she found a drugged delight in witnessing pain. Now she was very tired, wanted only to sleep.

Upon her dressing-table were three letters forwarded from Cajus. One was from Edward — she read it carelessly: it was exactly like the letters that Edward always wrote her when she was away: the latest case, the health of the children (briefly), Edward's plans for joining her on the Riviera in another ten days (at length). Really all this had very little to do with her. An invitation to a lunch party in another week: well, evidently she would not go and supposed she had better be too ill to answer. The third letter was from Mary. She began to read it carelessly, then grew intent. Suddenly she put it down upon the dressing-table, trying to believe herself so excited as not to understand what this meant. "Come, come," she remarked to herself, "no nonsense." She took up the letter, read it to the end. Then she read it again very carefully. "So," she said, "it has come." The end only mattered:

"I don't say you're doing anything wrong in what you are doing, though I can't say I think it right. I suppose it has to be, and I hope you will be very happy. After all, old G., you know that's what I've always wanted, for you to be happy, even if it doesn't look as if you were going the right way about it. You'll be wondering what I mean, but you know. I was feeling it all the time when you said you were going away alone. I don't know where you are, but somehow I seem to feel how it is with you. I wonder whether you will ever come back? Don't do it unless you feel you've got to: you know what I mean. Ask him whether it's really got to go on like this and try and be quite, quite sure that it's got to. I feel it as I write, I can almost see you. MARY."

After this was a postscript: "Oh, my poor little G."

For a long time Grace stood holding the letter. So it had come! Even here, a thousand miles away from her old life—even here! The uncanny, horrible instinct of a woman who loves another had pursued her and hunted her out. "I can almost see you," she quoted to herself from the letter, and then flung it down with a little sharp cry, as if there lay heavy upon her the placid gaze of her sister's eyes.

She was conscious of being watched. She stood as if in a market-place with everybody staring at her curiously, or callously, or with an air of pity, staring at the woman found in sin.

Suddenly she threw herself down, face upon the bed, and for many minutes there was no connection between her thoughts. It was as if hundreds of preoccupations had been bound upon a wheel within her brain and as if that wheel were racing.

Then one idea began to emerge. Bolt! yes, they must bolt at once. She had made an effort to get up from the bed, but it did not succeed; some weakness seemed to have settled upon her muscles. "Hallo," she thought, childishly, "can't move. How funny!"

It was a good many minutes before she related this queer inability to move with her mental state. The fierce stimulus of the bull-fight helped her no longer. She was afraid. Bolt! Well, yes, to fly together still further, to be together far from all those other people and to make happiness. Yes, that was all right. But at once she knew it was no good. Had she not already bolted to the coast of Spain and been followed by a thought? They could never get away. Of course they could break all links, make another life. But that wasn't what they wanted; they wanted the life they had, not a new life to make. Her brain grew clearer. They could make only a life similar to the one she had led with Edward; they could not maintain the one she had led with Enoch, the secret, passionate, dangerous life. She would only exchange one respectability for another respectability. Publicity had cooled their passion and it could not rise again. Her face pressed into the pillow, she seemed to see Enoch. He was very silent and sad, and in his eyes she could read the same thought: If they had come together in the flush of youth, they might have managed to preserve for a while, not their passion, for that was impossible, but something precious, to preserve it a little longer than she had preserved it with Edward. But they knew that they could not have saved it for ever, saved it from the preoccupations of children, money, society, rates, wine bills.

And it was not even worth while trying; thirty-eight

and thirty-four, with different habits and circles, different responsibilities and separate desires, it was too late even to try.

X

She told Fenor the next morning when she got up, her eyes dry and burning with the tears she had not shed. He listened quietly and sadly, just as he had listened in her vision. Silently they went to the edge of the plateau to face the sea that was calm and oily, like an elliptical cup full of blue paint. Without any misery or any relief Grace observed him. She knew. Then she said, quietly:

"You don't love me any more."

There was no pain in her voice. She spoke aloud the thought that had come to her weeks before in the Underground, and he could not reply. She knew that she loved him no more, at least not as she had. And so she repeated cruelly, illogical and yet sincere:

"You don't love me any more."

CHAPTER THE FOURTH

MONDAY, TUESDAY AND WEDNESDAY

I

A DYING flower hangs long upon its stalk, and a passer-by may say: "Here is a flower," and not know that it is dying. On the Monday morning Grace and Enoch Fenor stood before their old passion, still more subtly ignorant, for they knew that it was dead, yet did not want to know it, and, by avoiding this knowledge, managed for a few hours to believe that it was not dead. They had not resumed the discussion of Mary's letter, but separately they had thought of nothing else; they had mingled in their mind Mary and her letter. They had realised her not as an enemy, but as a friendly intruder, one whose affection was as dangerous as would have been her hatred. The millstone of her complicity hung from their necks and they understood that what she felt for them was keen enough, deep enough, to overcome all barriers of distance and of time. Nowhere and not even in the course of years could they get away. She would always know, she would always watch, she would always be with them, witness of and participant in their guilt; even if they made their lives regular she would still be the witness and still be the accomplice. She must follow them to the grave because she loved them. Her placidity threw out long waves of emotion which must touch them wherever they were because she loved them; their spirits were commingled and they who would have been two in one were eternally one in three.

They went down to the sea that morning, talking brightly; Fenor translated a few foreign cables out of the "*Heraldo.*" They were not eluding the shadow, they were trying to ignore it. They tried bravely; they laughed at an old woman who rode upon a donkey that had a rounded ridge to its back so that every now and then, after she had slipped back with her saddle far enough towards the donkey's tail, an extremely small brown boy had to stop and shove his ancestress back on to the donkey's culminating point. This happened about every fifty yards as they followed the group down the slope. And they managed to laugh again, a little later, upon the strip of yellow sand that lay before the sea at the bottom of the southern hill, at a rather gross political cartoon in that day's issue of the "*Pais.*" But, little by little, as the morning passed, they found the oppression which they had at first overcome grow more powerful. They talked, but in bursts, and there were intervals now between those conversations which did not resemble the old, long intervals in the past when they had said nothing to each other because to be with each other was enough. Now conversation was a bridge between them; when they talked they were cheerful, and indeed that morning Enoch was more paradoxical than usual: he was trying. Grace had for him her usual ready response, but perhaps it was a little too ready. Somehow her smile was too sweet; it had that quality of exaggeration which a smile has when one wants to smile. They were not acting, either of them, but they were conscious of what they were doing; at different times in that morning both wondered how the three days would work out. They did not just then want those three days to end; they merely wondered, instead of taking for granted, what those three days would mean.

The afternoon gave an indication. They had adopted the local custom of the siesta, and now it was two o'clock, threateningly hot, for no breeze came off the sea, and the sky had a queer, greenish tint as if some yellow heat-haze had mixed with its blueness. Albacin seemed from the windows of the *Fonda* to look darker; the cobblestones of the street and the low houses at the bottom of the slope did not bear their usual colour: the brown and silver effect seemed to have turned to black and yellow, and the pier, that was all green with seaweed, looked silvery grey. Behind the two hills, as the heat-haze moved, was the bottom of a cup which swept up with a misty rhythmic roll to the hills far away, the hills that were sage and blue under their little caps of pink cloud. An air of storm no doubt or, worse, of a heaviness threatening, concealing storm, yet not realising it.

So far they had taken their two hours' siesta in their separate rooms, but with the door open. For the first four days it had been a convention that they should pass through Fenor's room, declare that it was very hot and that they felt very sleepy; then Grace would go into her own room, leaving the door open so as to have as much air as possible. They did that again. There was the usual salutation; the usual words were said, but when Grace remarked: "Well, I'm going now," Fenor opened for her the door of communication, held it open; she passed out, put her hand upon the handle. On the other side of the door his hand was also upon the handle. And then, for the first time, the door was closed between them: neither of them knew which one had closed the door, or whether both of them had until the last moment kept on it an active hand.

They slept very heavily that day because of the growing heat perhaps, or because of the weight of this thing they carried, this June wreath of roses that had unaccountably grown so heavy though they had not felt its burden when they danced under it, crowned. When they woke up they met naturally and again asked each other what they should do. Both of them knew that to ask made a difference, for each day at that hour, except on the Sunday when they had been to the bull-fight, they went along the path of crunching little pink stones between the three palms to the great boulder and its patch of shaded sand. They looked at each other, embarrassed rather than sad, for the desert of rock where they had been so alone, where no beast, or man, or even bird could live, it would be peopled now: she who knew would mix her shadow with their shadows; and when the sun set and their own shadows died, hers would still be there, for she could outstay the sun.

It was Fenor cleared up the situation.

"Oh," he said, and his tone was casual, "I want to go up into the town and buy some tobacco. Coming?" She hesitated. He added: "Rather a pull in this heat, isn't it?"

"Yes," said Grace, "I suppose it is. You go and buy it and you can meet me after; I'll be here, just outside the hotel or down at the bottom by the sea."

He nodded, and she watched him out of sight as he walked down the hill, crossed the street and passed the Eusebio Bar. As he passed the little bar where, it seemed to her, an hour ago they had sat together watching the amber bullocks drawing their loads, the first pang shot through her. She violently desired that at that point he should stop, turn to look back at her and with a gesture call her down. He stopped. He looked very small at that distance, but she was frightened: "If he stops and calls me down," she thought, "what shall I do?" Then she knew that she would not go, but she was not brave enough to pull herself to the test. She turned away from the northern hill and looked at the sea. As she so did Fenor too turned from the bar to look up at her: "Oh," he thought, "so her eyes did not follow me." He shrugged his shoulders: "Perhaps it's as well." And quickly he walked away up the precipitous Calle Mayor.

II

The storm still hung over the town; it was darker and hotter now, and the pink caps of cloud over the little hills had turned to pale brown. Grace and Fenor had slept badly, and both put that down to the storm, for they were still determined not to acknowledge to themselves, though they so might to each other, that all was over and that what they did now they were doing out of courtesy. Tuesday seemed endless. Everything seemed to conspire against them, for in the heat the people of Albacin were more listless than ever and few of them appeared in the streets; the little tug, instead of busily doing nothing, did nothing at all; upon the sea, that was now like an old grey looking-glass, that day not a sail appeared. They had come to a place where there was nothing to do save to love and they could love no more. Because they could love no more, very vaguely each one began to want to get rid of the unloved one. They were still courteous, but they were aloof. Grace was one of those women who are jealous of their own bodies and are not given to familiarities of touch but, during the three years, Fenor, who was more superficially sensitive, had educated her. He had taught her to be demonstrative. He liked her, when she was with him, to put her hand upon his shoulder or, in a country lane, spontaneously to take his arm. Now, carried away by those three years of association and quite unconsciously, as they stood together looking at the sea, she took him by the arm just above the elbow. He did not resist or withdraw, but simultaneously hand and arm knew that there was discomfort in the contact. It was not repulsion, it was awkwardness. They did not belong to each other any more; it was not like the contact of two people who do not belong to each other at all and who casually indulge in it because they like it; it was the contact of two people who had belonged to each other deeply, and who felt it to be indecent to touch each other now that they were parted.

Grace's hand dropped away from his arm. Nothing was said. But, that day, when they sat together, almost naturally their chairs were set a little further apart than they had been set before and, without intent, if one at a meal passed the other bread or salt, it seemed to be done carefully. Finger-tips that do not commune are hostile.

The day managed to be busy. There was a tiny draper's shop at the top of the Calle Mayor where Grace had to buy something. She did not say what, but made it clear that Fenor was not to accompany her. They had often visited a draper before, and this had never happened. But he did not press her to let him accompany her even to the door, nor point out that she spoke no Spanish. She was conscious of that. "I suppose they speak French," she remarked rather curtly as she went. But, strangely enough, when she returned after an hour from an errand which could have been accomplished in about twenty minutes, she met Fenor coming down the slope as she walked up. "Going to the post-office," he said, and gave her a cheerful smile. He did his business at the post-office, then he felt thirsty: "I don't think I'll go to the Eusebio," he thought. He looked about him. Opposite was a dreadful *bodegon* into which he went and where, for a long time, he sat before an earthenware bottle of red wine while two fishermen watched him with that Spanish air of insolence which always seemed to him so Scotch. He knew his own heart better than Grace knew hers; he told himself half-sorrowfully, half-cynically, that the Eusebio Bar could be seen from the *Fonda's* terrace, while this little place could not.

When he returned to the hotel a maid told him that his *señora* was tired and was lying down. He too was tired. Well, he would not disturb her. He lay down upon his bed, staring at the pearl-white ceiling. He was tired. But yet somehow he was impatient. "Let me see —" he thought. "Yes, this is Tuesday." A clock struck — four o'clock.

A very long time seemed to pass and then again the clock struck — half-past four. He started a little: Well, yes, half-past four. But what about it? He hadn't been waiting for it to be half-past four; or had he? Then, with a little thrill, half-horrible, half-delightful, he reflected that soon it would be five.

III

Dusk falling and both of them aware of each other so vividly that, every now and then, they thought that they could hear each other, though each one lay passive upon beds separated by a wall. Each one was aware of the other and anxious. It was like having a dead body in the house, that just does nothing and lies there, is significant by the fact of so lying. And if it is a body that one has loved, slowly the anxiety grows: how dare it be dead and love one no more? It is an offence almost. Let it soon be taken away, as soon as possible, and all that belongs to it be destroyed so that nothing may remain of it save its own sweet memory while there is time for the memory still to be sweet.

When at last they met that evening, because they knew they had to meet and that not to do so would be a greater manifestation of discomfort than to do so, there was a little remorse in their attitude.

"After all," Grace thought, "he's done me no harm. It isn't his fault, poor fellow."

"I oughtn't to have left her this afternoon," he thought. "Why should I? I'm not afraid."

There was still enough left of their old harmony to make it unnecessary for them to tell each other these things. Indeed as just before dinner they stood at the edge of the plateau, looking towards Albacin, their hands were linked and they were close together; the maid, who admired the beautiful English *señora,* stood for a moment in the porch and wondered how long they had been married; she sighed rather sentimentally, thinking that the Englishman was much more attractive than Pedro who every morning and evening brought the letters.

But their intercourse was not easy. Her effort was to maintain over him the solicitude for health and happiness that lover feels for lover. She was grave, almost motherly; she wanted to know whether the heat affected him, whether he was tired. She recommended a hot bath, and this annoyed him. It was intolerable now that she should try to take possession of him, to dominate him and manage him, in a sense to hang over him. He tended to react against her, for once he had dominated her and now he wanted to preserve the integrity of his personality. Her hands, which he had wanted to lay upon his most intimate thought and desire, now intruded. Grace did not feel that when he told her that she was looking pale and that he would give her champagne that evening. Jarred as they were, they were still man and woman, and she found it easier to be taken care of than he did; while he wanted to be free from any woman she tended to fuse with any man.

Both of them together wondered whether the strain would not be too much for them, whether they would not burst out into angry words, whether they would not manage in the twenty-four hours to spoil everything that had been and to leave each other a bitter heritage of insult and reproach caused by nothing, based on nothing, illogical, cruel, feverish. In the evening Fenor came very near to speaking that fear. They had gone out in the night to the three palms. There they stopped. They felt that they could not go beyond, for these were the taboo trees. Beyond lay their past symbolised by the wilderness. Behind them lay civilisation which had thrown them into each other's arms and was about to absorb them again. They knew they could go as far as the taboo trees, but not beyond. They stood for a long time, looking at the three black shadows, for it was clearer now, and a solemn moon, the colour of salmon flesh, hung over the little hills.

"Russet," said Fenor, "let's try — " She looked at him quickly, and he made himself clear. "Let's try not to quarrel. There's nothing to quarrel about, you know."

"No, of course not," she said, with a forced laugh.

"I can't — " said Fenor. "Well, it's no use pretending — this can't go on, can it?"

"No," said Grace in a low voice.

"Then there's nothing more to be said. You've got to go to-morrow — that was arranged — only you can't catch the morning train from Barcelona."

"Oh, the night train will do," said Grace. The harshness of her voice surprised her, but she had felt a vague regret in his voice as he said: "You can't catch the morning train," and then she had hated him because he wanted her to leave early and not to have to bear with her almost a full day. Then she had hated herself for wanting to cut loose from him. He understood a part of what she was thinking. He became nervous, hurried.

"I'll make it all right at the other end," he said. "I suppose you're going to Cajus?"

"Yes."

"Well, that's all right. I've made all the arrangements. To-morrow morning the man at the Hotel des Étrangers will have telegraphed your change of address to London; you're going to the Hotel d'Angleterre. Like that, nobody will —"

"Yes, yes," said Grace, angrily. "I don't want to talk about that."

"Well, you've got to know," said Fenor, dense as are all men when women become emotional.

"Oh, write it down," said Grace, "I can't stand any more of this sort of thing. Write it down, it'll be all right. Don't let's talk about it, let's end this as well as we can." She gave him a poor little smile. "Remember what you said, Enoch, about yourself — well, I want it to be true about me. I want to be able to say that I won you like a woman and lost you like a lady."

He was silent for a long time.

"All right," he said, "it's no use talking about it. We must try and make the best of it, but don't forget, Grace: even when it's all over there's hope."

"Hope!" repeated Grace, bitterly. Her eyes were full of tears. It was not because she doubted that there might still be hope, she was not thinking of that; but he had called her "Grace" this time, not "Russet."

IV

It was very late in the night and the sullen moon had risen. A long rosy beam lay along the floor. A little wind had risen in the evening, and as the windows were open it floated through the room, shaking little objects, swinging the curtains. She lay awake listening to the sounds. Suddenly all her senses leapt to attention. She had heard a click, as if a door opened. Yes, it was the door of communication between her room and Fenor's. It was ill-closed, no doubt, and the wind had opened it.

It was a little after midnight when the door opened; with open, fascinated eyes Grace watched it. It swung a very little, just opening and shutting an inch or so with every puff of wind; it swung, and every time it opened her heart gave a leap; then it closed and somehow she felt dull, as if each time she were being cast away. The half-hour struck, then one o'clock, and still, her limbs all numb, she watched the door opening and shutting, connecting and disconnecting the lifeless future with the living past. . . .

At last she could bear it no more. She leapt out of bed, ran towards the door. An instinct told her to be careful, to tread lightly. With fingers of velvet she took the handle and turned it, but as she so did she heard a footfall on the other side, cautious like hers, stealthy. She gripped her jaws together, molars to molars: yes, she would close that door. She closed it, and made an enormous effort to restrain a scream, for it closed all too easily. It seemed to her as if another movement, which did not quite espouse her own, animated the handle upon the other side of the door, combined with hers to close it.

V

They were conscious on the last morning of needing activity. They satisfied it at first with packing; somehow they managed to make this packing hurried and busy, to lose things and to find them, to cause a little clamour in the Fonda and to keep the servants employed. Activity of any kind did them good and both of them regretted, though neither of them confessed it, that they had so few things to pack that within an hour all was done, that all they had to do was to wait. For a while they waited together in the detached, forlorn way in which people wait when all their goods are packed and they have nothing about them to connect them with the world. They stand quite free and wondering what to do with their freedom, waiting for a train, unable to do anything because books, clothes, golf sticks, tennis rackets, all the things that make life so busy have been put away. They waited for that train as soldiers in the trenches nervously wait for the artillery to begin.

They tried to talk, they tried to be natural; and the more they tried the more artificial they grew. They suffered, and laughed louder; they were horribly strained, and from casual they grew slangy. At first it was a coldness creeping upon them, just that feeling of detachment for each other which they had had at first for their love as it lay in the house like a corpse. From coldness grew something else: a captious, critical quality as if now, with the veils off, they saw each other for the first time: they had stripped each other of the mantle of love, that mantle so thick that it excludes the world, so thin that through it the lover can glimpse a light more radiant than the sun's. They did not see each other as they were, but they saw all the ugliness, the meanness of each other, and much they thought mean and ugly that was not there. It was indeed the reaction from their over-great love. Because they had loved so much they were beginning to hate each other; it was not dislike, that feeble objection to minor faults, but something hotter and fiercer which came, splendid in its way, out of the ruddy passion which had been theirs. So rich was the soil in which had flourished the flower of their passion that now it could readily feed a big, poisonous weed.

Grace saw that the whites of Fenor's eyes were too large, that they made him stare and look, she thought, almost stupid. He was not stupid. That she had to confess. But as soon as she agreed to her own confession she told herself that his cleverness was cruelty, cold, cynical, sensual cruelty. And, as she looked at him, with the beautiful humid film gone from her eyes and their pupils hard, he too saw her differently. This attitude of hers, this slow, languid walk, how self-conscious it was! And her way of walking with her head in the air, not looking where she was going, how vain! How saturated with her self-importance! And she was justified by very little in the intellect, save a capacity to absorb not much nobler than that of a sponge which you flung into a bucket, and by physical beauty — He hesitated. Well, perhaps already that faint line under the chin meant some little degeneration of the beautiful curve —

Together they realised what was happening, pulled themselves up. As usual it was Fenor explained.

"Grace," he said, "don't let's forget. We've had a big thing, you and I; don't let's spoil it. It couldn't go on — I hardly know why. Perhaps it was because others knew, or perhaps we'd run our course, so we must bless a fate that parts us before we ourselves want to part."

"D'you think we'd ever have wanted to part?" asked Grace.

He shrugged his shoulders: "How am I to know? I'm not responsible for to-morrow, and you know what I think — There may be no to-morrow, so why trouble about it? There's joy and pain enough in the day's work."

She did not answer him. He was right, she knew. But could she save this thing which with every moment was shrivelling up and drying like a cut lily in the sun?

"Don't let's talk about it," said Fenor, "let's leave it as it is. It's been the most beautiful thing in my life and it'll always be. Only one thing makes me anxious: without it what shall I be?"

"Oh, you'll get over it," said Grace, suddenly cruel. "I don't mean just you, Enoch. All men are like that. I don't say one woman's just the same as another to you, but almost. If the princess is unkind there's always her maid."

He shook his head: "No, it's not true, not quite true. There's always the maid, as you say, but somehow we never forget that the princess was unkind and, believe me, it's quite as tragic to fly to the drug of a mean little attraction because the great love has gone, as it is to mourn the great love all alone. You see, it has less dignity." He smiled. "When you're being dignified, you know, you're just a little pleased with yourself. The more you suffer, the more your self-esteem grows." His smile grew quite merry. "People who have a broken heart get intolerably stuck-up."

She threw him a look that was almost tender: here was the old Enoch again, and for a moment she wondered whether she would ever get away from this odd charm, half-seductive, half-repulsive. "But no," she thought, "it's too late. There's the charm. Don't let me forget it, that's all. But how?" The idea came to her as she spoke:

"Look here," she said, "we'd better not talk about it any more. Just leave it like that and remember it, as you say, as beautifully as we can. And now let's do something else."

"I can't think of anything to do," said Fenor. "I suppose you wouldn't like to — come down to the Eusebio?"

"Oh, no, no," said Grace, nervously, "let's think of something else."

"Well," said Fenor, "Albacin's not exactly Margate Sands. There's neither kursaal, nor golf, nor tennis, and I don't know the Spanish for cockshy — There's absolutely nothing to do."

"Then why stay?" asked Grace, suddenly. "My train doesn't start until nine. Why shouldn't we go to Gerona now — sightseeing?"

Fenor laughed. "All right," he said. "I suppose after all you *ought* to see Gerona. What a pity you won't be able to send off picture post-cards there."

She took up his mood. "Never mind, it shall benefit my inner consciousness, as they say in intellectual circles. Come along."

VI

They did Gerona all the afternoon. They did all the proper things: walked the banks of the Ter, visited the cathedral and were told by the guide that the nave was twenty-two metres broad. They did San Feliu and they did San Pedro, and they did a number of other places the names of which they did not know because they were not mentioned in the guide-book. They even did the Museo and found it agreeably cool, for the storm still hung heavy over the country. Little by little the sky had turned a curious shade of saffron, melting near the horizon into an ugly brown the colour of broth. But, when four o'clock came and when all the things that could be done were done, the heavy consciousness of each other began once more to lie upon them. It was so hot that when they walked the streets Fenor often stopped to mop his head, and Grace suddenly felt that she hated men who mopped their heads, that she had always hated them at dances; there was something almost indecent in a man mopping his head. When he did it for the fourth time she could not restrain herself.

"We'd better sit down if you're so hot," she said. Her tone was acid. He threw her a sulky look and nearly said: "Can't I mop my head if I like?" Instead he kept silent and reflected that woman apparently had only one desire, which was to gain mastery over man. Well, she wouldn't, that was all. Then both together they reacted. This would never do; in five hours they were going to part for ever. Surely they could be civil to the end. The severity slowly turned into a quiet hostility during which they had a sort of conversation they had never had before.

"They ought to have trams here," said Fenor. "This place is so sleepy that one day it'll go to sleep for good and never wake up."

"I shouldn't wonder if it did," said Grace. "It's so hot, no wonder it's sleepy."

"Yes, it is hot," said Fenor, "I expect we shall have a storm by and by."

"I hope we will," said Grace, "it'll clear the air."

There was a long pause. A man passed in a frock-coat and white beach shoes. That made them laugh and relieved the situation a little. For a while they remained at the top of the hill, looking down upon the close-packed houses on the slope that made Gerona look like an old brown honeycomb as it clustered up to the castle. Like stripes down the hill went the steep, narrow streets, making silver shadows along the walls that were yellow and dull like dirty gold. They discussed the city a little. Then Fenor showed his acquaintance with Spanish literature, with Ibañez and Perez Galdos; he spoke of the drama of Benavente and Echegaray. Little by little it was time for dinner. But Grace had had to make a few purchases in the town and Fenor had stood aimlessly, chafing a little, in the perfumer's shop and at the shoemaker's, while, it seemed, she took endless time to buy what she wanted; she made him translate incomprehensible reasons why this did not suit, and explain what she did want only to have it shown, then to say again that that was not what she wanted. He chafed badly. He was a man — that was not his way of shopping. Time passed, and anxiety seized him. It was hardly after seven and yet he was haunted by the idea that she might miss her train. Another night — no, not that. For two hours the thought lay heavy upon him, and as the minutes sped he found that he was hurrying her, until at last she turned on him.

"There's no hurry," she said, "we've got an hour and a half."

"Oh, well," he said, ashamedly, "there are so few trains, you see."

They did not speak for a while. They hated each other and themselves because each one could not bear the thought of missing the train, and could bear still less the idea that the other one feared that the train might be missed.

Dinner was abominable, for Gerona, it seemed, was not ready for visitors. They entered the restaurant at a quarter past seven, and by twenty-five past even *hors d'œuvres* had not yet come. Fenor called the waiter only to be soothed and, he felt, lied to. Then there was a long pause. The waiter, summoned again, merely remarked that the fish was being fried. They sat, anxious and raging, hearing in the distance the faint sounds of the frying which it seemed would never cease. There were breaks in the conversation, which was polite and strained. They watched the clock and neither suggested that this could not go on. A vile thing, a rump steak the waiter called it, about a quarter of an inch thick, was served dripping with olive oil. Still they waited and waited until the clock pointed to ten past eight and Fenor lost his temper, asked the waiter whether they were digging for the potatoes in the garden —

It was horrible because neither of them had the courage to say: " Let us go." They had to be dignified to the end, and because they were dignified they had to torture each other and be courteous.

Then they were on the platform, waiting for the train. They had ten minutes to wait and nothing to do. " Oh," thought Fenor, " if only there were luggage to register, or something! " But there was nothing to do except to wait. There was not even a crowd to notice, no curious native; there was nobody winding up a private affair: just two or three black-clad men, probably commercial travellers, sitting stodgily by the side of their bags, and an old couple upon a bench, almost asleep. So they stood on that platform as on an island, horribly alone. They were alone and they suffered from it, they who had risked so much to be alone. Then they heard a clicking: the signal! And suddenly a wave of excitement passed through them. At last! The station became busy, officials appeared, porters made noises. It was better now, for the strain was over and both of them were invaded by a shameful joy because now there was to be no more waiting, but action. Then, in that last minute, a sorrow fell upon them, not the bitter blinding sorrow that brings tears, but something soft that was almost sweet. They held each other's hands, looked into each other's eyes.

" Good-bye," Grace murmured. " We've been very happy, haven't we? " He nodded. He did not want to speak. Grace was more anxious. " Good-bye," she said. Then after a pause: " Enoch, say you won't forget me."

He shook his head; being a man he feared himself. It was all right for her to talk. If she cried it wouldn't matter, but how ridiculous he would be if he didn't keep a stiff lip to the end. In the distance they heard a sound, a rumble, low and growing. They listened. Yes, there was not a minute left.

"Good-bye," said Grace again, very close to him.

Fenor spoke, very close to her. "Must we?" he murmured. Then, answering himself: "Yes, of course." They remained so standing for a moment as slowly the train pulled up in front of them—

A few minutes later Grace sat alone in the carriage, her hands loose upon her lap, trembling, for she still felt about her the last clasp of his arms, and that last kiss upon her cheek, so soft and so violent that she could still feel it hurting her.

VII

Grace looked out of the window of her little white bedroom at the Hotel d'Angleterre. It was ten o'clock in the morning; over the sea that was smooth and light as aquamarine little barks with brown lateen sails chased each other. She found herself without spirit; tired, she thought. That was likely after fourteen hours in the train. "I'd better lie down," she said aloud. She turned towards her bed, but before she undressed she considered, thinking vague thoughts. A big jar upon the dressing-table was full of heavy, full-blown roses. They were very beautiful. As she looked, a petal detached itself from the greatest of the roses and fell silently upon the wood. A little later another petal fell, as the rose blooming to fullness began to bloom towards its end. Grace remained standing for a long time, head down and hands clasped behind her, watching the slow fall upon the wood of the petals of the rose.

CHAPTER THE FIFTH

HOPE

THE thin, grey rain had ceased to fall. It was October, and the three sisters were gathered together in the drawing-room of the house near Sevenoaks where Clara had passed the last five months. The room opened out into the garden. The gravel paths were strewn with dead leaves, the gold of which had by rain been tarnished until they made a brown carpet everywhere. In a big, sheltered bush hung a spider's web, and in the midst a great, sulky October spider, the light markings upon its back obscure. It did not move, and its long limbs seemed drawn closer to its body than the day before, as if it felt in the air the coming of winter and of death that made it languid and careless.

Clara stretched her thin limbs upon the sofa, sat up to look into the garden, and spoke half to herself:

"I shan't mind going back to town."

"No," said Mary, "I suppose it's been dull for you?"

"Well—" said Clara, and hesitated, "I don't know. It hasn't always rained, you see, and it's been rather fun watching the dahlias, seeing them bud, and then become flowers, and the flowers fall and all that."

Mary did not reply for a while, but examined very carefully the piece of fancy-work which she was engaged on. "So you haven't been bored," she said.

"No," said Clara, "I think I've been too tired to be bored." Grace turned to looked at her sister. She thought that Clara spoke queerly, considering what she had been; somehow she would have expected her to say that she was jolly glad to get back to town, not that she "wouldn't mind." But then a complete nervous breakdown involving a convalescence of five months, during the first three of which Lady Govan had not been allowed to receive a letter or read a newspaper, must have worked a change. A physical change she perceived: Clara, who had always been slim, was now very thin. One could see clearly the bones of her wrists, and over the woolly white coat she was swaddled in the line of her jaw had almost a cutting edge under the skin; the neck was stringy; the whole face had changed; it had been reduced to its simplest elements of skin, tendon and bone, out of which the eyes shone wonderfully blue, not like lobelias, so shy, but almost violet, very large in the shadow of the brows that seemed to overhang more now that the eyeballs had receded a little.

"D'you think you ought to go back yet? You don't look very fit."

"I don't know," said Clara, "but I don't mind. The doctor's sending me back—I suppose it's all right. In fact, he says I must get about a bit and not be slack."

Mary laughed contentedly. "Oh, he needn't have told you that, Clara, you'll be on the run in a week." There was a very long pause, and then Clara said: "Oh, no." After another pause, Mary replied: "Oh, you'll have to; London's so busy, it's catching. Why, I couldn't stop if I wanted to."

"It's all right for you, Mary," said Grace, "with your seven children, or is it eight? I really forget the number of that August one."

"Don't be silly, G.," said Mary, still good-tempered, while Clara gave a high little laugh at the elementary joke.

"I'm not being silly," said Grace, quietly. "You think I'm joking, Mary, but I'm not. It's all right having eight children (I make it eight until corrected); it gives you something to do."

"Sure enough," said Mary. "Bother! This stitch is too much for me."

For some time, while she struggled with the fancy-work, Grace looked at her. Yes, Mary was all right. Then, with a little sigh, she got up and went to the window.

Once more the rain had begun to fall and she could hear it very gentle, drop by drop, making sodden the wet leaves. Beyond the garden she saw the side of a quarry, all white, with ruddy brown streaks of clay flashing through it, and a veil of rain that slowly grew across it, thicker and thicker; she watched the veil become dense, turn the white of the quarry into grey, then blot it out. When she could see nothing before her save the pall of rain that was now like a tenuous wall, bluish and in its higher parts pearly, she ceased to see the world without and was able to look within herself. She was calm and she was not unhappy. She was in that state which is the common ease of man, between joy and misery. It was not suffering, that was all over; indeed she was conscious of a health, a strength she did not quite understand. It was not boisterous health; she had no desire to sing or play tricks on anybody. She just had a sensation of setness; of being there and knowing that she was there.

"It's funny," she thought, "I feel so established, like the Albert Memorial." She smiled at herself. "Somehow it's as inconceivable that I should move as that the august monument could be blown up by the suffragettes." She turned to Clara. "I wonder — " she said, then she stopped a little guiltily, but Lady Govan was no longer pettish and did not say in an injured tone: "Oh, do stop wondering."

Grace missed the repartee; as a result, she found that she did not know what she was wondering about, and almost told herself: "Well, what are you wondering about now?" Still, after a time, Mary said:

"You wonder what?"

"Well," said Grace, "I hardly know."

"Then," said Mary, comfortably, "there's nothing to wonder about, G., unless you're wondering what you're going to do now."

"Now?" said Grace, and her voice sounded a little frightened. "Oh, I don't know, don't let's talk about it. Let's talk about something interesting; about you."

"I'm sure that's not interesting," said Mary, "except

to me." Both her sisters laughed at the naive egotism. "I suppose you think that's very smug," said Mary. "But still, it's like that, we all do think about ourselves; we only pretend not to just because we're polite."

"Or because we're fat," said Clara, with a touch of her old aggressiveness.

"Perhaps," said Mary, "I like being fat. In a sort of way, d'you know, I think one's happier when one's fat."

Grace smiled. "There may be something in your theory, Mary. I know I've lost a few pounds in weight this summer, but you look happy enough."

"Yes," said Mary, seriously, "I'm all right; I suppose I always have been — never had much time to be anything else. Oh, it hasn't been exciting, but all those babies, one after another — well, it's been rather fun. And the way Tom goes on with Jack — it's like the monkey house."

"It's a good thing you got Jack," said Grace.

"Yes," said Mary, "though in a way I was sorry to have him because if I'd lost him — think what Tom would have felt. Fortunately there's Elba now."

"How's Elba?" asked Clara, listless, alluding to the new baby-boy.

"Splendid," said Mary, enthusiastically. "D'you know? he weighed ten and a half pounds when he was born."

"Is that very much?" asked Clara.

Mary gave an audible sniff at her sister's ignorance. "Of course it is. You surprise me sometimes, Clara." Lady Govan did not reply and Mary returned to the thread of her idea. "Yes, it makes a difference having Jack and Elba. Still, it makes me feel more comfortable. It would never have done for Tom to have had only one boy and then lost him; he'd never have got over it."

After a long pause Grace said: "Is that quite true, Mary? Can't one have had something precious and lost it — and get over it?"

Mary looked up quickly; for a moment her face looked sorrowful. "Yes," she said, hurriedly, "I was wrong

— it's better to have something and lose it than not to have had it." Then, after a pause, as if with an effort: "You may not think so, G., but you're not so much to be pitied after all."

"Pitied," said Grace. "Who knows? I thought so at the time, six months ago. I thought — Oh, dreadful things."

Clara looked up, interested. "What sort of things, G.?"

"I hardly know. Drugs — and — well, you see — I thought that if I began to take veronal one day I might take too much — everybody'd have thought it was an accident."

Mary shivered. "Don't even talk like that; it's worse than silly, it's wrong."

"Yes, I suppose it is wrong, but then I'd done such a lot of things that were wrong. I felt I might as well do another and be done with all complication."

"Two wrongs don't make a right," said Mary, sagely. "There was only one thing for you to do after — that, and that was to go on and make the best of it, the only way to put things right."

"So you don't think I did wrong?" cried Grace, logically, for the Puritanism that was deep in her soul and had survived three years of illicit passion made her ask for approval.

Mary did not raise her eyes from her fancy-work. At last she said: "You know what I mean; you know quite well you did wrong. But then people are like that and the only thing is to go on as if nothing had happened."

"But something has happened," said Grace. "You know quite well I can't wipe out those three years, even if I wanted to, unless —" She paused, and a hot flush dyed her cheeks.

"Unless what?" asked Clara, listlessly.

"I sometimes feel I can't go on like this, hiding it. You know all about it, you two, and if you hadn't known it might have gone on. But just as I used to feel that nobody ought to know because it was going on, now I seem to think that everybody ought to know because it's over."

She shivered, for it seemed as if a very soft, caressing voice, coming from low down in a man's throat, had murmured to her: "Braggart!" But she closed her ears to the voice and went on: "Sometimes I feel I'd like to tell Edward."

"What!" cried Clara, this time genuinely excited.

"Don't be silly," said Mary.

"Yes," said Grace, courageously; "sometimes I feel I ought to. What's the good of hiding things? They only stay inside you and get inflamed."

Mary looked at her steadily. "Sometimes they do," she said, "But this isn't getting inflamed in you. It's just there and, little by little, you'll forget — "

"Never!" said Grace.

"No, not all — you'll forget some of it — all the bad parts. But you mustn't tell Edward; of course not. He's much too happy, he's going to take silk soon, isn't he?"

"Yes," said Grace, "it's about time; he's dreadfully pleased about it."

"Well," said Mary, "let him be pleased. Because you've done him a wrong it's no reason that you should do him another."

"Would I?" said Grace.

"Yes," said Mary, "he's so fond of you, you see, and he thinks such a lot of you."

"When he thinks of me," said Grace, rather hard.

"Yes," said Mary, "when he thinks of you, as you say. Perhaps you expect him to think too much of you. Have you ever thought as much of him as you did of — well, you know who I mean."

Grace shook her head. "No," she said, "and so you think I mustn't hurt him. I've done something which I knew to be wrong and only now and then I thought it was right, and you say I ought to hide it so as not to hurt him."

"Yes," said Mary, "you mustn't hurt him. It would

do him no good. After all, it seems to me that all you can do in life is to suffer what you've got to and to enjoy what you can."

"Mary," said Clara, from the sofa, "you're quite immoral."

"Perhaps I am," said Mary. "When one's got seven children to look after, one hasn't time to think of how one ought to do it; one just does it, and then somehow the day is done."

Grace was thinking while she spoke of the phrase which she unconsciously made more epigrammatic: suffer all you need and enjoy all you can. She had enjoyed and now she suffered, or rather had suffered. Well, that was all right, and perhaps it had been worth it. She considered her sisters. For a moment she thought of Mary, white, serene, and triumphant. Mary had done nothing in those years. But had she not? At once Grace realised that Mary, apparently quiescent, had travelled along the road of life just as fast or as slowly as her sisters; she saw that nothing one could do hastened or retarded the flight of time; and here was Mary, not very happy, not very unhappy, but established and content, having preserved her dignity, set off her pains against her pleasures. She was queen of the hive; certainly she had suffered less. Perhaps she had found the better way. Then Grace abandoned Mary, concentrated upon Clara.

"Clara," she said, "I suppose you've enjoyed yourself in your own way?"

"I suppose I have," said Clara.

"You must have enjoyed all those politics, and influence and all that?"

A flicker of animation came into the big violet eyes, then quickly died. "Yes, you did," said Grace, "I saw it in your eyes just for a moment."

"Well, I'm not going back to it," said Clara. "It's not that I can't; I expect I shall be quite well enough in a few months. I don't want to, somehow. It's all a bit of the past."

"A bit of the past!" said Grace. "All our life, I suppose, is just made up of bits of past — Why, the moment we perceive a delight, it's just past. We're already separated from it by that tiny little moment of time which is necessary for us to feel it. It seems almost as if there was no present at all, but just the past and we remembering it."

It was a long time before Mary replied and then she said:

"You were both happy, you two, each in your own way. I don't quite understand you, G., your talk's too clever for me, but I think I know what you mean: that you had your good time, both of you."

"I mean something much more than that," said Grace, dreamily, "it's just striking me that if it's always the past that delights us, what does it matter if it's a second old or ten years? It's only a question of remembering enough and well enough."

"I don't quite know what you mean," said Mary, stupidly. "I suppose I too remember things, nice ones most of them — one forgets the others, or even the nasty ones seem nice when you think of them, because they're over. But there, I won't bother myself with those things; I suppose I haven't been very happy or very unhappy: I married, I've had children, and, after all, marriage being what it is -- "

There was a very long break during which Grace abandoned the general question and thought of Enoch Fenor. He had completely disappeared from her life, and for a long time she had missed him in a peculiar way. Accustomed to the quickening influence of his mind, she had been bored; that had been the main feeling, and she had been ashamed of herself because she was bored instead of being heart-broken.

"I suppose," she thought, "that the modern young lady indulges in intellectual atrophy instead of going into a decline, as they used to do in the days of Trollope." But she knew that was not quite true, for there had been many moments, the moments most empty of mental stimulus, when she had wanted him and needed him, when she had stood alone in a field and called for him — like a lioness roaring for her mate.

But that was all over, and now she was as used to not having him as she had once been used to having him. He was the past, the glowing, beautiful past. And as she thought this, some warm current seemed to flood her veins. She was filled with a splendid realisation that it had all been so fine, so clean, so bold up to the end, that together when the thing which the world hated was exposed to the world they had smashed it rather than allow it to become mean. She had loved and she had piled up memories which would inflame her life, irradiate the future. It was as if she had turned her back upon a light so brilliant that still it shone upon her and still lighted her path as she plodded on away from it. So much had she loved that love must always be present with her, always be significant, and never abandon her. And now, whatever happened, when she saw young lovers, she could always tell herself that she too had been in Arcadia. Perhaps in an Arcadia so splendid that, in their first fervour, they could never hope to enter such an one. "Yes," she thought, "I am marked just as if I had been branded with a hot iron. I have had love, and so much and so strong that nothing ever can take it away from me, that it is always with me, that it is not a memory at all, that it is something actual which I carry, something that folds me in like a warm mantle that cannot wear out." Then she spoke aloud: "It was perhaps the best for me," she said, "just as what happened was the best for you, Clara." Clara threw her a surprised look. "I mean what happened to me and to you, Clara: my man and your success."

"There's not much left of my success," said Clara. "Here am I, lying on my back on a sofa and nobody bothering much about me. Not that I care. I don't want to take up those things again."

"You don't understand," said Grace. "Didn't you have splendid moments? Not only the big ones like the meeting at the Albert Hall, but all sorts of other little moments: the first time you took the chair, and that day when the Premier said to you that he wished you had married a man on his own side."

Clara smiled. "Yes, it was rather fun now and then."

"Don't you ever think of it?"

"Perhaps I do — sometimes quite a lot." Her smile broadened. "Yes," she said, almost sentimentally, "those three or four years, they were really rather good — but they're over."

Grace's voice came suddenly loud. "Over? Of course they're not over, Clara. Those three or four years of yours, your successes, all that — it's all with you now, piled up inside you ready to cheer you up. Oh! Can't you see it? You tell me you think about it now and then quite a lot. It's your reserve of happiness, your reserve of glad memories that you're drawing on just as I do on mine. Don't you think so, Mary?"

Mary did not raise her face. Then she remarked: "Well, thank heaven, there's not much more to do in this stitch."

Grace did not notice, for now she was speaking aloud to herself. "All that is life," she said, "the real thing. There's a difference, you know, between riding a bicycle and remembering the day when you rode a bicycle. You do all those things after and you like 'em — and so you go on — "

"You go on doing the same thing over and over again," said Clara.

Grace shook her head. "No, life isn't a circle. People are always saying that, but it isn't true. You change, and every time you see things a little differently. That's why the things we used to suffer from we won't suffer from them again — We go through them to become — well, bigger and finer. You, Clara, you too, you had to have a bad time — to want things and to have them, and to pay for them. Oh, it was pretty beastly, I know, having to pay for them, but it made you sort of nobler."

"D'you think I'm any the better for it?" asked Clara. "What's the use of being nobler, as you call it?"

"I'm not quite sure," said Grace, "but somehow I feel that by having had to sacrifice our joys we can now face life much more clearly, more serenely. That is our hope."

"Hope?" said Clara, rather bitterly.

"Yes, hope," and Grace's voice was ringing. "Hope because we've enjoyed things: you your triumph, and I my — love. It's made us braver and fitter, don't you understand? Braver and fitter for the things that are coming — fitter for the joys and braver for the pains. And we shan't be so afraid when the next thing comes, whatever it is, and it doesn't matter what it is: love or motherhood, or politics, or business, or art. I don't care what it is, we'll be bigger and finer people because we won't be afraid of having a bad time and because we took our licking — like men."

Clara looked at her steadily. "Like men," she said. "How funny you are, G.! We're not men."

"We should be," said Grace. "If men have beaten us, it's because they were finer. They could do things better and they could stand them better; what we've got to do is to do them and to stand them as well, and then women will be big serene people too, and they won't be afraid. They won't be afraid because they'll know that the whole of life is a thing to be taken bravely, as a sort of store of memories that are going to make one still bigger and still serener."

"It sounds all right," said Clara. "Perhaps you're right. But what have we got left, after all?"

"We've got our old happiness," said Grace, "that can't die. We'll just carry it on into the next years, and we'll pile the years, one upon the other, abler to take with them what they bring us: the good and the evil mixed — all that. And even if they don't bring us much, we've still got what the dead years brought us. Somebody said to me once — " She flushed, then suddenly became bold. "Oh, let me speak the truth: Enoch said to me once, 'he that hath the ashes of a friend hath an eternal treasure' — that's about it."

Mary suddenly put down her fancy-work and looked up. " What's that you say, G.? "

Grace repeated the phrase.

" Oh, I suppose you mean the ashes of anything that's been good? "

" Yes, that's it," said Grace.

" Well, I've had good things too." She smiled. " A pretty good thing, now you come to think of it; I've made something of marriage. It isn't easy, you know, being what it is. I've heard people talk of free-love and all that sort of thing; I don't know, I'm not clever, but it seems to me we've got to take it as it is and see what we can do. Perhaps it means that we've got to find the thing to do when we're married — I hardly know. Anyhow not to be lazy or have a good time. Children, that's a way — that's how I look at it. One can't help being fond of them if one has enough — a sort of habit. So I'm not sorry. Sometimes I think it wasn't the best thing I could do, and sometimes I think it was the best thing in the world, and then the baby cries, or something, and I stop thinking, and it's all right. Marriage is pretty difficult, you know, but it strikes me that if you take it in my way, well — there's hope."

" Hope? " murmured Clara. " I wonder whether there is hope for anybody."

" Yes," said Mary, very gentle, " there's hope for everybody — even for wives."

THE END

John Gunther

4223 Kenmore Ave

Chicago